Acclaim for the novels of
BRENDA JOYCE

BEYOND SCANDAL
"Master storyteller Brenda Joyce weaves
threads of mystery, intrigue and passion
into a tale that Gothic fans will relish
and romance readers will devour."
Romantic Times

THE GAME
"A stunning tale of power and passion set against
a rich Elizabethan tapestry. Don't miss it!"
Virginia Henley

AFTER INNOCENCE
"An extraordinary woman…
an emotional roller coaster."
Publishers Weekly

PROMISE OF THE ROSE
"A powerful story, rife with compelling characters,
political intrigue and steamy sensuality."
Los Angeles Daily News

BRENDA JOYCE

Innocent Fire

AVON BOOKS  NEW YORK

AVON BOOKS, INC.
1350 Avenue of the Americas
New York, New York 10019

Copyright © 1988 by Brenda Joyce Dworman
Published by arrangement with the author
Visit our website at **http://www.AvonBooks.com**
Library of Congress Catalog Card Number: 87-91461
ISBN: 0-380-75561-0

First Avon Books Printing: June 1988

AVON TRADEMARK REG. U.S. PAT. OFF. AND IN OTHER COUNTRIES, MARCA
REGISTRADA, HECHO EN U.S.A.

Printed in the U.S.A.

WCD 10 9 8 7 6 5

To
Michelle and Sid
for absolutely everything.
And a very special thanks to
Meg O'Brien.

Prologue

London, 1830

She pressed her small body against the wall. She could hear his shouting, and her mother's soft sobs. She was frozen with fear, too afraid to run down the hall and into the kitchen, to the safety of nanny, cook, and the serving maids. Her small, pinched white face, with the huge violet eyes, was almost level with the door frame, and without meaning to, she moved her head slightly forward and peered into her father's study.

He was a huge man. Tall and broad with black hair, he was dressed impeccably, as always. He was still shouting at her mother, who, like Miranda, was dark and pale and petite. She was standing in front of him, trembling and fighting back tears.

Miranda tried to understand their words. She rarely saw her father. When he was home, he was locked in his study, but he was often out, not coming in until past her bedtime. On the very few occasions she did see him, he was like this, huge and loud, terrifying both herself and her mother.

"When I say you will come, you will come!" he roared.

"Please, Edward, please," her mother whispered. "Yes, all right, yes, I promise—"

"There is no promise to make! Am I not the head of this house?"

"Yes, yes, Edward. Would you like some coffee, or

1

something to eat?'' She looked at him hopefully, her eyes every bit as large and violet as her daughter's.

''Are you accusing me of being drunk?'' The new roar was the loudest. ''You slut!'' He backhanded her across the face, and she flew against a chair, almost collapsing.

''Edward, please,'' she whimpered.

''I can't stand the sight of you, you faithless bitch!'' Edward bent down and yanked her to her feet, lifting her off her toes and holding her face close to his. She began to weep softly.

''Where were you yesterday afternoon? Where?'' he shouted.

''I was at Lady Burrows's.''

''Liar!''

''Edward—I swear it! That one indiscretion—so many years ago—a few kisses—*mon Dieu, s'il vous plaît . . .*''

Miranda heard the sound of material tearing as her father ripped open the front of her mother's gown. Her mother cried out in protest as he began touching her.

''So you play the frigid virgin with me, bitch?'' Pushing her onto the floor, he grabbed her thick black hair, coiled in a knot, and held her head still while he began to kiss her wildly. She struggled and moaned, but he ignored her flying fists.

Miranda could stand it no more. Her papa was killing her *maman!* She ran into the room, anger overcoming her fear, and grabbed her father's arm. ''Papa, no! Papa! *Arrêtez-vous! Papa, non!''*

The struggling couple ceased all movement, and her father lifted his head. His eyes were glazed, and then a look of rage crept into them, making Miranda shrink and drop his arm.

''*Ca va petite, tout va bien, vraiment,* leave now, quickly,'' her mother said, her voice strange and choked.

But before the words were even out, her father had risen, grabbed her, and smacked her across the face. ''Never interfere with me and your mother, Miranda!'' he shouted. ''Never!''

The slap knocked her off her feet. She had never been hit before. Her face throbbed painfully, and tears sprang to her eyes. ''I hate you, Papa,'' she sobbed, and then she ran out of the room, as fast as her long, skinny legs would take her.

Her father stared at the doorway, a stricken expression on his face. "Oh my God," he moaned. "What have I done?" He turned to look at his wife.

She was sitting on the floor, making no attempt to cover her full breasts, which were heaving from exertion. She was staring, stricken.

His whole body tensed. "Get up," he snarled. "I will deal with you later, Angeline. But know this. You go nowhere from this day forth without Whit to escort you. To *protect* you," he added mockingly.

Angeline rose shakily. "It is your unfounded jealousy that makes you such a monster and destroys any chance of happiness in this home," she whispered bravely.

"Get out of here, you slut!"

Angeline gathered her torn bodice together and fled.

Miranda cried for a long while, hating her father more than ever, not so much for herself as for her *maman*, whom she loved and adored with all her heart. Poor Maman! She finally fell into an exhausted sleep, and soon the entire town house became silent and dark.

It was her mother's gentle touch that awakened her, and at first Miranda was confused, because blackness shrouded her form. "Maman?"

"Shhh, *ma petite*. We must make no noise, *chérie,* and be very, very quick. Come."

"Maman, but what?" Miranda was confused. Her mother had lit one lamp, and Miranda saw that she was dressed for travel. She was holding a similar gown for Miranda. Miranda became instantly awake as her mother helped her to dress. "Maman? Are we—running away from Papa?"

"Don't ask questions, *petite*. Come."

Miranda was afraid, and she could feel her mother's fear as it coursed from her hand to her daughter's. They moved swiftly and quietly downstairs, and out the back entrance of the house. A carriage was waiting, and a man descended. "Hurry, Angeline," he said, and his familiarity—not addressing her mother as Lady Shelton—struck Miranda with shock.

They all climbed in and the carriage moved off.

"Thank God you came," Angeline said to the strange gentleman.

"For you, dear heart, I would risk everything, even my life." He took her hand. In the darkness of the coach, Miranda could only see that he was slim and well built.

Her mother started to cry.

"Angeline, please, dear, don't cry," the man whispered. "You and your daughter will be safe, I swear it. You will never have to endure that bastard again!"

Angeline moaned.

"You still love him, don't you?" the man said after a moment's hesitation.

"Oh, Harry! No, no, you're wrong! It's not true! I hate him!" Angeline began to sob uncontrollably.

Harry put his arms around her. "Oh, dearest, how I wish that were true. Hush, Angeline, you are frightening your daughter."

Miranda was frightened because her mother was trembling with fear, and because this strange man had put his arms around her. Would he hurt her? Her mother's words were ringing in her ears. Maman hated Papa too! Her mother disengaged herself from Harry, and moved quickly to her daughter, pulling her close.

"*Chérie*, everything will be fine, I swear it. We are going home, to France, to a convent, where we will both be safe." She stroked her daughter's hastily braided thick, black hair.

"I hate Papa, too, Maman," Miranda said, clutching her mother. "He will be so angry! He will try and find us!"

Angeline choked back another sob, but her fear was completely communicated to her daughter.

The soft whispering between Harry and her mother, and the rhythmic motion of the coach, soon lulled Miranda to sleep. The next day they crossed the Channel. Her mother was deathly ill, but Miranda was excited, excited enough that she forgot her fear of Harry and stood next to him on deck, laughing with excitement.

That night they reached the convent. Miranda watched with fascination as Harry, who was blond and fair and so opposite her hard, bronzed, huge father, kissed her mother on the cheek. It was not the same kind of kiss that her father had given; it was soft and gentle. Miranda shuddered at the memory she wanted to forget forever—the memory of her father on top of her mother, pulling her arms over her head, his mouth on hers while she struggled.

"Angeline," Harry said, "if you ever change your mind—write me. I love you. I will come to you. We could go to the Americas, Mexico—I would make a fine husband, and a better father."

"You are so kind," Angeline said, touching his cheek softly. "You are such a fine, fine friend. You know I would never run away with you, *mon cher*. This"—she gestured in a French way at the convent—"is different."

"How can you love that brute?" Harry said. He turned to Miranda, who was listening to everything, puzzled. Why did Sir Harry think Maman loved Papa? She hated him!

"Come here, little one, and say goodbye." Harry's eyes were warm and brown. "Maybe I shall wait for you. You are the image of your mother, sweetheart, and one day you will be the most beautiful lady in all France."

"No, I shall be a nun," Miranda announced with conviction.

He laughed and tousled her hair. "I hope not! What a waste that would be!"

The next few days passed in a strange haze for Miranda. Her mother seemed to know many of the sisters, and when Miranda asked, her mother told her that she had been raised at this convent, and had, indeed, wanted to become a nun before her father had arranged her marriage. Miranda was no longer frightened. And her mother, although very sad, no longer seemed frightened either. Miranda's spirits rose. The convent had beautiful gardens, which she would play in when she was not praying. To her seven-year-old mind, everything here was peaceful and safe, although of course she did not put her feelings into those kinds of words.

Then one day, almost a week later, when Miranda was wandering in the gardens, she heard *his* voice. She was seized by a terror unlike anything she had ever known before. Papa had found them!

Her mother came to her many hours later, her face deathly white and her eyes red and swollen from weeping. "*Petite*, we must talk."

"Maman, I'm so afraid!" Miranda rushed into her mother's arms.

"You know? *Chérie*, Papa has come. But listen to me. He will let you stay here. I have told him—" Angeline stopped. She could not tell her daughter that she had bargained with her husband, that she had promised her body to him willingly so long as Miranda could remain at the convent. No, that would never do. "Papa will let you stay here. You will be raised the way I was raised, *ma chérie*. But I must go back to London with your papa. Do you understand?"

"No!" Miranda cried. "No, Maman! Please, *s'il vous plaît*, I beg you, no, don't go back with him, we can both stay here, please, please—"

"*Non*, be still now. Your papa has decided. Be brave, *ma petite*. You will be happy here. And safe."

"I wish to say goodbye to my daughter." A hoarse voice came from the doorway.

Miranda gasped and clutched her mother's skirts, burying her face.

"*Non, non, chérie*, please, be nice, and say goodbye to your papa." Angeline gently pushed her away.

Miranda started to cry. The earl stood in front of her, and when she looked up, she gasped, hardly recognizing him. His face was covered with black whiskers and his eyes were red, with dark circles beneath them. He knelt in front of her. "Miranda," he whispered, then broke off.

Miranda cringed against the bed.

"Oh dear God," Edward cried. "You are afraid of me! I never meant to hit you! I am so sorry! Don't you understand?"

Miranda chewed on her lip, trembling.

"Your mother wants you to stay here, Miranda," he said with a sigh, standing. He spoke aloud, but to himself. "God forgive me, but she is right. If I ever struck you again—no, this is better." He stared at her for a long moment, and Miranda was compelled to gaze into his dark eyes.

"Please let Maman stay," she whispered. "Please." She tried bravely not to cry, but failed.

"I can't," he said hoarsely. "I can't live without her." Edward reached out and touched a tendril of her hair. "It is not forever, daughter." Then he turned abruptly and strode away.

Part One

The Bride

Chapter 1

Natchez, 1840

Miranda was afraid.

They had stayed in Natchez four days, waiting for her fiancé to show up to escort her the rest of the way to his ranch just east of San Antonio. He had not appeared. Miranda was very, very glad, because all she wanted to do was to go home, to France, not England, back to the safety and security of the convent. She prayed, selfishly she knew, that the man her father had betrothed her to had changed his mind.

Miranda was as frightened of marrying this stranger, who had to be a barbarian—he was a Texan, was he not?—as she was of the country she was going to. It was a land she knew of only vaguely from her studies, but upon her father's startling disclosure, she had made a point of learning all she could about it. *Mon Dieu!* Her father was banishing her to a wilderness of savage Indians, wild animals, and barbaric men! How could he do this to her!

The shock had come so suddenly. One day Miranda was content—although maybe a bit restless—performing her duties at the convent, and the next she was being sent home, upon her father's request, with no explanation. She had been reluctant to leave, dreading the thought of seeing her father again, although she had been excited at the prospect of seeing her mother. Angeline had come to visit her several times over the past decade. She had seemed quite different, with a glow on her face, her eyes bright and sparkling. Miranda didn't understand it. She didn't understand, either, her mother's sadness when she'd asked Miranda if she wanted to return home and Miranda had replied that she preferred to remain at the convent.

Angeline couldn't have guessed that Miranda would have chosen anything to avoid going home—her childhood memories were vivid and insurmountable. Home was a place of terror. The convent was a haven of comfort, security, and affection. She was loved there, even if she was occasionally the despair of the mother superior, who thought her too curious in some ways for her own good.

There had been nothing but shocks, one after the other. Her father in his study, looking exactly the way he had the last time she had seen him, ten years ago. He was huge and animallike, his face was covered with unkempt growth, and his eyes were red, very red, as if he had been weeping.

"Papa," Miranda said, curtsying formally. She held in check her fear of this monster—she would never forget what he was. "Is Maman here?"

Her father rose unsteadily. "No. No. I am sorry." His voice was hoarse, barely audible. "She's left me, Miranda. Left . . ."

Miranda started, thinking that her mother had run away again, finally, after all these years.

"She's dead," Edward cried in anguish. "She died in childbirth—and God, I killed her! I killed her!" He reached out suddenly and drew her into his embrace. "Your mother is gone!"

Miranda couldn't believe it—no, not Maman! Not beautiful, gentle Maman! "No!" she screamed, twisting away. "No!"

"I'm sorry! Miranda, God—"

"You killed her!" she cried in uncharacteristic rage. She had never felt such rage; in fact, anger of any kind was a totally unfamiliar emotion to her. "I hate you! You killed her! Oh, Maman!" Without waiting for permission, Miranda fled from his study.

Her father didn't speak to her for a week. Miranda lived in a state of extreme fear. How could she have talked to her Papa like that? He would surely beat her, maybe even whip her—and it was no more than she deserved. She had been rapped on the knuckles a few times by the nuns, when she had been too wordly or too mischievous. And then there was that one time, when she was so young, when her father had struck her. But she had never been beaten before. He was a monster, a beast, like most men— Sister Agnes had told her horrible stories about what had happened to *her*. She had been raped!—not that Miranda knew what that was. She didn't know anything about the facts of life, she did not know how babies were conceived, she did not know that men and women coupled. But she had heard her father's agonized, guilt-ridden words: *I killed her!* Papa had killed Maman! She hated him, feared him, and grieved for her beautiful mother all at once.

Edward called her into his study a week later. He had shaved and dressed neatly, and his eyes were no longer red. His face was lean and hard, and his virility, his magnetism, frightened her. His presence was overpowering. She couldn't help trembling.

"I have chosen a man for you to marry," he said bluntly.

Miranda gasped.

"I want grandchildren. A grandson. Your mother would want that, too. You are too beautiful and too rare to rot away in that damn convent." His dark eyes held hers and she could not look away, although she was stunned by his sacrilegious manner. "If you are at all like her, you will not regret my doing this."

Miranda couldn't speak. Her entire world had been crumbling piece by piece, and now lay in ruins around her feet.

"I met him a few years ago. He lives in Texas. He has a ranch, and thousands of acres of land. He is a gentle man, educated, and he will not hurt you. You only have to please him and he will worship you, believe me."

"Marriage! *Texas!* Papa, no, please . . ."

"You will not change my mind. He is already in love with you. He saw your portrait, the one Angeline gave to me two years ago, and he fell in love. He asked me then for your hand, but you were too young. I told him I would think about it. Last year, I agreed. Your mother didn't know—but I know she would have liked him.'' His voice broke off. ''This is for the best, Miranda.''

Although her entire life she had tried—sometimes unsuccessfully—to learn obedience before anything else, she couldn't accept this. But, God, what could she do? She was so afraid. This man was her papa, and if he wanted to marry her off to some strange barbarian, he could. Miranda closed her eyes and began to pray, even as she stood right there in front of her father. She knew that God had chosen this as her punishment for not being as docile and obedient as she should have been.

''What are you doing?'' her father asked.

''Praying,'' she told him honestly.

Edward seemed to hesitate, but then he said, ''There is one thing, Miranda.''

What more could there possibly be? Miranda wondered, waiting.

''Your eldest son must return upon his majority to take his title and his lands.''

Miranda shut her eyes briefly. He was sending her to Texas to breed her to some barbarian for a grandson. She could not believe that this was happening. ''Papa? Why this man?''

The earl of Dragmore smiled grimly. ''There are several reasons, Miranda. Your husband to be—John Barrington—is the grandson of Lord Barrington, the fifth earl of Darby. His lineage is impeccable. He is also a man—not some London fop. You are as delicate as your mother. I want to see you bear strong children, Miranda, not weak, fragile ones.'' He turned away, his word final. ''You will travel next week with my sister Elizabeth. Your fiancé will meet you in Natchez.''

''Are you daydreaming again, dear?''

Miranda was brought back to the present as her Aunt Elizabeth, a thin, tall, kindly widow, bustled into their room. It was the best lodging in Natchez, although crude compared to what Miranda was used to. Thankfully, their room was clean. Even the town of Natchez was crude, full of big, brawny men—all of whom carried guns—and colored people, so many colored people, all slaves. The very thought of slavery revolted her.

"I suppose."

"A man has arrived to take us to your fiancé, child."

"What?" Miranda gasped. Why hadn't her fiancé come? What kind of a man was he that he would promise to come and then not appear?

"It seems that John Barrington has suffered a bad accident and could not come. The man who has come for us carried a note for you, and for me. Here, dear." Elizabeth handed her an envelope.

Miranda's hands were trembling as she read it. It was brief, but expressive.

My dearest Miranda,

Please forgive me, but I have met with an untimely accident, and am temporarily bedridden. My very close friend, Derek Bragg, will escort you to my ranch. I entrust you to his care, knowing he will guard you with his life. You have nothing to fear, for he is a captain of the Texas Rangers. He was born in this country, and thus knows the land and its inhabitants well. I await with great anticipation your arrival.

All my love, your betrothed,
John Barrington.

Miranda looked up. "When do we leave?" she asked.

"First thing in the morning, dear," her aunt said kindly. "At the crack of dawn, I'm afraid."

Chapter 2

Derek Bragg wanted a woman.

He surveyed the boisterous, trail-worn patrons of the saloon, and the barmaids. What had happened to that lovely quadroon, Sherisse? Had she been sold? It was going to be a godawful long trip to San Antonio, over two weeks with two women and a wagon—two women he could not touch. Christ! If John wasn't his best friend and his blood brother, he would never have agreed to this insanity. What in hell had gotten into John? Marrying some English lady, one who had been raised in a convent, for crissakes! It was going to be a bitch of a trip, he felt it in every bone. John had obviously lost his mind, no matter how pretty he thought this woman was.

Bragg sighed and downed the sweet bourbon. He had made the trip in just over six days, but he had been traveling alone, not pushing it either. Hell, he could do it just as fast on foot if he had to, like any Apache worth his salt. He could make seventy-five miles a day on foot, if pushed. Of course, he wasn't Apache, he was white—in his mind. He had been called "breed" numerous times—because his mother was a squaw—and he had killed almost every man who had dared to label him half-breed.

Bragg leaned against the bar, a tall, broad man rippling with muscle and clad from head to foot in buckskins. His frame came from his father, a mountain man, one of the

16

original trailblazers through Texas, and so did his coloring. Golden was the only way to describe him. His hair was six different shades of gold, his skin was a golden bronze, and even his eyes were gold—glinting topaz. Only his brows and lashes and body hair were darker, not black, but brownish—a deep, dark shade of gold.

Bragg saw Sherisse and smiled. She was coming downstairs, meaning that she had been with a customer, but her face lit up with a real smile when she saw him. She swayed over, hips swinging, and he threw his arm around her waist, pressing her close to him.

"Sherisse," Bragg murmured, "I was hoping you were still here." He smiled at her, heated already, remembering very well her soft, voluptuous body, a body a man could get lost in for hours and hours.

"Derek! When did you arrive? How long are you here for?" She regarded him with blue eyes, her long chestnut hair flowing around her peach-tinted face. She looked whiter than some whites, he had thought on more than one occasion.

"Let's talk later," he said, his lips brushing hers. He ran his hands down her back, caught her buttocks, and pressed her against his ready manhood. She opened her mouth and accepted his tongue eagerly.

"Do you want me for the whole night?" Sherisse asked coyly after the long, long kiss had ended.

"I sure as hell do, but dammit, I'm hitting the trail tomorrow. Oh, what the hell!" he decided. "There won't be any trouble till we hit the Sabine. All right."

An expression of pure pleasure crossed her face.

"You like that, huh?" Bragg laughed huskily, pulling her against him again.

"Very much," she breathed. "I don't have to pretend with you, you know."

He chuckled and let his hand slide up her waist, cupping a full breast. "We'll talk later." He proceeded to half pull her upstairs to a room, where he promptly stripped her, ripping off her skirt in his eagerness.

He was up well before sunrise, and so was Pete Welsh, the man he had hired to drive the wagon that would carry the women and their luggage. They checked and packed up their supplies, and finally Bragg left Welsh hitching up the team. He nodded to the innkeeper's wife, who was up and fixing breakfast for all the travelers, and he silently moved with a sinuous, coiled grace up the stairs. His wariness wasn't purposeful; it was instinctive. Not a board creaked.

He rapped three times very sharply on the ladies' door. "Rise and shine, ladies," he called loudly. "We're moving out in thirty minutes. Grub's downstairs."

He paused, about to leave, but he didn't hear any sounds from within. He was just about to knock again, this time more forcefully, when he heard a soft voice say, "Who's Grub?"

Christ!

Bragg turned swiftly and went back outside. He finished saddling his own horse, a high-strung palomino stallion. He found Welsh relaxing with a cup of coffee. "That's about it," Welsh said cheerfully. " 'Cept fer the ladies' bags."

"Let's eat," Bragg said.

They had just finished when they heard the rustle of skirts, notifying Bragg that his charges had arrived. He stood abruptly, shoving his plate away when the serving girl bustled over.

"You want some more, Derek?" She flashed him a big smile. "Or anything else?"

He smiled back and patted her round rump. She was a cute, plump thing he had bedded in the past, and would certainly bed again in the future. "You know what I want," he teased in a low voice. "Next time, Lettie."

She giggled and fled back into the kitchen. He straightened to find the aunt, Lady Holcombe, staring at him with disapproval. Behind her stood her niece, but all he could see was her dark green skirts—she was obviously short and small.

"Ma'am, morning," Bragg drawled. "Why don't you two have a bite, and fill up good. We won't be stopping until nightfall. We'll be loading up your bags." He touched two fingers politely to his hat and swept past them with a snapped "Welsh."

The women had enough trunks to clothe an army. Bragg was disgusted. There were four large trunks, and six smaller ones. The wagon would be completely full, and the mules would have to work too hard.

No, this was insanity, and it wouldn't matter if she were the princess of England! He told Welsh to stay put, and strode back inside. He stopped in front of the two women, his face grim. "Ladies."

They both looked up. For a second, Bragg stared at the girl—because that's what she was—and forgot everything he was about to say. She looked him in the eye for a second, just long enough for him to glimpse huge violet eyes set in a flawless, pale face, before her long, black lashes swept down and she pinkened again. His heart had begun a dull thudding.

Sweet Lord, he thought inanely. She's a beauty! No wonder . . . I had no idea. . . .

He was dying to see the rest of her, but she was seated, and all he saw were small shoulders and arms—she had to be tiny—and the top of her bent head. Coils and coils of sable black hair glistened in the lamplight.

"Mr. Bragg?" her aunt said, and he tore his gaze away from the young woman, wondering again what her body looked like. He was very aware of his strong stirrings of desire.

"Ma'am. Look, we've got close to five hundred miles to travel, and we've only got two mules. Half the luggage has to go. Once we get to Comanche country—hell, we won't stand a chance loaded down like that." He frowned.

The young woman gasped and turned her lovely, pale face toward him. Her full, red lips were parted, and he saw her wide-eyed fear. "Indians?" she whispered.

Bragg hated himself for scaring her with the truth. But before he could speak, her aunt patted her arm, saying "Don't worry, dear, remember what your fiancé said about Captain Bragg. We'll be safe."

Miranda's gaze had gone to her aunt, but when he spoke, she looked back at him.

"I'm sorry to frighten you, ma'am. We're losing time. I need you to show me which half of your luggage you'll leave behind to be sent for later."

"Now see here," Lady Holcombe flared. "That's insane! My brother spent a fortune on Miranda's trousseau! I—"

"Aunt Elizabeth," Miranda said, trying to forget what he had said about the Comanches. "Please. Captain Bragg?" She stood, holding out her hand. "I don't believe we've been introduced properly. I'm Lady Miranda."

Bragg stared at the extended hand. She was no longer looking at his face, but at his chest, as if meeting his eyes would be too intimate. He grinned. He took her hand, turned it over, and pressed a moist, warm kiss onto the tiny, soft palm. She gasped, drawing her hand away as if she'd been burned by a flame. The touch of her hand and her scent, jasmine, had excited him further. Damn me, he thought, this is going to be the longest two weeks of my life. "Your bags?" he drawled coolly to hide his discomfort.

"You may choose," Miranda said, her face flushing again.

He noted irrelevantly that her waist could easily be spanned by his hands, and then some, and that she had some curves to her—a bit more than a faint swell of bosom and hip. Maybe without her clothes she isn't all skin and bones, he thought, fascinated with that idea. "Very well." He brushed his hat with a finger again and turned.

"Miranda!" Lady Holcombe gasped. "Well I never! How can you let him choose which bags to take?" She was already on her feet and hurrying after Bragg, calling his name.

Miranda sat very still, not hungry anymore. She was trembling. She was no longer thinking about the Indians, but about Bragg. That awful, crude man! Not only hadn't he removed his hat, a shocking insult, but the way he had kissed her hand—dear God! She shuddered again. She hadn't been able to see his face, just his mouth, a cruelly sensual mouth, which, when bared in a grin, seemed indecently suggestive, even predatory. She placed her hand on her bosom. Her heart was fluttering wildly. I should have slapped him, she thought. How could I have let him get away with that? How could John Barrington have sent such a crude lout to escort me?

He was an animal—like her father. Miranda could feel

it. She couldn't explain why she felt that, but she did, and she knew it deep in her heart. He frightened her. His presence was overwhelming. It wasn't just his size, although that was overwhelming, too. His buckskin shirt, beaded and painted around the neckline, strained across his broad shoulders and massive chest. She hadn't missed the dangerous-looking gun strapped to his right thigh, bound there with rawhide. And tucked in another belt, that one tooled and boasting brass conchos, was a long, sheathed knife. Miranda shivered. The man looked deadly. And he was dirty! His buckskins were stained; to her alien eye, they were repulsively barbaric and crude. And—he smelled. When she had offered her hand, she had inhaled his scent, his male scent. . . .

Five hundred miles, she thought, dazed.

"Ma'am?"

She almost jumped at that insolent drawl. She hadn't heard him approach. "Yes?" She refused to meet his shaded eyes. She focused instead on the intricate beading around the neck of his shirt.

Bragg smiled. "We're about ready." He took her elbow, ignoring her gasp, and guided her outside. Dawn had broken, and faint rays of sunlight were filtering over the streets of Natchez.

Miranda tried to control her fear. Or was it agitation? Why did this man frighten her so? Why was her father putting her through this? God, give me strength! she prayed silently.

Her aunt was already sitting beside another brawny man, although he was nowhere near as tall or graceful as Bragg. He was also clad in buckskins, and he smiled at her. As they passed, Miranda realized that he was dirtier than Bragg, and her sensitive nose could detect his odor, something quite different from Bragg's masculine scent, and rather offensive. She choked, wanting to bring her handkerchief to her nose, but unable to do so as Bragg rudely propelled her toward the wagon. Then Bragg did the unspeakable. He placed his two hands on her waist, completely enclosing it, lifting her up and settling her next to her aunt before she even knew it. This time the gasp died in her throat.

Against her will, Miranda watched him spring effortlessly into the saddle of a big palomino stallion, her heart pounding so hard against her ribs that she could barely breathe. "Move out," he said with a motion of his gloved hand.

The wagon moved forward. Bragg's mount pranced beside them for a few paces, Bragg sitting gracefully and easily, and then the stallion leaped forward and galloped away.

Chapter 3

They didn't see Bragg again until noon, and Miranda was more than relieved. Welsh kept up a running dialogue with her aunt, for Miranda was too immersed in her thoughts to participate. What was her fiancé like? How would he treat her? What was her new home like? And how was she going to adjust to all this?

Welsh, just as most other Americans they had met, seemed impressed that they were aristocracy. He asked many questions as he spouted trail lore and Texas adventures. Welsh had explained that Bragg would always be riding ahead of them, scouting for Indians and other hostiles. He assured them that Bragg was a Texas Ranger, one of the best, and that they had nothing to fear—he had traveled the Camino Real hundreds of times.

Miranda stared at the passing countryside—lush, dark cypresses, dripping moss, fragrant flowers, a mystical kind of beauty—and soon became lost in God's creation. Louisiana was a beautiful state.

Bragg appeared out of nowhere, raising his hand, and Welsh slowed the wagon. "All right, ladies, ten minutes. Stretch your legs and take care of any business you have." His golden eyes glinting beneath the wide-brimmed hat found Miranda and settled on her tense form. Her face was pinkening in what was fast becoming a familiar way. Had he embarrassed her again? Not that he'd meant to. Damn,

23

but she was so sensitive. "This is our last stop before camp," he added.

Welsh was helping Lady Holcombe down and, unable to resist, Bragg leaped off his stallion and quickly approached Miranda. "Ma'am?" He smiled and held out his hand. Then he frowned when she stiffened involuntarily. "We don't have all day," he snapped, angry at her reaction to him.

She extended her hand and he pulled her close enough to grasp her familiarly again. He could feel every muscle and fiber in her body go rigid at his touch. The Ice Princess, he thought with irritation. He swept her off the wagon seat and set her on the ground.

But, he had to admit, he had forgotten just how stunning she was, even if she was a fragile thing, and as he let her down, he held her close enough that her small breasts touched his shirt for just a second. He quickly stepped back, thoroughly annoyed with himself. She's John's fiancée, he reminded himself sternly.

Miranda stood indecisively in front of him, her face red, biting her lip and staring at the ground.

She's a mouse, Bragg thought. Poor little mouse! She'll never make it in Texas, not ever! And just as he thought that, she looked up at him and said softly, "Captain, I do beg of you, please treat me with some respect. It is going to be a long journey." Her eyes pleaded openly with him, and then she dropped her gaze and hurried after her aunt.

He thought about her words and was angry with himself again. She's a real lady, damn you, he thought, not some cheap hussy—what's wrong with you? But his eyes, of their own volition, settled on her small hips, enjoying their natural, unaffected rhythm as she moved hurriedly away. I'm going to have to watch myself, he thought, suddenly confused. He had never been around a real lady before. The only women he encountered were cheap whores, squaws, and the wives and daughters of settlers. Except for the last, they were women for the taking.

Bragg frowned. The rules he knew no longer applied. He was used to taking what he wanted when he felt like it, and women had been no exception. Anger rose in him. The situation was ridiculous, insane. He had work to do, and instead he was babysitting some spoiled, pampered virgin aristocrat. Just what the hell was he supposed to do? Bow down and kiss her regal hand every time she swept by? He rode on ahead.

By the time they made camp that night, Miranda was exhausted. She sank stiffly to the ground, Bragg having helped her down again, and this time she was grateful for his assistance. There was nothing she wanted more, at that moment, than a hot bath and a bed. But here she was in the middle of the Louisiana wilderness—it seemed like wilderness to her!—on her way to an even more hostile and savage land. Oh, Papa! she thought miserably. Why, oh why, did you do this to me?

The sun was still high, but slowly setting. Her aunt had disappeared—to relieve herself, Miranda thought—and she watched Welsh quickly make a fire. Where was Bragg? The next moment she saw him stride into camp with two rabbits, the hooded gaze beneath his hat going directly to her. Miranda looked away. Why was he always looking at her? He was so insolent! Did he never take off that hat? When she dared to peek at him again, he was squatting and skinning the rabbit quickly and efficiently. At the sight of the blood and the entrails he tossed into the fire, Miranda felt nausea rise up in her. She struggled to her feet with a gasp and ran into the forest, where she sank to her knees and fought the urge to vomit.

Bragg scowled and looked at Welsh. "John is insane," he said quietly, angrily. "That little chit will never make a Texas wife. Never."

"Poor thing," Welsh agreed. "So small. How old do you think she is?"

"She's seventeen," Bragg muttered. What kind of man would send his frail, sheltered daughter to a savage land like Texas, to marry a Texan? He shook his head. When Miranda appeared a bit later, he studied her quickly to see if she was all right. She needed protecting, he realized, washing his hands, and felt the urge rise up in him, hard and strong. It was not a familiar feeling. Frustrated, confused, Bragg skewered the rabbits and handed them to Welsh. Standing, he tossed his hat aside and ran his fingers through his hair. When he glanced at her again, he found her staring at him, seemingly mesmerized. He scowled and walked away.

Miranda held a hand to her breast. Her heart was flutter-ing wildly. As sheltered and innocent as she was, she knew a handsome man when she saw one. Except, she thought in panic, he's not handsome, he's too savage to be handsome, even if his features are strong and clean, straight and even. Good Lord! Never had she seen a man with such coloring. He was gold, from his head to his toes—literally. His hair was gold, his skin was gold—a dark gold, to be sure, but gold. Even his eyes were the color of topaz, and his clothes were golden-tanned buckskins. She laughed a bit hysterically. Her face felt warm, and she knew that she was flushing uncontrollably, although why, she had no idea.

And why had he looked at her so darkly? As if he despised her?

Silence reigned in the camp throughout the meal of roasted hare, beans, and coffee. Miranda couldn't eat the rabbit. Just looking at it made her ill—in fact, she wasn't hungry at all, just tired, so utterly tired. She set down her nearly untouched plate, and before she knew it, a pair of muscular legs, clad in buckskins and moccasins, were planted in front of her face. Miranda looked up.

Bragg squatted, his face worried. "Are you feeling all right, Miranda?" His voice was a low, husky drawl, and his topaz eyes searched hers.

He was so close. Of course, he was being insulting, by using her name so familiarly. A small, unaccustomed spark of anger flared at his insolence. But she could feel his magnetic pull, smell his masculine scent, and she couldn't look away from his gaze. She was trapped by his hypnotic stare, helpless, and she let out a long-held breath through parted, quivering lips.

"Ma'am?" He broke the spell. "Are you feeling ill?"

Miranda flushed and looked down, away, anywhere but at him. God, how could he kneel so close to her, it was so improper! She trembled. "No, I'm just not hungry," she whispered. "I'm too tired to be hungry." Her gaze was pointedly averted.

Without looking, she knew when he had left, and a huge

tide of relief swept over her. But then, before she could count to three, he was there again, wrapping a blanket around her shoulders. His touch sent another shudder through her. Mistaking it for fear and repulsion, she shrank against the tree.

Bragg studied her, scowling darkly, then he stood up. Was the little mouse afraid of him? The thought irritated him. "You're too skinny already," he said brusquely. "You have to eat. We travel all day, every day." With the tip of his toe, he pushed her plate at her.

She tensed, fought briefly for control, then gave in to her baser nature. She looked up with a smoldering glare. "You're here to escort me to Texas, sir! But don't tell me what to put in my body, thank you!" The minute the words were out, Miranda couldn't believe that it was she who had spoken them. Why was she angry? But how dare he presume to order her to eat?

Worse, he chuckled. "So the mouse has some spine," he said, laughing as he walked away.

The insult made her stiffen even more. Is that what he thought she was—a plain, drab, timid mouse? This man had done nothing but insult her from the moment they had met—treating her like a cheap tart, now calling her a mouse—it was too much!

Chapter 4

"Excuse me, Captain Bragg. When can I bathe?"

Bragg stared, startled, then he grinned, imagining her naked in the creek below. "Why, any time at all, ma'am. The creek's that way." He pointed through the trees. They had just made their camp for the night after traveling another long, hard day.

Her violet eyes widened and she gasped. "In the creek?"

He chuckled. "You didn't expect me to lug along a nice brass tub for you now, did you, ma'am?" He started away, then abruptly turned back. "If you intend to bathe," he said, no longer smiling, his features hard, "you must tell me first."

Miranda couldn't believe what she'd heard, and she went to her aunt, who was sitting wearily, rubbing her spine. "Aunt Elizabeth! Captain Bragg just told me we're to take our baths in the creek!"

"We will do no such thing," her aunt responded grimly. "You will do no such thing," she added.

"Of course not!" Miranda gasped. "*Je voudrais . . . mon Dieu!* I'm so dirty—I smell!"

Her aunt patted her shoulder. "Ignore it, dear. From what I've gathered, in a few days we'll be at Natchitoches, and there's lodging there."

"A few days!" Miranda sighed. "I guess I'm just going

to have to get used to this. *Mais*—oh! I wish I could dare bathe in the creek!''

"Miranda!"

Miranda bit her lip. She had never been unclean a day in her life. Cleanliness was next to godliness. She stood. "Well, I'm going to go down to the creek and wash my face and arms and anything else that I can. Will you come with me?"

"I'll be down shortly, dear. I need to rest my poor bones."

"Are you all right?" Miranda was worried. After only two days on the trail, her aunt was looking wan and pale.

"Yes, go ahead. Wait! Is it safe?"

"The captain told me I could use the creek. I assume so." She shrugged in a very French way, then gathered a change of clothes. She paused at Welsh's side as he stirred beans—not again!—and told him where she was going. He nodded.

Miranda took her clothes, a sponge, a towel, and a bar of scented soap with her and tentatively made her way to the stream that lay just in sight of the camp. She stumbled on exposed roots and rocks. Suddenly feeling eyes upon her, she looked back to see Welsh watching her with undisguised male interest. He immediately turned away. Miranda flushed. She didn't know exactly what his look meant, but it disturbed her greatly. Dear God, there was no privacy at all on the trail! Once she reached the creek, she wandered up the bank a bit until she was just out of sight.

It was so beautiful here, Miranda thought wistfully. Almost eerie in the twilight. The air was fragrant with honeysuckle and something else she couldn't identify. She unbuttoned her dark green jacket and removed it for the first time that day. She glanced over her shoulder, but there was not a soul around. She wanted to remove her high-necked blouse so that she could scrub her arms and chest and throat, but that would be scandalous. She settled for unbuttoning the top six buttons instead and pushing the sleeves up to her elbows. She bathed her arms, the top of her chest, under her arms (without removing the shirt, of course!), and her throat and face. She felt so much better.

Miranda hesitated. She cast another quick glance over her shoulder, but of course no one was watching. She pulled her heavy muslin skirt up to her knees, wincing at the thought of what would happen if her aunt appeared at that moment. She carefully rolled down her stockings and removed them, quickly bathing her feet, ankles, calves, and knees. Then she replaced her stockings, fastened the garters, slipped on her kid boots, and stood, turning.

Bragg smiled. "Finished?"

Miranda stood as still as a cornered hare, her heart going wild. "How long were you watching?" she managed stiffly, her face flaming.

Bragg shifted the rifle in his hand and shrugged, but a wide grin lit up his face. "You have very pretty legs," he said easily. "But—"

Miranda took three strides over and slapped him as hard as she could across the face. "You go too far!" she cried. "You have done nothing but insult me and treat me like some cheap harlot since we've met! How dare you spy on me while I bathe?"

He was staring, shocked, then he started to laugh. "Miranda! First off, it's not safe for you to ever be alone—and, sweetheart, you couldn't kill a fly with your strength!" He was still laughing. "And if you call that bathing, well . . ." His laughter trailed off.

"You're repulsive," she whispered stiffly. "You're barbaric, completely uncivilized." She realized she was getting a reaction, for his face had grown hard and his laughter had stopped abruptly. "You disgust me—although I know it's uncharitable for me to feel so. I should feel sorry for you, for how could you know how to treat a lady?"

Bragg's face had been growing darker by the second, and his eyes were glittering dangerously. Miranda felt fear then, and all her anger and indignation fled. She took a quick step to go past him—to flee—but his arm whipped out and he grabbed her, pulling her roughly against his side.

"I'm the trail boss here," he snarled. "And my word is law. I told you to inform me when you want to bathe. You never leave camp without supervision." His grip tightened, and Miranda cried out. "Is that clear? *Lady* Miranda?" He pronounced her title mockingly.

"You're hurting me," she whispered, trembling. She could feel his body against hers, as hard as a rock. He abruptly released her and she stumbled slightly. She wrapped her arms across her chest, hugging herself, and tears welled up in her eyes. He was so cruel! She bit back a sob and ran blindly to the camp.

Bragg stared after her, frowning with agitation. Stupid twit! He had given a direct order, and she had disobeyed. Of course, the danger here was only from a stray wolf, but in a few days there would be Indians to worry about. He could not let anyone start to disobey him now.

He followed her back to the camp, his jaw clenched. The image of her long, willowy legs came to his mind, making his groin ache. I'm lusting after my best friend's fiancée, he thought angrily, directing his anger at her. She was a little twit of a woman—a child, really—all skin and bones. Why in hell did he have to be so stirred by her? Was she afraid of him? She looked at him so strangely, as if she were both fascinated and repulsed, as if he were a two-headed monster. . . .

With a foul curse, one that caused both ladies to gasp, Bragg squatted by the fire to give Welsh a hand.

Chapter 5

The next three days passed without incident, and soon they were approaching Natchitoches. Miranda had taken to dreaming about a bath, until it had become the most important thing in life to her. Both Bragg and Welsh obviously bathed in the creeks and rivers they camped by, and their smell, she had come to realize, was not so bad—a smell of horse and smoke and musk. She was getting used to the barbaric Texans! It was too much. Would her husband dress and act and smell like these big, strong men? Would he also be a six-foot giant? Miranda shuddered at the thought.

Bragg had avoided her since she had accused him of treating her like a trollop, although his eyes still roved insolently over her body when he thought she was not aware of it. But the moment he turned his gaze on her, she could feel it, and a strange heat would spread across her body while her cheeks flushed uncomfortably. She would clench her fists and wonder why this rude, crude man was sent to humiliate her like this. Had she really been so disobedient at the convent? It was the only answer she could think of.

What if her husband treated her so rudely? She could not think that—it was too upsetting.

Miranda had grown used to the wagon and Welsh's incessant, endless monologue. When he wasn't chattering away, he was humming some ditty. Once Miranda asked him to teach her the words, so they could sing to pass the time. Welsh actually went red, and Bragg burst into laughter as he rode alongside the wagon.

"The words for that tune are not for a lady's ears," he told her, laughing and clearly enjoying her embarrassment. "Especially not a convent-reared lady like yourself." And he'd had the gall to wink lewdly at her. Miranda had then had a very ungodly thought—maybe lightning would smite him right then and there, on the spot. She prayed for forgiveness an instant later.

Now, suddenly, the wagon stopped short, jerking all of them forward. "Damn!" Welsh exclaimed, already leaping off.

"What happened?" Lady Holcombe asked with concern.

Miranda felt her heart fluttering nervously. "Did something break?" she called down, worried, then her eyes searched the horizon. As usual, Bragg was riding ahead, and there was no sign of him.

"Goddammit! Excuse me, ladies!" Welsh bit down hard on his lip, and Miranda knew that if she and her aunt hadn't been there, he would have uttered a most foul string of epithets.

"What happened, Mr. Welsh?" she asked again, fanning herself. It was hot and muggy and almost unbearable. But she was so close to her bath!

"Got the wheel stuck in a deep rut," Welsh said, shaking his head. "It's my fault. I was thinking about whiskey and wo— I was thinking about reaching Natchitoches tonight," he corrected hastily.

"Aunt Elizabeth, I think we should get down," Miranda said, rising and cautiously gathering her skirts. "So Mr. Welsh has a better chance of getting this wagon out of the rut."

"Here, hold on now, little lady," Welsh said, hurrying over. He helped her down, then her aunt.

"Where is Mr. Bragg?" Lady Holcombe asked. "Shouldn't he help?"

"I hope he never knows about this," Welsh muttered, jumping up on the wagon with surprising agility. He slapped the reins. "Harrah! Harrah! Get up!"

Miranda and her aunt stood back and watched with consternation as the mules strained to free the wagon. The wheel only dug deeper into the rut.

"Oh, stop, Mr. Welsh! Stop!" Miranda cried. "You're sinking deeper!"

Welsh sighed and climbed down. "We'll just have to— here comes Bragg!"

Miranda heard the pounding hoofbeats and watched as he came cantering in, his face dark. "What's going on?" he called, but already his eyes had found the offending wheel, and he cursed beneath his breath. He leaped down from the stallion.

"It's my fault," Welsh said miserably.

"You're damn right it is," Bragg snapped.

Miranda's eyes widened. "Mr. Welsh is only human," she objected. "Everyone makes a mistake—"

"You be quiet," Bragg said, turning on her, his eyes dark with anger. He threw his hat on the ground. Miranda couldn't believe how angry he was—all over a little accident.

"You're insufferable," she breathed, not meaning to speak the words aloud.

He whirled on her, fury etched on his face. "Insufferable, am I? Accidents mean death, lady, when you're on the trail! Do you understand now?" He was shouting.

Miranda stepped back, frightened by his barely leashed fury. "But—it's just a—"

"And what if we were in Comanche country?" He had lowered his voice, but his mouth was white. "What if this had caused a broken axle? Huh? What if we were stuck immobile for many hours fixing it—and a war party came upon us?" He turned away from her in disgust.

"It won't happen again," Welsh said quietly.

"You drive, I'll push," Bragg said in a calmer tone.

Miranda understood now, but it didn't make his temper any more bearable. And then, right before her very eyes, he shrugged off his shirt, tossing it carelessly aside.

She gasped, her heart stopping in her throat, choking her. Her face began to burn, and she felt light-headed and dizzy. She was scandalized. The man was half naked in front of her! She reached out weakly and found the wagon wheel, leaning on it for support and fanning herself wildly.

"Captain Bragg!" her aunt exclaimed, aghast. "How dare you disrobe in front of my niece!"

Bragg had been oblivious to Miranda's reaction, for he had begun studying the wheel the moment he had discarded his shirt. Now he straightened, his lips twisting in amusement as he glanced at Lady Holcombe, then Miranda. His smile died.

She was very, very white, fanning herself rapidly, staring straight ahead at some object far in the distance. Her aunt was objecting loudly again to his bare torso and, dropping to her knees in front of Miranda, she began chafing her wrists.

"Good God!" Bragg exclaimed. "Hasn't she ever seen a man's chest before? Is she going to faint?" He was disbelieving.

"Of course not," Lady Holcombe snapped, her face red with fury.

Miranda glanced at him for the briefest of instants, saw his broad, hairy chest, and went crimson. Her fan moved faster. Bragg started to laugh—it was too much. He walked over. "You're in the way," he said, not unkindly.

Poor John! What was he going to do with this frigid little virgin? He touched her shoulder to move her aside, but she inhaled deeply and fled from the spot as if he were the devil come to claim her. He stifled his laughter and got behind the wagon, bracing himself. "All right, Welsh, get these mules moving," he called, trying to forget about Miranda.

But Miranda couldn't forget about him. All she could see in her mind's eye was his golden, gleaming, naked flesh, thick and corded with sinewy muscle. Her face flushed again. And he had all that dark hair—it was indecent! She swallowed drily and heard Bragg grunting, while her aunt patted her shoulder soothingly.

Miranda didn't know what had come over her. She peeked above her fan at him. She was standing almost directly behind him, and a new rush of hot color flooded her face. He was leaning over, his shoulders and arms braced against the back of the wagon as he drove his entire body against it. His back rippled with his efforts. His buttocks and thighs strained beneath soft, tightly molded buckskins that were so revealing, it was as if he were naked. This time, she couldn't take her gaze away.

"Miranda!" her aunt cried. "Stop staring at Captain Bragg!"

Miranda flushed and quickly dropped her gaze. She was mortified that her aunt had caught her looking at him, and even more embarrassed that she had been reprimanded loudly enough for Bragg and Welsh to hear. But even as she stood staring at the ground, she heard Bragg groan again—a deep, animal sound that caused her body to ache warmly, sweetly, strangely. Again her gaze rose and rested upon his huge, fascinating form, and this time she saw that the wagon was moving forward.

"Miranda! What is wrong with you! What has possessed you?" Her aunt was astounded and horrified.

Uttering a little cry, Miranda dropped her fan and ran into the woods just as Bragg turned to look at her. An expression of amusement and comprehension came upon his face as he leaned back against the wagon, sweat pouring off his body.

"Sir, I must tell you, I have never—"

"You've already told me," Bragg cut her off. He wasn't in the mood for a lecture from some frigid, priggish, English widow. "We've lost time. Let's get going." He straightened.

"Miranda?" Her aunt called toward the woods. "Miranda? We're ready to go. Miranda?"

Bragg picked up his shirt. They would make Natchitoches just by dark, if they left now. But that was only a small, insignificant thought right now. Jesus! Miranda had almost fainted at the sight of a man's chest! She was so innocent. . . .

And John, his best friend and blood brother, was going to take that innocence and change her. That fact made him unreasonably angry.

There was no sign of Miranda, and she hadn't responded to her aunt's calls. Bragg slipped on his shirt and began to worry. Now what! Had the foolish twit run into a tree and been knocked senseless? Or worse?

"Why hasn't she responded? Oh dear, if anything's happened to her . . ."

"Relax, Lady Holcombe," Bragg said. "I'll find her in a flash." He strode into the forest in the direction Miranda had fled.

He kept up a rapid pace as he followed her easily, deeper into the forest. Tracking was one of the things the Apache did best. She'd left a trail a mile wide, and if she had beribboned it, it couldn't have been simpler. He found her curled up on the ground, hugging herself, beneath a huge fern.

"Miranda!" Irritation washed over him now that he saw she was safe. "You're holding us up."

She looked up, wiping her eyes, and he realized that she had been crying. A strange, unidentifiable feeling engulfed him—an unfamiliar softness. He squatted down next to her, but she wouldn't meet his eyes, and all he could see were her long, thick, black lashes on tear-stained cheeks.

"Why are you crying?" he asked softly, not recognizing his own voice. He instinctively placed both hands on her shoulders. She pulled away from his grasp and leaped to her feet.

"It's nothing," she said, brushing distractedly at her face, which was pinkening again.

"No, something's wrong," he said, more sharply this time. Did his touch offend her so much? Or did he repulse her? He stiffened at that last thought.

"I'm so ashamed," she whispered, glancing up at him. Her eyes were moist and held his directly for a moment. Her color deepened and her gaze fell to his chest. Her mouth parted slightly.

A feeling of triumph washed over him and he grinned. "Feeling desire for a man is nothing to be ashamed about," he told her easily. How could he have thought that she found him repellent? She was a woman, after all, and now her eyes gave her away. Bragg was delighted. He felt like strutting before her—taking off his shirt again and holding her against his bare chest. Holding her and stroking her . . .

Miranda gasped, her eyes widening. She stepped away from him. "Oh! *Vous êtes impossible! Bête! Sauvage! Vous êtes fou. Stupide! Vous retrouvez . . . vous m'en pensez . . . ohhh!*"

Bragg grinned. He didn't know what she was saying, but her French was adorable. When she spoke English, her accent seemed entirely British, and it was only when she slipped into French that he remembered she was half French. But there was no mistaking the import of her words. "Time's awasting, princess," he said, chuckling. He took her hand before she knew it. "C'mon."

He pulled her along with him, clearly feeling the taut fury of her body. She may not even know what she's feeling, he thought, dazed with delight. She probably doesn't even recognize her desire for me. He was smugly pleased with the day's revelations. Suddenly he realized that her incipient attraction meant nothing in the larger scheme of things.

He dropped her hand, frowning, and his stride lengthened. After all, Miranda was taboo, hands off—she was marrying John. Why did he hate that thought so much? It was none of his damn business! Or, if anything, he should be happy for his friend, who had often confessed his loneliness and his desire for a wife and family. Bragg was grim when they reached the wagon.

Chapter 6

The rest of the way to Natchitoches passed in a whirlwind daze for Miranda. She was very upset. Her mind was spinning and racing and wouldn't stop. Her aunt sat in frozen silence, very angry with her. Welsh was morose, and for once said not a word. Bragg, as if to show his complete displeasure with them all, rode right in front of the wagon. Miranda kept staring at his back. For some insane reason, all she could see when she looked at it was his naked, rippling flesh. Several times he suddenly looked over his shoulder, his gaze hot and hard, to catch hers. She would flush and quickly look away, but of course it was too late.

What was wrong with her? She didn't understand why her pulse was pounding in her ears, why she kept picturing his broad, hairy chest or his lean, powerful back. She finally decided that she had been greatly shocked today, and that her interest was natural curiosity. She had always been an avid student, eagerly drinking up new studies, new sights—and she had never seen a man's bare torso before. What she had witnessed today was a new lesson. She now knew something of the difference between men and women. Men were not only bigger and stronger, but built very, very differently. Did all men look like Bragg?

She didn't think so. Some men were fat, others dainty and foppish. Bragg was all rocklike strength. She shuddered. Her thoughts were almost lewd. In fact, she had an insane urge to touch him, to touch his bare skin. Would it be soft and smooth? Or . . .

Miranda stifled her thoughts, feeling heat rise again in her face. She realized that she was staring at his buckskin-clad back again, and her aunt whispered "Miranda!" very disapprovingly. At that instant—for the third or fourth time—in a lightning-quick movement, Bragg turned his horse sideways so that his gaze met hers. For a brief, hypnotic moment, she couldn't look away, she couldn't even breathe. She was unable to swallow, her mouth completely dry. She licked her lips without even thinking about it.

What does he think I'm thinking? Miranda felt miserable. She knew what he thought. The arrogant boor thought that she found him attractive. How had he reached that ridiculous conclusion? All men were awful, hurtful beasts, as she well knew, even her father. Men raped helpless women, like Sister Agnes. She didn't know what rape was, but she knew that it hurt, very, very much, and was humiliating and violent. She had guessed that much when Sister Agnes had told her about it; she could see the raw pain in her eyes, even after so many years.

Miranda shivered. No, she would never find any man attractive, she knew that. Men were different from women, crude and controlled by baser instincts, like wild animals. Bragg was no different. The way he looked at her made her pulse pound in fear. She didn't know what the look meant, exactly, but she knew it was rude, insolent, and related to the unspeakable things men did to women. She shivered again, at the same moment involuntarily wondering how his skin felt.

"Aunt Elizabeth?"

"Yes?"

Miranda knew that her aunt was furious, for she had not called her "dear." "Maybe there's a church in this town. I would like to go to church tonight. Or to Mass tomorrow morning."

"That is an excellent idea," her aunt said. Although Elizabeth was Protestant, she was very religious. "Mr. Bragg?"

"I heard," Bragg said, riding up to them. Miranda wondered how he could have possibly heard their low whispers. His gaze found her face, and their eyes met just for a moment. "The answer is no."

Miranda gasped. "But I must go to confession," she cried, angry and dismayed.

He scowled. "You have nothing to confess, princess," he said. "And there's no mission in Natchitoches. You'll have to save your confessions for San Antonio del Baxar." He clucked to his horse and rode ahead.

Miranda felt tears come to her eyes. "Oh, Papa," she whispered, "why did you do this to me?"

Bragg wheeled his horse again, having heard her anguished comment, and he stared at her. But she was brushing a tear from her cheek while her aunt took her hand in a gesture of comfort.

"Don't be angry with me, Aunt Elizabeth," Miranda cried brokenly. "Please don't be angry. I'm so . . ." She leaned against her aunt's shoulder, fighting the urge to cry in exhaustion, despair, fear, and confusion.

"Hush, dear, everything will be for the best, you'll see." She stroked Miranda's back.

"Why does Papa hate me so? Why? Why wouldn't he leave me be?" She couldn't help letting a few tears escape her tightly shut lids.

"Your papa loves you, Miranda, very much."

"Papa is a beast!" Miranda cried. "I hate him, I've always hated him for what he did to Maman—for killing her!" She started to cry in earnest. "And God is punishing me by sending me to this barbarian because I have such hatred in my heart."

"Your father didn't kill your mother!" Elizabeth gasped, horrified. She shook her niece. "How can you say that?"

"He did! He even admitted it." Miranda gulped and pulled herself together.

"Your mother died in childbirth, Miranda," her aunt said sternly. "It was God's will. Your father loved her deeply . . ."

"No! Do you think I'm a child?" Miranda whirled on her aunt. "I saw how he treated her—how he hit her. She hated him. He forced her to return to him. I know it."

"You are nothing but a foolish, frightened child," Elizabeth said. "And you are talking nothing but nonsense. I will write to your father and tell him that you harbor these ugly misconceptions!"

Miranda bit her lip and looked ahead, to see Bragg staring at her strangely. She frowned at him, upset that he had heard their private conversation. That was her fault, not his. The topic should have never come up in public. She stared at the forested hills on either side of them.

About an hour later they pulled into the courtyard of an inn in Natchitoches, which was a rambling, wooden town. The inn was one of the best the town had to offer, but it was rough and shabby compared to England's fine old establishments. Bragg left Welsh with the team and wagon, and led them into a common room.

"Why don't you eat while your baths are readied," he suggested pleasantly. "I'll take care of it now." He smiled at Miranda almost warmly.

Miranda felt surprise as he walked away, and she sat down with her aunt at an empty table. The dining room was quite full, and she was embarrassed about her appearance until she realized that nearly everyone was as travel-stained and weary as she. Still, she decided she would rather eat in her room, after her bath, and she told her aunt so.

"A wonderful idea," her aunt agreed.

"I'll go tell Mr. Bragg," Miranda said, and Lady Holcombe nodded tiredly. Miranda followed in the direction he had gone, out of the dining room and into a front room where there was a desk for registry, a sofa and chairs and table, and a few lounging occupants. They were all male, and they eyed her with blatant interest. She flushed, feeling disgraced at being seen looking so ill-kempt, and wondered where Bragg was. She inquired at the desk. The clerk told her that he had gone back outside and she headed off in that direction.

The team and wagon and Bragg's horse were gone, and she wandered into the stable. It was very quiet inside, except for the sound of the animals moving, snorting and eating. She thought she recognized their team of mules, although she wasn't sure. There was a lit lantern hanging on one wall, so she knew that someone was still in the barn. She was about to give up when she heard a noise. Staring down to the farthest end of the barn, she thought she saw the white mane of Bragg's stallion. She started down the hay-strewn corridor, and soon Bragg's broad back came into view.

Miranda heard his husky murmur just before she saw the woman. Bragg must have heard her because he turned abruptly, and his features softened as he came toward her. Miranda looked past him at the woman, wondering what they were doing there alone, feeling something like jealousy rise up in her. The woman smiled, pulling straw out of her hair and smoothing down her skirts. Miranda had the uncharitable thought that she was quite fat.

"Are you looking for me?"

Miranda's gaze moved back to Bragg, and she noticed that his eyes were bright, his shirt unbuttoned, his chest massive and glistening. She flushed. For a moment she couldn't remember why she had come—she could only stare.

"Y-yes, Captain. My aunt and I are tired. We'll be dining in our room tonight."

Bragg smiled. Then he said something, but she was already hurrying away, running. She reached the safety of the courtyard and breathed in deep lungfuls of air, unbuttoning the top three buttons at her throat. She was trembling. What had they been doing, alone like that?

And why did she care?

A moment later she heard him right behind her. "Miranda, wait." She grabbed her skirts and fled.

Chapter 7

"Miranda, what's wrong?"

Miranda forced a smile. "Nothing, Aunt Elizabeth." Stop thinking about that fat woman, she admonished herself.

"Dear, you're out of breath and flushed."

Miranda turned away, testing the bathwater.

"Are you ill?" Elizabeth asked, with concern.

"No, I'm fine."

"Did you find the captain?"

Miranda felt the heat rising in her cheeks, and her aunt didn't miss it. "Miranda?"

"Yes, I did. In the barn," she mumbled. Then it burst out. "He was in there with a woman, Aunt, alone with a woman." Elizabeth pursed her mouth in a severe line.

That night, Miranda had the most awful dream. Bragg had her in his arms, and he was stroking her body, her breasts. She was afraid, but didn't have a voice with which to cry out. She wanted to struggle, but her limbs wouldn't move. His touch made her body throb in the most peculiar way. She awoke in a sweat, a bittersweet ache between her thighs in her most intimate place. It took her a long time to fall back to sleep, and still she did not understand—not any of it.

Miranda and her aunt were eating a breakfast of hotcakes and sweet syrup when she felt his eyes upon her. She felt her face flaming but didn't look up. How can I look at him

44

after dreaming about him last night? she asked herself desperately. She looked at her plate and concentrated on eating every last bite. She wasn't hungry at all, but it gave her something to do.

"Good morning, ladies," Bragg drawled lazily.

"Captain Bragg." Elizabeth rose. "I would like a word with you in private."

Bragg stared at the top of Miranda's bowed head. He had an inane thought. How long was her hair? He realized that Lady Holcombe was waiting, and he gave her a casual glance. "Let me guess," he muttered. He made a gesture with his hand. "After you, ma'am."

They stepped outside into the courtyard. Bragg sighed and braced himself as the tirade came forth. "Mr. Bragg! I don't understand how John Barrington could have chosen a man like you to escort his betrothed five hundred miles, but I must demand that you exercise strict restraint upon your own baser nature, sir! My niece is an innocent. She has been greatly agitated, having had the unfortunate luck to stumble upon you and one of your . . . paramours last night. Please, sir! Have a care for the sweet, young girl! I beg of you!"

Bragg met her outraged eyes. "Ma'am, let's get things straight. No one is sorrier than I that she happened across me and my friend and was upset by it."

Elizabeth was startled into speechlessness.

Bragg smiled. "But a man's appetites are a fact of life in this land. Just how long do you think your niece is going to stay sheltered and innocent living in Texas? Is she to be a virgin wife?"

Elizabeth gasped at his rudeness.

"I will try and be more discreet." Bragg grinned mockingly and swept her a bow. "Now, shall we be on our way?"

"I'll get Miranda," Elizabeth replied stiffly, in high indignation.

Bragg lounged on the porch. He had meant every word he'd said. He was sorry Miranda had seen him and that wench. But they hadn't even been doing anything. Yet. They had only been alone together—certainly no sin. He

shrugged. After all, it wasn't his fault. He hadn't expected
Miranda to come seeking him out.

"Derek."

He was startled by Louise, the woman he had bedded
the previous night. "Morning." He flashed her a relaxed,
natural smile. She had been very accommodating last night,
and quite skilled as well. She wasn't too bad looking
either, even though her breasts were already sagging. She
stepped next to him, pressing that particular part of her
anatomy against him.

"I'm sorry you have to go so soon." She smiled up at
him.

"So am I," Bragg said, not meaning it but not lying,
either. Then his smile disappeared. Damnation! Miranda
had just stepped out and was staring at him and Louise.

"Next time you come this way, will you come see me
again?" Louise flirted openly, placing a hand on his chest
and slipping it into the open vee of his shirt. She stroked
his flesh.

"You know I will," he said, glancing from her to
Miranda, who was staring unblinkingly at them. He saw
her expression and realized that it wasn't exactly shock
that held her frozen and staring. She was fascinated—
although she probably didn't even realize it.

He took Louise's hand and removed it from his chest.
"Not here," he said.

Louise glanced scornfully at Miranda. "What do you
care about that little virgin?" She laughed, throwing her
arms around his neck and kissing him hotly. Bragg heard
Miranda gasp as his hands slid down Louise's back and his
mouth opened to her kiss.

Then he caught himself ruefully and pushed her away.
He patted her behind. "Until next time." He grinned,
stepping down from the porch. He smiled at Miranda, who
was now as red as a rose. He had never seen a woman who
blushed so much. "Good morning, Miranda," he said
politely. "How did you sleep last night?" His gaze raked
over her of its own accord. God, what a beauty!

Miranda swallowed. Could he read her mind? How did
he know that she had been dreaming intimately of him last
night? Completely speechless, she hurried past him to the

wagon, her heart pounding wildly. Would her husband touch her like that? If he did, she would die!

"Morning, Miss Miranda," Welsh said with a friendly smile. "Here, let me help you up."

Bragg had been approaching, and Miranda quickly accepted Welsh's offer. She thought she would die, too, of mortification, if Bragg ever laid another hand on her!

Chapter 8

Bragg was annoyed, even angry.

Tomorrow they would reach Nacogdoches, the last town before San Antonio on the Camino Real. They had left Natchitoches two days ago, and Miranda had been studiously avoiding him. Although he caught her looking at him with frightened fascination whenever he was not riding ahead, when they were in camp she seemed to go out of her way to keep a great distance between them. If he spoke to her casually, and was not asking her a direct question, she made no response. When he looked at her, she blushed. Sometimes he would look at her and find her staring back, and he could see the pulse beating wildly in her slim, white throat. When she unconsciously wet her lips with her pink tongue, he wanted to grab her and devour her mouth.

He wanted to talk to her. He was angry because she was avoiding him, making talk impossible. It didn't help that she seemed haughty, too, as if he repulsed her. Or maybe it was just a mask for fear. Whatever it was, they had a long trip ahead, and this kind of infantile behavior didn't suit him.

However, her aunt was watching him like a hawk, and was quick to ward off his attempts to approach Miranda.

He knew she was an innocent. But how could she be that embarrassed by what she had seen? Or did she think

him a crude lout? Hadn't she already called him an uncivilized barbarian? Was she afraid of him? Sometimes she
looked at him like she was afraid, with a kind of mesmerized fear. How in hell could he get that aunt out of the
way?

The problem solved itself. They had made an early
camp, because they were less than seven hours from Nacogdoches. Miranda and her aunt had disappeared into their
tent. Bragg had already supplied game, which was roasting
on a spit. Welsh was smoking tobacco on his bedroll.
Miranda appeared at the flap to the women's tent, looking
at him.

Bragg straightened from where he was lounging against
a boulder. Miranda stepped out, and he saw that she was
carrying a towel, soap, and some clothes. He smiled as she
approached. Her eyes were wide, and her voice tremulous.
"Captain Bragg?"

His gaze searched hers. Once again, he was struck by
her beauty—it seemed that she was more beautiful every
time he saw her. "Yes?"

"I would like to perform my ablutions," she said in a
strained voice.

"Where's your aunt?" Bragg asked casually, standing
close to her. For some odd reason, his heart was hammer-
ing as if he'd run a long distance.

"She's sleeping." Her violet gaze locked with his.
"This trip is hard on her. I'm worried."

Bragg nodded, now sober and understanding. "Unfortunately, it will only get tougher. Follow me," he said.

He heard her stumbling behind him as he walked down
the embankment, and he automatically turned to her, taking her arm. She sucked in her breath and pulled away as
if he were a leper. Bragg let her go, his face darkening.
Miranda swallowed, dropping a frightened gaze, and said,
"How much farther to the ranch, Captain Bragg?"

He continued down the path, past some cottonwoods
and palo verde. The little chit *was* frightened of him! It
aggravated him no end. Did she think he'd rape her?
"Almost three hundred miles," he said, stopping.

"Oh! A pond!" Miranda was delighted.

Bragg smiled despite himself. "Miranda? I would like to talk to you."

She looked slowly at him. "About what?" Her words were so soft they were barely audible.

"About what you saw in Natchitoches." He watched her face. The revealing pink tide flooded her features and she averted her face.

"No," he said softly, "don't look away." His fingers gentle, he tilted her chin to meet his gaze. She seemed to be holding her breath. He had a nearly uncontrollable urge to kiss her.

"I'm sorry," she whispered. "I wasn't spying. I was looking for you."

"You've been avoiding me. Why?"

Miranda tried to look away, but he wouldn't release her chin. "What were you doing with that woman?" she asked quaveringly.

Bragg looked at her in complete surprise, then he laughed, dropping his fingers from her silken skin.

She started at his laughter, her eyes widening.

"She enjoyed herself," he said, chuckling, "very much."

"Then she's a . . . bad woman," Miranda said seriously. "A . . . harlot."

Bragg stared. "I think we need to talk, really talk," he said, feeling angry as hell. "Louise is not a whore."

She gasped at his crude language.

"She's a woman with normal appetites, that's all."

Miranda gaped disbelievingly.

"Miranda, what happens between a man and a woman is good and natural—and very, very enjoyable."

She was shocked. "No well-bred lady enjoys a man's . . . attentions that way!"

"Poor John," he said, before he could stop himself. "What drivel have they been feeding you? If lovemaking were so sinful, then why did God make it the way to conceive babies?"

She stared in a complete lack of comprehension.

Bragg stared back. He couldn't believe that she didn't know what he was talking about. "You don't know, do you? You don't know how a woman conceives?"

"No," she whispered, swallowing hard. She wet her lower lip. "How?"

If she does that one more time, I'll kiss her, Bragg thought as desire surged through him. A wave of anger immediately followed. "Ask your husband," he said, too harshly. "Believe me, he'll tell you . . . no, he'll show you." Their eyes held.

Miranda was the one to turn away, trembling. "I'm going to bathe. Could you possibly turn your back?"

Bragg already knew that there were no Indians lurking about, so he nodded shortly. He was thinking that she had probably never been kissed. Well, it sure as hell wasn't his place to kiss her; it was John's. But she needed a kiss, a good one. Hell, she wanted one, he was sure of it. He gazed up at the sky, his back to her, and heard her clothes rustling. He froze. She was undressing.

His hearing was keener than any white man's. He was aware of each item of clothing that she discarded. In fact, he could tell that she had been wearing three petticoats. Then he heard her wade into the pond. What had she left on? Her chemise and a petticoat, he guessed, fighting an urge to look.

"I'm surprised you trust me." He laughed harshly.

The splashing sounds of her bathing ceased. He strained his ears and could hear her breathing. "My fiancé trusts you," she said finally.

So innocent, he thought. So goddamn innocent! And John was going to take away her innocence. *He* wanted to be the one to teach her passion, instead.

The pond wasn't deep, and he knew she was squatting as she bathed. He heard her rise to a standing position as she said, "Don't turn."

He didn't bother to answer.

Suddenly she cried out and there was a great splash. Bragg was immediately at the edge of the pond. She had slipped, and her head popped out of the water while she sputtered for air. Bragg didn't smile. He was straining to see if she was okay.

Miranda cried out again. "Oh! Something—something's in here!" She stood up, and he caught a glimpse of hard nipples through her wet chemise before she fell again, disappearing beneath the water.

Bragg scooped her up in his arms as she choked on the water, carrying her out of the pond and falling to his knees on the grass. "Are you all right? There's nothing in the pond."

Miranda trembled in his arms.

Suddenly he realized exactly what was happening. Miranda was in his arms. She was clad in only a chemise and petticoat. Her breasts were small, softly rounded, and beautiful, and her pink nipples begged his mouth to touch them. Her hair had come loose; it flowed in gleaming black waves to her small, rounded hips. Her lips were parted, and she was staring at him with the same shocked awareness of their compromising position.

He could no longer think. The hand that was on her shoulder slid up to the back of her neck, wrapping itself on a thick strand of hair, holding her head immobile. He lowered his face. Her body went rigid. His lips brushed hers, then again and again, softly, delicately. She pressed her lips tightly together and wouldn't open them, even when his tongue teased their joining. He held her crushed against him in such a way that she couldn't bring up her hands to pry him away. He pulled at her mouth. His tongue traced its outline. His breathing became harsh and ragged. He wanted her more than he'd ever wanted any woman.

She suddenly, furiously, began to struggle.

He released her abruptly, so abruptly that he dropped her onto the damp grass while he sat back on his heels, his blood racing furiously. She scooted out of his reach, giving him the tempting view of her wet petticoat clinging to a round, delectable behind. He stood up slowly, exhaling. She was struggling into her dress, and he heard fabric rip.

He reached out and took her wrist, stopping her frantic movements—in fact, she froze at his touch. "Relax," he said raggedly. "I won't hurt you." He dropped his hand, glancing at her body one last time.

He was about to avert his gaze when he saw her hand flying through the air, and he caught it before she could strike his face. She was panting. Her eyes were black with fury. Flags of color marked her cheeks, and her breasts heaved. His grip tightened and he started to jerk her toward him, following old habit and reflex. Instead, he collected himself, reminding himself who and what she was. He threw her away from him. Miranda stumbled and tripped and went down on her hands and knees. "I'm sorry," he said, not realizing that he looked anything but sorry. In fact, he looked thunderous with rage.

Miranda pulled up her dress, shaking. "You animal! *Cochon!* How dare you! I won't—I won't travel another day with you! *Mon Dieu!*" Her voice broke and tears welled up in her eyes.

"For crissakes!" Bragg was furious at his lack of control. How had it happened? "Don't be a twit!" He was shouting, and he lowered his voice. All he needed right now was for Miranda's aunt to come marching down here with a lecture.

"How could John send you?" she said with a sob. "How could he put me in the company of a savage like you? How?"

"Grow up, Miranda! Don't tell me you've never been kissed before." He watched as she buttoned her blouse, her fingers clumsy and trembling. She stopped and stared at him in disbelief. He must have known she'd never been kissed before—she'd been as stiff and unyielding as a board, her mouth all but glued together.

"Never!" She was horrified that he could think anything else.

Bragg opened his mouth to apologize, but only a sound of disgust came out.

"We will find a new guide in Nacogdoches," Miranda declared.

"Oh no you won't," Bragg warned, his expression becoming dangerous.

Miranda backed away. "Oh yes! After I tell my aunt what—"

He grabbed her and shook her, not meaning to hurt her, and when she whimpered he wanted to kick himself. She was so fragile! "You listen to me," he said in a low voice, his eyes blazing, releasing her. "I gave John my word I'd see you safe and unharmed to his ranch and, goddammit, I will.''

"Safe?" her eyes were incredulous. "Safe? You call kissing me returning me safe and unharmed?''

Bragg clenched his jaw. "I'm taking you all the way to San Antonio, Miranda, and that's that.'' Their gazes locked. "No matter what you and your aunt want. If you like, I'll hogtie you both for the rest of the trip.''

Miranda paled. "You brute!''

Bragg gave a smile that was close to a sneer. She turned and fled back toward the camp. Bragg picked up the items she'd left behind, cursing. He kicked a tree. So much for their talk. She was more frightened and disgusted with him than ever.

Chapter 9

Miranda felt ill again, actually feverish. There was a warm flush engulfing her whole body, and her heart still fluttered painfully. She glanced at her aunt. Praise God, she was asleep! Miranda was afraid her face might give away her agitation, and she did not want to answer her aunt's prying questions.

Bragg had kissed her! Her face burned even more. She lay on her bedroll and hugged herself. Dear God! Was she ruined? Should she tell John? Would he send her home in disgrace? She sat up abruptly.

If John knew that Bragg had held her half naked and kissed her, he would surely send her home. Her eyes sparkled and she almost laughed aloud in glee. Home! Oh, how much she wanted to go home, to get away from all this—these strange, barbaric men in a wild, untamed land. It was a wonderful idea.

Miranda knew she was a good girl—mostly—for Bragg's kiss had repulsed and terrified her. That was the only explanation for the way her heart had threatened to burst from her chest at his touch. How could that man have touched her? How could her fiancé have sent him, a complete beast, with no control over his baser instincts, to escort her to his home? She didn't understand it. What if John was no better than Bragg?

It was a bit later when Bragg had the audacity to call to

her from outside the tent and tell her their supper was ready. She bit her lip, wanting to shout back that she wasn't hungry, but she didn't want anyone, especially her aunt, to know what had happened. Her aunt would tell her it was all her fault for going to bathe in a pond, in public, practically in front of a man. No, she couldn't tell Elizabeth. She didn't dare.

Miranda ducked out of the tent cautiously, feeling his burning gaze upon her. Why was he always looking at her in that strange, hungry way—the way a starving child looks at a piece of cake? She kept her lashes lowered, filled two plates, and without looking at anyone disappeared back into the tent. She did not step out again that night, dreading his gaze, resolving to wait to take care of her needs until the next morning.

Because of her resolution, Miranda was up at dawn, before any wakeup call, and slipped out of the tent. Above the prairie, the sky was a peachy pink, turning the brown grass golden. In the distance, jagged, mauve mountains crested a darker sky. Miranda took a moment to inhale the sweet, morning-fresh scent of the raw land, enjoying the majestic sunrise. Then she glanced around. Fortunately there was no sign of Welsh or Bragg, and she assumed that the men were taking care of their own needs. The team was still hobbled, their packed gear lying unloaded on the ground. The coffee was heating, and she wrinkled her nose in distaste. What she wouldn't give for a bit of tea!

Miranda hesitated, wanting to wash at the pond, when Welsh appeared from the opposite direction, startling her. Surely by now Bragg had finished washing up, too—if that was what he was doing, or maybe he had been with Welsh. She headed down the embankment.

The sun gave forth a sudden burst of light as it crested higher, suddenly warming the cool morning, brightening the dawn to day. Miranda smiled and was even more pleased when she found the pond unoccupied. She washed her hands and face, brushed her teeth, and was about to stand when she heard a foul curse and was yanked up by her hastily braided hair.

"You never leave camp without my permission!" Bragg roared.

Miranda's heart was pounding in fear. "You're hurting me!"

"Good!" he shouted, deafening her. He was still holding her braid cruelly, and now an iron hand gripped her shoulder. He shook her roughly. "Foolish twit!"

"Let go of me," Miranda managed, not knowing where the words of bravery, spoken so calmly, came from. In fact she was deathly afraid that he was going to beat her.

Bragg must have seen the terror in her eyes. He suddenly released her, and she wheeled abruptly and fled. She was brought up short, however, after only three steps. This time he had grabbed her wrist, and he whipped her around to face him. She could see that he was fiercely fighting back his rage. "Stand still," he finally said, his nostrils and mouth pinched and white.

Miranda froze obediently. She had a sudden vision of her father striking her mother, and she flinched. It made his eyes grow darker. "Please," she whispered.

"We're in Comanche territory," he said, in a cold, hard voice. "Do you know what the Comanche do to pretty white women like you?"

Miranda shook her head mutely.

"They strip you naked," he said cruelly. "All the braves who want to take their pleasure with you do— touching you, hurting you, raping you." She was staring at him, transfixed with terror. "Then, if you're lucky, someone, like John, pays a ransom, and you're released." Bragg's expression was murderous. He smiled grimly. "Of course, if you're not lucky, a Comanche decides to make you his second or third wife."

His eyes bored into hers. "A Comanche woman is treated like a dog. She's taken when her husband feels like it, beaten on whim, worked like oxen. A second or third wife doesn't even have the protection that a first wife enjoys. She gets beaten continually by the first wife—who is cruel because she's jealous—as well as by her husband."

Miranda couldn't breathe.

"Of course, if you're really lucky, they sell you south of the border. Do you know what happens then?"

She could hear her own heart suddenly, pounding like a drum.

"You spend your time on your back—in a brothel. You become a whore."

Miranda swayed, fighting to clear her head of the strange light-headedness that had descended. A whore . . . a third wife . . . many braves . . .

"Until we reach John's ranch, you never go anywhere without my presence. Is that clear?"

His voice was coming from far away. The ground seemed to be coming up at her. Finally, a welcoming blackness enveloped her.

Chapter 10

Bragg caught her just before her head hit the ground.

"Miranda!" His anger had fled. He shook her face and slapped her gently. Dammit! He had scared the little chit into a faint! He felt overwhelmed with guilt and anger at himself—he couldn't believe she had actually fainted. He dabbed cool water on her face, and she moaned, her lashes fluttering.

"Are you all right?" he asked hoarsely, wondering why his heart was pounding so hard.

Miranda looked at him blankly, vaguely, and then fear welled up in her violet eyes, and she stared at him with frozen terror.

He wanted to stroke her hair. "I won't let anything happen to you, Miranda," he said gruffly, and almost placed his hand in her thick tresses. "But you need my permission to go anywhere, is that understood?" He was brusque to hide his relief, his agitation, and another confusing, unfamiliar feeling—fear. Miranda nodded mutely.

"Can you stand?" She was still staring at him, and he remembered how she had flinched at his rage, as if he were going to hit her. Had she really thought that? Only a husband could hit a woman, for then it was his right, whether he was white or Apache. However, he knew John would never hit Miranda—it wasn't in his nature. Absurdly, that thought pleased him. He helped her to her feet.

* * *

59

Nacogdoches was only a few hours away, but Bragg
scouted ahead anyway, trying not to think about Miranda,
that girl-woman. It was hard not to. He had had a sleepless
night last night, stiff with desire for her—his blood brother's fiancée. It was an unacceptable situation. He seemed
to have no control over his lust for her, but he had
promised himself that he would never touch her again, and
he wouldn't. Miranda belonged to John. In all fairness to
himself, the kiss had been an accident. What virile man
could have stopped himself from kissing a woman clad
only in wet underclothes, especially when that woman was
as beautiful as Miranda, and was suddenly, unexpectedly,
in his arms?

In an effort to quell his attraction for her, he reminded
himself that she was not his type at all. He remembered his
dead wife. She'd been slender when he had married her,
yet he had always preferred women with ripe, voluptuous
figures. Like Louise, who had breasts a man could bury
his face in forever. She was soft and accommodating. No,
Miranda was not his type at all.

Nacogdoches had always been a rough town, and it was
even more so since Texas had gained independence from
Mexico in '36. There were no longer Mexican Rurales to
keep peace, and although the Texans had elected a sheriff,
violence ran rampant in the town, outlaws and drifters
competing with immigrants, and the sheriff could not keep
the peace. Because it was high noon when they rode in,
Bragg secured them lodging at one of the more reputable
establishments. He was glad they had only a half day of
travel that day. He was worried about Lady Holcombe,
who was thinner than when the trip had begun, pale and
wan. She needed a bed, food, and rest.

"There is nothing to see in this town," Bragg announced to the ladies as they stood in the front room. The
common room was already half full with patrons, and
Bragg immediately saw two hard, dangerous men. He
instinctively stepped closer to Miranda.

"What do you mean, Captain Bragg?" Miranda met his
eyes briefly, innocently.

"This is a hard town. Dangerous men, outlaws, ride

through. I want both of you to keep to your rooms until we leave tomorrow." He settled an unflinching gaze on her. "Understand?"

"Yes," Elizabeth said, taking Miranda's hand.

"Anything you need—food, drink, bathwater—have brought up." Bragg stared at Miranda again. Then he glanced at the common room and immediately met a dark gaze in a shadowy, bearded face. The man looked from him to Miranda with open lust. Bragg restrained the urge to beat the man to a pulp for his insolence. He unconsciously noted that the man was as tall as he, brawny, and exuded a reckless, lawless confidence. He took Miranda's elbow, ignoring her gasp, and said, "I'll escort you upstairs . . . *now*."

Unfortunately, the stairs to the rooms were on the other side of the common room, and there was no way to approach them except by entering that male domain. They had taken no more than three steps within when a hush fell over the room, and every eye turned to Miranda. Bragg felt her tremble beneath his hand.

There were only a dozen men in the room, but another man stood out. A tall, dark, ruggedly handsome Mexican, possibly a Comanchero, caught Bragg's attention. As with the dark, bearded man, the Mexican was also a worthy opponent—possibly trouble. The Mexican, clad in buckskins like everyone else, devoured Miranda with cold, black eyes.

They had started up the stairs when the room began to buzz excitedly.

"Did you ever see anything like that?" someone said hoarsely.

"What a beauty! What white skin!"

"Did you see her eyes? They're purple! I saw 'em!"

"She's skinny."

"Who cares? With your rod buried deep in her, would you give a damn?" Excited laughter greeted this last remark.

"You wish you could bury your rod in her!"

"She looks like a virgin," a cool voice commented.

"Who's the man?"

"Bragg."

"You think he's getting it?"

"He's a Ranger," someone warned.

Miranda was shaking when Bragg opened the door to the room.

"It's all right," he said softly.

Her eyes, wide and filled with horror, held his. Bragg wanted to sweep her against his chest and protect her, but he shrugged off that ridiculous, womanly urge.

"How could you bring us to this place?" Elizabeth gasped, her face flushed with outrage and indignation.

"I told you," Bragg said coolly, suddenly wondering if it wouldn't have been better to camp on the trail, "it's a rough town. I guess I won't have to remind you to stay in your room?" He quirked a brow.

Miranda turned and fled inside.

Bragg regarded her aunt soberly. "I'll be downstairs, and I have the room next to yours. No one will try anything, don't worry."

Elizabeth gasped. "Try anything? Good Lord! What do you mean?"

Bragg saw Miranda standing frozen by the window, her face a mask of raw terror. He wanted to kick himself. "Just don't worry," he said harshly. "You'll be safe if you lock the door." He closed the door and left.

The crowd downstairs was worse than he had ever seen, and it was just his luck. He had no intention of moving from that common room, he decided, unless it was to sleep outside Miranda's door.

Chapter 11

Bragg settled himself comfortably at one end of a trestle table, his back to the wall. He met the Mexican's assessing eyes. The man held his stare for a moment, long enough to show that he was not afraid. Then, smiling slightly, he gazed casually about the room. In that instant, Bragg felt a deep foreboding. The man looked like a half-breed, and if he was, he was a deadly foe. His glance moved to the brawny, bearded man, who was studying Bragg openly, also unperturbed. He suddenly smiled, said something to his companion—a thin, oily blond man—and they both grinned lewdly. Bragg knew who they were talking about, but ignored them.

"Is the beautiful girl your wife?"

Bragg turned to the lanky redheaded man on his left. "Yes," he said, his eyes sharp.

The man, clad in buckskin pants and a cotton shirt, smiled amiably. "You're very lucky. She's a rare beauty."

Bragg nodded, not smiling. He decided to be pleasant. "Do you know any of these men?"

The man shrugged. "I've met a few of them on my travels."

"You pass through these parts often?"

The redhead nodded. "I'm an impresario," he said. "The name's McDermott, Tim McDermott."

"Bragg," he responded. "So you're scouting land for settlement?"

"Yes. In fact, I've filed on four hundred thousand acres north of here, way up by the Red River. I hope to find three hundred families to settle it."

"Good luck," Bragg said. "That's very wild country up there."

"Good farming and cattle land," McDermott said.

Bragg nodded. "Do you know that man?" he asked, not quite so casually.

"Ah, one of your wife's ardent admirers." McDermott glanced at the dark, bearded man. "No, I'm afraid not."

"What about him?" Bragg turned a cool gaze on the Mexican, whose black eyes, just as unperturbed, met his glance in a slight salute—or a challenge.

"Yes," McDermott said, grimacing. "He's a Comanchero."

Bragg tensed. So he had been right; the man was half Comanche.

"His name is Chavez. Or that's what he calls himself. He's very dangerous."

"Was his mother or his father Comanche?"

"His father was a chief. He is not the eldest son, however. It is rumored he has a Comanche wife. It is also rumored he has extensive land in Chihuahua, that his mother was a Spanish aristocrat."

Bragg lapsed into silence and fell into a waiting game.

About an hour later, Chavez rose gracefully to his feet, sending Bragg a nonchalant smile. Bragg recognized the challenge. He watched as Chavez sauntered out, then, through the window to his right, he watched Chavez mount a magnificent black stallion and canter out of town. He felt no relief. He knew, beyond a doubt, that their paths were destined to cross again.

It was much later when the bearded man rose to his feet and started up the stairs. Dusk had fallen. The common room was full. Bragg rose too, and quietly followed.

At the top of the stairs, the man turned to look at him. Bragg stared back steadily. The man paused in mid-stride, then kept on walking down the hall, opening a door at the end and disappearing inside. Bragg knocked softly on Miranda's door and Lady Holcombe cracked it open.

"Is everything all right?" Bragg asked.

"We're fine. Miranda's sleeping. She seems exhausted."

Past Lady Holcombe's head, Bragg saw Miranda's form curled on her side beneath a tattered but clean blanket. Her hair was loose and thick, wavy tendrils falling over her shoulder and down to her hips. He couldn't tear his gaze away.

"Good night, Captain Bragg." Elizabeth closed the door in his face.

Bragg frowned. The woman had obviously read his expression. God! He had let down his guard—which he could not do. He sank to the floor in front of their door and leaned his head back, removing his wide-brimmed hat. He dozed fitfully.

Sounds in the middle of the night woke him three times, but it was just other patrons stumbling tiredly or drunkenly to their rooms. The night passed without incident. Bragg woke the women at dawn and escorted them downstairs for breakfast.

"I'm not hungry," Miranda said, gazing up at him pleadingly. "I can't eat in that room."

Bragg regarded her steadily. "No one will say a word in my presence."

"Please," she whispered.

"It's out of the question, Captain Bragg," her aunt said firmly. "We ate a huge meal last night and we are not hungry. We will not suffer the intolerable company of uncivilized, brutish men. That is final."

"Fine," Bragg said. It really was for the better. He led them outside. "Wait here, and don't move while I help Welsh finish hitching up."

Miranda and her aunt nodded, and he left them on the porch, striding across the courtyard to where Welsh was harnessing the mules. There was a team of oxen being hitched to his left, and a man was leading a pair of sturdy bays out of the corral. A thin, gaunt woman and a small boy waiting not far from Miranda and her aunt belonged to the man with the bays, Bragg decided. The man hitching up the oxen had another male companion, and they looked like prospectors. Bragg moved around to the far side of the team, slipping a bridle on a mule.

Another man came out on the porch, and Bragg looked up just as he was pushing the bit against the mule's closed mouth—one of his hands forcing open the stubborn animal's jaw. It was the bearded man. He had stopped next to Miranda and was smiling and talking to her. Bragg dropped the bridle and strode over.

Lady Holcombe was trying to push herself between her niece and the stranger, but the man planted himself firmly at Miranda's side, taking her arm. Miranda was frozen. All her worst fears, it seemed, were coming true.

"Where are you heading?" he asked pleasantly.

"Please unhand me, sir," she said.

His hand slid up her arm. He pulled her against him, pressing his male hardness against her hip, saying, "I just want to talk, pretty lady."

In a red rage, Bragg saw what the man was doing. He yanked him away before the man even knew what was happening, landing a crushing blow to the man's abdomen. He doubled over. As he did so, Bragg lifted his knee into the man's face. He had already planted one leg behind him, and used his body and the leg as a lever to flip the man onto his back. He straddled him an instant later, digging one knee into his ribs. He yanked up his head, hitting him again. Bragg's knife appeared in his hand, and he pressed the blade against the man's throat, breaking the skin. Not more than thirty seconds had passed.

"Say your prayers," Bragg rasped. "Because I am going to kill you now."

"No!" Miranda screamed. "Don't! It was nothing!"

Without taking his knee from the man's broken ribs, and keeping the blade at his throat, Bragg raised his head and looked at her.

"Don't kill him," she pleaded. "He only touched my arm. Please, I beg you, have mercy!" Tears trickled down her face.

Lady Holcombe came into action, pulling Miranda away. "Don't look, Miranda!" she cried. "Come, come with me."

Miranda wouldn't be pulled away. She broke her aunt's

hold, panting. "If you kill him, you're an animal," she cried. "He only touched my arm—*mon Dieu! Quel espèce d'assassin est cet homme? Je lui en pries . . .*" She was babbling hysterically.

Bragg sheathed his knife and rose. She didn't understand what the man had been doing, but Bragg had seen it. He wanted to kill, but he would not. It was the hardest thing he had ever done.

Miranda turned away from him, and her aunt pulled her into her arms, patting her while she choked back her sobs. Bragg scowled, trying to ease his bloodlust, then stared past their heads—at Chavez.

Studying him without a smile, Chavez was standing in the shadows of the inn. Bragg had never even seen him arrive, he had just appeared, with the stealth of a Comanche. Their gazes locked. Chavez's contemptuous glance said clearly, *I would have killed him, no matter what she said.*

"We ride out," Bragg said. "Now."

Chapter 12

Miranda stole another glance at Bragg. He was eating rapidly, using his fingers, gnawing on a bone. He's an animal, she thought, unable to look away. He was squatting in what looked like a very uncomfortable position, but he always ate in that position on the trail. He suddenly tossed the bone into the fire, rubbed his hands on his thighs, and looked over at her.

She wanted to look away, but couldn't. His gaze had been masked, but as she stared at him, even from across the fire, she could see it changing. She could see his expression of raw hunger, as if he hadn't just eaten half a haunch of venison. Miranda realized that she was holding her breath. She expelled it, forced her eyes away, and daintily picked up a bone with her fingers. She was starved for the first time in ages, it seemed, and she had already tried to carve the meat, unsuccessfully, with a knife and fork.

Bragg had almost killed a man today! A man who had simply touched her arm. She still could not get over it. His hypocrisy astounded her. At least she thought that was why her pulse raced whenever she thought of the incident. Bragg had done much worse to her. He had kissed her and held her while she was clad only in her underclothes. But he had beaten a man badly, and been only a second away from slitting his throat, all because the man had held her arm intimately.

She had not realized Bragg was so lethal. Good heavens, she thought, what kind of a man is he? Her glance slid to him again. A savage, an animal, her mind whispered. A beautiful animal, another voice said.

Startled, Miranda dropped her plate with a cry.

"What is it?" her aunt asked solicitously, while Bragg and Welsh stared at her with open curiosity.

"Nothing," she said quickly. Wherever had that thought come from? Then, as her mind raced, she grew calm. Bragg's stallion was a beautiful animal. A wolf, a bear, they were all beautiful beasts. They were beasts, and they were beautiful. Bragg was the same. It was all right to see him that way, as dispassionately as she saw his stallion. Yes, he was beautiful, but frightening, because he was crude and uncivilized.

"Miranda? Are you listening? I asked if you are ill."

"Oh no," she said hastily, looking away from those golden eyes. But when he got up, her glance was drawn to him again, and she watched him leave the glow of the small, smokeless fire.

The next day, as usual, Bragg rode ahead, disappearing from sight. By high noon, he had not returned, which was unusual. Several hours passed, and there was still no sign of him. The garrulous Welsh had ceased his chatter some time ago, his face wearing a dark frown, and Miranda and her aunt had begun exchanging very frightened glances. Lady Holcombe finally asked what had happened.

"He's run into trouble," Welsh said bluntly.

Miranda gasped, a crazy, sudden fear tearing through her. "What do you mean?" she cried. "How do you know?"

"Because we'd already discussed this," Welsh said. "Don't worry. Bragg probably ran across a raiding party of Comanche, and the plan was for him to lead them away. A decoy, so to speak."

"Oh God," her aunt moaned.

Miranda's heart was pounding. "What if they catch him?" she whispered, her eyes wide with fright.

"That won't happen." Welsh smiled reassuringly. "You

watch. We'll make camp like usual, and he' ome riding in by dawn.''

Miranda didn't believe him. "But he's only one man! How many Comanche ride in a raiding party?''

Welsh didn't tell her that he had lied and that Bragg had probably run across a war party. "Ten to fifty,'' he said.

Miranda gasped.

"Now don't you worry,'' Welsh said, reaching over her aunt and patting her hand. His impropriety was lost in the shock of their fear. "Bragg's half Apache. No Comanche can track an Apache unless he wants him to. Bragg will lose them when he's good and ready.''

Elizabeth had begun to mop her brow with her handkerchief. "Half Apache?''

"Half Apache?'' Miranda echoed. "Captain Bragg is half Apache?''

Welsh was annoyed with himself for revealing that fact. "His ma was Apache. Mescalero. Mostly up in the New Mexico Territory. Don't you worry, ma'am. Everything will be fine.''

Miranda was dazed. She was worried for Bragg, as worried as she was for herself, because suddenly she felt very insecure and unprotected without his presence. Half Apache. No wonder he was so savage.

"We'll make camp here,'' Welsh said. "No fire tonight, ladies, as an extra precaution.'' He slowed the team.

They made a silent, small camp. They ate dried beef and cold beans. Miranda wasn't hungry. She kept thinking about Bragg leading fifty fierce, savage Comanche away from them, risking his own life to do so. Dear God, protect him, she prayed.

She was sleeping when they attacked. She felt hands upon her, strong hands, male hands, and then something was being shoved in her mouth. Sudden awareness electrified her. She was being abducted from her own tent! She began to struggle, but she was being held in an iron grip, against an iron body. One of her feet kicked over a pitcher and it clanged against an unlit lantern.

"Miranda?'' her aunt asked sleepily.

Miranda screamed into the gag, making muffled noises.

Lady Holcombe saw a tall, dark form in her tent holding Miranda, clad only in a white cotton nightgown, and she shrieked.

The man carried her out the back of the slitted tent with rapid strides. A shot sounded. Miranda twisted wildly to see over the abductor's shoulder. Welsh lay sprawled on his face on the ground, yards from the front of her tent. A man stood over him, sheathing his pistol in a holster.

She looked ahead, squirming wildly, pounding on the man's back. He chuckled. Three men were holding horses.

"Chavez!" one of them cried.

Chavez turned to look just as one of his men shot Lady Holcombe. She crumpled to the ground, a small derringer slipping uselessly from her hand. Miranda saw her aunt murdered, and with a muffled cry, she fainted.

Still holding Miranda, Chavez leaped onto his stallion, and he and his four men rode away into the night.

Chapter 13

Miranda awoke to the early morning sunlight. Something wet and cool was on her forehead, and then it slid down to her throat, to her chest. She sighed. The cool cloth went lower, over her breasts, making her nipples harden and tingle. She was suddenly wide awake, and her eyes flew open as she cried out.

A dark face with glittering black eyes was peering at her. "So you are awake," he said.

Miranda realized she was lying on a bed in a pine-planked room, clad only in her flimsy nightgown, which had been unbuttoned to her waist. The man was holding the damp cloth that had been touching her breasts. With a cry of anger, she clasped the edges of her gown together.

"So beautiful," he murmured. "Miranda. Even your name is beautiful."

Her momentary outrage fled as everything came back. Her face crumpled as tears of pain streamed down her cheeks. "Aunt Elizabeth," she moaned. She rolled onto her side. "Dear God. No, *non, pas man tante. Mon Dieu! Je vous en pries . . .*" She broke into huge, heaving sobs.

Chavez regarded the beautiful girl silently for a moment, understanding her grief. He was sorry that his impetuous man had killed the older woman. In fact, he had backhanded the man when they had reached their hidden camp, causing him to lose two teeth. He had given strict orders that the elderly woman was not to be hurt. Now he understood that the dead woman was the girl's aunt. He stroked her shoulder.

"I am sorry, little one, about your aunt. It was an accident."

Miranda ignored him and kept crying.

Her sorrow did not ease his desire. He had rarely seen such beauty, and he had been able to think of little else except this girl since he had seen her the other day in Nacogdoches. The moment he had seen her, he had known he would have her. But he was human, after all, so he decided he would give her time to grieve.

"You are going to be my woman, little one," he told her as she lay on her stomach, sobbing. "Maybe even my wife. I have no wish to harm you. You are too rare, too precious. My men will not touch you. But there is no escape. You are constantly watched; do not even try to leave." He rose and regarded her steadily. He was taut with desire. He had been that way all night as they rode southwest toward Coahuila.

Miranda didn't seem to hear him. He shrugged, reached down, and covered her with a blanket, for he had no wish for his lecherous men to stare at her delicately beautiful body visible through the thin gown. He left.

Miranda cried all morning. Eventually, when she had no tears left, she rolled to her side and peered with swollen eyes at the crude room. She saw that she was in a shack, lying on the single bed. There was a table with two chairs, a fireplace, a dull iron pot, and that was all. Miranda wondered what was going to happen to her.

She also wondered what had happened to Bragg. He must be dead, she thought dully. A new stab of pain pierced her. Then she remembered what Welsh had said. Bragg was half Apache. No Comanche could track an Apache. If Bragg was alive, would he be able to track the men who had abducted her? It was her only hope.

She sat up and walked to the shack's one window. Outside, she saw two Mexicans sleeping. She tried to remember what her abductor looked like. All she could remember was that he was tall, and his voice had been soft and slightly guttural.

"So you are better."

Miranda gasped and turned, pressing her back against
the wall. He was as tall as Bragg, and as dark as Bragg
was golden. He was sinister, she thought, shuddering. His
eyes had a naked, hungry look.

"You are cold," he said, striding over to her. He took
her hands and chafed them.

Stiffening, she tried to jerk them away.

"No, *cara*," he murmured, and lifted them up to kiss
them. He nibbled her knuckles. Miranda choked on a huge
sob.

Chavez stopped and looked at her. "Don't be afraid,"
he said.

"Please," she whispered. "Please, let me go. I beg of
you."

He smiled. "No, *querida*. That is not possible."

Miranda began to cry.

"Why are you so eager to leave?" he asked, looking
angry. "Am I not handsome? I am rich, too. Did I not tell
you I would marry you? You could do no better, believe
me!"

She gazed at him through tear-filled eyes, startled.

"Or are you already married?" His eyes flashed. "To
that Ranger? Eh? Is that it? I think not. I think you are a
virgin. You have that innocent look."

"I can't marry you," she whispered, seizing the opportunity. "I am already married, to Bragg."

His face grew taut and rage flooded his features. "So be
it," he said harshly, pulling her into his arms.

"No!" she screamed as he lifted her and carried her to
the bed.

"You will be my mistress, my woman, eh?" He placed
her on the bed, holding her still as he leaned over her.

"Bragg will kill you," she cried, unable to move beneath his hold.

"No, *cara*. Bragg is far from here. Your husband—if
indeed he is such—has been taken prisoner by Comanche." At her frightened look, Chavez grew angrier.
"So you do care for him! Is he a good lover, eh? Do you
think I do not recognize a dangerous man when I see
him?" He shook her. "I arranged for my friends, led by

my half brother, to lead him away from you, *cara*. I am no fool!''

Miranda had no time to absorb that before his mouth came down on hers, hard and demanding. He clasped her in his arms as he plundered her tightly pressed lips. She lay beneath him like a board.

"Open your mouth," he said harshly, lifting his head. He slid his hand over her breast, rubbing her nipple.

"No! No! Please!"

Chavez laughed, rolling the hard nub between his thumb and forefinger. "I think you lie, *cara*. I think you are very innocent." His lips found hers again.

Miranda struggled, overwhelmed with revulsion and horror. This was so different from how she had felt about Bragg. She felt bile rising in her throat and writhed uselessly.

His hand caressed her breast while he rained kisses over her frozen face, ignoring the tears that streamed down her cheeks. *"Madre de Dios!"* he cried, ripping open her gown. "I am like a boy . . . I cannot wait!"

He tossed the gown aside, breathing raggedly. Miranda screwed her eyes tightly shut as he ran his hands up and down her body, over her breasts, her belly, her hips. He stroked the hair over her secret woman's place, and she knew that she was going to throw up at any second.

"Open your thighs, *cara*," he cried. He pried them apart. "So beautiful," he breathed.

She flinched and began to moan in agony as his hand touched her most intimate spot. Her moans were half sobs, and no man could mistake them for passion.

"You're bone dry," he said angrily. "Am I so distasteful? Eh?"

Miranda lay limp and sick and tried to block her mind from what was happening. But when he pushed his fingers into her—actually inside her!—her eyes flew open and her nails came up with a scream of rage. She slashed his cheeks, drawing blood.

Chavez growled, catching her wrists and pinning them over her head. He searched her again, thrusting his fingers inside her. Miranda turned her head, panting as the bile tried to rise again.

"You are a virgin," he said harshly, withdrawing his hand. "I knew it!" It was a triumphant cry.

Miranda vomited over the side of the bed. When her heaves became dry and finally stopped, she was aware that he was no longer touching her, aware of her naked body on the bed, of her vulnerability, of the horror. . . . She slowly raised her face.

Chavez was standing rigidly beside the bed, his face dark and tense. "I disgust you."

She collapsed weakly, her face buried in the pillow.

"I do not like rape, *cara,*" he said, after a long moment. "Maybe if I court you, you will find me not so ugly, eh?" His words were bitter. "In my country, even with my Comanche blood, I am considered a prize catch among the noble young ladies. Women are eager to give themselves to me, even out of wedlock." He studied her beautiful, slim curves. His voice grew harsh. "God, I want you," he rasped, running a gentle hand over her smooth flanks.

Miranda shuddered at his nauseating touch. She felt his breath on the back of her spine, and then he was moving her hair aside and kissing the nape of her neck. The bed creaked with his weight. No, God! And she felt his trousers, the muscles of his thighs, as he pressed himself on top of her with a moan. Something hard and rodlike pressed through his trousers against her buttocks, and found the valley between them. He groaned. "I don't know . . . I don't know if I'm strong enough . . ."

An instinct honed by thirty years of survival made him look up.

Standing in the doorway, Bragg fired.

Chapter 14

Chavez rolled off the other side of the bed, taking Miranda with him and crying out as Bragg's shot hit him in his side.

Bragg ran for him. "I will kill you, Chavez," he roared.

Chavez had a knife at Miranda's throat, and he held her tightly against him while he rose slowly to his feet. "I will kill her."

Bragg didn't lower his Colt. He didn't look at Miranda, even though her eyes were upon his face. He never took his eyes from Chavez's black gaze. Very little of Chavez's anatomy was exposed for him to hit. Worse, Chavez was a Comanchero. He could slit her throat as fast as Bragg pulled the trigger.

Unless he was bluffing. Bragg could not read his eyes. They were masked and ruthless.

Chavez, with Miranda shielding him, inched along the wall and toward the door. "I am leaving and taking her with me," he said.

"No." Bragg watched, helpless and frustrated, as Chavez reached the door and backed out of it, protected by Miranda's naked body. The blade at her throat glittered.

"No," Miranda moaned, and the movement of her throat caused the blade to cut her skin. She whimpered as a thin line of blood appeared from beneath the blade.

"Do not speak, *cara*," Chavez ordered with a flash of anger.

It was too late; he had given himself away. Bragg knew he would not hurt Miranda. And Chavez knew that Bragg knew. They stared at each other in silent, uneasy understanding.

Bragg smiled ruthlessly. Chavez whistled and his stallion trotted over, bridleless and barebacked. Bragg waited eagerly. For only the slightest moment Chavez hesitated, and Bragg knew the dilemma he was facing. He had to decide whether to shove Miranda aside and escape alone, or attempt to mount with her. With his arm around Miranda, Chavez backed around the stallion, his eyes never leaving Bragg's. So that was his game, Bragg thought. He didn't move. He didn't have to.

Chavez leaped for the stallion's back, holding Miranda in one arm. She screamed and the stallion took off. Bragg fired as the man was still finding his seat. A bright red flower blossomed on Chavez's back, and Miranda went tumbling to the ground.

Bragg fired again. Chavez was leaning low on the stallion's neck, despite his two wounds, trying to make a smaller target. At that precise moment the stallion crashed down an incline, and Bragg did not know if he had hit Chavez again or not. He ran to Miranda.

She was crouched on the ground, panting, her thick sable locks covering her naked body. Bragg reached her in an instant, sending a quick, searching glance around the perimeter of the camp, then dropping to his knees beside her. "Miranda," he said huskily, pulling her into his arms.

The urge to comfort and protect her was overwhelming. She was quivering against his chest and began to tremble violently. "Miranda, it's all right now, I'm here." Tremendous pity welled up in him for what she had suffered, and along with it, guilt. Cruel, harsh guilt. He had failed her.

Her shaking was steady and convulsive. "It's all right," he said, stroking her hair. The words were ridiculous, but he didn't know what else to say.

The rustling sound of leaves and branches was faint but

piercing to Bragg and made him jerk up his head. He
could not comfort her now. He doubted that Chavez would
be back, but the man was Comanchero. This site could
also be a rendezvous point. He didn't like it. Rising, he
said, "We're leaving," then realized she wasn't paying
attention to him. She remained crouching where he'd left
her, and a terrible pang seared him. But he didn't pause
again. Bragg had sacrificed his palomino to decoy the
Commanche, tracking Miranda at a dog-trot on foot. He
chose the best animal of the remuda, a big, rangy chestnut
stallion with a deep chest and strong legs. The horse would
not have a lot of speed, but he would be long on endurance
and tough. Bragg saddled him quickly and led the horse to
Miranda.

She hadn't moved. She wasn't shaking convulsively
anymore, but every now and then a tremor would seize
her. He pulled her upright. "We have to leave now," he
said, his eyes searching her face. Like the rutting bastard
he was, he couldn't help but notice her white, slim, but
beautifully curved body, and the sight stirred him. He
searched her face. Her eyes were on his shoulder, it seemed.
"Miranda! Look at me!"

She raised her eyes, violet and lifeless. They gazed
vacantly into his face. He cursed, deeply perturbed by
what he had seen, and swung her into his arms. Leading
the horse, he retrieved the rest of his gear and slipped his
buckskin shirt over her. It came to her knees, and that
satisfied him. He lifted her into the saddle, mounted
behind her, and they set off rapidly north.

Chapter 15

They rode until dusk. Bragg did not head directly north, back to Welsh's camp. Instead he headed west, for they were far south of the Camino Real, almost on a direct tangent with San Antonio. There were several towns on the way, but Bragg had no intention of stopping at any of them. He could not ride into a settlement with John's fiancée clad only in his buckskin shirt. He intended to protect her the best way he could from this point on, which meant that no one but John would know what had happened. Although the young nation of Texas boasted a population of several hundred thousand, mostly American and European, it was still a small community where gossip flew as fast as any current news. Indeed, gossip was a good deal of the current news.

Miranda sat slumped in his arms, wearing the sombrero of one of the dead men. Occasional tremors shook her. Bragg tried to talk to her several times, but it was as if she was deaf and dumb. He was alarmed by her condition, if not downright frightened. He could not forget the vacant look in her eyes, as if she were far gone from reality, withdrawn from the world. His guilt tortured him. He had given his word to John that he would protect her with his life, deliver her to the ranch unharmed. He had failed miserably. And the evidence of his failure was Miranda's silent agony.

It was a great relief to him when she slumped fully against him, falling asleep in the saddle. Finally, those awful shudders no longer wracked her.

He stopped at twilight, setting her down carefully without waking her. She stirred and moaned. Bragg rolled out the bedroll, then lifted her onto it. Despite her condition, her soft, feminine warmth made him acutely aware of her as a woman, a desirable woman. He hated his own lust. He left her sleeping, then he sat staring at her for many hours—even though he had not slept in almost two days. That ability, too, was a part of his Apache training.

He awoke at daybreak and saw that she was still sleeping. She had had bad dreams during the night, whimpering and moaning, but had not awakened. He had gone to her and soothed her, feeling awkward, but what else could he do? Let her dream about being raped by Chavez? She really was a child, he assured himself—not at all comfortable with what he saw as a weak, maternal urge to comfort her. He reasoned that any man would soothe a hurt, frightened child.

He came back from relieving himself and saw her sitting up with a look of confusion. He studied her closely, and when she met his gaze, a vast relief washed over him. That awful vacant look was gone. He squatted beside her. "Miranda?" His voice was so gentle that he didn't recognize it and was embarrassed. She flushed and looked away.

He took her hand. "It's all right," he said steadily.

She looked at him, and he saw that huge tears were welling in her eyes and spilling over. "No," she moaned. "Oh dear God, no." She hugged her knees and rocked herself.

He laid a tentative hand on her shoulder. "I'm sorry," he said harshly, hating himself for his failure. "I am so damn sorry."

She lowered her eyes, then looked up at him, biting her lip. "It's not your fault," she said, her mouth trembling. She took a deep breath. "Thank you. I—I thought you were dead. But you saved me." New tears rolled down her cheeks. "You saved me from that—that—" She moaned.

"Unfortunately, I was too late," Bragg said grimly, furious with himself. He felt like hugging her, but wasn't sure if he should. He hated himself so much at that moment that he was sure she hated him, too.

"Oh, Captain Bragg, thank you for rescuing me," she cried, sobbing now. She leaned forward into his arms.

He caught her and held her gently, awkwardly, not knowing what to do or say. "Did you think me some kind of bastard, that I'd leave you to the likes of Chavez?"

Miranda looked up at him, her breasts soft against his chest, her hair teasing his jaw. "How—how do you know him?"

Bragg grew dark with self-recrimination. "I saw him in Nacogdoches and didn't like the way he was looking at you. Goddammit!" He looked down at her, his hand caught up in her long tresses, delighting in the silky softness. "I asked who he was."

She had caught her breath.

"I know I can't make up to you for what happened," he said harshly. "But no one will ever know about this except John, I assure you."

"Now I understand," she murmured, and suddenly she stiffened in his embrace.

"What is it?" he asked with concern.

Miranda pushed his arms away and scrambled out of his grasp, yanking the bedroll up around her bare calves. "We forgot ourselves," she said, her face scarlet. "I have no clothes. I need my clothes." With horror, she had realized that she was wearing nothing but his shirt.

A small smile twisted Bragg's mouth. He was so glad to see some of the old Miranda! "There's no one here to know if we're improper, princess," he teased gently.

Her blush rose anew. "But we know," she said, fixing her huge violet eyes on him. "Where are my clothes?" A note of panic rose in her voice, and she looked around with desperate urgency.

Bragg leaned back on his heels. "I'm afraid it would be an invitation to disaster to go back to the wagon to fetch your things."

She looked extremely dismayed.

"Look, Miranda. I've seen about every portion of a

woman's anatomy that there is, and I promise you, the sight of your lovely legs isn't going to turn me into a bastard like Chavez."

Miranda flushed again and looked down. "Is—is he dead?"

"I don't know," he said harshly, rising, his face grim.

"I hope he's dead," she whispered raggedly, her eyes still downcast.

"I know," Bragg said, wondering why her pain hurt him so much. He had never been a compassionate man, not really, and never toward women.

"God is punishing me," she said, looking up at him. "Everything—"

"That's ridiculous," he snapped.

"No! Don't you understand? I wasn't obedient enough, not humble enough! And I had too much worldly curiosity!" She moaned. "I have sinned so much! And now I hate this man. If I were truly Christian, I would forgive him with love and kindness."

"I personally don't know a single Christian who loves his enemies," Bragg said. "That kind of teaching only belongs in the convent, princess, not in the real world."

Miranda gasped, looking as if she expected to see him struck down for uttering such blasphemy. "No!"

"Oh yes. Here in Texas, if you love your enemies, you die. To live, you kill your enemies before they kill you." His gaze was hot and angry. She would never survive in this raw land if she believed such nonsense.

"No," she said, standing unsteadily, still clutching the blanket around her waist. "No, I beg your pardon, but you are wrong!"

The force of her voice, revealing the strength of her conviction, surprised him. "Listen to me," he snapped, unable to believe he was arguing with her, a mere girl, especially after what had happened. "What do you think forgiveness will bring you with Chavez?" He knew he was being cruel, but he was too angry to help it. "You pat him on the back and tell him he's forgiven, and he'll just rape you again!"

Miranda gasped, growing pale.

"If Chavez is still alive, Miranda," Bragg said in a

somewhat calmer tone, "he will never forget what I did, and he will kill me without a second thought the next time he sees me—unless I kill him first."

Miranda clapped her hands over her ears and turned away.

Bragg kicked at a rock and sent it flying through the air. He strode away to saddle the horse, furious with himself for yelling at her—but someone had to teach her the facts of life. Was she going to welcome the Chavezes of the world with open arms and blind innocence, time and time again? But what did he care? This wasn't his problem—it was John's problem.

No, he thought, flinging the saddle on the startled chestnut's back. I owe her. Because of me she was brutally used. I owe her protection. It was that simple.

"Captain Bragg?"

He turned at her approach, unable to smile at the ridiculous look of the blanket clutched around her waist. "Yeah?"

"I think you should know something about Chavez." Her eyes were fixed on his. He stiffened.

"I mean, if he is going to try to kill you sometime in the future . . . you should know how smart he is." She gazed up at him, her face pale.

"Go on."

"Chavez's half brother was the chief of those Comanche you were decoying. It was a trap, to get you away from me, so he could abduct me." She shuddered uncontrollably. "It was planned."

He stared at her with growing comprehension. And in that moment, he hoped that Chavez was alive . . . so that he could exact vengeance, Apache style. The man would die—oh yes. But very, very slowly, and in great pain.

Chapter 16

. . . .y was nothing like the one before. Miranda sat stiffly in front of him, her every muscle tensed, trying to hold herself away from his body. After a long fight Bragg had finally let her keep the wool blanket thrown over her legs to hide them from his view. If she had not been abused so badly, the situation would have been almost amusing. Unfortunately, her discomfort only matched his. Her firmly soft little derriere nestled between his thighs had elicited an unavoidable physical reaction from him, of which she seemed—thankfully—oblivious. He intended for her to remain ignorant of his disgusting lust—although he had never been disgusted with his own natural appetites before. He did not want her to equate him with Chavez.

Because of their mutual discomfort, they did not talk. Miranda was thankful. Today she was numb and exhausted, as if she had been undertaking a very strenuous task for a very long time. Her mind had blocked out all memory of her abduction and encounter with Chavez. She knew she had been hurt and touched, but could not recall exactly what had happened, nor did she even try. She could still feel numbly the horror and the terror, way back in the farthest depths of her mind. She knew that her ordeal had been a punishment from God, but she didn't feel guilt, as she should. She still grieved for her aunt, although not as strongly as she knew she should. She had not even known her aunt until she had returned from the convent to England, but that was no excuse. All she could think about were two things. The man upon whose lap she was sitting and her fiancé.

Miranda was very uncomfortable. Bragg's body heat made her own body throb—not unpleasantly, but feverishly. It was not a new feeling, and she wondered if she was becoming ill from everything that had happened. She was aghast at the impropriety of their riding arrangement, indeed, of the fact that she was no longer chaperoned. It was not that she did not trust Bragg. His one, brief, accidental kiss was virtually forgotten—insignificant compared to the humiliation and agony she had endured since then. He had risked his life to save her, and she trusted him completely.

But there was no escaping the fact that Chavez had ruined her, and that now she was traveling in a completely scandalous manner with a strange man. She knew she was ruined, that John Barrington would never take her as his wife. She would certainly be sent back to the convent as soon as she arrived at the ranch. That thought should have relieved her immensely—she wanted to go home. But instead she was filled with anxiety.

They halted for the night in the mountains beneath lush oaks, next to a tumbling creek. There were a few hours of sunlight left as Bragg lifted her down, still clutching the blanket. Her legs itched unbearably, and her knees and inner thighs were sorely chafed from rubbing against the leather of the saddle all day. She was utterly exhausted.

"Make a fire, Miranda," Bragg said, untacking and hobbling the chestnut. "I'm going to catch us a nice fat pheasant for supper." He smiled. "How does that sound?"

His golden eyes were kind. She found herself smiling back. "All right," she said, then stopped. "Wait! I don't know how . . ."

He stared at her, then laughed. "All right. I'll show you when I get back. I'll only be fifteen, maybe thirty minutes." He started to go. "Oh. And don't worry. There's not a soul around for twenty miles."

Miranda smiled at him, not knowing how it affected

him. "I'm not afraid. I know you wouldn't leave me here if there was danger."

Bragg hurried away with a strange look on his face.

Once he was gone, she immediately shed the blanket. The cool air on her legs was a blessed relief. She stretched and walked a bit to ease her cramped muscles. She decided to collect firewood, without roaming too far. At least that was something she could do.

Afterward, Miranda wandered down to the creek. She suddenly had a compulsive urge to scrub herself clean. She raced back to their gear and searched through Bragg's saddlebags for soap. She found a long, rectangular piece of buckskin, the size of a small blanket, gunpowder for the rifle, caps for the six-shooter, a small jar of grease of some sort, dried jerky, a strange beaded necklace with brass conchos and something that looked suspiciously like a cross on it. There was also coffee and tobacco and a small bottle of whiskey, but no soap. Damn, she thought, then slapped her hand over her mouth, truly horrified for even thinking such a word. She went back to the creek empty-handed, thinking that she would have to ask Bragg to watch his language around her.

Miranda waded into the creek wearing Bragg's shirt, afraid that he'd return soon and catch her bathing. The water stung her raw blisters. The urge to scrub herself clean became compulsive. She sat on a rock, the water racing about her shins. She picked up a handful of coarse sand and began to scrub her leg violently, from toe to thigh.

She began rubbing harder and harder as a frightening, sickening image came to mind—Chavez stroking her naked body. She fought the vision, chased it away. The grains of sand abraded her skin, but the pain was a relief, and she welcomed it. Her heart was pounding painfully and it was hard to breathe. She started on her other foot and worked her way up that leg, determined, driven. She kept seeing Chavez, kept seeing his face looming over her. She scrubbed herself harder, viciously. She rubbed her inner thighs, already raw from riding. Chavez was thrusting fingers into her, into a place she had not even known she had. She tore off the shirt and began to scrub her belly, her breasts, every part of her body he had touched. . . .

Chapter 17

Bragg stopped whistling the moment he saw her. True to his word, he was holding a plump pheasant. Miranda had her back to him, and her long, thick tresses shielded her completely, but he knew she was naked. He could see she was washing herself furiously, no doubt rushing so he wouldn't catch her in an immodest state. He stood frozen, his mind telling him to back away. He fought with himself, and was about to turn away and give her a little more time, when she turned to the side and began to scrub her arm.

It was then that he realized something was terribly wrong. He glimpsed a long, slim leg, the curve of her belly, one soft, high breast. Her skin wasn't white, it was red—an angry red. He instantly realized she was rubbing handfuls of coarse sand on herself. From the vicious, frantic look she wore he saw that she was performing a kind of self-flagellation.

A cry of outrage came from his lips. Dropping the pheasant, he grabbed her hands to stop her from inflicting more pain on herself.

"No!" she screamed, wrenching free with a hysterical strength that took him completely by surprise. "No! No!" Before he knew it, her nails had raked down the side of his face, drawing blood.

He caught her wrists firmly. "Stop it!" he yelled. "Stop

it, Miranda, stop!'' He shook her. She was twisting like a
wild animal, panting and giving little cries, trying to kick
him. They had both risen to their feet, and he shoved one
leg between her thighs and wrapped the other behind her
right leg, pinning her to him. "Stop it!''

Miranda froze against him and began to weep softly, her
head falling limply against his chest. He relaxed his hold
and lifted her to carry her to the blanket. Then he saw the
extent of what she had done. Her skin was an angry red
from her neck to her toes, even her breasts. And the
insides of her knees were bloody. He felt sick. Her quiet
weeping gave way to a moan, and he laid her gently down
on the blanket. "Why, Miranda?'' he said. "Why did you
have to hurt yourself like this?''

"Chavez,'' she moaned. "He touched me.''

Of course Bragg understood. He rose and went to his
saddlebags. He knew she'd gone through them, although
he didn't know what she'd been looking for. He took the
loincloth he carried as a spare blanket and laid it on top of
her, covering her from her thighs to her breasts. He brought
water back from the stream, and when he knelt at her feet,
she had stopped crying, although tears glistened on her
face.

"I'm going to clean up these blisters,'' he told her
evenly. He reached down and gently tried to move her legs
apart.

"No,'' she said, sitting up, holding the buckskin cloth
over her breasts and trying to push his hand away. For
once, she didn't blush. "I'll do it.''

"Don't be ridiculous,'' he said sharply. He tucked the
loincloth between her thighs, ignoring her gasp. He was
careful not to touch her womanhood, but his hand trembled, and he brushed her by accident. "You're completely
covered,'' he said harshly, dismayed with himself once
more. "Goddammit! Why didn't you tell me you were
getting blisters?''

"I didn't know,'' she whispered.

He studiously avoided her face, knowing that she was
embarrassed. He was determined to clean her up and
ignore his own involuntary desire. He bathed her legs and
rubbed on grease containing healing herbs. He could feel

how tense she was at his touch, but he was glad that her fragile skin was no longer so red. He was furious with her for hurting herself.

"Miranda, I want you to put this all over your body." He handed her the jar.

She gasped.

"I'm going to make a fire. I want you to do it. It's healing," he added, standing.

She stared at him, looking aghast.

"Everywhere, Miranda, and if you don't do it, I will." He started to turn, then put his hands on his hips, facing her. The thought had occurred to him that Chavez had probably hurt her while raping her. "Everywhere Chavez touched you," he said. He looked right into her eyes. "Do you understand what I'm saying?"

When she flushed, Bragg knew she understood. He knelt and made a small fire, all the while listening to her movements, as quiet as they were. He kept his back to her and began to prepare the pheasant. Finally, he said, "If you take off that damn loincloth it will be easier, Miranda."

She gasped. She had left it on and was rubbing the grease onto her belly beneath the buckskin cloth. "You're looking!"

"No, I just know you, that's all," he retorted. But he was pleased when he heard the sound of the soft material falling aside. It was hard to concentrate on plucking the pheasant, though. He had a very clear image in his mind of her stroking her own soft skin, massaging in the grease, and he was throbbing with untimely desire.

"I'm finished," she said softly.

Bragg brought her his shirt. "Why don't you put on the cloth too, as a skirt. You can fasten it with some vine."

Miranda nodded.

Later, they ate in silence, Miranda wearing the loincloth as a skirt, with Bragg's shirt tucked into it. Bragg saw that she had no appetite. He didn't understand why she had seemed fine all day and was now suddenly so withdrawn. "You need to eat," he said.

"I'm not hungry." Her voice was barely audible.

"Please try," he said, surprised again at the words that came unbidden to his mouth. The word *please* was completely foreign to him. He was a man who took, not asked. He rose abruptly.

Of course she didn't eat, and he wondered if she'd be nothing more than skin and bones by the time they got to John's. With his back against a tree, he stared at the stars while she crawled beneath the single blanket they possessed.

It was cool in the mountains, but he could survive a blizzard with nothing but a loincloth if he had to. He sighed and closed his eyes, worrying about Miranda until sleep overtook him.

He was awakened by her cry of pain. He knew immediately that she was dreaming; her moans were anguished exactly like those he'd heard outside of Chavez's tent. He went over to her and shook her gently. She was thrashing about restlessly, lost in her nightmare.

"No, please," she moaned, her eyes flashing open.

He gave in to his urge to put his arms around her and sank down onto his side. "It's me, Miranda. Bragg. You're just dreaming, princess, just dreaming."

"Ohhh," she moaned, curling up hard against him.

Like the beast she had accused him of being, his body caught fire. He ignored it and held her gently, but she burrowed against him. "It was so real," she cried. "I'm ruined, ruined . . ."

What could he say? "You have to put it all behind you," he said, relishing the feel of her body pressing against him even as he tried to control himself. He shifted slightly so that she wouldn't feel his body's treacherous but unmistakable response to her closeness, her softness, her scent.

"I'm ruined," she cried. "Oh, this is so silly! Can't you just take me back to Natchez?" She was talking into his buckskin-clad chest. "John is just going to send me home anyway, after he finds out what Chavez did."

Bragg was completely startled. "Miranda, John is in love with you. I can't tell you he won't care about what happened, but he will still want to marry you—gladly." He grasped her shoulders and moved her away so he could look down into her face. In the moonlight, he could clearly make out her expression—and she was so close.

I'm lying in my bedroll with a woman, he thought derisively, a woman I can't touch. Is that ever a first!

"He will?" Her eyes searched his, still glimmering with moisture.

"Absolutely." He tried a smile but failed. Their position was beginning to torture him.

"But you don't understand," she said haltingly.

"I do."

"No—Chavez touched me."

"I know."

Miranda shook her head. "He touched me! In—my—" She broke off.

"I know," he said, a tremor overtaking him.

"I think he raped me," she whispered, closing her eyes.

Bragg sat up, abruptly releasing her. "You think?" His mind was racing. How could she not know? Could an innocent, ignorant virgin not know when she was raped? Impossible! "Miranda? What do you mean, you think?"

She lay on her side and shook her head mutely.

He pulled her up into a sitting position. "Don't you know?"

"No," she whispered.

He sat there a moment, thoroughly confounded. There was no question in his mind that he was going to find out whether she had been raped. He didn't for a moment stop to think that it was John's concern, not his. "How did Chavez touch you, Miranda?" he asked bluntly.

She gasped, her eyes widening.

"Please, this is important," he said evenly.

"With his hands," she finally said, her voice barely audible. He was sure her face was crimson. "His fingers."

Bragg stared. "Did he mate with you?"

Miranda gazed at him blankly. "I—I don't know."

"You said he hurt you. Did you bleed?"

She stared. "I don't think so."

Bragg cursed. "Miranda, did he put his rod in you?"

Her mouth fell open. "His—what? Where?"

Bragg stood. "His rod, dammit. Men have rods." He pointed at his own evident bulge. Her eyes followed his hand, and she gasped.

"Christ," Bragg said. "I take it the answer is no."

She nodded mutely.

He took a deep breath, laughed shakily, and gazed down at her. "I think you'd better stop staring," he said hoarsely.

Miranda uttered a horrified cry and fell onto her side, curling up with her back to him.

"Miranda, I think you should know, you're still a virgin. I can't believe any woman could be so ignorant," he added, and walked down to the creek.

Chapter 18

Miranda had never felt so completely alone in her life.

She lay huddled in the bedroll, alone, her mind overwhelmed with everything she had found out. She was still a virgin. John wouldn't send her back.

She could remember, now, how Chavez had felt when he had been lying against her back. She remembered very clearly the rodlike thing pressing against her buttocks. She flushed in the darkness at the image of Bragg pointing to himself—at the bulge she had seen. She still wasn't sure exactly how the act of mating was accomplished.

If John didn't send her back, he was going to do things to her with that male part of him. It would be much, much worse than what Chavez had done. She stifled an anguished moan. Why wouldn't he send her home? Why?

Miranda closed her eyes tightly. Her loneliness overwhelmed her. She had no one to turn to—no one to help her face this marriage to a complete stranger, a barbaric Texan. No one to ask questions of . . . no one . . . no one . . .

She felt tears, those endless tears, starting again. "Oh, why can't I go home?" she whispered to herself. *"Why?"*

She hadn't known where Bragg was, nor did she hear him approach until she felt his strong, warm hand on her shoulder. "Don't cry," he said gruffly.

"I want to go home," she said brokenly, fighting the urge to weep.

He stroked her shoulder through the blanket, but she didn't turn. "I know," he said finally. "I'm sorry."

"I hate Texas." Miranda sobbed, giving in to her fear and anguish.

"Miranda, please don't cry," he said, distress in his voice. He didn't know what to do. She was so fragile, so young, so vulnerable. He had never faced a woman's tears before. His mother, an Apache, had never cried, not even when his father had slapped her for some wrongdoing. His wife, now dead, had never cried either, or at least not in front of him. Even after he had found her, sold to a brothel by the Comanche, she had not cried, not even for their son. . . . For some reason, at that very moment, Bragg felt like crying with Miranda. From deep inside, the long-buried grief of his life welled up and threatened to burst.

He had never cried. Although Apache men did cry when in mourning, Bragg's white father had told him at an early age that crying was a womanly weakness—he would not stand to see a son of his cry. Even the time he'd been badly hurt as a boy, Bragg had learned to control himself—a lesson he would carry with him forever. As a young boy growing up, he had thought his father a giant among men, a god.

Bragg knelt helplessly by Miranda, touching her shoulder gently. "You're not alone, Miranda," he tried. "I'm here."

"Maman is dead," she wept. "Aunt Elizabeth is dead. Papa hates me. The sisters are in France. I'm marrying a man who won't be able to bear the sight of me, not after . . . after . . ."

"John isn't like that." Bragg said quietly, his voice soothing. He felt very tense with the unmanly, commiserating grief he was feeling as he struggled over whether to hold her or not. "And you can always turn to me, Miranda, always."

She rolled over to face him, then sat up and wiped away her tears. Her face was almost on a level with his, and their knees touched. He patted her shoulder. She was looking at him with such trust, and it yanked at him, disturbed him. "Why?"

"I feel responsible," he said, and shrugged. He started to rise, but she grabbed his shirt. Startled, he felt his heart start to hammer and sank back down by her side.

Miranda stared at him, wet her lips, then dropped her hands. "Are you sure?"

He couldn't remember what they'd been talking about. He now knew that she wet her lips in that unconscious, sensuous way when she was nervous. Still, it didn't lessen the impact on his senses. He had a brief fantasy of her running her tiny pink tongue over his lips, probing past his teeth. "Sure of what?" His voice was hoarse. Any other woman would have known how aroused he was becoming.

"That John won't despise me." She searched his face for the truth.

"I know he won't," Bragg told her, coming back to reality with difficulty. "What happened wasn't your fault, it was mine."

Miranda started. "It wasn't your fault," she protested.

He held up his hand. "I refuse to discuss it."

She sighed, rubbing her eyes with a childish gesture.

"We have a long day tomorrow," Bragg said softly, touched despite himself. "Why don't you get some sleep?"

He stood and turned his back to her, hoping she wouldn't cry herself to sleep and hating the feeling of vulnerability she aroused in him.

Chapter 19

The next morning Miranda rode with both her legs dangling over the chestnut's right side, settled firmly upon Bragg's lap. He kept one arm around her waist to hold her in place. She was hotly aware of his arm pressing against her stomach, his fingers lightly splayed. She was even more aware of the contact between her derriere and his thighs. Although she didn't know it, Bragg had her strategically placed so that she wouldn't touch any sensitive, revealing part of his anatomy.

"I'm not comfortable," she said about two miles out of their camp.

"I'm sorry." He replied curtly, not exactly comfortable either.

"This is so improper," she said a few moments later.

"Forget propriety, Miranda," he snapped, and felt her body tense as if he'd smacked her. He didn't apologize. "This is Texas. Not England. Not a goddamn convent."

Miranda gasped, thoroughly shocked and angry. "Mr. Bragg, I've been meaning to tell you, your language is abominable, and I would greatly appreciate it if you'd refrain from using such . . . uncouth . . . curses in front of me."

"What?"

"Please don't use the Lord's name in vain," she said, her voice tight.

Bragg chuckled. "That was a pretty speech. I'm sorry to offend you, but what the hell—er, excuse me, I'm only a backwoods barbarian, and I've never met an English lady before."

His breath, soft and warm, tickled her ear. "You're making fun of me."

"Never."

"You are."

"You're too beautiful to ever be made fun of," he said, and his voice dropped, becoming a soft caress.

A tingle ran all over her. "I'm not beautiful," she said. "I'm skinny."

"Now that's a fact! Skinny and beautiful. John's going to want to fatten you up." He chuckled again.

Miranda stiffened and flushed. She was remembering how Bragg had seen her naked in Chavez's arms. How he had come upon her naked the day before, bathing. Her color deepened. Her pulse raced. Her only coherent thought was: He thinks I'm too skinny.

"I didn't mean to insult you, princess," he said softly in her ear.

Miranda didn't answer. Why did his breath make her body tremble and ache, in such a painfully sweet way?

Suddenly Bragg's arm tightened as the chestnut stumbled, and she felt herself being pulled back fully against him, from her buttocks to her head. The heat of his body burned her. Then his hold loosened, and they sat easily again as the chestnut continued on its way. Her face was burning.

She didn't know why she was so nervous, but she quickly spoke to hide her confusion. "Where do you live, Captain Bragg?"

"Derek," he said. His voice seemed hoarse to her. "I think you should call me Derek."

"Oh no," she returned primly. "That would be so improper."

"John wouldn't mind," he said.

"Where do you live?"

"Anywhere I care to throw my bedroll."

"No! Really?"

"Really."

"What do Texas Rangers do?" she said, after having absorbed the fact that he was something of a vagabond.

"Fight Indians and outlaws," he said easily. "You're full of questions today." He sounded pleased.

"But you're half Indian!"

He tensed. "Now who in hell—oh! Welsh!"

"Captain Bragg! Is every word out of your mouth a curse?"

"Are you trying to convert me or reform me?" he asked suspiciously.

"You are a lost lamb," Miranda said seriously.

He roared with laughter. "That's very funny! Me—a lost lamb!" He chuckled again.

She twisted so that she could see his face, peering up at him. "But you are! You're heathen. I mean . . ." She flushed.

To see him, she had shifted her left shoulder fully against his right side, her derriere slipping comfortably into his crotch, her hip against something uncomfortable—yet somehow familiar. Something hard and rodlike . . .

Their eyes held, hers widening with understanding. His golden gaze was liquid and bright, like flames, burning and flickering. She swallowed, tried to push herself up slightly, and felt his maleness pressing harder against her hip. "Oh!"

"I'm sorry, princess," he said, swinging her into her original position. "I am sorry."

Her heart was racing wildly. Why was it like that? She knew for a fact that this morning when they'd mounted there had been no bulge in his pants. She had looked discreetly, wanting to know if she'd dreamed what she had seen last night. Worse, why was her body reacting to his as if she was ill with a fever? She could barely breathe.

"Relax," he said huskily. "I won't hurt you." He mistook her tense silence for fear.

"Why . . ." she began, and trailed off. Her body ached unbearably.

"Men can't control it, Miranda, not always. I'm sorry."

She took a deep breath. "Derek? I think I'm ill."

"What's wrong?" he said quickly, pulling her hard

against him so that he could look down into her flushed
face. He reined in.

"I think I have a fever," she breathed, staring up at
him, unable to close her mouth, her gaze liquid and smoky.
And then, for some reason, she found herself staring at his
mouth. She heard a low, strange sound, a whimper, not
even realizing it had come from her.

He gasped as coherent thought and all self-control disappeared in the face of her all too apparent desire. His arm
tightened, pulling her up higher, harder, against his straining manhood, while his other hand dropped the rein, found
her hip, and slid up to her waist. She was staring at his
mouth with hungry eyes, her red lips parted breathlessly.
He lowered his face.

She knew he was going to kiss her, and she couldn't
move, couldn't protest, couldn't even think. She didn't
know if she wanted him to or not. She sat frozen in his
arms, unable to breathe, her body on fire. His lips came
down on hers, softly, gently, and the tip of his tongue slid
into her open mouth. Miranda closed her eyes, her hands
finding his shirt, clinging. His mouth became more demanding. She didn't kiss him back—the thought never
entered her dazed mind—but she opened her mouth wider
and pressed her hands harder against his chest. His tongue
invaded her mouth—strangely, deliciously exploring her
teeth, her cheeks, her own tongue. His hand on her waist
caressed her flesh.

The kiss was endless and intimate and devouring. His
hand slid from her waist to her hip, paused, then went
lower. He stroked her buttock, the back of her thigh,
kneading along the way, coming back up to cup her buttock again. She whimpered, pressing her derriere back into
his hand, straining for his seeking fingers.

Suddenly she found herself sliding off the horse and
onto her feet. She stumbled, panting, realizing that he had
slipped her off the horse, and that he had leaped off the
other side. Her legs were so weak that she crumpled to her
hands and knees, trembling wildly.

Suddenly she became aware of what had happened. She
gasped, covering her face with her hands, ashamed and
mortified. Bragg had been kissing her! Bragg had been

touching her! Dear god! And it had been . . . wonderful . . . exciting.

Miranda sank into a sitting position as she tried to collect herself. Harlot! an inner voice shrieked. Trollop! You let him touch you, let him kiss you. You liked it! Whore! She gave an anguished cry and covered her face with her hands.

That was how Bragg found her when he had gained sufficient control to approach. He was dark with anger at himself. "We have to talk," he said harshly, glaring at Miranda as she sat hiding her face behind her hands. At the sound of his voice, she leaped to her feet and backed away, her eyes huge and wary.

"Miranda, we have to talk," he said again, angrily.

She looked around wildly. She had to escape! Was he going to rape her? Would she enjoy it? Oh God! With a cry, she turned and ran toward the woods.

"Oh, goddammit!" It was a bellow. He watched her race from him as if he were a monster, across the rocky ground, toward the shelter of oaks and juniper. "You're going to cut your feet," he yelled, fury overcoming him. "Where the hell do you think you're going?"

He took off after her and caught her a moment later. Miranda struggled as he wrapped his arms around her, and he saw that her eyes were wide with horror and fright. "I'm not going to hurt you! What are you doing? Where the hell do you think you're going?"

She stopped twisting and stood stock still. Her enormous violet eyes seared his. He frowned darkly and released her. "Look," he began, "I'm sorry. Dammit! Why the hell am I always apologizing to you?"

He saw it coming, but he let her slap him anyway. He felt he deserved it, and besides, her strength was pitiful. The smack stung—barely. "Feel better?"

"I am sick of your language," she said tersely.

He straightened in surprise. "Is that why you hit me?"

"Yes! I can't stand your cursing! I—"

Bragg laughed. "You know, every now and then you surprise me when you show some spunk, Miranda. I thought you hit me because of the kiss."

They both became very silent and tense, each thinking about what had happened.

"It was wrong," Miranda whispered.

"Yes."

"Why did you do it?"

He stared at her, then scowled. "You wanted me to."

Her eyes widened. "Never! That's not true!" She hugged herself and stepped back a pace.

"Da— Darn! You don't even realize what you want, you foolish child!"

"I know what I want," Miranda said shakily. "I want to go home."

"Now you really sound like a child." He grimaced in exasperation. "Look, Miranda, I accept all blame for what happened. You're a woman, and I'm a man, and my appetites are too damn lusty, I guess."

She met his penetrating gaze, waiting with anticipation for she didn't know what.

"Anyway, from now on you'll ride and I'll walk. No sense in testing my willpower anymore." He laughed bitterly. "Especially since I don't seem to have any." He stared at her. "Why did you run off just now?"

Her mouth trembled. "I was afraid. Afraid you were going to—" She bit off her words.

He looked black with anger. "Afraid I was going to rape you?" Fury swept over him. He felt like exploding, like shaking some sense into her—how could the little fool think he'd force himself on her? "Get on the horse," he said, his words cutting like a whipcord. "And stop being afraid of me—I don't like it."

Chapter 20

No matter how often Miranda asked, Bragg would not let her take a turn walking. The problem was, her knees hurt terribly, for riding alone meant that she had to sit astride. She tucked the edge of the loincloth under her knees the best she could, and knew she was bleeding again. She didn't want to complain. She didn't want any attention from Bragg. She had trusted him and he had violated that trust. He was able to become a beast like Chavez. She was afraid of him. But in a different way than she had ever been afraid before.

She was lost in a kind of fascination. A few hours after the shocking kiss, Bragg had slipped off his shirt and tied it around his waist. Miranda gasped aloud without meaning to, and tried to tear her eyes away from his broad, gleaming, bronzed back. She did not know how to ride, so Bragg led the horse, apparently tireless. She couldn't stop staring.

They didn't stop once until nearly dusk. Bragg asked her twice, without looking at her, how she was doing. She replied both times with an abrupt "Fine." She wasn't fine. Her knees hurt terribly. Her hair was thick with sweat from the sombrero, which she wore to protect her face. Her body ached from using different muscles to hang on to the horse, even at a walk. When they finally stopped, Miranda was desperate for relief on all accounts.

Bragg came over to her for the first time since that disastrous morning. He barely glanced at her as he pulled her out of the saddle, setting her on her feet. He led the horse away while he unsaddled him.

Miranda could barely stand, and she couldn't walk. Tears of pain came to her eyes. She sank as gracefully as she could onto the ground, gingerly stretching out her legs. She would much, much rather sit on Bragg's lap than go through another day astride. At that thought, a tear spilled over her cheek. Had she really liked his touch, or had she imagined it? She couldn't have liked it! No well-bred lady did, and she was a gentlewoman!

Miranda decided that she hadn't liked it. She remembered very clearly how she had felt sick to the point of nausea with Chavez. Bragg had just taken her by surprise, she decided, and he had been gentle—hence her passivity. Yes, that's all it had been—passive acceptance. She felt greatly relieved.

"Are you going to sit there all night?"

Miranda looked up, met his golden gaze, and quickly looked past his shoulder. "I . . . I'm just tired."

He squinted at her. "Are you all right?"

"Yes."

"I'm going to get some game," he said, staring down at her. "Are you stiff?"

"A little," she lied. She was so stiff she couldn't move.

He frowned, clearly displeased, and strode away.

Miranda tried to ignore his cold anger. She debated wandering over to the riverbank, which was about thirty yards away, then decided it was too far. Sighing, she stretched out and fell asleep.

She was awakened by Bragg's harsh, angry voice as he shook her. "What?"

"You stupid twit! Why didn't you say something if you were bleeding! What's wrong with you?"

Miranda became instantly awake, and she struggled upright. He had bared her lower legs. "Stop it!" she cried, feeling sudden panic.

Bragg had noticed the blood on the loincloth. "You have no common sense," he said, pulling her to her feet.

She groaned involuntarily.

"That bad?" He grimaced. "Why didn't you speak up? If you were so sore—come on." His tone grew softer, and he started to lead her to the river.

"Please, no. I'm fine." Miranda stopped, refusing to take another step. Her body hurt unbearably.

Instantly he swept her into his arms, tearing off the loincloth and tossing it aside. He grumbled beneath his breath, then dumped her unceremoniously into the river. The water first stung her raw flesh, then it became soothing. She just sat there, looking up to see Bragg staring down at her, his legs spread, his hands on his hips.

"Are you stubborn or stupid, Miranda?"

"Stop insulting me! Stop insulting me because you're angry with yourself!" She glared up at him.

"You're right," he said unpleasantly. His eyes were cold. "I am angry with myself—and with John. I'm angry at myself for wanting you, and angry at him for bringing you out here in the first place. You don't belong in Texas. You belong in some fancy duke's castle, tucked away nice and cozy, in fine dresses and silk stockings."

Miranda stared, her mouth open.

"John is a damn fool." His eyes held hers fiercely. "And so am I," he added as an afterthought.

Chapter 21

"Sun's coming up, Miranda," Bragg said cheerfully. "Up and at 'em, princess."

Miranda groaned as she tried to stretch, and opened her eyes to see him staring down at her with a strange look. The look disappeared, and he grinned, then sauntered off. She felt a rush of relief. He was apparently in good humor. She couldn't have taken another day of his coldness, which was practically cruel. She sat up and moaned.

She knew she couldn't ride. Every muscle in her body ached. Just sitting up hurt. The only places that didn't hurt, and were merely sore, were her neck and shoulders. Cautiously she rose to her feet, gasping as pain knifed through her hips and legs.

"You're in pretty bad shape, huh?" Bragg said, sounding sympathetic as he approached and handed her coffee. He was smiling.

"It's not funny," Miranda said, taking the foul brew and sipping it. She wondered if John would have tea at the house. She had not had coffee in the convent and hated it. But Bragg's brew made Welsh's seem like beans roasted for the queen. It was like sipping thick, bitter mud.

"You're too weak, Miranda, woman or not," Bragg said with a frown. "A woman has to be strong in this territory to survive."

"Oh, go away," she grumbled, then was instantly shocked at her lack of manners.

He chuckled, raising an eyebrow. "That bad, huh? Look, I've been thinking. If we ride hard, we can make John's ranch in two and a half days."

Miranda stared, devastated by the idea. "I can't even sit to a trot," she cried.

He waved at her impatiently. "I'm talking about the way we were riding before. And when I say hard, I mean hard. We only stop for a few hours of sleep."

Miranda stared, debating this idea. He wanted her to sit on his lap. What if he kissed her again? He did not seem too good at controlling his male appetites. What if . . .

"I can read your thoughts," he growled.

"Can't we take the day off and sleep late and rest?" she asked hopefully.

"What?" He stared at her in disbelief. "Rest?" He said the word as if it were foreign. Miranda realized that it probably was, to him.

"Look. If we go on like this, it'll take a week. If we ride hard, believe me, there's not going to be the kind of distraction between us that there was yesterday. And even though we'll ride half the night, you can sleep in my arms." His gaze held her. "We might as well get this over with, Miranda."

She felt a funny kind of sadness at his last words. He disliked taking her across the country, she thought, hurt. "All right," she said, looking up. But he had walked away, silently, as usual.

Miranda understood quickly what Bragg meant by riding hard. At first she was frightened. They rode at a canter or a trot, up and down gullies and ridges, splashing through creeks, over rocky trails, across stretches of flat valley. Bragg kept his arm tightly around her, and she soon realized that she was secure. He had cut off strips of the loincloth and bandaged her knees, for she had to ride astride in front of him, he told her. Now she knew why. He never slowed the horse—and he was right. Her concentration, instinctively, was on her seat, while his was on the horse, the terrain—both underfoot and all around them—and on holding her.

Once his grip seemed precariously loose, and she cried out. "Captain Bragg! You're going to drop me!"

The chestnut had settled into a loping canter. Bragg chuckled. "Never, princess. Relax. You're too stiff. Try and go with the rhythm. Move your body a bit. Like this."

He exaggerated the movement his own hips made with the horse, back and forth, but Miranda wasn't ready to try it. In fact, for some reason, her awareness of the movement of his body with the horse, pressing back and forth against her, caused her color to rise and her pulse to race.

"I guess that wasn't a good idea," he said in her ear, his hold on her tightening as if he could feel her reaction.

It was past midday when Bragg pulled the chestnut to a complete halt. Miranda thought they might have been riding for five or six hours. She was thrilled that they were stopping. "Oh, thank God!"

Bragg urged the chestnut over the rise. "Don't thank Him yet," he said quietly.

"But aren't we stopping? Just for a bit?"

"For ten minutes, to rest the horse," he said curtly, and then Miranda saw why.

Her heart lurched. Below them a swollen river raced furiously. "No," she said with true fear. "We're not going to cross that!"

Bragg dismounted, then pulled her down. "We are. Don't worry. Walk around a bit and stretch your legs. I'm going to scout a better crossing."

Miranda stared miserably after him as he set out in a steady trot, running parallel to the river. They had crossed rivers like this before—the Mississippi, the Red, the Sabine—but there had always been a ferry. Was he crazy?

He appeared ten minutes later, running like a deer, easy and loose-limbed, barely breathing harder than normal. He had stripped off his shirt, and sweat made his chest gleam. He stopped in front of her. "Looks like we'll do it upriver about a mile," he said easily.

Miranda realized that she was staring at his chest. The muscles were like huge, hard slabs, the heavy fur between his nipples trailing into a delicate vee before disappearing into his waistband. She flushed and looked at his face.

Bragg didn't laugh. His eyes glowed like embers, then

he turned and walked away. He began to put some things in a watertight oilskin: his Colt, his rifle, and other water-damageable items. Miranda realized what was about to happen and ran to him as he tied the parcel to the saddle.

"No! You're crazy! How are we going to cross?" There was panic in her voice. "I can't swim!"

He turned to her slowly. "You're not going to swim, the horse is. You're not going to drown, Miranda, I give you my word."

"Like you gave John your word I wouldn't be harmed?" she cried hysterically, not thinking.

He stiffened, hurt coming into his eyes, until a dark mask covered his pain.

"I'm sorry," she cried, grabbing his arm. "I . . . I didn't mean that! Oh! I can't!"

"Don't start crying, dammit!" Bragg glared. "Show some of that spine I know you have, Miranda." He grabbed her hand roughly, and she had no choice but to follow as he led the horse.

She knew that crying wasn't going to help, and she fought the tears of terror. Her life was in God's hands. Hadn't she been taught that long ago? Trust in the Lord. He would protect her. Unless this was her final punishment . . .

Miranda realized they had stopped. Bragg had his hands on her waist and was about to lift her into the saddle. "Wait!" she cried, panic-stricken. "I want to pray."

He swore. "You're not going to drown. You don't— All right. Hurry up."

Miranda sank to her knees, wishing she'd been to Mass and confession since Natchez. That was the first thing she'd do when she got to John's ranch. There was a mission in San Antonio, thank God! She knelt, closed her eyes, and prayed.

Bragg stood and watched her. He was truly annoyed that she trusted him so little that she had to get down on her knees and pray. He was even angry. But then, why should she trust him? Hadn't she hit the nail on the head just a moment ago? He had failed her once. Little did she know that he had no intention of failing her again. He watched her rise unsteadily, her face white beneath the sombrero.

He placed her firmly upon the chestnut, then took the rawhide lariat off the pommel, unwinding it.

"What are you doing?" she asked, trembling.

He slipped the lariat around her waist. "I'm tying you to the saddle, princess."

"But . . . why?"

He looked up into her huge violet eyes as he secured her to the horse. "Do you think I trust you to keep your seat while the horse swims?" There was a teasing note in his voice.

"But . . ." She was breathless. "But you're going to hold me!"

He tightened the knot and clasped her hand. "No, Miranda. I'm going to swim alongside."

"No!" It was a scream. "No, Derek, no!"

"Stop it," he said calmly. "I want you to sit still and hold on to the horse's mane and the saddle, like so." He placed her hands where he wanted them. "And you don't let go, no matter what."

Tears streamed down her cheeks. "No! *Non! Sale bête! Je vous en pries.* Please, Derek, please, Derek . . ."

She was shaking uncontrollably. Derek smacked her across the face, and the tirade stopped. A pink mark marred her cheek. He was angry that he'd had to hit her, even though it had been the weakest of slaps. "Grip with your legs. Hold on like you're doing now. Don't let go. Lean forward, like so." He pushed her over the horse's withers. She didn't move.

"Good." He slipped his knife out of the sheath and placed it between his teeth. The odds of the horse losing his footing were minuscule. But if it happened, he would have Miranda cut free in a second. He led the horse into the river, and the water rose quickly from his toes to his shins.

Miranda wasn't breathing. She was terrified. He wished that he could speak to her, but of course he couldn't, because of how he was carrying the knife. He patted her knee as the water rose to his hips, his waist, his chest. The horse lunged forward, swimming, and Bragg placed one hand on the saddle and let himself be pulled alongside.

The current was fast. But as he'd known, the horse was

a strong swimmer, and had no interest in floating endlessly downstream. Bragg was on the downstream side anyway, using his body to guide the horse at an angle to the opposite shore. He'd swum alongside a horse hundreds of times, and there was nothing to it. He glanced at Miranda and smiled. She didn't even notice. She was hanging on for her life, her face buried against the horse's neck.

The horse hit the riverbed first, stumbling slightly. Bragg found his footing next, released the saddle and grabbed the reins. Now running, he and the chestnut lunged out of the water and up the bank.

"Whoa, steady up," Bragg said, throwing his hip into the excited horse's chest while he pulled on the reins. He was in no danger of being stepped on. Instinctively, he knew exactly where each lethal hoof was—it was as natural as knowing where his own next footfall would be.

The horse quieted, snorting and blowing. Bragg dropped his reins and went to Miranda. She was in the same position, her face pressed to the horse's neck, clutching his mane and saddle, frozen stiff.

Bragg untied her rapidly. "Good girl, Miranda. See? Nothing to it!" Wait until she finds out there's two more like this to cross, he thought. "Miranda?" She hadn't moved, and he pulled her off the horse.

She clung to him. He enfolded her in his embrace as if it were the most natural thing in the world. "It's all over now, princess," he murmured. "You did just fine. Just fine." His hands immediately slid over her slim back, caressingly. Then he became aware of her body, warm against his, and her hair, teasing his chin; her softness and her musky, feminine scent. A dull roar swept through his veins. He pried her arms away.

Miranda gazed up at him and started to breathe.

"You did fine," he said, forcing himself to remain calm.

She smiled.

"I'm proud of you," he added.

Her smile widened. "I did it! I crossed the river!"

He grinned. "Now, that wasn't so bad, was it?"

The smile disappeared, and she stared at him aghast. "It

was awful, awful! I never want to have to go through that again!''

''I think we'll take a rest,'' he said easily. ''I have a feeling you just spent more energy in ten minutes than you did all morning.''

Part Two

The Promise

Chapter 22

"That's it," Bragg said casually as the horse shifted beneath them.

Miranda stared down at the valley. The slopes were forested with juniper and pinyon and oak. The land was rocky, but lush and green. A lake sparkled across the valley, bounded by flat, green grazing land on one side and pine-covered slopes on the other. At the far end of the valley, and across the rolling slopes, brown cattle flecked the countryside. And directly below the ridge where they stood was the JB ranch. Her fiancé's ranch. She was tense with anticipation and anxiety.

"The whole valley is John's," Bragg said, lifting his arm from her waist to gesture.

"It's beautiful," she breathed, no longer afraid when Bragg didn't hold her. After the past two days of riding, she thought she could ride alone if she had to—and yes, even swim a horse across a raging river!

"God's country."

"I didn't know you believed in the Lord, Mr. Bragg," she said pertly, twisting around to glance at him over her shoulder. It was impossible. The brim of her sombrero caught his jaw, even though he had long ago taken his knife to it and trimmed it down.

He chuckled. "Your Lord? No, I don't think so."

"He's the only Lord there is," she said primly.

He placed his hand back on her waist, guiding the horse forward. At his touch she became blind to the panorama spread before them, momentarily forgetting her apprehension at meeting the man she was going to spend the rest of her life with. Her belly knotted, a sweet pain flooding her.

Miranda didn't know why the warm, hard feel of this man, his scent, his voice, caused such an ache, a physical yearning she didn't understand. This sensation, while new, had occurred with more and more frequency during the past few days—in fact, the more she got used to riding, it seemed, the more she became aware of him. She had never in her whole life spent so much time with a man, any man. In fact, Bragg was the first man who had ever touched her, and other than her father and a priest, the first man she had ever had a conversation of any length with. She blushed, just thinking about the intimacies they had shared.

Fortunately, they had ridden hard for the past two and a half days, so hard that he had been right. He had not shown the least interest in kissing her again. She wondered why she remembered his kiss so vividly. They rode so long each day that she had spent half of the past two nights asleep in the saddle, the other half asleep on the ground, too exhausted to awaken even when he stopped and wrapped her in the bedroll. And now it was over. No, now it was actually beginning! What did the future hold in store? As the horse scrambled down the stony slope, her body stiffened, and Bragg increased the pressure of his hold.

"I thought you were getting used to this, princess," he said with amusement.

"I am," she replied quietly. "I was thinking about my fiancé."

Bragg was silent behind her.

Her heart had started to pound the moment he told her this was it, and now perspiration began to collect on her brow. She was about to meet the man who would be her husband for the rest of her life. She prayed he was kind and good. She prayed he would not hate her for what had happened, that he would not be a brute like her father, or a man with appetites like Chavez . . . like Bragg.

But above all, Miranda wondered how she could face

him looking as she did. She was wearing Bragg's huge buckskin shirt tucked into his loincloth, which was draped around her like a skirt. It reached to her ankles, but her small feet were bare and black with dirt. Her hair was pulled into one snarled braid. Her face was dusty, and she hadn't bathed since she had tried to scour Chavez's touch from her skin. The hat on her head was a bashed, decrepit version of its original self.

"Stop!" she cried, suddenly panicking, yanking on Bragg's hand as he held the reins.

He slowed the horse, the hand on her waist giving her a soft squeeze. He said, "You can't put it off, Miranda."

"I'm filthy," she said brokenly. "I can't face him like this."

Bragg took the sombrero from her head and tossed it to the ground. "You're beautiful," he said, his voice a painful caress. "And John will be devastated by your beauty, I promise you." He wasn't lying.

"I need to at least wash my face and rebraid my hair," Miranda cried, twisting to look at him. Her panic and anxiety were written all over her face. "There's a stream back there, I remember seeing it! Please!" Her eyes held his urgently. Bragg nodded, turned the chestnut, and urged him into a trot.

The stream was clean and fresh, running deeply. Bragg helped her down and sucked on a blade of grass, watching her. Miranda washed her hands and her face very carefully, then her feet. She smoothed down the skirt and shirt, then swung her long braid, almost as thick as a man's forearm, over her shoulder and unbound it. Bragg watched impassively, his pulsebeat rising as she combed the shining ebony locks with her fingers, again and again. She had not combed her hair since he had braided it for her after Chavez, and he watched, mesmerized. He noted that her fingers were trembling as she rebraided it, but finally she completed the task. She raised a tremulous gaze to his.

"You're not going to your funeral," he said brusquely. He wanted to kiss her—one last time. Of course he wouldn't—it was out of the question. It made him angry.

At his cruel tone of voice tears welled up in her eyes. He felt rotten and mean, but he didn't care. He'd had enough of this torture. He wished he'd never set eyes on her. As soon as he dropped her off at the ranch house, he was going to ride into San Antonio and bed a lusty wench. He'd wipe her image out of his mind.

"Let's go," he said harshly, and he lifted her onto the saddle, leaping up behind her. He wheeled the chestnut around and urged him forward, into a canter. The horse scrambled down the slope surefootedly, and the ranch buildings grew larger and larger.

The ranch house was made of rough-hewn logs, but it was one of the finer homes in the vicinity. The chinks were plastered, the fireplace was stone, the roof was steep and shingled. It was two-storied and had four bedrooms, kitchen, dining room, living room, and study. It was a large home for a bachelor, but John had always known he would marry and have children one day. Bragg had a fleeting vision of riding up to the door some years hence and being greeted by John, his arm around Miranda, three children tugging at her skirts. The image made him unreasonably surly.

There were two large barns, a large bunkhouse, and a smokehouse at some distance from the house. It was unusual that John had the kitchen in the house itself, for most settlers had a separate cookhouse. Oaks and pine were clustered everywhere, and wildflowers, pink and blue, grew in the meadows beyond the barns. A well stood between the ranch house and the cluster of other buildings. Grass grew right up to the veranda, except for a wide dirt path lined with stones, that all visitors and hands had learned was the sole means of approaching the house. John wanted a lawn for his wife.

Bragg reined in at the front of the veranda and slipped down, then he turned and easily lifted Miranda down. Her anxiety was apparent in her tense body and her fearful eyes. He felt sorry for her. He put a hand on her shoulder, and they walked up the porch. Bragg banged on the front door, opening it with casual familiarity.

"John Barrington," he shouted. "Come out and greet your fiancée!"

Miranda hung a bit behind him, chewing on her lower lip, afraid, yet wanting to see him—ready to get it over with once and for all. They heard limping footsteps, and John appeared, an incredulous expression on his face. "Derek! You're here!" His eyes went eagerly to Miranda.

He was as tall as Bragg, and much bigger. Bragg seemed like a sleek bull, John like a big bear. His hair was curly and unruly, a dark brown; his mouth wide and friendly, his teeth white and even. He was not handsome, but he wasn't unattractive either. It was his eyes that held her and made her sigh with relief. They were brown and gentle, full of tenderness. He limped forward, using a cane. "Miranda!"

Bragg had told her about the accident, which had occurred while John was breaking horses. He had fractured his leg, but it had been set properly, and there were no complications. Miranda could only wonder how he had found a cane big and strong enough to support even some of his huge bulk.

He stopped, an incredulous expression crossing his face as he saw her garb. "What happened!"

"Easy, John," Bragg said, smacking his shoulder. "She's in one piece," he said significantly.

John shot him a look.

"We had a bit of trouble, which I'll tell you about over a whiskey, while Miranda bathes." He kept his hand warningly on his friend's shoulder.

John turned his full attention to Miranda. "Are you all right?" His voice resonated with genuine concern.

Miranda flushed, casting her eyes down. "Yes. I'm glad to meet you, sir." She held out her hand and raised her eyes to his.

He smiled. Then, still taut with worry, he took her hand and kissed it. "Miranda, no 'sirs,' please. It's John—we're not formal over here." He searched her face.

Miranda lowered her gaze, incredibly shy and embarrassed. "I'm so sorry . . . I wish to apologize for my dress . . ."

"There's no need," John cried. "Good God, I'm so glad to see you, I'm trying to stop myself from giving you the best hug you ever had! You must be tired and hungry! Bianca!" he shouted.

"A bath," Miranda murmured, averting her gaze. She glanced at Bragg, who was studying her intently.

"Of course," John said.

A young, voluptuous Mexican woman appeared. "Señor?"

"Send up bathwater to Miranda's room. And anything else she needs. And tell Elena, if she doesn't already know, that my fiancée and Derek are here. Tell her to fix up the best feast she can on such short notice." He turned back to Miranda, smiling.

Bianca disappeared. Miranda felt doubly awkward in the silence that ensued, especially because both men were now studying her so avidly.

"I'm being rude," John said. "Come, let me take you up to your room." He gestured with his hand. Unsure, Miranda followed him. "Derek, you know where the red-eye is."

They went up a curving stairway off the foyer, pine-planked like all the floors and walls in the house. The hallway had six doors leading from it, and John opened the second one on the left. "I know it's not much," he said, "compared to England."

Miranda gasped. The room was a beautiful, sumptuous haven completely unexpected amid the casual rough-hewn style of the rest of the house. The four-poster bed was canopied in beige muslin striped with pink, matching the coverlet, shams, and dust ruffle. The curtains were a dusty rose silk. There was a stone hearth, with a plush, brightly upholstered chair set before it. The bureau and wardrobe were mahogany—European—and they gleamed from many coats of wax. There was a mirror above the bureau. A Chinese screen stood to the side of the fireplace, undoubtedly hiding a tub and chamber pot. A thick Persian rug in a cherry pink covered the entire floor.

Miranda had seen much finer furnishings, even in her father's home. But she had spent most of her life in the stark convent, and she knew the trouble John had taken to provide her with this touch of home. Tears of gratitude came to her eyes. "Thank you," she said softly, "thank you so much."

John beamed. "I've been planning on this all year. I didn't want to hope too much, not after your father said you were too young. I also . . . well, look." He opened the armoire. It was half full.

Miranda's surprise showed. "But you must have expected that I'd have a trousseau! I lost some of it on the way here, but the rest is still in Natchez."

"I just want to make you happy," he said, then flushed. "Elena is real good with a needle, and even Bianca's not bad. These things are all small, but you're even smaller than I thought."

"Thank you." Miranda had been wondering what she was going to do about clothes. Then she noticed the door to her right.

John followed her gaze. "That's my room."

She turned crimson.

"You come on down when you feel like it. If you want to nap, why, go right ahead. If you're hungry, or you want anything, just ask Bianca. Or me."

After he left, Miranda dropped weakly into the chair in front of the hearth. She was so relieved—he was kind.

Chapter 23

Bragg poured himself another brandy, sipping this one. The living room was large and sparsely furnished, with only a sofa, two chairs, and a footstool. A huge stone hearth dominated the room. Bragg imagined that Miranda would enjoy adding her own touch. He knew John would be only too glad to give her the moon.

He looked up at the woman who had appeared in the doorway and realized vaguely that she must be Bianca. He hadn't paid attention to her before, but he knew Elena, and this was someone new. She smiled at him in a very inviting way. "Señor? Is there anything I can get for you?"

He turned his attention to her for the first time, briefly wondering why John had seen the need to hire another servant. She had curly, almost wiry, shoulder-length hair, and big, black eyes. She was no beauty, but she had a great body—big, full breasts, a small waist, round hips. Bragg smiled lazily, knowing she would like him to bed her. "Not right now. Maybe later." He stroked her insolently with his eyes, enjoying the teasing sway of her hips as she left. He wondered what Miranda was thinking, and how she was holding up.

John appeared, looking very grim. He closed the door behind him. "What in hell happened?"

Bragg doffed his own glass and poured John a hefty snifter. "Drink this. You're going to need it."

John downed half in one gulp. He waited anxiously.

Bragg told him about Chavez.

"Goddammit!" John cried, interrupting him as Bragg explained how he'd decoyed the Comanche and ridden back to Welsh's camp, to find Welsh and Lady Holcombe dead—and Miranda gone.

"Take it easy," Bragg said softly, and he finished the tale.

"The son of a bitch! Did he rape her?"

"John, I'm pretty sure he didn't."

"What in hell does that mean?"

"Your fiancée is about the most sheltered woman I've ever met. I had to explain what rape was, quite literally, and from what she said, he didn't rape her. He touched her, though—intimately, I'd say." Bragg frowned. "She was in shock when I rescued her. Too much so even to talk. The next day she came apart. She seems fine now. John—she's real innocent where men are concerned, even now. I just think you should know that."

John covered his face with his hands. "I'll kill that son of a bitch, if he's not dead already."

"Leave that to me, John," Bragg said, swiftly downing the rest of the brandy. "It's between me and him." He didn't relish what he was going to tell John next.

"Poor Miranda," John groaned. "God, you can tell by just looking at her how sweet and innocent she is—it kills me to think of that monster touching her!"

Bragg was silent.

"I owe you," John said heavily, looking up.

"I didn't do a very good job of protecting her," Bragg said quietly, evenly.

"Derek, you're the toughest man I know when it comes to living Texas-style. No man could have done better."

"I kissed her, John," Derek said, almost casually. "Twice."

John stared.

"Both times were an accident," Bragg said.

John roared, lunging to his feet. He grabbed Bragg by his shirt and lifted him up out of his seat. Bragg didn't resist. "It was—" he began, then John punched him in the jaw.

Bragg hadn't intended to duck, or fight, but he turned his face reflexively as he saw the powerful fist coming, deflecting the blow and saving himself a broken jaw. As it was, the blow sent him flying backwards over the chair, and he landed on his back on the floor.

"You rutting bastard," John shouted, kicking the chair aside as if it were made of paper. He reached down, yanked Bragg up, and hit him again, this time in the stomach. Bragg grunted, but still didn't defend himself.

"An accident," he managed, gasping.

John yanked him up by his shirt, and threw him against the wall, hard. Bragg saw stars, his stomach and face throbbing, and he slid down the wall to a sitting position.

John roared inarticulately and spun away. He limped back and forth as Bragg moaned. "Son of a bitch," John spat out. Picking up the decanter of brandy, he threw the contents into Bragg's face.

Bragg sputtered and coughed and fought his dizziness. He hurt, but he'd hurt worse. He opened his eyes, taking a second to focus. Eventually the room righted itself. He struggled to an upright position. "I'm sorry, John, but it wasn't anything."

"If I didn't owe you my life twice over," John said, standing with his legs braced, "I'd kill you."

"You do owe me," Bragg agreed, not attempting to stand.

"How could you do it!"

"I told you, dammit, it was an accident!" Quickly, sparing details, he told John how he'd found Miranda in his arms by the pond, and how he'd kissed her when they'd been astride together. "I'm a man, John, and being forced so close to her . . . her being so beautiful . . . it wasn't thought out. Hell—put yourself in my place!"

John sat down, spent. "Did she kiss you back?"

Bragg struggled to his feet. "The woman was a board, John, better yet, a block of ice. She smacked me, in fact." Bragg had forgotten about that, but he knew it would mollify John. He was right. John smiled.

"I guess I'm not going to be the best man at your

wedding anymore," Bragg said, trying not to sound as hopeful as he felt.

John looked at him darkly. He thought about it. "No, you're not getting out of that, my friend. We've been through too much together for me to hold a kiss against you." He rose and limped out.

"Shit," Bragg said.

Chapter 24

Bragg sank deeper into the tub, thoroughly relaxed, and became aware of the wet, somewhat fleshy woman in his arms. He couldn't help comparing her to Miranda. He couldn't help wishing that she was Miranda—as traitorous as that thought was. He patted Bianca's buttock, giving a little push with his hip. "Tub's a bit cramped," he said.

She stirred and glanced at him.

He smiled charmingly, kissed her briefly, and stroked her back. "Be a good girl, Bianca, would you? I'm a bit sore from your boss's right hook."

"I'm sorry, señor," Bianca said. She had brought him the compresses, so she knew what had happened. She climbed out of the tub. Her large breasts were hard-tipped and streaming with water. She glanced at him archly as she picked up her clothes, giving him an enticing view of her full bottom. Bragg ignored it.

"Can you wash these, Bianca?" he asked as he continued to soak. He glanced at his dirty buckskins.

Bianca frowned, slipping on her petticoat, her breasts dangling. "Certainly, señor." She smiled, eyes black, her interest evident.

"Use flour," Bragg said, taking a sip of the brandy, "so they won't be wet tomorrow. Could you bring me a change of clothes from John, too?" He flashed her a coaxing smile.

"Okay." She adjusted her blouse and pulled up her skirt, glancing at the bed.

He knew what she wanted, but he'd had enough. "A little later," he told her pleasantly, ignoring her frown. He felt relieved when she left with his buckskins, but he didn't feel sated. Not in the least. He felt empty, with a vague yearning . . . and he was perturbed that Miranda was still on his mind.

He was lusting after her. There was just no denying it to himself anymore. He didn't like it one bit.

Supper ruined any sense of well-being he had regained. Miranda appeared in a blazing yellow silk gown, her hair pulled back with a matching ribbon, breathtakingly lovely. She was shy, demure, every bit the unblemished, innocent young lady. John sat at the head of the oak trestle table in the dining room, putting Miranda on his right and Bragg on his left. He was openly besotted, and it irritated Bragg that his friend could act the lovestruck fool, drooling over her every word while Bragg had to sit back and play the casual observer. But when, by chance, she raised her eyes and their gazes met, it was stabbingly sweet. And when John reached out and covered her small hand with his own, Bragg felt red-hot jealousy searing through him.

The meal couldn't end soon enough for Bragg. When they all stood up, he nodded a cool, polite good-night at Miranda, and headed into John's study, pouring himself another brandy. He had been imbibing steadily since he'd arrived, but he felt, unfortunately, stone-cold sober. He was not surprised when he heard John's footsteps. He was about to pour his friend a drink when John stopped him.

"No, don't." He smiled. "I'm afraid I won't be joining you, Derek. Sorry." The smile broadened. "I'm going to take my fiancée for a stroll in the moonlight."

Bragg nodded, watching him disappear, and wondered if his mood could possibly get worse.

Chapter 25

They discussed the wedding the next morning. John was kind, and he understood all she had gone through, but she was living in his house now, chaperoned only by the help, and he was eager to marry her. Miranda understood. He confessed openly that he'd been in love with her ever since he'd seen her portrait two years ago, but he didn't want to press her. He offered to wait a few weeks, to give her a chance to get accustomed to things.

Miranda thought he was being very kind, and they set the date for three weeks hence, in February. He squeezed her hand affectionately, then told her she should rest and regain her strength. He was about to leave when Miranda called out.

"John, will we be going to Mass soon?"

He hesitated, then came back over to her. "I can take you in a few days."

She was immensely relieved.

"Miranda? Did your father explain to you—about me?"

She was completely mystified. "I don't know what you mean."

John sighed. "I am a Roman Catholic, but only in name. I don't practice."

Miranda was stunned. "I don't understand."

He put his hand on her shoulder. "I was raised as a Protestant, but I had to become a Roman Catholic and a

Mexican citizen in '25 to get title to my land. The Mexican government didn't ask us to practice; they told us we could still hold our old beliefs. Everyone did it. And I'm doubly glad now, because it makes marriage between us possible."

"Oh," was all she said.

"I'll come to Mass with you," John said suddenly.

Tears almost welled up in Miranda's eyes. He was more kind and thoughtful than she could ever have hoped. He promised they would go to Mass in San Antonio in a few days. When Miranda asked what her duties were, he told her she could do whatever she liked. She could oversee the servants, or she could let Elena continue to do so. She was amazed at his eagerness to please her.

That evening Miranda was dismayed when she sat down for supper and there was no place set for Bragg. "Isn't Mr. Bragg joining us?"

"He left," John told her, helping himself to a potato swimming in a thick, unappetizing gravy.

Miranda was shocked. Her face fell, although she didn't know how transparent her expression was. He had left without saying goodbye! Her heart was thudding painfully, achingly. How could he have left without saying goodbye? She was very hurt.

John studied her. "You look upset." His voice was quiet.

She blinked back tears. "I'm—disappointed."

"You like him." It was a flat statement.

She turned her brilliant violet gaze upon him. "He was my friend . . . I trusted him."

"But I'm your friend," John said, frowning.

Miranda realized how badly it sounded, how it must look. "I just mean I'm very alone right now. We became friends because circumstance threw us together. I have no one. I wish Aunt Elizabeth were here!" She hadn't meant to become distraught.

"I understand," John said, although he still looked displeased.

Miranda began to dread every day that passed, every day that brought her closer and closer to her wedding. It wasn't that she didn't like John. Her father had chosen well—he was a big, gentle, tender man. But . . . she knew he would touch her after they had married, and the thought disturbed her greatly. She had a pretty good idea now of what men did to women sexually, for Bragg had explained it well. She grew ill with fear when she thought that John would do what Bragg had described to her.

He didn't kiss her until the week of the wedding. She allowed him the kiss, even though it was improper—but then her whole life had been improper since the day she had set out from Natchez with Bragg. She kept her mouth purposefully closed. He only held her arms lightly, but his mouth was open and wet, the kiss becoming harder and harder. She could feel his urgency, and he trembled when he drew away. "I love you so much," he said hoarsely, stroking her hair. She could only give him a tremulous smile.

Sometimes she had nightmares. There was no one to turn to in the night when she awoke bathed in sweat, a scream on her lips. She remembered when Bragg had been there to comfort her. The dreams were always about Chavez holding her down and hurting her with his rough hands, or of her aunt's murder. They were awful, horrifying, and she would force herself to stay awake afterward, afraid she'd dream the same dream again.

Miranda began to recall locked-away memories of her father. She remembered him hurting her mother that one dark day in his study. She hadn't known what he was doing to her then, but she knew now. He had been about to rape her. She remembered his brutality, and how her mother had fought him and wept. She thought of Chavez. She grew more and more frightened thinking of her own wedding night, and all the nights to follow.

One night she had a different kind of dream. At first it was silly. She and Bragg were picnicking in an English park, she dressed like a lady, he in his crude buckskins. But they laughed, and his voice was warm and rich and slightly teasing. He smiled at her, his eyes golden, and she felt so secure—so warm and safe. Then his topaz eyes started glittering, and suddenly all she saw were his eyes. They became brighter and hotter, until they had that strange, hungry look. Then the dream became different—threatening but exciting. She was suddenly naked in his arms, and he was kissing her the way he'd kissed her before, his mouth hot and moist. Soft. She could feel his body, hard and firm on top of her. When she woke up her heart was beating wildly, and her thighs were cramped and aching. The dream and her physical reaction to it shamed her no end. She couldn't believe that she, Miranda, had had such a dream.

And as the wedding approached, as her apprehension grew, a part of her became eager, restless, anticipating. Bragg would be arriving any day now. He was not only John's best man, he was also going to give her away.

Chapter 26

The Texas Rangers were always busy. There were always Indians, usually Comanche, and Comancheros, robbers, and outlaws to track, pursue, and destroy. Justice was harshly dealt, and usually took the form of an instant execution. Even when there was no assignment of pursuit, there was always reconnaissance and patrol. As the saying went, a Ranger had to "ride like a Mexican, track like a Comanche, shoot like a Kentuckian, and fight like a devil." Usually they worked in small groups of two and three, or even alone.

Now, beneath the darkening sky, Bragg puffed a cheroot and gazed at the small, smokeless fire while his two partners, Pecos and Lakely, did likewise. An easy silence surrounded them, broken only by the whisper of the soft night breeze, an owl's lonely hoot, and far, far away, the yelping of a coyote pack closing in on the kill.

"Reckon we have to catch up to them redskins tomorrow, Cap," Pecos drawled lazily. He was taller than Bragg, as thin as a rail, and as fine a Ranger as any. Like Bragg and many other Rangers, he had ridden for Sam Houston in the Texas War for Independence.

Bragg had been thinking the same thing, with irritation. He had to finish this assignment soon or leave his two men to do it without him. All because of the damn wedding. "Reckon so," Bragg said harshly.

Pecos grinned. "You been in one bad mood ever since you got back from babysitting the English lady, Cap. I ain't heard you say one soft-spoken word in two long weeks."

"Your imagination is getting the best of you," Bragg returned, puffing on the cigar. In a few days Miranda was going to be John's wife. He hated the thought. He knew that was why he was in such a hard, angry mood. Selfish bastard, aren't I, he thought.

"Is she really as pretty as you said?" Pecos asked eagerly. "If she is, let's finish off these bastard Injuns, because I want to get a peek at her myself."

Bragg scowled at him. "She's the most beautiful lady in Texas," he said.

Pecos laughed and slapped his thigh. "So now it's not just pretty but most beautiful! What does she look like?"

Of course he was curious; it was natural for his men to want to know what the woman he had escorted looked like. Bragg sighed. "Small and slim, white skin, thick black hair that comes to her hips." He smiled despite himself. Memories assailed him. He felt his groin tightening.

"And her eyes?"

"Purple," Bragg said.

"I know what's wrong with the cap now." Pecos laughed. "He's horny for John Barrington's bride!"

Bragg clenched his jaw tightly and refused to be sucked into any more revealing talk about Miranda.

"I'm right!" Pecos laughed, enjoying himself.

"Shut up, Pecos," Lakely said. He rarely spoke, and now he was pulling up his blanket. He was fully dressed, from his hat to his boots. He even wore his two Colts. He lay flat on his back and would begin snoring in two minutes.

Bragg flicked his cigar into the flames, then he rose and began to put out the fire. He was aware of Pecos studying him from beneath the brim of his hat. Pecos knew him too well. Instead of denying Pecos's accusation, he would not bother responding. Without another word, he unbuckled his guns, placing them within an instant's reach, took off his hat, and slid into his bedroll.

They rode hard the next day. Bragg had kept the chestnut, for he had proven himself a tough, tireless beast. They were tracking a war party of twenty Comanche who had attacked the Bennetts a week ago. It had been a typical Comanche attack. The Bennetts were isolated, living halfway between San Antonio and San Felipe. The family had two sons—a teenager and a child—and a baby girl. The Comanche had appeared from nowhere and caught the menfolk in the fields, immediately killing and scalping the younger boy. The wife had barricaded herself in their log home with her daughter. The father and older son had managed to gain the sanctuary of the barn, the father wounded by an arrow in his shoulder. The Comanche had left as quickly as they had appeared, taking some cattle and grain.

There was a peace parley scheduled for March in San Antonio between three Comanche chiefs and Ranger Colonel Henry Karnes. Because the Comanche bands were so independent of each other, the Rangers could not know if this attack had been carried out by one of the chiefs intending to participate in the parley. Right now, that didn't matter—it was a question for the men who determined policy. Bragg's assignment was easier—seek and destroy.

They closed in on the war party around midmorning. Bragg promptly made quick plans, giving precise orders, and the three dispersed. They slipped past the Comanche and ambushed them in a gorge, each Ranger at a different vantage point. By the time the fighting was finished, half the party lay in the gorge below, wounded or dead, the rest having escaped, many wounded as well. The Rangers rode down to finish them off.

Bragg was hoping that one of the braves was conscious. They found a young brave of about sixteen, wounded, but that didn't make him any less deadly. He had been hit twice and was losing a lot of blood. Bragg disarmed him cautiously, searching him for a hidden knife. He found one in the Indian's moccasin and tucked it in his own belt. He heard a shot, then another, and knew that his men had finished off the wounded. It was cold-blooded, but a live Comanche was too dangerous—and this was war. He squatted next to the boy.

"Who's your chief?" he demanded in the Comanche language.

The brave looked at him with contempt.

Bragg smiled. "I'm half Apache. I have no qualms about torturing you all night long until you speak. You can die fast—or slow." He spoke only part of the truth. He would get the information out of the brave, and hurt him to do it, but he did not like torture and never practiced it. He did not allow any men under his command to torture, either. Fortunately, few Rangers liked to torture. Instead, when enraged, they killed quickly and fiercely.

The light of fear flickered in the brave's eyes, then grew masked. "Go ahead."

Bragg stood, and nodded at Pecos and Lakely. They pulled brush from beneath a tree while the brave watched stoically. Bragg was irritated. Very few Indians of any kind would break under threat of torture, or even torture itself. He himself would die a slow and painful death rather than betray his honor. Pecos and Lakely grabbed the Comanche, ignoring his pain, and hung him upside down from an oak, over the wood and brush.

"Who is your chief?" Bragg said.

The Comanche spit.

Bragg wiped the spittle off his face and looked at Lakely. Lakely lit the brush. The brave's thick braid hung about a foot over the wood, by plan. Bragg did not want him to be touched by the fire—he wanted information. The kindling caught and sparked and began to burn.

The Comanche twirled slowly upside down in the breeze.

"Who is your chief?" Bragg said.

The brave looked at him with fearless eyes. And even though the Comanche was his enemy—the more so because of what had been done to his wife and son—Bragg felt respect for him. The flames leaped higher, and soon his hair would catch. Bragg knew he would not talk.

"Is Chavez alive?" he heard himself say.

Caught by surprise, the brave's eyes showed confusion, but no recognition of the name. Bragg pulled out his Colt, seeing, in that split second, the relief in the warrior's eyes just before he killed him.

"I'm sure glad you don't have more of that Apache blood in your veins," Pecos drawled.

Bragg ignored him. He cut the brave down while Lakely doused the fire. They left the dead Indians; giving the brave a quick death was as far as he would go. They mounted and rode out.

"Who is Chavez?" Pecos asked as they cantered swiftly southwest.

Bragg frowned, but related the entire incident. His partners listened intently, with growing anger. Pecos's blue eyes sparked with fire, while Lakely's gray gaze became as cold as ice. His men were Rangers and Texans. They were outraged by what had happened to Miranda. Bragg knew that if any of them ever came across Chavez by accident, they would kill him.

"I want Chavez myself," Bragg said grimly after he had finished. "If either of you ever come across him, you save him for me."

Pecos and Lakely nodded, and then Pecos spoke. "Just what do you have in mind for him?" His blue eyes were very sharp.

Bragg smiled. It was not a particularly pleasant smile. "He will die a death no man would ever want to die."

Neither man asked him any further questions, and Bragg was confident that if they ever came across Chavez without him, they would capture him, or trail him, and send word to Bragg. It was a pleasant thought.

In that one respect, Bragg knew he was completely Apache. Vengeance was the Apache way.

Chapter 27

It was truly ridiculous, but as Bragg dismounted in front of the house, he could feel his heart thudding as if he'd just run a long distance or been in a long fight. He looped the chestnut's reins over the hitching post and walked silently up the steps and across the veranda. He had made the wedding with plenty of time—it would be on the day after tomorrow.

He knocked on the door as if he were a stranger and waited. It opened, and John's face broke into a broad grin. "Derek! You rascal! We were worrying you wouldn't make it!" He slapped him heartily on the back. "What are you doing standing on my front porch? You lost your wits? Look at the flowers," he added proudly.

Of course Bragg had noticed the neat, transplanted wildflowers the moment he had been within fifty yards of the house. They bordered the stone-rimmed path up to the house and the veranda.

"Miranda did that," John exclaimed. "In fact, she did it herself. I think she's out back in the vegetable patch right now. Come on in."

Bragg followed him in, immediately noticing her touch everywhere. Not only were there fresh-cut flowers, but there were drapes in the living room where before had been bare windows, and a plush, bright blue carpet bordered with roses and vines covered most of the floor. The sofa was missing, but there were other items of furniture in the room—end tables, a divan, lamps, a card table, and two chairs.

"Sofa's being reupholstered," John said, gesturing at the bare spot where it had stood. "I'll go get Miranda." He rushed out, walking a bit stiffly but no longer using his cane.

Bragg's heart increased its pace, and he turned to look out the window. He noticed that the furniture on the porch had been whitewashed and fitted with cheerful print cushions, and that there were flower boxes and planters, too. Inanely he wondered what would happen to the cushions when it rained or snowed. Someone would have to remember to take them inside.

He heard her light, running footsteps and turned as she burst into the room, a few paces ahead of her fiancé. The expression on her face made his heart stand still. Her eyes were bright with joy, and she was smiling with delight, a flush of pleasure on her cheeks. "Derek!"

For an instant, Bragg's own eyes betrayed him, lighting up with unbelievable pleasure. Then he suddenly quenched the feelings she had aroused, guarding his expression, thinking that the little fool was wearing her heart on her sleeve for the entire world to see—she looked as if she cared for him. John's face had become incredulous as he looked from his fiancée to his best friend, a dawning light in his eyes.

Bianca burst in. "Señor Bragg!" She stopped, beaming.

Bragg hadn't smiled, and he nodded coolly at Miranda, the urge to take her in his arms overwhelming. He glanced at Bianca and flashed a reflexive but nevertheless disarming smile, one that made Bianca's face light up. Bragg looked casually at Miranda and saw that she was stricken, her hurt showing in her wide, pained eyes and trembling mouth. She seemed about to cry.

"How's betrothed life treating you, John?" Bragg said easily, hating himself for hurting her.

John had gained control of his own expression, but now he looked grim. "Great," he said shortly. "You must be tired. Bianca, see to whatever Derek needs."

"A bath, señor? Food?"

"Fine," Bragg said, "Both. Up in my room."

She smiled into his eyes with anticipation and looked at John. "Should I bring you any refreshments here?"

"Only if Miranda wants something," John said harshly.

Miranda was pale, and her eyes seemed moist. "No," she said stiffly. "I'm glad you could make it, Captain," she murmured, forcing a pained smile.

"I wouldn't miss it," Bragg lied, wishing he were anywhere else.

"If you don't mind"—she turned to John—"I'm tired from all the weeding."

"Go ahead, dear," he said.

Bragg felt like wincing at the endearment and refused to allow himself to look at her as she went upstairs, holding her head high with dignity. He hoped she wasn't going to cry. Why had she acted so damn glad to see him?

John poured them both healthy doses of brandy, and they drained the glasses silently. He refilled them immediately. The silence was tense, heavy.

"To you and Miranda," Bragg said.

Chapter 28

Miranda finally forced herself to stop weeping. How had she ever thought that he was her friend? How had she thought that beneath his Texas exterior, there were touches of kindness, gentility? He was a man like any other, completely selfish. His only interest in her had been because he found her attractive and he wanted to do those unspeakable things men did to women. He had never even acted as if he liked her; in fact, he was always angry around her.

She punched her bedspread, her face in the pillow. Why did his callous attitude pain her so much? Why did she want to cry and cry, as if her heart was broken? What did it matter that he disliked her, or didn't even care at all about her? She wrapped her arms around the pillow and hugged it to her body. She had been looking forward so much to seeing him again, and he had come only because he was John's best friend.

She washed carefully before dinner, making sure that all the dirt from the garden was gone. Even though she used gloves, soil always managed to trickle down her wrists. She changed her gown, pulling an amethyst silk dress with a high neck and long sleeves from the wardrobe. The gown had lace trim and a collar, and matched her eyes exactly. As she smoothed it down, she noted that her eyes were pink from all the weeping. She briefly debated feigning sickness, but realized it would be unpardonably rude. Hopefully no one would notice her eyes.

She dreaded seeing that awful man again. She tried not to think about how he had smiled at Bianca.

She came downstairs feeling doubly miserable, for Bragg's visit had been the only bright light in her days as the wedding approached. Now she had nothing. Nothing . . . and no one.

Miranda sensed that something was wrong at dinner. Bragg was polite but aloof, and John was cold and withdrawn. Had they argued? she wondered. Both men seemed more interested in the wine than the meal. They spent the end of supper discussing a meeting that was to take place in March between the Comanche and Texas Rangers. Miranda excused herself, pleading a headache, and went to bed early.

She slept fitfully, not falling asleep until just before dawn, her mind wandering between Bragg and the wedding, the wedding and Bragg. She slept late, and it was just before noon when she awoke and bathed and dressed. John knocked on her door and came in.

"Are you all right?" he asked with worry. His face was soft and had lost the harsh lines of the night before.

"Yes." She smiled. "I had difficulty sleeping last night. I guess that's why I slept so late."

"Bad dreams?" he asked, taking her hand and squeezing it.

"No, I just kept thinking." Her voice trailed off.

"Well, I was worried, you're such an early riser. I was afraid you were getting sick or something." He patted her hand. His eyes were shining. Miranda knew it was because tomorrow was the wedding, and he couldn't wait. "I'm catching up on my ledgers this afternoon," he told her, "but we'll have a glass of champagne before dinner, to celebrate."

He left, and Miranda sighed, walking to the window and gazing out blindly. She knew she was extremely lucky. John worshipped her and would never hurt her. But . . . tomorrow night she would be sharing his bed. She shuddered involuntarily. He was such a big man. Maybe he would hurt her without meaning to.

She tried not to think about it and wound up thinking about Bragg again. She wished they could talk, alone, just the two of them, the way they had done before, on the trail. It was impossible—and she knew it! It was improper to even think . . .

Miranda saw him walking lazily across the yard toward the barn, his strides long and graceful. Her heart contracted at the sight of him. She wondered if he was going riding, but then he walked behind the barn and into a cluster of trees, where he disappeared. Her heart was thumping. She saw her chance. If she really wanted to talk to him, she merely had to follow him. She knew it was wrong, but she was so frightened, and she wanted nothing more than to be able to tell him her fears and hear his warm assurances that everything would be all right. Without pausing to deliberate, knowing that if she did so she wouldn't go, Miranda ran out of her room and hurried down the stairs.

She slowed her pace across the yard, so it wouldn't look funny in case anyone saw her. But John was holed up in his study, and the women would be doing their chores. The three men who worked for John spent almost every day out on the range. She passed the barn and entered the clump of trees. Ahead she saw brighter light, and she stopped, assuming there was a clearing. She had no idea where he would have gone.

Whatever was he doing in here, anyway? Had he gone hunting, on foot? Dismay welled up in her, and then she thought she saw something move in the clearing ahead. She pushed forward.

She came upon the clearing and saw him immediately, and had to grab the trunk of a tree to prevent herself from collapsing. Bianca was clinging to his arm, pressing her full breasts against him, talking softly, seductively.

Tears rose in Miranda's eyes, and pain stabbed through her. She knew she should move, run, leave, but she couldn't; she could barely breathe, and all the while her eyes were glued to the two of them. . . .

Then she realized that Bragg was angry. Bianca had touched his face lingeringly, but he pushed her hand away, his face and expression dark. His words carried to her ears. ''Not now, Bianca, dammit.''

The words echoed—*Not now, not now.* With her new knowledge, his implication was clear.

The tears in her eyes made everything blur, and they fell freely down her face. Her heart was beating so loudly she was sure they would hear it. Trembling, she shifted her weight. A twig snapped.

Bragg's head shot up and he looked directly at her. His eyes widened in amazement.

There was no need for her to sneak away now. With a small cry, she turned and fled noisily through the woods.

Chapter 29

John closed the doors to his study, and Bragg felt relieved. Still, his keen ears heard her footsteps as she went up the stairs to her bedroom. Although he had acted as if nothing had happened, as if she hadn't seen him with Bianca, dinner had been very difficult for him.

He didn't understand why she had been crying. He was sure she had followed him to the clearing—but for what reason? His mind ran riot with speculation, and a silly kind of elation. At the same time, her tears disturbed him greatly. It was ridiculous that he should care. She was getting married tomorrow, and what he did, and with whom, was none of her business.

He had never before given more than a brief thought to a woman's feelings. Like almost all men, he believed that a woman was there to serve his needs, to bear and raise children. He had never treated women unkindly, because it wasn't in his nature—he didn't treat his horse unkindly either. But since he had met Miranda, he had felt a most unfamiliar concern and compassion for her. He did care, terribly, that she had seen him with Bianca and had guessed their relationship. What was even worse, he was ashamed. He couldn't even begin to fathom why. He was a man, he had needs, it was natural.

Since he had met Miranda, he was very aware that his bouts of lovemaking had become more infrequent and that he never felt sated like he used to. In fact, he had turned down several women who had practically thrown themselves at him, much to Pecos's interest and shock. In the old days when a woman sat on his lap and grabbed him, it was all he could do not to take her right then and there, regardless of who was watching. Now he found it hard to become interested, and his desire was aroused only after days of celibacy.

For some men, this would be usual. For him, it definitely was not. He had always been the kind of man to have a woman to share his bed on a nightly basis. He had a favorite whore in almost every town. When he had been married he had come to his wife almost every night. How could he not be aware of what seemed to him a sudden lack of virility?

Why had Miranda been crying?

Had she somehow come to care for him? Had the sight of him with another woman hurt her to the point of tears? Or had she gone into the woods already crying, seeking privacy? And if that were the case, which seemed more likely, was she crying because of the wedding? Homesickness? What was upsetting her? Why did he care? Why did he feel like a caged wild animal, barely able to restrain his frenzied energy?

Bragg recognized his tension as frustration. He would die before hurting her. But he had been at the ranch not more than twenty-four hours, and he had already hurt her at least once. Sorrow, shame, and anger roiled together in one heaving, confusing mass of emotion.

Bragg accepted a brandy from John and sprawled out in a chair facing him. "Nervous?"

John smiled. "No. Excited, beyond belief."

Bragg studied his brandy, swirling it in the glass. John had been his old self today, cheerful and warm, so Bragg knew he had convinced himself that Miranda's joy at seeing him meant nothing. But did it mean nothing? Of course it did, it was just that she was a guileless young woman, glad to see an acquaintance again. It was just as well. He wanted Miranda to be happy, and he knew John could make her happy. As he never could. He was too crude and untamed; John was kind and caring.

John sighed. "I was hoping that Miranda would become more used to me, but she's still so shy."

Bragg reached for John's cigar box and opened it, extracting one. "You want a cigar?" He didn't want to talk about Miranda.

"Sure."

They lit their cigars and puffed together in silence for a few moments. "She's the perfect wife," John said. "This place has needed a woman's touch for a long time."

Bragg exhaled. "I'm happy for you both, John." His words were soft, and although he felt a deep hurt in his heart, he meant them.

John met his gaze steadily, searchingly. He didn't speak for a long time. "Let's talk," he said.

Bragg was instantly alert. "About what?"

"I have a few things I want to say to you, Derek, and something I want to ask you."

Bragg knew then that John hadn't forgotten at all how Miranda had greeted him. He wondered if John was going to ask him to stay away after the wedding. It didn't matter if he did. Bragg already planned on staying far away, if he could. "Shoot."

"I'd like to remind you that we're blood brothers," John said, surprising Bragg. "Apache blood brothers."

"What are you getting at?" he asked suspiciously.

John seemed at ease, but he set aside his brandy and leaned forward very intently. "I know you're a Texan before anything else. But sometimes you're very Apache, in some ways. I want to remind you of your Apache obligations . . . to my wife."

Bragg stared speechlessly.

"If something happens to me, Derek, I expect you to fulfill those obligations."

"Damn, John!" he erupted, finding his tongue. "Nothing's going to happen to you."

"Oh, crap! You know this land better'n me! That bronc could have killed me—and that was just an accident."

They stared steadily into each other's eyes.

"If I'm killed, Derek, it's your duty to provide for Miranda, marry her if she'll have you, or see her married to the man of her choice. I'm reminding you of your duty, right now."

Bragg stood abruptly. "Nothing's going to happen to you, dammit!"

"Relax. I intend to live a long and healthy life, but if something does happen, I can die in peace knowing you'll look after her. I want your promise."

Bragg felt uncomfortable, upset, and angry. "You know I'd look after her no matter what."

"Yes, I do." John's voice dropped.

Bragg turned and faced him, having heard the unmistakable inflection in his friend's voice.

John smiled a bit sadly. "I don't blame you. When I realized, I was upset. But you're a man, and how could any man help falling in love with Miranda?"

Bragg was stunned, then he laughed. "Don't be ridiculous! Where in hell did you ever get that idea?" But even as he spoke, he had an uneasy feeling.

John just shrugged, his gaze enigmatic, then held out his hand. "Let's seal it doubly, your word as a Texan."

Bragg's jaw tightened. The mere thought of anything happening to John was ludicrous. But John didn't withdraw his hand, so Bragg took it. The promise was sealed.

Chapter 30

Guests began arriving a few hours after sunrise. Miranda stayed in her room, but when she looked outside she saw that the grounds around the house had been transformed into a village of wagons and families, most of whom would camp there and spend the night after the celebration. She had stayed up half the night, trying to reconcile herself to her fate, and searching for the strength and goodness to do so as a lady—graciously. Now, as Bianca and Elena helped her dress, Miranda felt a bit like a sleepwalker. She was dazed from strain and fatigue and, yes, even disappointment. She was very pale, without a trace of color, and her eyes were huge. Her fear had congealed into a small knot in her stomach. She refused to eat, for she knew she couldn't keep anything down.

Elena was a thin, vigorous woman who was also kind and caring. She had doted on Miranda from the moment she arrived, and it soon became clear that she doted as well on John, Bragg, and the three men who were employed at the ranch. "You are beautiful, *querida*," she crooned, smiling. She was missing a front tooth, but it did not make her ugly.

Miranda didn't even try to smile. She stared at her reflection, a serious young woman in white silk covered with white lace and pearls. The gown fit her perfectly. Her cleavage was lace-covered, as were her arms all the way up to her elbows. Although it was beneath lace, she had never displayed so much of her skin before—except, of course, to Bragg. Sadness tugged at her heart.

"*Querida*, hold still while we pin this headdress," Elena said. There was no need—Miranda was hardly breathing.

"Tía Elena," Bianca said, "is she all right?"

"Bianca, you go and see to the guests, we are fine." Elena deftly pinned the seed-encrusted headdress, folding the veil back over Miranda's head. "*Querida*, you are marrying a fine gentleman."

Miranda nodded.

"Tell me, are you afraid of tonight?" The woman's dark eyes were kind and perceptive.

Miranda met her gaze. "A bit." Her voice was low and hushed.

"Do you know what to expect?"

Miranda nodded.

Elena smiled. "It will hurt the first time, but that is all. Do not be afraid. John loves you very much."

"How long?" Miranda didn't even bother to finish the sentence.

"A few minutes. I will go downstairs, unless of course you want me to wait. Already everyone is gathering. You wait here until I come back."

Miranda nodded and waited for what seemed like an eternity, although in truth it was only fifteen minutes. She didn't think. She could hear everyone downstairs, crowded into the living room where the ceremony was going to take place. There would be about fifty guests, John had said, including children. Miranda didn't care. She was too numb to think.

A Catholic priest, one of the priests from the mission, was performing the service. He was her confessor, a kind man with a big belly and merry eyes. Father Miguel had not sounded distressed when he heard her full confession, which included everything that had happened on her travels across Texas. She had been given a light penance: a day's fast and meditation and prayers, during which time she had kept to her room. He had reminded her last week that her duty to John as a single-minded, devoted wife was also her duty to God.

The knock came, and the knot in her stomach tightened. Elena opened the door, beaming. "Come, *niña*. Do not look so afraid. Señor Bragg is here to give you away."

Miranda floated through the door as if in a trance. She met his golden eyes and saw a bright light leap into them—worry? appreciation? distress? She realized that he was wearing a suit and boots, with a fine white linen shirt, the collar and sleeves slightly ruffled. He said, "Miranda. Are you all right?"

She looked into his eyes. "Fine," she said, her voice a bare whisper.

Bragg ignored Elena, sure that Miranda was going to faint at any moment. He took her shoulders in his hands, peering down into her face with concern. The Texas air had given her fair skin a soft ivory glow, but now she was as white as her gown. "Miranda? Are you going to faint?"

"No, of course not."

Her voice disturbed him greatly. He turned to Elena. "Loosen her corset, dammit," he snapped. "I'll tell everyone to wait a minute."

"It's not tight, señor," Elena said, scowling at his familiarity. "She is just afraid, poor baby. She is too young."

Bragg turned his worried gaze on Miranda and found her staring at him steadily. It unnerved him more than ever. He wanted to hold and comfort her and give her some of his limitless strength. Ignoring Elena's gasp, he cupped her face with one warm hand, running his finger along her cheek. He could smell the scent of lilies. A becoming flush rose in her cheeks. As if on cue, the piano began.

Her eyes widened. "Where did the piano come from?"

"Don't you play?" Bragg asked, pleased to see her coming out of her stupor. He held out his arm, and she took it.

"Of course, I love playing."

Bragg smiled. "I do believe you'll have to ask your husband." It was a gift, of course. They walked to the top of the stairs, and Bragg placed his other hand on top of her small one and patted it for a moment. "Don't trip."

The voices below were hushed. Bragg felt a ridiculous

surge of pride, on top of a gut-eating sickness. Everyone was awed by her beauty.

Bragg led her down the stairs and gave her to John, stepping aside. He couldn't take his eyes off her, so ethereal was she in her gown and veil. He barely heard the vows being exchanged. And then came the final words, "I now pronounce you man and wife." Father Miguel was beaming, the guests giving a wild Texas whoop and cry. John was smiling, his eyes full of love, lifting her veil and kissing her. Bragg looked away, hurting, and met Pecos's astute gaze from across the room. He wondered if the pain in his heart showed in his eyes.

Everyone congratulated the bride and groom, then wandered outside where a dozen tables had been set up with food and drink, and a fiddler and a harmonica player were waiting to begin. Children were already racing around, playing tag, filching food, and shouting gleefully. Bragg walked outside alone, and poured himself a glass of whiskey. He drained it quickly. It wasn't his first that day.

"Beautiful wedding," Pecos said. He helped himself to a drink.

Bragg nodded. He shifted uncomfortably—his feet hurt like hell in his stiff boots. It was a rare occasion that he wore anything but moccasins.

"You were right. Miranda is a beautiful woman," Pecos said. "She seemed half frightened to death."

Bragg didn't reply. There was nothing to say. He was leaving as soon as possible.

"I understand," Pecos said sympathetically and walked away to leave him to his own frustrated thoughts.

The party moved outside. In the yard people ate and drank and danced. John and Miranda held court to well-wishers. Miranda was flushed, and Bragg noted that she was sipping champagne. Good, he thought, it will make tonight easier for her. Then jealousy and anger knifed through him. He had a vivid image of Miranda moaning passionately in John's arms, and he didn't like it at all.

He made his way up to them when they were finally alone, walking stiffly in the boots. "Congratulations," he said easily, embracing John.

"Thank you!" John beamed. The expression of sheer happiness hadn't left his face all day.

"I'm leaving," Bragg said. "I wish I could stay, but duty calls."

John nodded, knowing it was a lie.

Bragg turned to Miranda. "Best wishes," he said softly. "You've married the finest man I know. I'm glad."

She stared up at him, her color high, her eyes bright. Her mouth was cherry red and parted slightly, breathlessly.

Bragg smiled softly, for a moment forgetting John, the wedding—everything and everyone except this woman who had somehow, insidiously, stolen his heart. He brushed his lips gently along the side of her face, almost lingering, his mouth touching the corner of hers. The urge to crush her to him and capture those lips with his own was almost uncontrollable. He smiled. "Goodbye, Miranda, John."

"Goodbye," she said softly, her eyes moist.

As he walked away, he wished they had had a chance to exchange a few words since he'd arrived. It was too late now.

Chapter 31

She eased under the covers, pulling them all the way up to her chin. She was in her own bed, but she could hear her husband moving restlessly in his room next to hers. She shivered, waiting with dread for him to come to her. Outside she could still hear the hearty laughter and conversation of a few staunch revelers, although the din had long since quieted down. She listened to the merrymaking and wondered if maybe John would not come. Maybe he was tired—he had been drinking quite a lot.

She had become ill earlier. The two glasses of champagne had gone right to her head, since she hadn't eaten, and she had had to run back to the house. She had made it just in time, fortunately, to keep from disgracing herself in front of the guests. Now her head throbbed, and she was perspiring faintly. She was also as sober as the day she was born. Was he coming?

Could she bear his touch?

She would never hurt his feelings by letting him see her distaste for his touch, never. She would not cry out when he hurt her. John was kind and good, and she wanted to please him. She would bear his lovemaking the way a lady should.

She heard the door open and stiffened involuntarily.

"Miranda?" His footstep was already familiar, heavy with his bulk. A match flared.

"Oh no, please," she begged, twisting away, wanting it to be dark.

"I want to see you," John murmured. He held the match, and for a moment they could see each other's faces. He saw her fear and cursed silently, shaking out the match. "All right, dear."

Miranda took a deep breath, truly grateful that they would do this in the dark. He eased his weight beside her, the bed groaning, and Miranda felt as if she was made of wood. Every fiber of her being froze against her will. He reached out and pulled her into his arms. His body was warm and hard, but not as hard as Bragg's.

"Darling," he whispered. He kissed the side of her face, then leaned over her, capturing her mouth with his.

Miranda stayed passive, fighting her urge to resist. Tears gathered hotly beneath her lids. His hand stroked over her body, over her sheer lace gown, from shoulder to hip. It paused on her waist, gentle and trembling.

His sigh was almost a groan. "Miranda, darling, I need you." He kissed her again, his mouth harder, more demanding. "Open your mouth . . . please."

She obeyed, trying not to show the revulsion she felt when his tongue invaded her mouth. She didn't mind his touching her half as much as this. Her stomach felt ill again.

"I love you," he said hoarsely. His hand found her breast, and he caressed her gently. "I want to go slow," he said, kissing her ear, his breath hot on her skin, "but I've waited so long . . . years . . ."

Miranda wished he would do it and get it over with. He slipped his hand beneath her gown, up her thigh, and she tensed even more, not breathing. He stroked her silken flesh, her hip, and found her breast again. He groaned, then eased the garment over her head before she knew it, and his mouth came down on her nipple, sucking frantically. One of his thighs covered hers, and something hot and hard pressed against her leg.

She fought the tears. She could stand this. If he enjoyed pushing her, sucking her, she could bear it. She hated his tongue in her mouth, though. She didn't want him to know and worried that if he kissed her that way again, she might become dangerously nauseated.

She began to relax, wondering how long it would take, wondering if he would do this to her again tomorrow, how often he would want to use her. She detached herself from the man sucking and stroking her, and thought about the beautiful piano. She couldn't wait to play it. She wondered if she would ever be able to play it for Bragg. She stiffened suddenly when she realized John had shifted his weight onto her completely and had spread her thighs with his own. His manhood pressed against her most vulnerable spot.

She was seized with instinctive fear. "No," she cried, but his mouth was on hers, ravenously, and his arms were beneath her like steel bands. That hard part of him was thrusting against her, seeking entry, hurting her. It was like a battering ram. The tears rose again.

By luck and instinct, he found the entrance, tested it, and thrust deeply. Miranda screamed as he tore through her tight, dry flesh. She felt as if she was being ripped apart, and tears flooded down her face. She bit her lower lip to keep from crying out again, ashamed and embarrassed that their guests might have heard her scream. He thrust again and again, breathing raggedly, each thrust a shaft of pain, almost unbearable, and then he shuddered and was still. The unbearable fullness inside her disappeared, and he rolled off her.

She turned away, onto her side, weeping silently. Never had she imagined that it would hurt like that.

"God, Miranda," he said hoarsely, leaning over her shoulder. "I'm sorry. I'm sorry." His voice was anguished, desperate.

She couldn't answer. She didn't want him to know she was crying.

"Darling, I didn't know it would hurt you so much," he said.

She took a deep breath and summoned all her will. "It's all right," she said brokenly. "It's all right, John."

"Forgive me," he said softly, placing one tentative hand on her stiff shoulder. "Please forgive me."

Miranda took another deep breath, fighting for control. "There's nothing to forgive," she whispered.

He lay back down beside her. She stayed curled up in a ball on her side, her back to him. She was still awake some time later when he silently rose and went to his own bed. But the need for crying was over. She was his wife now, in every sense of the word. She was resolved to be the best wife possible, even if she had to go through that experience again and again.

Chapter 32

John wanted to make love to his wife, but he was afraid to approach her. His desire had been growing all week, since the wedding night, but he could still remember her scream of pain, and the last thing he wanted to do was to hurt her again. Of course, like any man, he knew it always hurt a virgin the first time. But he had not been prepared for the depth of her pain. He had never had a virgin before—so how could he have known?

John had not had many women. He was a man, and had needs, obviously, but the times he had been with a woman could be counted on both of his hands. Now he wished he had more experience. He knew that ladies did not enjoy it. He had never been with a lady, of course, before Miranda. The whores he had been with were merry and eager, their bodies warm and wet. Miranda had been dry and tight. He knew she had not just disliked their love-making, but hated it. However, she was his wife, she would bear his children, and he knew the second time would not be as bad as the first.

He could not put it off, although every night he felt and saw her fear, anxiety, and apprehension. It dimmed his need and desire for her, but only fractionally. He did not expect her to enjoy their coupling, of course, but he did expect her to accept and not mind it.

Exactly seven days after their wedding night he came to

her bed again. By then, his desire for her was uncontrollable. To his shock, he hurt her again—although her cry of pain was muted, she couldn't restrain it. And there was blood again. He was frightened.

He knew that wasn't right, but he didn't know whom to discuss the situation with. What happened between a man and his wife was never discussed, not even by the couple themselves. Why had she bled again? Even he could feel how dry her passage was. She was so small. Was it possible she was too small for him? He was a big man. He had never compared himself to other men, but he assumed that his manhood was proportionately big, like the rest of his anatomy. Could his wife, being so tiny, be too small for him? Or was she ill? Or was she formed defectively?

He did not know what to do. He loved her so much he couldn't bear hurting her. Maybe, he hoped, the problem would resolve itself. Maybe over time, the hurt and bleeding would go away. Maybe some women bled twice. Whom could he ask? He wished he had the courage to ask his best friend, who was as experienced with women as he was not. Of course, he could never bring up such a sensitive topic, not even with Derek. He let the days go by, the weeks pass, until he was desperate for her, and so wishful that everything would be all right that he tried again. It was another disaster. How could he put himself inside her when he knew that every thrust was hurting her, tearing her? He was frantic with worry. Although there wasn't a lot of blood, there was some, and he knew it wasn't right. Something was definitely wrong. He didn't know what to do, so he stayed away and did nothing.

Chapter 33

Miranda didn't mind being married. There was plenty to do, and the truth was, she loved her home. Under her tasteful touch, the ranch was becoming a warm and welcoming haven. Some of the furniture came from St. Louis, via New Orleans and Galveston. Some was brought by custom order from the Swedish cabinetmaker in San Antonio. The Persian rugs had come from New York, imported from Europe. Some of the upholstery she did herself, some was done by the German upholsterer in San Felipe. She was working on a large tapestry for John's study, and, of course, she was always tending her flowers and her vegetable garden.

There was also the supervision of the household, which she took over in stages. Elena welcomed her input, even expected it, and surreptitiously drew her gradually into the running of the house by seeking her out with questions she had been answering herself for years. Did she want the bedding aired? Should Bianca damp-mop the floors? Did she want to mend John's shirts herself? Could she oversee the ironing? Bianca was so clumsy. Did the menu meet with her approval? Did they need these supplies? The questions were what any servant would ask of the mistress of the household, and Miranda soon became at ease in her role as mistress of John's house.

She knew they didn't need Bianca—she and Elena could

have easily run the house alone. But she was also aware that Bianca needed the employment, so she didn't say anything. Although John was often annoyed when he found Miranda with her delicate hands in hot water, or doing something that could blister them, she softly and subtly protested until she was allowed to resume her tasks. After all, she was no longer an English lady, she was a Texan's wife. All the other women she had met at her wedding had red, chapped, and callused hands, and she saw no reason why she should be any different.

Sometimes, for no reason, she would look at Bianca and remember her pressing against Bragg. Then a strange, unpleasant feeling would assail her, a painful ache—something like hurt mixed with envy. She always shoved the memory and its accompanying feeling aside. It was not her business.

The piano was her greatest solace, and she played for hours and hours, especially when her heart had a strange heaviness. She would lose herself in her music, playing Mozart and Beethoven with great passion, until she was soaring on the wings of their emotion, not even aware when someone would come and stand quietly, listening, in the doorway.

She dreaded the nights. John had only come to her twice since their wedding night, but neither time had been any better than the first. Since he no longer came, she assumed she had displeased him, and that shamed her, but her relief was greater than her shame. She hated coupling. She knew he knew it, and although she wanted to hide her revulsion, how could she? Every time he entered her it hurt unbearably. Still, she resigned herself to being available to John when he wanted her. After all, one day she would have his children. That thought enchanted her, and almost made their lovemaking worth it.

About a month or so after their wedding, when Miranda came down for dinner, John called her into the library. His eyes shone with love as he looked at her, touching her arm briefly. His gaze was hungry, too, and she knew he would come to her bed again soon. She couldn't help it; a wave of anxiety overtook her.

"Miranda, I've forgotten to tell you, but it's Eliza

Croft's birthday next week, and we're invited to the Crofts' for the weekend. I hope you want to go.''

Miranda was delighted, even though she didn't remember who Eliza Croft was. Since their wedding, she had seen no one except John and their help. ''Oh, I'd love to! Will there be a lot of people there?'' Even as the words came out of her mouth, she wondered if she would see Bragg.

''I'd say so. Eliza will be eighteen. That's a big one.'' He smiled at her fondly. ''The celebration will go on all weekend. A real Texas barbecue. We'll leave before dawn Saturday and arrive by midmorning. We'll come home Monday.''

''What should I bring? Will we be camping outside?''

He laughed at her enthusiasm. ''Elena will help you to pack. She knows exactly what you'll need. And no, I'll be camping out, but the ladies will all be sharing bedrooms. Do you mind? The Crofts' place is twice this size.''

''I don't mind,'' she told him. She was so excited at the thought of a party. Why did Bragg's handsome face keep looming in her mind?

John leaned down and kissed her on the mouth. ''I like seeing you happy,'' he murmured.

Chapter 34

"Wake up."

Miranda opened her eyes sleepily. For a moment she forgot where she was, then it came flooding back to her. She was at the Crofts' and had just taken a nap. They had arrived yesterday, by midmorning, as John had promised.

She had never had such a wonderful time as she'd had in the past day and a half. The Crofts were big, raw-boned people, but soft as silk beneath their leathery exterior. Beth Croft had introduced Miranda to everyone, shoving John into his crowd of friends. To her delight, everyone was warm and pleasant, whether young or old, male or female. Everyone accepted her. She especially enjoyed meeting a young wife like herself, Wilhemina Vereen. She was a year or two older than Miranda, a busty, almost stout blond who was always laughing.

Miranda had mentioned to Wilhemina that she had never dreamed Texans were so friendly. Wilhemina had laughed and answered in her usual blunt way. "But, dear, the men are friendly because you're beautiful, and the women are friendly because you're married and no threat. If you were single, none of the single girls would talk to you!" Although a little disillusioned, Miranda had to laugh.

The barbecue was actually a two-day party with a never-ending supply of food, drink, games, and dancing. John taught her to dance the fast-paced, wild jig, which she loved—so much so that he was relieved to give her up to other partners. The men held foot races, wrestling matches, and shooting contests. There were horseshoes and a game from England, cricket. There were swimming and sunning—segregated by sex, of course. About a dozen families were in attendance, of which four were young and childless, like herself and John. The children ranged from a four-month-old infant to Eliza and two other single young women.

"All that dancing tired you out," Wilhemina said, smiling. She had stripped off her dress and was changing her gown.

Miranda sat up. "Oh dear. It's almost dark."

"I didn't want you to sleep through all the evening's fun."

"No chance of that," Miranda said excitedly. She was wearing only a chemise, and she sponged herself all over with water and soap from a basin. From outside she could hear the sounds she had grown used to—laughter, animated conversation, shrieking children, a fiddler, a violinist, and a harmonica. She slipped on an emerald green gown of taffeta with short, puffed sleeves. Cream lace edged the modestly scooped neckline and cuffs.

"It's funny, but that green makes your eyes even more purple," Wilhemina mused. "It's odd how John married such a tiny thing like you."

Miranda smiled, knowing that she meant no offense. "You mean he should have married a big thing like you?"

Wilhemina laughed. "I've got my own man, thank you, and I wouldn't trade him for anybody, not even a handsome Texas Ranger like Derek Bragg!" Wilhemina smiled dreamily.

"Do you love your husband?" Miranda asked, trying not to think about Bragg. She was disappointed that he wasn't there.

"Very much." Wilhemina grinned. "He's handsome in his own way, I think. And when he touches me, my skin feels like it's on fire."

Miranda gaped.

Wilhemina shot her a look. "So you don't like that part of married life, huh?"

Miranda grimaced slightly. "I can live without it, thank you."

"Oh well, I imagine it's you being a lady and all. Now me, I'm from good old peasant stock." She winked, and the two girls went downstairs and outside.

Already couples were dancing. Wilhemina and Miranda stood side by side for a moment, glancing around the throng for their husbands as folks stood in merry clusters.

"Oh, there he is! See you later, Miranda." She darted off.

Miranda sighed, then reached down and caught a ball Ben Parker had dropped and was chasing. "Ben, you're going to trip and fall in the dark," she scolded the eight-year-old.

He grinned slyly, took the ball, and ran away bouncing it, a puppy at his heels.

Miranda smiled, searching the crowd for John. Her gaze came across a man she hadn't seen before, buckskin-clad like many of the men, tall, lean, and dark. His eyes held hers, and he tipped his hat—insolently, she thought. She frowned and looked away.

"There you are," John said, coming up behind her. He kissed her cheek. "Did you have a good rest?"

"Yes, I slept like I was exhausted."

"Too much dancing," John said, chuckling.

"Your feet aren't sore, are they?" she asked anxiously, her disappointment clear.

"Miranda, I would dance with you if I was still on crutches, seeing how happy it makes you."

"Now?"

"Can we eat first?" He laughed, leading her toward a table full of food.

They ate and chatted, and twilight settled in. The younger children were sent protesting to bed. John and Miranda danced. Miranda had never danced before the previous day, and she loved it. Swirling on her toes, the music seeping into every pore, her body swaying, moving gracefully—it was so much like playing the piano. She wished that she could dance forever.

Of course, John was not a good dancer, and he didn't really like it. But there were many men eager to dance with his beautiful wife, especially the younger, slightly awed single ones. Miranda was tireless. She danced for an hour without stopping, with one partner after another. Her hair had long since tumbled free of its careful chignon, and it flowed behind her like a shimmering black cape.

After one number, as another man claimed her, a rider cantered into the midst of the dancers, causing a murmur to rise up. Miranda's heart almost stopped. A rush of joy swept through her, even as the rider held up his hand for silence, not looking at her once.

John came up beside her, taking her hand. Miranda saw that Bragg's horse was heavily lathered. The rest of the revelers had begun gathering as people whispered his name and came to investigate.

"What's happened, Derek?" John asked gravely.

"Everyone quiet down," Bragg said, not raising his voice. Silence fell.

"I have bad news. Fighting broke out today in San Antonio. As you all know, a peace parley was to take place with three Comanche chiefs. They were to bring all prisoners to exchange as a prerequisite for the talks. They only brought one, a girl, Matilda Lockhart." He paused, his even gaze roaming over the crowd as mutters of surprise and indignation rose.

Again he raised his hand for silence. "Seven Texans were wounded in the fray, one was killed." He continued on through the now angry murmur. "Thirty-five Comanche were killed, about twenty women and children taken prisoner. Thirty or so warriors escaped intact. I'm here to warn you to expect an increase in hostilities, as of now."

Everyone began talking at once, angrily, trying to be heard.

"Bragg! Why did they only bring the girl?"

"What about the other captives?

"How did the rest get away?"

"What are the Rangers going to do?"

Bragg raised his hand again, and again the audience grew still. "I have a recommendation to make, and I urge it strongly. Everyone travel home tomorrow in groups for as much of the journey as possible. When you get back home, be prepared for raids and attacks. You all know the

Comanche style of war. Make sure your weapons are
always within reach, and have enough water and ammunition to withstand a short siege. That's all.''

"But what are the Rangers going to do?" someone
called out loudly. "Are you riding after them? Is Lamar
going to call out the militia?"

Bragg ignored the questions, moving his horse through
the crowd and dismounting. The men converged upon him
at once, asking the same questions, as the women hung on
to every word.

John gave Miranda a brief hug. "Don't worry, dear,"
he told her. "The Comanche never attack my spread. I've
got too many men who can shoot, and it's too well built.
They don't like those kinds of odds."

Miranda nodded, unable to speak, not sure if her heart
was racing from fear or something else.

"I'll be glad to chat later, over a whiskey or two,"
Bragg was saying.

"Leave the poor captain alone," Beth Croft shouted,
bustling through the men. "I think I know just what you
need, Derek."

A grin split his bronzed face. "A hot bath?" His tone
was hopeful. "Some of that barbecue pork?" He sniffed.
"I could smell it the moment I rode in."

"You come with me," she said, taking his arm. "Someone see to the captain's horse."

Everyone was talking in animated, tense murmurs, spec-
ulating on the Comanche trouble they might face over the
next few months. Standing in the background, Miranda
listened, then walked away, shuddering. She thought about
the poor girl who had been a prisoner of the Indians. How
awful. She remembered what Bragg had told her happened
to women taken prisoner, and she shivered again.

She was absorbed in her thoughts, marveling at the
authority Bragg had over these people. Was John right?
Were the Comanche afraid to attack their ranch, or was he
just reassuring her?

Suddenly a small form ran right into her, and with a cry,
they both fell. Miranda sat, reached out, and caught a
child's wrist. She pulled him close. "Who—? Ben Parker!
I told you you'd have an accident with that ball!"

"I hurt my knee," he cried, sniffling. "It's bleedin'!"

"Let me see," Miranda soothed, stroking his little shoulder and peering more closely at the raw knee. "Well, that can be fixed up in a flash. Can you walk? Come, we'll go find your mother."

"Ma will whup me for bein' up," he whispered. "Can't you fix it—please?"

Miranda was sure his mother would not whip him, but then she wondered. Lucy Parker was a grim, lean, haggard woman, and Ben was her youngest—and eighth—child. The woman probably had no patience left. "All right," she said. She took his hand and led him around the back of the house.

"Oh, wait, where's Spot? I've lost Spot!" With that he wrenched free and ran easily back in the direction from which he had come.

"Is that you, Miranda?" Beth Croft asked, bustling out of the kitchen.

"Oh, yes. Mrs. Croft, I need some linens for bandages. Where can I find them?"

"Everything you need's in the pantry, just off the kitchen—"

"Beth! Come over here and listen to this," her husband shouted, gesturing grimly.

Beth started to hurry away. Then she hesitated, looking over her shoulder. "Miranda, maybe you should wait," she called after her, then sighed and shrugged. What difference did it make? Miranda was married. She hurried over to her husband, guessing correctly that he and his cronies were in a serious discussion about defense against renewed Indian hostilities.

Miranda hurried into the kitchen, which was lit by a fire in the large hearth and one kerosene lamp. She paused, looking for the door to the pantry, and was about to move across to it when a casual drawl made her freeze.

"Hello, Miranda."

She gasped. Bragg was sitting in a tub in front of the hearth. Because she hadn't expected to find someone bathing in the kitchen, she hadn't noticed him at first. Her face flushed. "What are you doing?" she breathed.

His shoulders and chest were bare, wet, and glistening

above the tub. He grinned. "What does it look like?" He sighed. "I've never seen you look better."

Miranda swallowed. She tried not to look at his bare flesh, but it was exceedingly difficult not to. "I—I need some linens," she managed.

Casually, as if he had no care in the world, he began to soap his shoulders, chest, and lower body. "You don't have to worry about the Comanche," he said easily, his eyes holding hers. "They avoid big, well-manned places like John's."

Bragg was rinsing, and she watched, fascinated, as he splashed water over himself. He glanced up and caught her gaze. Quickly she picked up the lantern and went into the pantry. Her hands shook a little. How could she have stood there and watched a man bathe? Where were the linens? She finally found them on the shelf right in front of her face, realizing she had been seeing in her mind's eye only the man in the tub. She bit her lip, grabbed the bandages, and shut the door behind her.

"Mon Dieu," she said, with a long, soft breath.

He was standing with his back to her, toweling himself off, all long, hard, rippling muscle. At her voice, he quickly wrapped the towel around his waist, and turned to face her. "Sorry," he said. "What are you still so shy for? Hell, Mrs. Croft stood right here while I stripped." He grinned. "Of course, she refused to leave until I gave her my clothes to launder."

Miranda didn't hear a word he said. The towel couldn't hide his arousal. She practically choked as she whirled and fled. She couldn't get outside soon enough. But the fresh, cool air didn't make breathing any easier.

Chapter 35

Outside, Miranda found Ben, who was indeed getting a spanking from his mother. She left the linens and hurried away, trying to regain some calm, unable to fathom why Derek Bragg seemed to agitate her so. Why in God's name did he make her pulse race and her body heat up? And worse, why was she so happy to see him? She was no fool. It was clear that she had some kind of misplaced affection for the rugged Ranger. That was shameful. A woman who was a wife should have no room in her affections for an unattached man, even if he was her husband's best friend. Or maybe that made it worse. She leaned against a huge oak tree, sighing, confused.

"Hello, pretty lady. I was hoping I'd get a chance to talk to you."

Miranda hadn't even heard the man come up behind her, and now she recognized the stranger she'd noticed earlier. Up close, he seemed menacing. But he was obviously a friend of the Crofts'. "How do you do," she said politely.

"How do you do?" He laughed. "Well, if that isn't the purtiest voice I ever heard! What's your name? Mine's Earl. Earl Hollister."

"Mrs. Barrington," she said, just so he wouldn't get the wrong idea.

"Missus, it it? John's a lucky man. Tell me, how'd he

find a pretty thing like you?'' He leaned closer, grinning.
His arm brushed hers. Miranda stepped away.

''He met my father,'' she said. ''And it was arranged.''
She didn't want to talk to him. He made her feel uncomfortable. But that was probably ridiculous. There were
people everywhere, not more than twenty yards away.

''Arranged, huh? Now that makes me feel better.'' He
leaned close again, this time taking her hand. ''Maybe I
have a chance?''

''Please,'' she said, shocked, trying to wrench her hand
free.

''God, you even smell good,'' he said huskily. ''I ain't
ever had a woman as pretty as you.'' He pulled her close.

Miranda realized that he was drunk, even though he
didn't sound or act it. His breath was sour with alcohol.
And he was holding her improperly. ''Please release me,
sir,'' she said firmly.

He chuckled and pulled her into his embrace. ''Only
after a kiss,'' he said, and kissed her fully on the mouth.

Miranda cried out and struggled uselessly. His breath
was awful, the kiss worse. His body was hard and strong,
and she could feel his maleness against her, which frightened her. As he released her, she realized they were
completely in the dark, shaded by the tree. No one had
noticed, or even heard her cry through the noise of the
festivities. She slapped him. He laughed. ''I didn't hurt
you, you liked that!''

''My husband—''

''Don't be a fool, gal. You tell your husband and he'll
get hisself killed. I wouldn't—''

Miranda wasn't listening. She ran from him, furious,
and still a bit frightened. Just when she'd begun to think
Texans had some redeeming qualities, they became crude
louts! She ran right into John.

''Miranda, I've been looking for— What's wrong?'' He
held her and searched her face worriedly.

''A man named Hollister grabbed me and kissed me!''
she cried. ''I've never met so many uncivilized beasts—''

John cut her off. ''Where is he?'' His face was grim.

Miranda pointed, not even wondering if she'd done the
right thing in telling him. After all, he was her husband. If

he didn't protect her, no one would. She ran after him as he went after Hollister.

"Hollister!" he roared. "You bastard! I'll kill you for touching my wife!"

Hollister was leaning under the same tree, and he laughed. "I told you, gal, not to tell him," he said easily, as if he were having fun.

John lunged for him with all the fury of an aroused mother bear. Hollister sidestepped quickly and ducked, slamming a hard right fist into John's abdomen. John merely grunted, grabbed his shirt, and bashed him in the face. Blood poured from Hollister's nose.

But Hollister was tough, and he blocked the next blow to his face, following with a hook to John's eye. The two men grabbed each other and began to wrestle. A crowd had gathered, and Miranda became afraid of the violence she was witnessing.

The men broke free of each other and exchanged blows. Hollister fell. John lunged for him, yanked him up, and nearly broke his jaw with another punch. He was about to hit him again, when suddenly he straightened, stiffened, and fell onto his back, a knife protruding from his chest.

Miranda screamed.

"He's killed Barrington!" someone yelled.

Miranda ran forward and collapsed beside her husband. "John! Dear God, no!"

"Miranda?" His voice was faint. His chest was covered with his blood. "I can't . . . can't see you."

"I'm here," she cried, throwing her arms around him. She wept hysterically. "Someone, please, get the knife out—save him!"

"Come closer," John whispered. "I . . . can't see . . ."

Miranda was aware of someone pulling out the knife, saying something. She hugged her husband's head to her breast, weeping softly. "It's all right, John, it's all right," she kept saying. She kissed his hair as if he were a child and began to pray.

The crowd parted behind her, but she didn't notice. Bragg strode through, his face contorted, and dropped down on one knee beside them. One look told him that

John was dead. Miranda was murmuring to him. He stood up and looked around.

"Hollister touched her," someone told him. "John went to kill him."

Bragg had only one coherent thought: Avenge John. Kill Hollister. He knew the man—an ex-sergeant in the militia, a man who looked for trouble, usually found it, and enjoyed it. Hollister was standing ten yards away, beneath the same oak tree, braced, his gun hand ready.

Bragg didn't have time to think further.

Hollister drew, but his gun never got past its holster. Bragg's Colt fired, and Hollister fell without a cry, hit in the chest, killed instantly. A couple of the men ran over to check him. Bragg automatically sheathed his gun, then he turned slowly and looked at Miranda and John.

Beth Croft was trying to pull the girl away. She was weeping softly, still cradling her husband's head. Bragg glanced at the crowd and made eye contact with Will Croft and another rancher. "Please see to John," he said. "Put him in his wagon. I'll be taking him and Miranda back to the JB at first light."

He turned away. The night reverberated with quiet, shocked whispers and Miranda's crying. He walked into the woods. His grief was burgeoning from where it was tightly held, in a small, fierce knot, deep inside him. He had to be alone before it exploded and overwhelmed him.

Chapter 36

Bragg paused outside Miranda's bedroom door, his hand lifted to knock. He hesitated. She had not come out of her room all day, or the day before, except to attend the funeral. He had been sorely disappointed when Bianca informed him that she was dining in her room that night; disappointed and worried. But no matter how much he respected her right to grieve in peace and privacy, there were matters that had to be discussed. He also wanted to alleviate her fears about her future—surely she had given a thought to that?

He knocked. He heard no sound from within, until Miranda's soft voice bid him enter. He went in quietly, his eyes immediately finding her on the bed. She was sitting propped up, in a gown and wrapper, pale and wan. Her hair was loose, falling in thick strands over her shoulders, and gray circles were smudged beneath her eyes. She was momentarily startled to see him, and he saw her tiny hand clench the sheet, knotting it.

"Hello, princess," he said softly, smiling slightly.

"I—I thought you were Bianca," she said nervously, gesturing at a tray of uneaten food by her bedside.

He came over and gazed disapprovingly down at her. "Why aren't you eating? Do you intend to waste away and die?"

Miranda met his gaze, flustered, and he saw a faint pink

stain color her cheeks. "No, that is not my intention," she said, so softly he had trouble hearing her.

Concerned, he touched her forehead, feeling her stiffen at his touch, but her face was cool. He pulled up a delicate chair, turned it around, and straddled it. He smiled. "I guess I'll have to sit here while you eat."

She met his gaze and saw that he meant business. "I have no appetite."

"I'm sure John would be touched by your grief," Bragg said, "but he certainly wouldn't want you to starve yourself to death."

Tears filled her eyes. "You are . . . so uncaring!"

He stifled his anger at her accusation; no one cared, or had grieved, more than he did. "Eat some food, dammit, and I mean it." He picked up the tray and set it on her lap, looking grim. He did not want to be harsh. He only wanted to do what was right.

He studied her as she picked at the roast chicken, now cold, at the beans and potatoes and fried cornbread. She ate agonizingly slowly, he thought impatiently, but at least she was eating. He knew from Elena that she had barely eaten a thing since they had arrived back at the JB ranch three days ago. "Thank you," he said, removing the tray to the bedside table. "We have to talk, Miranda."

She gazed at him steadily, waiting. She reminded him of a child—a sad, vulnerable child.

"I want you to know that you don't have to worry about anything." He paused. "I'm going to take care of you." He hesitated, seeing her expression remain unchanged. "I promised John," he added.

A look of confusion crossed her face. "What are you saying?"

He didn't know why he felt so nervous, why the words were hard to formulate. "I promised John if anything happened to him, I'd care for you, marry you." He gave her a smile as her eyes widened in surprise. "Besides, it's the Apache way. If a brother dies, it's his living brother's duty to marry and provide for his widow. It's actually very sensible, if you think about it."

Her eyes just grew wider, an expression of shock freezing her face. "This is a raw land," he rushed on. "A woman has to have a man to provide for her, and more so, to protect her—from hostiles, from other men." He smiled coaxingly. "Believe me, this isn't in the least unusual. No one will be surprised."

Miranda stared, sitting straighter, and for a long moment she didn't say anything. "You're serious, aren't you?"

"Of course."

"You're going to marry me because John made you promise to look after me? Because of some Apache—some barbaric—custom?" Her voice was high-pitched, almost hysterical.

Bragg took her hand, which was icy cold. "I know you haven't been in Texas long enough to understand us, or this, but . . . it's for the best, Miranda, trust me."

She shook her head. "It's—improper."

"No, actually, it's very proper."

"You're not Catholic. We can't be married."

Bragg smiled slightly. "Actually, I am Catholic. I had to become one to get title to my land." He shrugged. "Just like John."

She stared.

"Do you have some objection to marrying me, Miranda?" He was tense. A wife did not fit into his life, not at all. But he had accepted his duty, his promise, without thinking once of trying to break his oath. Now, suddenly, he realized that he wanted to marry her, and the force of his desire stunned him.

Miranda hesitated. "I suppose not. Even if I went home, Papa wants grandchildren. He told me. I suppose he would just arrange another marriage." She stared past his shoulder at the crackling fire.

"I'm flattered," Bragg said stiffly. "Truly flattered you are so enthusiastic." He stood. "Believe me, this wasn't my idea."

He was at the door when she called out. "Captain?"

He turned, his expression inscrutable.

"I hate to say this, but even if it becomes general knowledge that you will wed me, you can't stay here for the year of mourning. It's improper. I—"

Bragg's laugh cut her off, and he strode back to her

bedside. "My dear princess, there will be no year of mourning."

Her mouth fell open in surprise.

"This is a rough land, Miranda, in case you haven't figured that out. You can't live here as a widow, alone. You need me and my name as protection. We'll be married next week."

Miranda gasped and fell back on her cushions, stunned.

Bragg strode out, slamming the door behind him. The door frame shook and trembled in his wake.

Chapter 37

Miranda stood in front of the hearth and stared into the leaping flames. Her confusion and shock were dying. There was no fear, either—she wasn't afraid of Bragg. He intended to marry her, and she knew him well enough to know that anything she said or did would make little if any difference. He was a powerful man, used to getting his own way. And did it matter? If not Bragg, she was sure her father would marry her to someone else. Perhaps next time his choice would not be someone as kind and gentle as John. At least she knew Bragg. And she respected him. He made her feel safe and secure—the way no one else had ever done before, not in her entire life. She was sure she would be safe as his wife—who would dare to harm the wife of a Texas Ranger?

She supposed it didn't matter, either, that he was marrying her with obvious distaste, because of his word to John and some Apache code of ethics. She knew him well enough to know that he was not mean or cruel. He would never hurt her—and wasn't that the best she could hope for in a husband? She refused to think about sharing his bed, about the pain that would bring—maybe he just intended it to be a marriage in name only.

She tried not to see John in the dancing flames. As usual, just thinking about him wracked her with guilt. She knew that his murder was her fault. She blamed herself.

She had never caused another human being to be hurt before. She had been the instrument of her husband's death. It tortured her. And—worse. She had denied him the love he had wanted so desperately from her. She had disappointed him in bed. She had not been a true wife to him—and those days had been his last on earth. The crushing guilt would not go away. Everyone thought she was grieving. She was, a bit, the way someone would for a new friend who had died suddenly. But it was not the grief of a wife for her husband, a woman for her man. She just felt so utterly responsible for John's death.

Yet there was one thing she would not be a party to, she decided firmly, her resolution strengthening. She would not desecrate John's memory and make him a laughing-stock in front of all his friends by marrying a week after his funeral. Oh no. That was wrong, entirely wrong, and she would not give in on this point.

Miranda hesitated, rebelting the robe tightly, debating the propriety of wandering downstairs in her sleeping attire. But this was her home. She marched to the door and down the stairs.

Bragg looked up expressionlessly as she knocked on the open study door. His eyes were narrow, and the golden glow of the fire in the stone hearth warmed his rich coloring even more. He sipped the brandy he was holding. "Are you seeking out my company?" His words had a sarcastic ring.

Miranda tightened her lips and closed the door behind her. She marched resolutely in front of him, debating the best way to bring up the topic.

A faint smile touched his mouth and eyes. "I have a feeling it isn't my company you want. I'm shattered. What's on your mind, Miranda? Have you changed your mind about our wedding?"

She ignored his dry, slightly derisive tone. "No, Captain, I will marry you. But not next week."

He raised a brow, and set down his glass. "No?"

"I refuse," Miranda said evenly, growing frightened by his cool manner. "It's scandalous. You say it's not improper, no one will care. Well, I will care. It's improper to me!"

Bragg seemed amused. "You always surprise me, princess, when your spirit shows."

She ignored the insult.

"How do you expect to survive for a year, unwed, in this land? In this house? You will be besieged by suitors, and being that you are a widow, Miranda, many will not have proper intentions in mind. It is not done. It will not be done. I have not changed my mind." He picked up the glass of brandy and appeared to have dismissed her.

"You listen to me, you bully!" she cried. "Don't you have any feelings toward your dead friend? How can you be so cold, so callous! How—"

He stood and grabbed her, hurting her, and she cried out. His hold barely lessened. "No, you listen to me, dammit! No one loved John more than I! No one is sicker over what happened! But he loved you—*you*, dammit! And I intend to see you safe, to keep you safe, if it's the last thing I do! You are not going to sit here and mourn for John for the next year! You're going to go on living, like all the rest of us!" He released her, fighting for control.

Miranda was ashen.

He glared at her. "I have my duties as a Ranger, Miranda, and even though I intend to curtail them as much as possible, I'm a Texan, and I believe in this land. When I'm not here you'll have an armed guard. And my name. That should keep you out of harm's way." He picked up the brandy. "Now. Is there anything else?"

Miranda stared, her eyes glistening, knowing she had lost. Well, what difference did it make? Hadn't she known all along that he would have his way? She turned to run out of the room.

He grabbed her from behind before she even knew it, one arm around her waist, one around her shoulders, hugging her to him. She tensed, but when he did nothing more than hold her, her body began to relax, and she became aware of the wild, frantic beating of her heart. His face was pressed against her neck, between her cheek and shoulder. She could feel his breath on her neck, warm and soft.

His hold tightened.

She sensed, then, that he needed and was getting comfort just by holding her. She could almost feel his grief, which she had forgotten because he kept it so well hidden. She relaxed completely, leaning back into him. The heat of his body seared her, making her skin tingle deliciously. His grip tightened, not uncomfortably, and a soft groan escaped him. Then he abruptly released her.

A huge disappointment flooded her. She saw that he had walked to the fire and turned his back to her. She started to approach, instinctively wanting to comfort him. She raised her hand, about to touch his back gently.

"Go," he said huskily. "Leave me alone."

Miranda could hear pain and desire in his tone. She wanted to ease the pain, but she was afraid of the desire. Silently she slipped through the door.

Chapter 38

Miranda was used to obeying. After all, she had spent her whole life obeying one form of authority or another. First her mother and father, then the sisters and the mother superior, then her aunt, Bragg, and her husband. She did not expect to make her own decisions; indeed, she never had. After a few hours of tossing and turning, she realized it was just as well that Bragg make the decisions that would affect her life, and not some man she did not know. No matter what Bragg was, or how crude at times, for some reason she trusted him.

She had lost sight of the fact that Bragg had been closer to John than anyone, and she felt very badly about being so insensitive to his hurt. She pushed aside the rebelliousness which was so ungodly and resolved to forgive his high-handedness and lack of manners. After all, he was a barbarian, half Indian—it wasn't his fault. She also tried very hard to forget that he really didn't want to marry her, that this marriage was his duty. For some reason, that thought bothered her immensely, so she quelled it by shoving it way into the back of her mind.

The next morning she lay in bed, awake, knowing it was late, thinking about him. She remembered how he had held her the night before, how his sorrow had been a tangible thing, communicating itself to her through every pore and fiber of his body. She rose resolutely and got dressed. He needed her right now, and she intended to help ease his grief.

It was a new role for her, one she was enthusiastic about playing. No one had ever needed her before. Inspired by an idea, she dressed in a riding habit and hurried downstairs. Elena was the only one about, kneading dough in the kitchen.

"Señora! I was just about to bring you breakfast." She was beaming. "I am so glad you're up. Come, sit. Eat."

"I'm not hungry, Elena," Miranda replied, a bit breathlessly. "Where is Captain Bragg?"

"He is out riding with the men across the valley."

Miranda's face fell. Then her expression brightened. "Did they go far?"

Elena was already cracking eggs into a black iron pan. Bacon followed, sizzling. "No, not far. Why?"

Miranda didn't answer. She knew she could handle Daisy, the gentle mare she had ridden with John, but she wasn't thrilled about riding alone. Still, she wanted to see him. She wanted to be with him, to make him smile. She knew he was hurting deep inside, hiding it from the world, and she wanted to take some of the hurt away. It was an urge to comfort as old as time.

She forced down some eggs and a strip of bacon, as well as a cup of the scalding coffee, which she was coming to appreciate. When Elena wandered out to the smokehouse, Miranda quickly packed a picnic lunch—an inspiration. Then she hurried outside, knowing that Elena would disapprove of her riding even just a few miles out to find Bragg.

Daisy welcomed her with a snort, shoving her velvet muzzle into her hand. "I didn't bring you anything, girl," Miranda said, patting her. "I'm sorry."

Saddling and bridling the mare was not an easy task. Although she had seen it done a hundred times, she had never done it before. The saddle was heavy, and she was short, but she finally managed to heave it onto Daisy's back. Cinching the girth was easy, and Daisy accepted the bit readily. Miranda was very proud that she had tacked the mare all by herself.

Mounting was another problem, but she was becoming

excited at the thought of surprising Bragg. She led Daisy to a bale of hay, climbed up on it, and from there slid on. They set off at a trot.

By now she was used to riding, although she did bounce a bit. Both Bragg and John had told her that the secret to sitting well in the saddle was to relax her spine, but it was easier said than done. She slowed Daisy to a walk, which was much more comfortable, and they ambled leisurely through the endless meadow.

The house disappeared behind them. Miranda had never been alone outdoors, and it was a heady feeling. She breathed deeply of the rich, crisp air and gazed with awed eyes at the splendor of the forested mountains, the jagged peaks, all around her. She imagined being a man like Bragg, able to come and go as he pleased with no fear of the wilderness, strong and free. It was exciting. She liked riding alone.

Not for the first time since she had arrived in Texas, she felt a majestic sense of awe at this savage land. This time the feeling was strong, unquenchable, uplifting. She decided she would ride every day and explore the valley. Of course, she wouldn't go far. Even now, she was only a few miles from the house. Although everyone said that no Indians bothered the ranch, she was not a fool. She had no intention of stumbling upon a band of Comanche.

Exhilarated, the way she felt when she played the piano or danced the wild jig, Miranda urged Daisy into a lope. It was a brave thing for her to do because she knew she was no horsewoman. But, actually, it was easier sitting to the gentle canter than it was to the bouncy trot, once she got over her fear of going faster. Color rose in her cheeks. It was a magnificent morning, a magnificent day.

Miranda heard the pounding hooves when he was almost upon her. She felt a flash of fear, wondering who could be racing up behind her like a madman, then looked over her shoulder and instantly recognized Bragg. The chestnut was going all out, lathered, and as Bragg came abreast of her he reached out and grabbed her reins, pulling up both his mount and the mare so abruptly that she almost lost her seat.

"What's wrong with you?" he shouted, his expression

furious. He had urged his horse against hers so his knee touched hers, and he still held her reins. "Miranda, are you a fool? An idiot?"

The pleasure of the morning fled. She looked at him mutely, feeling like crying under the harsh onslaught of his words.

"Dammit," he yelled, reaching out and shaking her by her shoulders. "You're not allowed to ride alone, do you understand? Never! *Never!*"

Miranda felt a tear creep down her cheek and fought as hard as she could to control herself.

"Don't you have a goddamn thing to say?" His voice was still hard, although he was no longer shouting. "You *should* cry. I hope you feel bad. You can't possibly feel bad enough for doing such a stupid thing."

She wiped at her tears.

"Dammit," he said, and before she knew it, he had pulled her off her horse and onto his, wrapping her in his arms. "You scared the hell out of me," he said, holding her tightly against his body, his mouth against her ear. "Don't you ever scare me that way again."

"I just wanted to see you," she said, her voice broken.

"God, if something had happened . . ." He squeezed her, and she thought she felt his mouth pressing briefly against her neck.

A warm, hot flood rose up in her. She snuggled closer, her face wet from tears. His embrace was so warm. His body was so hard. There was something fiercely possessive about the way he held her, and something infinitely tender, too.

Miranda raised her face to look at him and saw that his eyes were closed. He opened them to meet her wide gaze. "I'm sorry," she whispered.

"You'd better be," he said gruffly.

"I brought you lunch."

His eyes widened, then he smiled grudgingly. "You little fool! Did you really bring me lunch?"

She felt him softening, saw that he was unable to hide his pleasure. "Yes."

He smiled openly then as she straightened in his embrace. "Why did you bring me lunch?"

Miranda flushed. "To make you feel better," she said after a pause.

He gazed at her with surprise. She wriggled out of his arms and slid to her feet. "Are you too angry to have lunch with me?" She hesitated. "I am sorry. Everyone kept saying the ranch is safe."

"It is, usually," he said, staring at her, then dismounting. "But a woman never rides alone, never. And you don't handle a horse well enough yet, either." He shook his head.

"But . . . it was wonderful," she said, holding his gaze. "I . . . felt so happy."

He gave her a crooked smile. "If you want to ride, Miranda, you certainly can. But with an escort. Also, I think it's time you learned how to shoot and had your own pistol." He thought about that idea for a moment, then grinned. It was the kind of smile that made her heart flutter. "I'm starved."

Miranda accepted the basket he took down from her mount and watched as he spread his bedroll out beneath two shady oaks. "What do you have in there?" he asked, a happy note in his voice as he sprawled casually on the blanket.

Miranda sat down, careful not to sit too close, and placed the basket between them. "Sausage, cheese, bread, and peach cobbler," she murmured, realizing that she was alone in the middle of the great sprawling valley with this rugged man. Her pulse seemed to be racing. "And wine. I hope you have an appetite," she said softly.

His gaze was golden and intense, holding hers. "I do," he said, and for some reason the way he was looking at her, the melodious timbre of his voice, made her flush and wonder if he was referring to the food.

Miranda laid out the food and served them while he opened the wine, pouring two glasses. As she handed him a plate, her hand brushed his, making her nerves tingle.

"Thank you," he said.

Miranda watched him eat. He wrapped the sausage in the bread and bit hungrily into it. Before her very eyes, half the sandwich disappeared. He took a swallow of wine, then glanced at her over the rim of his glass, his eyes sparkling with good humor.

Miranda felt unaccountably nervous, and she drained half her wine.

Bragg finished the food she had given him, and the wine, and refilled both their glasses. "What else is in there?"

"Peach cobbler," she said, handing him a huge slice.

"How come you're never hungry?" he asked, his eyes on her.

"I just ate, before I went riding." She smiled. "Elena wouldn't let me out of her sight until I'd eaten." She was feeling very relaxed.

"How am I going to fatten you up?" His voice was teasing.

Miranda blushed. She was remembering that he had said before that she was too skinny, and it bothered her. She resolved to eat more. The wine was making her feel dreamy and wonderful.

"Elena is a great cook," he said, studying her intently. "Can you cook?"

She wondered why he was always looking at her with such great interest. Suddenly she had a thought, and she laughed.

"That's funny?" he asked, smiling and leaning closer, lying down and propping himself up on one elbow.

"No, I was just thinking—if the mother superior saw me now . . ." She giggled, imagining that woman's despair—no, horror.

"I think you're drunk."

Miranda gasped. "I am not. Ladies don't get drunk!" Highly indignant, she finished the rest of the wine.

He smiled, reaching out lazily and taking her hand. His hand was so big it swallowed hers easily, and it was warm and strong.

Her laughter trailed off. The look in his eyes was so sensual, and in spite of herself she was warmed and mesmerized.

Miranda wasn't sure how it happened. He was lying there, so close, too close, holding her hand, pulling on it. The next thing she knew, she was on her side, facing him, his arms around her, his hands stroking her back. He was smiling slightly, and he kept staring steadily into her eyes. She knew beyond a doubt that he was going to kiss her. She wanted his kiss desperately. She ached for it.

His face lowered slowly, too slowly. "You are so beautiful, Miranda." His words were a husky caress.

She closed her eyes, barely breathing, her lips parted—waiting.

His mouth was soft and moist as it brushed her jaw. His breath tickled her ear. His lips played lightly over her cheek, one fluttering eyelid. His breath was warm, uneven. His hold tightened as his mouth caressed hers gently.

Delicious sensations, exciting sensations, feelings such as she'd never experienced, ran through her. She opened her mouth, pressing against him, her arms going around his neck. He pulled her hard against him then, throwing one thigh over hers, his mouth demanding. His tongue probed through her lips. She gasped with pleasure, wondering dimly how she could ever have found this act revolting. She could feel her heart pounding fast and erratically against her chest—or was it her heart? He held the back of her head with one hand, holding her still so he could better plunder her mouth. She strained against him eagerly. She couldn't think; all she could do was feel.

His hands were everywhere, roaming her shoulders, her arms, her back. She gasped with surprise, wanting to protest when he captured one breast, cupping it, but the jolts of electric pleasure that shot through her destroyed all such intentions. She heard a strange sound—and it had come from her. Bragg groaned heavily, rubbing his palm over her stiffening nipple. She arched herself more fully into his hand.

He rolled her beneath him, his full weight upon her. A warning voice tried to pierce the haze of wine and sensual delight. He had fit himself so intimately against her that she could feel his hard, hot manhood pressing against her belly, and the ache it brought was both sweet and painful, and very, very insistent. His kiss was savage. His hips moved against her. Her thighs opened, and he took the opening, pressing his own thighs between and moving hers farther apart. His hold tightened around her.

"Miranda," he whispered raggedly. "Darling, we have to stop, or I'm going to take you right here, right now." He kissed her again, lingering, pulling at her lower lip. He groaned. She clung to him. With great effort, he pulled himself free and stood up.

The withdrawal of his warmth and touch was like a splash of cold water. Her eyes flew open, to see him standing and staring at her with such a look of hunger that she couldn't swallow. She couldn't breathe, couldn't move. All she could do was stare back.

Chapter 39

Bragg whistled tunelessly as he walked across the clearing between the bunkhouse and the ranch house. His mood was fine, his spirits even better. He laughed out loud, feeling more than self-satisfied—almost smug. He thought about the coming night, about the kisses he would steal. His grin broadened. He tried not to think about his wedding night, which was still a week away. No, six days. He could barely wait.

He had thawed the Ice Princess. Miranda had melted.

He entered the house and strode into the kitchen, startling both women. "When's supper?" he asked Elena, watching her slicing freshly baked, steaming bread. He sniffed a huge pot of stew, then lifted up a spoon to taste its contents.

"Very soon, señor," Elena told him, waiting expectantly for his reaction.

"God, that's good! Is Miranda still asleep?" He felt a bit foolish. Since the afternoon, he had not been able to stop thinking about her, lasciviously, of course. He was acting like a boy about to bed his first woman.

"*Sí.*"

Bragg turned and trotted up the stairs. He knocked on her door, listening intently to the sounds coming from within. Miranda told him to enter.

He stepped in, grinning. "Hi, princess. I thought you were going to sleep right through dinner."

She was clad only in her chemise and petticoat, and she flushed, reaching for a wrapper and slipping it on modestly. "I thought you were Bianca," she murmured. She did not meet his eyes.

She was too tempting. He reached her in two strides. Before she could move, he had wrapped her in his embrace, pulling her intimately against him, his mouth seeking hers. There was nothing lazy or easy about this assault. She devastated his control, his very senses.

To his complete shock, Miranda stiffened, then began to struggle. He lifted his head but didn't release her. "What's this?" he asked, confused.

"Let go," she cried. "Good Lord! Have you no manners, no sensibilities? Captain! Release me." Her eyes were blazing, and so were her cheeks.

He let her go, still confused. "Miranda—"

"How dare you treat me like some trollop," she cried, clearly upset and angry.

He stared. "But—"

Her face crumpled. "But how could you not? The way I acted this afternoon . . . like some harlot . . ." She turned away, her voice breaking.

His reaction was swift. "No, Miranda, don't do this to yourself." He grabbed her shoulders from behind, but she wrenched out of his grasp. "Miranda!"

"No! Don't touch me, I mean it!"

Angry now, he whipped her around to face him. "You liked my touch this afternoon," he said bluntly. "You loved it!"

"I was drunk," she whispered, looking stricken.

"What kind of excuse is that? We're going to be married next week, Miranda. What's wrong with sharing a few kisses? You're going to be my wife, dammit."

"Everything's wrong, that's what! John isn't even cold in his grave, and you're lusting after me! If I didn't know better, I'd think you didn't even care that he was dead!"

He tensed, fighting hard for control, trying not to hit her. "You know how I loved John," he finally said, many moments later.

"Then act like it," she said evenly. "Show some respect. Stop acting like some wild beast!"

Her words stung. "I forgot you were such a lady, Miranda," he said, his words cruel and mocking. "Excuse me, but after this afternoon, how was I to remember?" He whirled and slammed out of the room.

God, would he ever understand women? Then he quickly reminded himself that Miranda was not any woman, but a lady, the kind of woman he had never had to deal with before. So just how was he supposed to act? He could stay away from her for the next week, because, as much as he hated to admit it, she was right. But what about after that, when the lady became his wife? Just how was he supposed to treat her then?

He had no idea.

Chapter 40

Miranda had risen at the crack of dawn, after a mostly sleepless night, to ask Derek if he would take her into San Antonio so she could go to confession. The answer had been a short, rude, and very unequivocal no.

At first she was stunned, but she had no chance to argue the point, for he was gone all day. Apparently this was the time of the spring turnout, when all the cattle were driven to higher pastures for better grazing. She broached the subject again at dinner. Clearly in a foul mood, Bragg told her that she would have to wait until their wedding day, for he had no time or men to waste on a trip to town now.

Finally Miranda refused to think any more about her shockingly unladylike behavior.

The hours Bragg and his men worked were long, and Miranda didn't see him at all the next three days. She performed her usual chores around the house, spending extra time in the kitchen with Elena, canning and preserving vegetables and jams. She did not dread this wedding as she had her wedding to John, even though she didn't fully realize it. She knew Bragg. He wasn't the stranger John had been when she'd married him. Besides, he was marrying her out of a sense of duty, to give her his name as protection. She assumed that was as far as their marriage would go. In fact, she was surprised he was even working the ranch, instead of riding with the Rangers. She asked him about it the next evening, when he returned in time for supper.

"I'm curtailing my duties as a Ranger," he told her, digging into a thick slab of steak. "This is a big spread, and now it's yours. Someone has to run it or it'll go into the ground. I'll only ride with the Rangers during an emergency."

Miranda was shocked. "John left the JB to me?"

Bragg smiled, studying her, his gaze momentarily soft, although a bit tired. "You were his wife, princess. Who else would he leave it to?"

"But—didn't he have any kin? Surely some cousin or brother would deserve it more than I!"

"He left everything to you, Miranda. In fact, he had quite a few business holdings outside of the ranch, in Galveston and elsewhere. You're actually quite a catch." He grinned.

His playfulness, as usual, took her by surprise. It was so rare, and so incongruous to the deadly man she knew he was. Miranda smiled. "But, do you mind it? Staying here, not riding with the Rangers?"

"Not at all," he said. "It's funny, but my vendetta against the Comanche suddenly seems a bit old."

"What vendetta?" She was highly curious.

"Why so many questions?"

"You're going to be my husband," she said softly.

Bragg smiled, looking pleased. "Well, I guess you might as well know, it's common knowledge to a lot of folk." He drained his glass of wine and poured another. "Sure you don't want any?"

Miranda shook her head, blushing, and sliced a piece of steak.

"I was married," he said casually. "She was Apache. We had a boy."

Miranda stared, registering the past tense, but he spoke as if he were discussing the weather. His face was relaxed, and he was eating as if he didn't have a care in the world.

"They raided my spread." He glanced at her. "Didn't know I had land up the Pecos, did you? I was riding the range that day. I had left them behind, alone—Comanche don't war that far west, it's Mescalero country.'' Seeing her confusion, he said, ''The Mescaleros are my people.''

Miranda nodded, barely able to breathe.

He shrugged, draining the wine. ''I found my wife a year later. After they took her, the Comanche sold her to a brothel in Natchez. I took her home, but she died a few months later—wouldn't eat, just wasted away.'' He leaned back in his chair, meeting her gaze.

He was having trouble, she knew, maintaining his calm poise. His eyes were hooded, but she could feel the sadness, the unexorcised grief. ''And . . . your son?''

''He was only six when they took him,'' Bragg said, his jaw clenching. ''I never found him. They would have taken him into their tribe, raised him as a Comanche. He had his mother's coloring—even her eyes.'' He looked away.

Miranda wanted to weep. She reached out to cover his large hand, but he pulled it away and attacked his potatoes. She wanted to ask more about what had happened, but she didn't want to upset him any more. It was so tragic. So very, very tragic. She wondered how long ago this had taken place.

''Eat up,'' he said, glancing at her very briefly, with a forced smile.

Eager to distract him, Miranda toyed with her food.

''Didn't you learn obedience in that convent?''

She met his gaze and saw that he was amused. ''Of course.''

''Then it's an order. Eat everything. Jesus! A strong wind could blow you away.'' He grinned. ''Then what would I do?''

''Captain,'' she reproved, ''please don't use the Lord's name in vain.''

He pushed his plate aside and watched her. ''I was praying,'' he said, smiling.

''You add one sin on top of another,'' she accused, almost choking on the bite of meat she had swallowed.

He reached out and thwacked her on the back.

''Thank you,'' she managed.

''You're too Catholic.''

"Nobody can be too godly," she said, regarding him as sternly as she could.

"Are you lecturing me?" He started chuckling.

"Aren't you afraid to go to hell?" She studied him and saw his smile broaden. "Oh no! You don't even believe in heaven and hell, do you? Or God?" She was stricken. The thought of Bragg someday going to hell upset her greatly.

"Sure I believe in God," he said, pouring himself the last of what had been a full bottle of red wine.

"God the Father, the Son, and the Holy Ghost?" She was hopeful.

"I have a feeling I shouldn't get sucked into this discussion," Bragg said, clearly enjoying himself.

"What do you believe, Derek? Can't you be serious?"

"Are you going to try to convert me?"

"Maybe."

He laughed. "I refuse to have a wife preaching religion at me."

"Tell me your beliefs. Do you really believe in God?"

"You have the tenacity of a bulldog, princess. Yes, I do. In my own way." He gazed at her with open, golden amusement.

Miranda had to ask. "And? In what way is that?"

He raised a large hand and gestured at the dining room. "I believe that God is the wind and the trees, the mountains and lakes. God is you and me."

She gasped, scandalized.

"You look like you expect me to be struck down by lightning at this very moment."

"I . . . I wouldn't be surprised," she managed. "That's heathen blasphemy!"

"Not quite. I suppose, though, some might say it's a perversion of Apache beliefs."

Miranda was afraid to ask about the Apache religion. Instead she said, "Would you go to confession with me next week?"

"Absolutely not," he said, throwing his napkin on the table, but he was smiling. "I'm a tolerant man, Miranda, and if you want to pray and confess and practice your religion, you can." He straightened ominously, becoming very serious. "But—and it's a big but—the day your religion interferes with me, this household, or us is the day I stop being tolerant.'' He stood up and held out his hand. ''How about a walk in the moonlight?''

Miranda stared, her mind positively racing. Then she saw his hand and, a bit shocked, she rose and accepted it. They walked outside under the cottonwoods. The moon was big and white and bright, streaming through the newly leafed branches. They strolled in silence. Miranda couldn't stop thinking.

At least John had been a God-fearing man. Although he said he was really a Protestant, he had gone to Mass with her . . . even if it was just to make her happy. But Bragg was truly a heathen. Should she ignore it? Let him die a heathen and go to hell? And what about his threat—for that's what it had been, a threat. If she were to convert him, she would have to do it so subtly he wouldn't even know what she was doing. Oh dear!

His soft, musical chuckle broke the silence. ''I do believe I've given you a shock.''

''Just a bit,'' she said.

Chapter 41

"I now pronounce you man and wife," Father Miguel intoned. "You may kiss . . ."

Miranda was fully aware of every word the priest spoke, and even more aware of the man standing at her side. Bragg was clad in a black frock coat with a plain white shirt and gray cravat. He seemed uncomfortable in his formal attire. She was aware of his closeness, his even breathing, his presence—his body heat. When he slipped the gold band, so simple and plain, on her finger, she felt a rush of warm happiness. However, that emotion fled quickly. Before she could absorb the fact that she was indeed married to this enigmatic, powerful Ranger, he had pulled her against him. With no thought of modesty, his mouth captured hers. The kiss was not soft or gentle. As his lips played demandingly upon hers, hard and insistent, she felt a tremor shake him. Then he released her. He caught her as she swayed slightly, taking one of her arms and holding her securely against his side.

The church echoed with silence.

There were no guests, out of respect and mourning for John—only the newly wedded couple, Father Miguel, and the two Rangers, Pecos and Lakely. Pecos had given the bride away. They approached with smiles to congratulate the couple.

"You lucky devil," the tall, lanky Pecos was saying. He was grinning.

"I think so," Bragg said, confusing Miranda. His arm had now gone possessively around her shoulder.

"Congratulations, ma'am," Lakely said.

"Thank you." Miranda was suddenly, inexplicably, exhausted.

"Ma'am, if I do say so, you are the prettiest gal I've ever seen, and I do mean that," Pecos said gallantly, grinning.

She smiled. "Thank you, Pecos."

"And if you ever get tired of ole Cap, you just let me know. I'd be more'n happy to help out."

This time, she blushed.

"Are you all right?" Derek whispered in her ear, his breath warm. A pleasant tingle raced down her spine.

"I'm a bit worn out, Derek," she confessed.

He chuckled. "Say that again."

She was puzzled. "I'm a—"

"No, my name." His gaze was so warm and so intent upon her face that she felt color rising to her cheeks.

"Really, please," she murmured.

"You are so shy," he said huskily. "I want to kiss you again . . . but I think you'd faint from embarrassment."

"Oh no, please!" Miranda was truly alarmed. It was bad enough that John was barely cold in his grave. And she was still very aware of the reasons for this marriage— duty, responsibility. Her new husband would be taking advantage of their situation if he kissed her again. She could not allow it. Fortunately, he seemed to be only teasing her.

Of course he knew, just as she hoped everyone else did, that this was a marriage to give her the protection of his name—and that was all.

They walked to the hotel, and Derek said, "Miranda, I'll see you upstairs, but then I'll leave you for a bit. I'm going to have a few drinks with the men."

"That's fine," Miranda said, wanting nothing more than to change out of her lavender silk gown and crawl into bed. Why was she so utterly exhausted?

Bragg walked her to the hotel and upstairs to their suite.

"I won't be long," he promised, opening the door but then reaching for her.

Again he caught her by surprise. She opened her mouth to protest. No words came out; instead, he held her head still with one large hand while his lips plundered hers, his tongue exploring the space she had granted him. Bolts of lightning-sharp heat swept her—and then, just as abruptly, he released her.

"I will see you soon," he said, not smiling. His voice had a husky catch.

Miranda began to protest, but found herself facing the closed door. She placed a palm over her breast, turning away. Her heart was racing. Good God, he didn't think . . . He did! He obviously expected them to consummate this marriage!

Miranda stared at the beautifully appointed sitting room without seeing a single detail of the furnishings. Was it possible Bragg thought to sleep with her? With John not two weeks dead?

Of course not! She felt a huge, overwhelming sense of relief. A barbarian Bragg might be, but he had loved John, in a man's way, and he certainly had an innate respect for his dead friend. He was just being—Bragg. Feeling relieved, she began to remove her clothes.

By now, she had gleaned all the information about him that she could from Elena. His wife and son had been abducted by the Comanche eight years ago, and it had taken him close to a year to find her and free her. She had died not many months after he had brought her back to their people, where they had lived, for his spread had been burned out and he had never rebuilt it. His son would be about ten now; he would have been raised as a Comanche, and by now would think he was one. Indeed, if no one told him differently, he would never know the truth about his parents.

Bragg had joined the first, earliest Texans in their fight against Mexico shortly after his wife's death. He'd participated in all the bloody rebellion for Texas's independence. He had ridden with the first Rangers, when their duties were not yet clear. His life for the past eight years—since his family's abduction—had been nothing but an extended

campaign of bloodshed and war, first in the fight for
Texas, then in his vendetta against the Comanche.

Could a man like Bragg possibly settle down? Miranda
wondered. He seemed to think that was what he was
doing. She wanted to see him release the past. He didn't
seem like a man driven by hatred, but she understood him
well enough now to know that he kept his feelings buried
deep inside.

He was such a confusing man, she thought, sliding into
bed clad in a flannel nightgown that buttoned to the throat.
Sleep promptly overtook her.

Chapter 42

Boisterous male laughter rang out, deep-throated, a bit inebriated. Bragg leaned back in his chair, looking every bit a gentleman, although he had unbuttoned his coat and loosened his cravat. His feet were starting to throb, a sure sign that he'd worn his damn dress boots long enough. It had been about an hour since he'd left Miranda. He was still so damn excited. He didn't want to be excited, he wanted to have control, he wanted to make love to her leisurely and languidly all night long. He wanted to make her happy, very happy.

"He's mooning again," Pecos said, grinning. "Lovestruck calf!"

Bragg smiled, not in the least insulted, and poured himself another shot of rye. "To envious dogs and other vermin," he said, raising his glass. "To the color green—it suits you." He drank.

Pecos laughed, and Lakely smiled. Jed Barnes, a neighbor, said, "Who wouldn't be moonstruck? I'm moonstruck, and I don't mind admitting it."

"To honest men," Bragg said blandly, trying not to think of her—of her white, slender body ready and eager for him. "Damn," he said. He stood. "Linette! Where's that champagne?"

"Goddamn! I wish . . . right now, I'd sell my soul to be you," Pecos said, meaning every word.

"God, I ain't ever had a sweet, good woman," Jed said. "Damn, maybe I'll get married too."

Bragg ignored them, but only after sending Pecos a warning glance. He didn't feel like hearing any ribald comments, and to his surprise, Pecos didn't make any. Linette appeared with a champagne bottle, nice and cold, and two glasses. "Thank you, sweetheart," Bragg said.

"Don't you want to thank me proper before you go up?" she asked, standing with her hip thrust out, a long leg revealed. "As a proper goodbye?" She smiled seductively.

"Sorry." Bragg grinned, pleased, of course, that Linette wanted him. "But Pecos can stand in my stead." He winked at his friend, who laughed.

Bragg hurried out of the saloon and up the stairs, his heart racing. He wanted to slow down. He wanted to be in control. He just couldn't keep a check on his vivid, sensual thoughts. He couldn't wait to have Miranda in his arms.

She was his! It felt incredibly good. Had he ever felt this good before? That was too complex a thought, he decided, setting down the champagne and glasses to unlock the door. He slipped in quietly, wondering what she was doing. The suite was completely hushed.

He moved stealthily into the bedroom, his burden in both hands, and paused in the doorway. It was dusk. The light in the room was dim, but not so dim that he couldn't see her asleep in the middle of the big four-poster bed. He saw she had braided her hair. Now why in hell had she done that?

He set down the champagne and glasses on a table by the fireplace. He pulled off his boots and slipped off the jacket and cravat, feeling much more comfortable. He proceeded to light a fire, prodding it until the flames caught. Then he rose, turning to look at his wife.

Miranda was awake and staring at him. She looked surprised and afraid.

A warm melting began in his heart and spread all over. "Hi," he said softly, smiling. Beauty incarnate, he thought absurdly. He noted, too, that she was holding the covers to her throat. He moved and lit a candle, and carried it to her bedside table.

"What—what are you doing?"

It took every ounce of willpower he had not to pull her into his arms and ravish her. The past week, having her so close, knowing that she was his but not being able to touch her, had been sheer hell. He wondered if he should have had a woman, any woman, to relieve some of his intense need. He had sent Bianca away with great annoyance the very first night he had brought Miranda home with John's corpse. He had not minced words, either. He had no intention of bedding Bianca under his soon-to-be wife's nose.

"Getting ready for bed," he said, wondering if he was really hearing his own voice—it was strangely tender and gentle.

Miranda sat up. "What?"

He stared at the ugly, childish nightgown. "After tonight," he said, "I want you to throw that thing away."

She was momentarily confused. "What? What are you talking about? What do you mean, you're getting ready for bed?"

He forgot about the nightgown—he would buy her a hundred nightgowns, even if it broke him. Sheer, lacy silk things to enhance her beauty, not hide it. He cupped her face. "This is my room, too," he murmured, trying to ignore the rush of blood to his loins. His hands slipped behind her, and he found the ribbon of her braid, untying it.

She pulled back. "Derek! What are you— Stop!"

He had freed her hair, and it fell in glorious, thick strands around her delicate oval face. He heard the panic in her voice. Why is she afraid? Certainly not of me? And the other question—had she learned passion? He stood and moved to the champagne, grateful for the dim light. He didn't want her to see how eager he was. He realized she was still untouched—she hadn't learned the joys of lovemaking. It fed his excitement. He was going to be the one to teach her.

With his back to her, he poured two glasses of champagne. His hands trembled slightly. He carried them over, sitting beside her on the bed, holding one glass out to her. Her violet eyes were huge in the flickering candlelight.

"Here," he murmured.

"I don't believe this," she said, looking stunned. She took the glass and set it firmly on the bedside table. "What is wrong with you?"

Bragg blinked at the indignation in her tone. "Excuse me?"

"Champagne? What, pray tell, are we celebrating?"

He felt as if she'd slapped him in the face, and he sat straighter, his pleasure draining away. "This is our wedding night," he said coldly, to cover the hurt he was feeling.

"Have you forgotten the reason for this wedding?" Her voice was an incredulous whisper.

Anger was etched on his face. He drained his champagne, then flung the glass at the hearth. At the sound of the glass shattering, Miranda jumped. He took her arms and pulled her close. "I refuse to share our bed with a ghost, Miranda."

She cried out, and he loosened his hold. "Our bed!"

"Yes, dammit, I don't care how much you loved him, life goes on, and our life starts now, tonight." He smothered her protest with his kiss, his passion erupting in the storm he had wanted to control, holding her tightly, too tightly. Forcing her mouth open, he kissed her so hard his teeth caught hers, grating. He thrust his tongue in, forcing her down on her back, covering her with his own body.

He was so close to being out of control—and that was not the way he wanted it. However, he was aware enough to feel her body stiffen like an unyielding board beneath him, until she began to struggle. Then she became wild, though her strength was pitiful. Abruptly he released her and jumped to his feet, stepping away. He was aghast at himself, and furious at her, at everything.

Had she loved John?

"How dare you!" she cried, her eyes blazing.

"How dare I?" he asked, panting like an animal. "How dare I what? How dare I take what's mine?"

"In name only," she shrieked. "You married me to protect me, you said, not to rape me!"

He stared, shocked, his desire abruptly dying. "I have no intention of raping you, Miranda," he said, his voice level. What in hell was she raving about? Did she really think he was some kind of bastard? "I believe there's been a misunderstanding."

"Yes, I think so," she breathed heavily.

He couldn't help but notice her breasts rising and falling rapidly, stretching taut the ridiculous gown. Her nipples were hard. He looked at her face. "You are my wife, in every sense of the word. Yes, I gave you my name to protect you, but I intend to enjoy all my husbandly rights."

Miranda sat back, the color draining from her face.

"Am I distasteful?" Another stabbing pain.

"I thought . . . I thought it was just in name . . . a marriage in name only."

He laughed bitterly. "I'm afraid you thought wrong."

Tears fell from her eyes.

Bragg cursed. "I intend for you to be my wife, Miranda, completely, and you won't deny me."

"I refuse to allow you to—to exercise your rights, not until a proper period of mourning has passed."

He scowled. "Really?"

"If you have no respect for me," she cried, "then at least show some for your poor dead friend! I will not have you satisfying your lust on his barely cold grave! Don't you have any sensitivity? Or are you completely selfish?" Her voice had risen to a scream.

He moved slowly, pulling on his coat. "Of course," he said stiffly. "I had forgotten propriety, again." He sat and pulled on the boots, cursing clearly as he did so. He ignored her flaming face. "And what, Miranda, is a proper time of mourning?" His voice was heavy with sarcasm. He was angry, hurt, and bitter. "Pray tell," he said mockingly, "so I do not offend your delicate sensibilities by coming to your bed too soon."

"A year, of course."

He stood abruptly, staring. "I will give you three more weeks," he said curtly, harshly. "This is Texas, not London, not Paris. A month of mourning is proper here."

Miranda looked ready to cry again.

"And since you deny me," he added cruelly, wanting to hurt her, "you can have no complaint should I not return to you this evening?'' He raised a brow, waiting for her reaction.

It took a moment for her to understand. Her color rose and she averted her eyes. ''No, of course not. Do what—you must.''

''I intend to,'' he said, furious. He picked up the champagne bottle and drank deeply until it was almost empty. ''To you, Miranda, a true lady. How dare I forget?'' He finished the bottle. His mouth set in a hard line, he hurled it at the hearth. The bottle exploded, and he heard the bed creak as Miranda leaped in fright, but he felt no satisfaction. He stalked out, slamming the door behind him.

Chapter 43

Bragg did not come to fetch her to return to the ranch until midmorning. Miranda could not forget his temper of the night before, in fact, she could not forget anything about the night before. She remembered his curiously soft voice—until they had argued about his rights as a husband. She shivered again, thinking about his violent temper. His temper frightened her. But even that sensation was lost to another, stronger one. True to his word, he had not returned that night, or that morning, not until close to ten o'clock.

Then he had come in looking very rumpled, and quite red-eyed. He had told her in one sentence to be ready to leave in fifteen minutes. Ignoring her, he had changed into his buckskins. They had left fifteen minutes later.

Miranda didn't understand why she felt so sick inside—and she couldn't stop wondering about where he had been the previous night. Had he really been with a woman? But then, what did it matter? Hadn't she wanted a marriage in name only? Why was she so upset?

They were traveling back to the ranch with a very gruff, hard-looking older man riding alongside their wagon. Bragg briefly introduced him as Brown. He was tall, buckskin-clad, of course, and heavily bearded. Miranda didn't dare ask Bragg anything. His face was a mask of tightly con-

207

trolled anger. He also reeked—of alcohol. He seemed oblivious of her presence.

Miranda found out later that day from Bianca that Brown was her personal guard. She was shocked. Why did she need a personal guard? It was disconcerting that the man was outside her door when she was in her room, and followed her about at a discreet distance. This was only the first day, and she was annoyed, feeling his black eyes constantly upon her. Had something happened that she didn't know about, to warrant this? Or was Bragg preparing to leave, maybe to ride with the Rangers?

He came in late that afternoon, but his expression was still so hard that she was afraid to ask. He didn't even seem to see her as he strode through the house and upstairs to his room. She heard him bellow for Bianca to bring hot water. Then, to her surprise, she noticed that Brown had disappeared, and she ran to the door and saw him walking toward the bunkhouse. She was confused, until she realized that she wouldn't need a guard while Bragg was in the house.

It took her a while to get up the courage to approach him. She knew that Bianca had brought the hot water for a bath up to his room, but she had not come back down. A stab of anxiety seized her. She had a vivid memory of Bianca clinging to Bragg in the clearing in the woods. Oh no. She gritted her teeth and marched up the stairs. She didn't knock.

Bragg was standing naked in the room, facing the door— and Bianca. Miranda felt a murderous rage. He glared at her with a flash of light in his eyes. Miranda closed the door behind her, then saw that her husband was handing Bianca his dirty buckskins quite disinterestedly. She averted her gaze from his naked body, flushing. "Please go, Bianca," she said calmly.

Bianca left.

Bragg stood there, staring at her, and folded his arms across his chest. "Did you want something, Miranda?"

She realized that she was standing in his room, not five feet from him, and he was stark naked. She had only had brief glimpses of his body in the past, and never a full view. For a moment she couldn't talk as she stared fixedly at his shoulder. "Yes."

He waited.

Her gaze traveled over his body of its own accord. Even with his arms crossed negligently, she could see that his chest was broad and hard and hairy, his muscles bunched. His belly was hard and smooth, banded with muscle, the hair narrowing into a delicate line. She gasped when her gaze found a thick, swollen member, and abruptly she turned her back to him.

Her face was burning. She had never seen that before. Her heart was pumping, wildly, madly. She forgot the entire reason she had come to his room.

Bragg felt a rush of amusement, then stepped into the steaming tub. "You act like you've never seen a man before, Miranda. Did you want something?" Against his will, his tone was not as frosty as he'd have liked. He knew he was sulking, but, damn—he wanted to sulk. He was still hurt and angry over her rejection, her obvious lack of desire for him.

She turned, her face as usual giving away her every emotion. "It's not proper that Bianca be in here," she said stiffly.

Bragg searched her face hopefully for a sign of jealousy. He smiled when he found it. It was indignant, but undeniably there. "She's seen plenty of men naked, Miranda, believe me. It doesn't bother her."

"I insist," she said, looking ready to cry.

He suddenly realized what she was thinking, and he straightened in the tub. "Miranda! Don't even think it. I am not sleeping with Bianca under your nose—and never will. Put it out of your mind."

She was relieved.

His face softened. "I'm not such a cad, am I? Come here."

She hesitated.

"I can't scrub my back," he complained. "Can't you perform that one little wifely chore?" He flashed her a mischievous smile. "I promise not to bite."

Miranda approached, taking the washcloth and soap. "Derek, about that man. Brown."

He leaned forward, showing her a long expanse of broad, sinewed back. She began to soap him, surprised at the feel of his warm, bare skin. He was so silken—and so hard.

Bragg sighed and closed his eyes. Heaven, he thought.

"Derek? Is Brown necessary?"

"Yes."

"Why?"

"I want him around you—ahh . . ."

She froze at his sensual moan.

"Don't stop," he said, trying to sound casual but failing.

"Your back is clean," she said, rinsing it with her hands. They trembled. She had a crazy urge to lean her cheek against his warm skin, to nuzzle him. She quickly shoved the inclination away, shocked at herself. She stood up.

But he caught her wrist. "Don't," he said, twisting to look up at her. He smiled lazily. "Wash my hair, my chest. Wife."

"Really, Derek, you can manage yourself." Her voice sounded funny, cracked and shrill.

"Is it really so much to ask?" His tone was husky, seductive. "I give you my name and all I ask in return is a woman's gentle touch—a bath."

"You had a woman's gentle touch last night," she said before she could help it.

"Jealous?"

"It's your right," she managed. She was jealous! The thought shocked her.

He still held her wrist, and he smiled, his golden eyes strangely bright. "You fool," he breathed.

"Please," she said, barely able to breathe herself. She had, by mistake, glimpsed down, and the water had magnified and reflected that male part of him, seemingly straining toward her. She couldn't believe she had ever had a thing like that inside her. Could John have been that big?

Bragg suddenly wanted her to know the truth—it was so important. "There was no woman last night, Miranda. I don't want another woman, and I want to make myself very clear. Do you understand?"

His words, his tone, so serious now, forced her to look

into his eyes. She flushed again, furious at having been caught staring, then realized what he'd said—and was unaccountably thrilled. "But where were you?"

"Getting drunk," he rasped, and closed his eyes. He wanted her—now. He had promised her three weeks to mourn, but he had only done so because he was fair enough to know that she was right. Despite what she thought, he did have some sensitivity. But if he tortured himself this way, he would go back on his word. . . .

"Why don't you change and meet me downstairs," he said.

Relieved, Miranda extracted her hand and quickly crossed the room, feeling his eyes on her. It wasn't until she had closed the door behind her that she realized she felt something suspiciously like disappointment. But that was ridiculous, of course.

Chapter 44

The next few days passed exceedingly slowly. Bragg was gone all day, every day, riding with the men. She had the feeling he enjoyed it. She was surprised to recognize her feelings of loneliness, and her eagerness when he returned. After their first night back, he had missed supper three times, to her great disappointment. She had remained downstairs, ostensibly engrossed in a book, waiting for him, wanting to see him if only for a few minutes before she went to bed. He had seemed surprised and then pleased on each occasion, but had behaved properly, sending her upstairs with a brief kiss on the cheek.

Miranda denied that the touch of his lips on her skin had any effect. She was in mourning for her husband. She was also a properly raised and well-bred English gentlewoman, and a devout Catholic. It was the strangeness of his touch that made her body taut—with dread, not anticipation.

She was delighted when he returned that day in the late afternoon, and smiled brightly as he strode in. "You're home early!" She beamed.

Bragg stopped, a funny expression crossing his features. Then he grinned, the corners of his eyes crinkling in an adorable way. "I like the sound of that, princess," he said. "I'm tired of beans and the boys." He started up the stairs. "Tell Elena to outdo herself for us, will you?"

Miranda felt a warm thrill watching him climb the stairs

so effortlessly, so gracefully, as if he hadn't been working the range all day. She informed Elena that Derek was joining her for dinner, then hurried to her own room to change. She wanted to wear something special, something he would like, something he hadn't seen before.

The gown she chose was a rich, vibrant turquoise, a color that was striking on her. It was low cut—immodestly so, she thought, a wonderful taffeta with full, billowing skirts. She left her hair hanging, tying it away from her face with a matching ribbon. The blue made her eyes seem even more purple, dark and mysterious, almost black. For some reason, her face was flushed, glowing.

Bragg was sipping a brandy in the study when she paused in the doorway. He immediately jumped to his feet, the look in his eyes telling her that he approved—very much. He smiled, still staring intensely, his topaz eyes gleaming. "You are exquisite."

"Thank you." She curtsied. She was overflowing with joy—everything in the world ceased to exist at that moment, except for the man standing before her, and his appreciation.

"Hungry?" he asked, taking her arm.

"Starved," she said.

"That's a first! Do you mind how I'm dressed?"

"Of course not, Derek, this is your home!" She meant it, and he smiled. He was clad in clean buckskins, his moccasins, and a plain linen shirt, open at the throat. She had become used to the way he dressed—it suited him. For her benefit, he removed his guns and knife when he was in the house in the evenings.

They sat, and Bianca served them roast pork, dumplings, sweet potatoes, collard greens, and carrots in a sweet sauce. Bragg filled both their glasses with red wine, then raised his. "To you, Miranda." His words, so simple, were spoken quietly, but his gaze was so intense it was almost unnerving.

Miranda hesitated, remembering the last time she had so foolishly imbibed, then lifted her glass, touching his. "Thank you," she said, sipping carefully. She put her glass down as Derek drained half of his. He drank too much, she thought. But it never seemed to affect him. She frowned.

"What, princess? Why are you frowning?" His voice was soft, questioning.

"You drink quite a bit," she said bluntly.

Bragg laughed. "Oh no! Do you intend to change my drinking habits, too? Will I always be judged and molded by my wife?" His tone was playful, teasing.

"Oh, Derek, I didn't mean you to think— I don't judge you." She stopped, flustered.

"Of course you do," he said, unperturbed. "You judged me the moment you met me, don't you remember? I believe you called me a savage, uncivilized brute, a crude lout, and, oh yes, a barbarian?" He smiled.

Miranda flushed. "I take it all back."

He chuckled, the sound warm and pleasant. "Don't. You are right, and I'm sorry when I forget just how genteel and fragile you are." His tone had become serious.

To cover her dismayed confusion, and the warmth racing through her body, she sipped her wine. Then she began to eat. The pork was delicious. Bragg told her about his work on the range, and she listened with real interest. She realized that she had been right, he did enjoy it, and she asked pertinent questions. He refilled her wineglass and his, and she was surprised that she had drunk the whole glassful. The evening was so warm and pleasant, so wonderful, it was like a dream. She felt safe, secure, and . . . cherished. When had she ever in her whole life felt this way?

After dinner he took her hand and they walked out onto the veranda to lean against the rail. The moon was an exact crescent, almost white, set amid a thousand twinkling, glittering stars in a blue black night. There was a faint breeze, the tinkle of wind chimes, a horse's nickering. She leaned against the man standing next to her without thinking about it, and was aware of his scent— brandy and buckskins, musk and soap. His arm went around her waist, and before she knew it, he was turning her toward him, pulling her against him.

She melted into his body, her face resting on his chest. His other arm went around her, and he held her like that for a long time, the night suddenly becoming very, very still. She inhaled his scent. His warmth throbbed against her. She could hear his heart thudding. She slipped her hands from his chest and slid them around his neck. She could stay in his embrace forever. His hold tightened.

"Oh, Miranda," he said huskily, his mouth pressed to the top of her head. She thought he kissed her hair, but she wasn't sure. His hands roamed her back, gently. Something long and hard rose between them, pressing into her belly. She wanted to stay there forever. Her pulse began to quicken.

His hands began to quicken, too, becoming harder, stroking insistently. One moved over her shoulder, catching her chin. She opened her eyes, saw his hot, golden gaze fixed upon her, and felt his breath on her face. She closed her eyes, sighing, arching toward him. She wanted him to hold her tighter.

Bragg growled, a male, animal sound. His mouth touched hers, gently, softly. His tongue traced the shape of her lips, which opened of their own eager volition, then darted just barely between them, teasing, tempting. She opened her mouth wider, wanting his violation. His lips brushed hers barely, lightly, fluttering over her face, her eyelids, her nose, her ear. He nibbled her earlobe. A soft, weak sound came from deep within her.

His mouth returned to hers, hard now, and she welcomed the assault. She pressed against him. His tongue demanded entry, and she gave it eagerly. He explored with a growing frenzy, thrusting his tongue into her rapaciously, cupping her buttocks, urging that strange, delightful hardness against her in the same rhythm.

His mouth moved to her throat, kissing, nibbling, and she arched her head back to give him more skin, her hands in his hair, holding tightly, guiding him down to she knew not where. He gasped, accepting her invitation, his mouth descending, making her whimper. Then he nipped lightly, causing her to groan, and he buried his face in the soft swells of her bosom above the bodice of her gown. His breathing was loud and harsh and ragged.

She was trembling from head to foot.

He touched her breasts, gently at first, but she was

mindless with wine-freed passion, and she arched herself toward him. He cupped her, teased her nipple, and she shuddered. She felt his bare hand, so warm and large, slipping into her bodice, cupping the bare, swollen flesh of her breast.

A sane voice suddenly intruded upon her consciousness. What is he doing?

Had she spoken aloud? Because suddenly, abruptly, Bragg was gone. She almost fell, opening her eyes and clutching the railing. She tried to catch her breath. She was light-headed, warm and unbearably achy. She wondered, disappointed, where he was. She realized stupidly that she was tipsy. She turned and saw him behind her, looking as if he was struggling with the devil. She realized how she'd acted—again. It was like cold water being thrown in her face. She straightened, horrified.

"Release me from my word," he said raggedly. He took a step toward her, then stopped. "Damn! Even if you do, it's because you drank that wine. Damn!"

Miranda stood there a moment longer, horrified and yearning all at once. The two feelings were so strong, so equal that she was overwhelmed with confusion and dismay. With a gasp, she rushed past him. She didn't know if she was relieved or disappointed when he didn't follow.

Chapter 45

"When are we going to San Antonio?" she asked cautiously, flushing despite herself. He had been gone when she'd awoken that morning, and she had been very, very thankful. Later she had been torn between her desire to see him and her inability to face him.

His glance was piercing. "I had no plans to do so, not until we need supplies." He had bathed and changed, and smelled strongly of soap and cigars.

Her face fell.

He put his hands on his hips and stared at her. "There is nothing for you to confess, Miranda. Do you intend to go to confession every time I kiss you—or only when you like it?"

She grew defensive. "I didn't like it!"

He laughed incredulously.

"It was the wine! And you gave me your word!"

His face grew tight. "If I hadn't given you my word, princess, you would have woken up in my bed this morning—a much wiser and happier woman."

Miranda blushed and turned away, but not before she heard him cursing. She didn't want to reprove him; she was too burdened by her own guilt. And he was wrong—she hadn't enjoyed it. It had been the wine. She would never drink again!

Dinner was a strained affair. She was too upset with her

own reprehensible behavior to carry on the light conversation Bragg tried to sustain, so he gave up, and they ate in silence. She was concerned enough to glance at him from time to time, certain that he was in a black mood, but he wasn't—he was just inscrutable.

"Let's walk," he said after they had finished.

"I don't think so," she said quickly, looking away. "I'm tired."

"Let's walk," he repeated firmly, taking her hand. He placed a shawl around her shoulders and slipped his arm around her waist, and they strolled beneath a row of cottonwoods. A fragrant scent she couldn't identify hung on the twilight, sweetening it. He was holding her too closely.

"Don't squirm," he said easily. "I know my touch isn't repulsive."

She had no answer.

They walked on in silence. She knew beyond a doubt that he had brought her out here to kiss her. Her heart was pounding with indignation. How dare he try to seduce her? What about his promise?

He turned her toward him, smiling slightly, his hands on her shoulders. "Now tell me you don't like this," he said, and he bent and kissed her.

Her heart leaped wildly in her chest. She stiffened and tried to draw away. His mouth was warm, soft but firm, insistent. His tongue touched the joining of her lips, teasingly, fleetingly. A warm, wet ache spiraled through her.

He raised his head and smiled. "Stubborn, aren't you? Shall we try again?"

"You promised!"

He pulled her closer. "I promised not to make love to you, princess," he said, then claimed her mouth with his own again.

She struggled this time instead of remaining passive. He ignored it, his hold merely tightening. She tried to twist her face away, but he caught the back of her head easily in one hand and continued to kiss her, without forcing her mouth open. She released an anguished sob. He released her.

Miranda stumbled but didn't fall, nor did he try to help

her. She watched his back cautiously as he leaned against a tree, staring at the jagged line of distant mountains. She began to breathe easier. She was angry, insulted, indignant—and there were so many emotions roiling around in her that she couldn't even identify them all. She ached.

"Let's go back," he said, sighing heavily. She thought she could feel his disappointment, it was so strong.

He didn't return for supper the next two nights, and Miranda didn't wait up. Instead, she sought the sanctuary of her bedroom. But she didn't fall asleep until long after he had come in.

She was awakened by the thunderous sound of many, many horses pounding up to the house. She blinked and fought sleepiness. What time was it? She heard male voices, taut and tense, but she couldn't make out the words. She slipped to the floor, throwing on a robe and peering out her window. There were at least a dozen heavily armed riders in the yard, their horses wet, their faces grim. She grew frightened and rushed downstairs.

She heard a voice, not Derek's, coming from the study, and didn't hesitate to burst in.

". . . a full day's start . . ." a tall man was saying, but he broke off the moment she entered.

"Derek! What is it?" she cried.

"Miranda, go back to your room, and I'll be up shortly," he said, his voice quiet and even, his expression implacable.

She opened her mouth to protest, but saw his gaze—hard and unflinching. Truly frightened, she obeyed. Back upstairs, she peered out her window again. This time she recognized Pecos and Lakely sitting easily amid the riders. Rangers. Something terrible had happened, she thought, for so many Rangers to ride together. She began to tremble. She wanted to cry.

She knew he was going to go with them.

She heard his footsteps and rushed to meet him at the door. "Derek! What's happened!"

He guided her into the room, gently, firmly. "Shhh. There's been some trouble. Nothing for you to worry about. I'll be gone for a week or two." He held her hands and smiled into her worried face. "Don't worry, princess, you have four good men here, and nothing will happen to you. Brown will stay by your side twenty-four hours a day. And no riding, at all.'' He smiled. ''Promise.''

''I promise,'' she cried, gripping his hands tightly. ''What trouble? Comanche?''

He nodded reluctantly.

''Where?''

He hesitated. ''Miranda, you'll be safe. But we've got to catch these bastards and get rid of them.''

''You said your vendetta was old! Don't go!''

He grew grim. ''They killed Hewlitt, Miranda. And his three boys, one only eight. They took Beth Hewlitt and her daughter captive. Her daughter is your age, Miranda, unmarried. We're going to get them back.''

Miranda sat still, ashen and terribly afraid.

He stroked her face with a surprisingly gentle hand. ''Nothing will happen to you. I've got to go.'' He stood, pausing, then he kissed her briefly on the lips. She was so frightened that she sat like a stone, unable to move, barely able to think.

He stared at her for a moment, disappointment flickering in his eyes, then he turned and walked into his room. She heard him dressing, gathering his guns, his saddle-bags, and the rest of his gear. Her mind began to shriek. Derek was leaving! He could be killed!

She realized he had already gone down the stairs, that she might never see him again. With a cry, she fled after him. ''Derek! Wait!''

Someone had saddled his horse, and he was about to mount. The other riders were waiting impatiently, their horses moving restlessly. He turned, startled.

Miranda flew off the veranda, her robe flying open around her legs, her hair loose and streaming like a flag behind her. She threw her arms around him, clinging tightly. His warm, strong arms held her tightly against him. She raised her face, tears swimming in her eyes.

''Don't be afraid,'' he said softly. ''You'll be fine.''

''I'm not afraid for myself,'' she said, her tears falling helplessly. ''I'm afraid for you!''

His breath caught, and his eyes blazed like golden fires. Miranda slipped her hands around his neck, grasping the thick hairs curling over his collar, pulling him down. She kissed him shamelessly. She clung, her mouth on his, demanding, seeking, frenzied. She heard him emit a deep sound in his throat. Someone laughed, and someone else suggested that Derek meet them later. Derek wrapped his hand in her hair, deepening the kiss, and she opened her mouth eagerly. She accepted his tongue desperately, urging him deeper. She could feel the whole length of his body against hers, hard and hot, even his manhood.

"Let's go, Bragg," someone yelled.

Bragg released her, putting her firmly from him. His gaze was smoldering. Miranda didn't look away. She was breathless. He smiled. Their eyes held as another voice shouted at him to mount up. He turned and swung effortlessly into the saddle. She hugged herself tightly, miserably. She couldn't take her eyes off him, wanting to memorize every last detail.

He was so magnificent, broad-shouldered, tall, powerful, the buckskins rippling over his body. He sat easily, gracefully, as the chestnut pranced in excitement. His face, so bronzed and lean, was incredibly handsome, and his eyes, golden like citrines, were tender.

And then he was gone, in a thundering cloud of hooves and dust.

Chapter 46

A noise awoke her.

It was dawn. Derek had left just two days ago. The morning was unusually quiet—no birds, no horses, no sounds of the men rising and tacking up, their soft, drawling conversation punctuated with laughter. She strained to hear. She had heard something. But . . . what? She fought for conscious recall. An animal? A grunt? A thump?

Why was the morning so quiet?

Miranda sat up, pushing her long braid over her shoulder, hesitating. There were no sounds from downstairs, either, but then she realized that of course there weren't; it was Derek who made noise downstairs in the morning, joking with Elena as she waited on him hand and foot while he ate before riding out. Sighing, a strange loneliness gripping her, Miranda sank down under the covers and tried to fall back asleep.

She dozed. Her light sleep was punctuated with images of her husband, a warm, fluttery feeling mixed with a sick fear for his well-being. She dreamed he was leaning over her, smiling, his breath warm on her face. Derek. She would welcome him into her arms now. She had been a fool to deny him. What if he didn't come back? No, she would never deny him again.

He took her in his arms, and Miranda snuggled against

his warm, hard body for a moment. Then her eyes flew open, and she opened her mouth to scream.

Something was shoved into her mouth, something like cotton, and she was flung over a hard shoulder. Indians! The man was moving silently, rapidly, out of her room. Her face was pressed against his bare waist. He was wearing only a loincloth and high moccasins. Her view was upside down and distorted. She struggled, but realized instantly it was fruitless. The man was too powerful.

In the hall she saw Brown, lying on his back, his eyes open in death, his chest covered with blood. She choked on hysterical sobs.

The man was taking her downstairs. Where were the rest of the men? Elena? Bianca? Oh God! He carried her outside and threw her on a black horse, jumping up immediately behind her. Wild war cries suddenly rang out, and dozens of Indians appeared from the woods, carrying torches, riding for the buildings, setting them on fire. Miranda tried to scream, but only a muffled sound came out through the gag. The man held her tightly with one arm around her waist, urging his horse forward.

Rifle shots rang out of the bunkhouse. Miranda exulted. She saw one, two braves hit, tumbling from their horses. She turned her head frantically. They had torched the big house, too, and flames were licking at the corners. She heard a woman scream.

Bianca was running toward the woods. A Comanche bore down on her at a gallop, and Miranda closed her eyes, thinking he was going to run her down. Her scream sounded again. The brave effortlessly whipped her astride his mount, and when she fought, he backhanded her with a resounding thwack across the face. She slumped over the horse's neck.

It had become a melee. Her captor was shouting words she did not understand, but he was giving orders, and the Comanche began to disappear into the woods from where they had so suddenly come. Miranda shuddered with another sob.

They followed the warriors rapidly into the woods, branches flying in their faces, horses' hooves thundering, bridles jangling. Miranda began to think.

Something was definitely wrong. She had lived in Texas long enough to know what to expect when Comanche attacked. They did not sneak into homes to abduct women. They attacked and sieged. It was as if . . . as if *she* had been the target!

But that was silly!

She twisted her face away when she suddenly felt his hand, then she realized he was removing the gag. He tossed it aside. The gravity of her situation hit her full force. She would be raped by many braves. She could be made a wife of one of them. She could be sold as a whore. She closed her eyes. Another shudder wracked her. No, think! Stay calm! Bragg will come!

She was seized with the dread certainty that when he came, it would be too late.

She trembled all over.

"Are you cold, *poquita?*"

Horror overtook her. She knew that voice. She would never forget it. Twisting, she looked up into Chavez's smiling face.

Brenda Joyce

Part Three

The Squaw

Chapter 47

Miranda wanted to weep, but she didn't. Tears were an indulgence, she realized for the first time in her life—although the sisters had told her that many times. Nothing would save her now except the Lord.

"What are you going to do with me?" she cried.

His hand on her stomach lightly caressed her, and her horror increased, for she was wearing nothing but her flannel nightgown. "I already told you, *poquita.*" His voice was rich, but so frightening. "I will make you my woman, my wife."

"They'll come after me," Miranda said desperately. "Those cowboys—"

"No, sweet, I'm afraid not." His voice was in her ear. "They will have to leave the bunkhouse or burn to death. Once all three have come out, the men I left behind will pick them off."

"Bragg will kill you!"

She could feel the man behind her grow tense. "If he can find me, I welcome him."

His tone was soft, ruthless, and she was afraid.

His voice became a silken caress. "But, *cara,* you give me no credit. Do you think I would come to you while he was still there? Eh?"

Miranda closed her eyes briefly. "You knew the Rangers were riding out."

"After Comanche—yes, of course. I am no fool." His hold on her tightened.

Miranda prayed. It was her only hope, and it gave her comfort. She was not conceited, but she did not think her sins were great enough that she should be raped by Indians or sold into a life of prostitution. Then, unwillingly, she thought of her behavior with Bragg. No, no, no! She couldn't succumb to despair and guilt now. She needed faith—faith and hope.

She had thought she had ridden to the limits of her endurance with Bragg on the last leg of their journey from Natchez, but she had been wrong. The Comanche, two dozen of them, rode for two days straight, stopping only to water the horses. They rode at a steady trot, up one river valley after another. Miranda was such a tenderfoot that it took her a day to realize they were heading almost directly north. She knew that northern Texas was the most uncivilized and wild part of the entire land.

The third night they stopped and made camp. When Miranda dismounted she would have fallen to the ground had Chavez not caught her. She couldn't walk. Her body was screaming with pain.

Everyone ate pemmican; there was no fire. Miranda prayed that she would be safe that night, that Chavez would be too tired to touch her. She prayed for Bianca, too, whom she had only glimpsed as they traveled. The woman was stoic, but Miranda knew she was terrified—it was in her eyes. Miranda wondered if her own fear was so apparent.

Her prayers were answered, it seemed. Apparently the braves were as exhausted as any human beings would be, and within moments the camp had become silent with deep sleep. Including Chavez, who lay beside her on his back. They were sharing a bedroll.

Miranda debated escaping. She knew she would die if she tried. She had no gun, even if she could use one, and no knife. She had no idea how to survive. She didn't know where to go. But . . . maybe this quiet camp was a gift from God, a sign. Maybe He would guide her. She was afraid, but she was more afraid of what waited for her with Chavez than of dying in the wilderness.

She rolled cautiously away from Chavez, onto her side, listening to his deep, even breathing. The fool, she thought, wondering why he hadn't tied her up. Or was what she was doing so foolish as to be incomprehensible? She thought of Bragg. She knew he would approve. She got to her knees slowly, glancing around. The camp was an expanse of bodies and soft breathing, some snoring. She rose and, on tiptoe, not wanting to make a sound, she edged toward the forest.

She was way past the camp, stumbling through the dark woods, suddenly wondering about snakes, spiders. She wished she had shoes and a knife. She walked into first one tree, then another. Branches cut her arms, her face. She was not going in any particular direction, just away from Chavez. She tripped over a root and fell on her hands and knees. She suddenly began to understand the immensity of what she was doing. She moved on blindly. There was no moonlight and she wanted to curse. She stubbed her toe on a rock and gasped aloud. The sound seemed to echo ominously.

She stood very, very still, frozen, listening. She heard nothing except an owl, and what seemed to be the breeze rustling leaves. She took another step. Too late, she realized that there was no breeze. He grabbed her.

"No!" she sobbed. "No! Let me go! Let me go! Damn you!"

He shook her. "Little fool! Do you want to die?" Chavez pulled her closer. His eyes gleamed in the dark. "Is death by wild animals or starvation preferable to being my wife?" Angry, he shook her again. "Answer me!"

"Yes!" she shouted. "Yes! Death is preferable."

He slapped her.

Miranda was stunned, and the blow carried her backwards against a tree. Her breathing was suddenly very loud.

"I do not want to hurt you. I should beat you. You are now mine, Miranda, mine. Understand it. Accept it."

"I'm married to Bragg!" Her voice was broken, but she lifted her chin, seeking courage. It was so hard to pretend to be brave.

"I do not care. Many Comanche take wives of other

men. Come. I must tie you up now, because I, at least, must get my sleep this night." He took her arm. She expected him to be rough, but his grip, although firm, was gentle. "Do not make me hurt you again, *poquita*," he murmured, leading her through the forest as if it were broad daylight.

The next day they rode for another thirty hours straight. The Comanche were tireless, superb riders. Miranda was sore, exhausted, and almost hopeless. Bragg had said he would be gone a week or two. Even if he were only gone a week, he would just be returning to the JB, and would be many days behind her abductors. She prayed. It helped to stem the hysterical terror that would rise and try to choke her, threatening her with insanity.

It was midday when they crested a rise and Chavez pulled up his black stallion. "Look, *cara*."

Miranda wanted to sob with despair. Below them, in the valley stretched a sea of teepees. There were a hundred—two hundred. So many! If she were ever going to be rescued, it would take the militia to do it. It was over, she thought. All the hopes she had clung to—hopes that Bragg would come . . . He *would* come, she knew it. But he could not possibly rescue her from this.

They rode down into the Comanche village, the warriors whooping and screaming in obvious elation, other warriors, children, and squaws, rushing to greet them, clearly congratulating them. She refused to think about what would happen that night. Surely Chavez needed more sleep. The night that she had been so foolish to try to escape had been a day and a half ago. Surely he would want to sleep tonight . . .

A tall, big-boned squaw, broad-shouldered and very beautiful, came running up to Chavez, crying out ecstatically. Chavez chuckled, sliding to the ground, pulling Miranda down with him. He spoke in Comanche to the squaw, obviously pleased by her warm reception. She ignored Miranda, flinging her arms around him, kissing him. He responded for a moment, then pushed her away. He spoke again, rapidly, gesturing to Miranda, who looked around, dazed.

There were fires burning and food cooking, tended by

squaws of all ages. The braves had interrupted their activities, she could see. She saw hides being sewn, baskets being woven, skins being cleaned. Dogs barked and children raced around in a frenzy. Fathers lifted up youngsters and laughed. There was much animated conversation. Where was Bianca?

Her gaze fell upon two white women, and she gasped. They were pitifully thin, their hair was cropped below their ears, and they were dressed in rags. One had a black eye. They were working over a large fire, but they were staring at her. Their eyes were vacant, dead. Miranda wanted to go to them.

"Miranda, this is my wife, Colchikehatta. You may call her Walking Tall Woman."

Miranda noticed then that this woman had her hair cut short too, as did all the women. As if reading her mind, Chavez laughed. "Don't worry. I have told her to leave your hair alone. You must obey her, Miranda. She is going to take you to bathe and give you clean clothes. Then you tend to me," he said to the squaw, in English.

She nodded, flashed him a smile, and turned to Miranda. "Come, Me-ran-da. A strange name, no?"

Miranda gave the white women a last glance and followed Walking Tall Woman down to a creek. The woman handed her soap and held out her hand for the nightgown. Miranda hesitated, but there was no one around except another woman, and she was bathing also.

"Do not worry. This area is for bathing, and for women only." She smiled.

Miranda removed the gown and waded in. The water was frigid, and she gasped. Immediately, her teeth began to chatter. The squaw laughed, tossing her the soap.

Miranda bathed as quickly as possible. She washed her hair, too, but only rinsed it twice. By the time she rushed out, she was blue from the cold. Walking Tall Woman clucked and wrapped her in a blanket that was surprisingly clean.

The teepee she was led to was very large with a hole in the top for the smoke of a fire to go out. There were hides upon the ground, and all kinds of gear—rifles, spears, bows and arrows, a saddle, blankets, cooking and eating

utensils, a book, and a pile of white men's clothing—
Chavez's, of course. Walking Tall Woman handed her a
buckskin dress and moccasins, which Miranda put on
gratefully.

"You rest," Walking Tall Woman said. "Soon you eat.
I tend to my husband now." She left.

Miranda leaned back upon the hides. Tears threatened,
and she gave in. She was doomed. Soon Chavez would
come, and there was nothing she could do.

Chapter 48

"He's daydreaming again," the rider said, chuckling.

"Hell, I'd daydream too if I had a sweet little filly like that waiting for me!"

Laughter greeted this comment.

"Hey, Bragg! What do you say?"

Bragg jerked himself out of his wonderful if not downright erotic reverie and smiled at Brett Lincoln, who had ridden his horse against Bragg's, knocking the chestnut rudely. "What's the question, Lincoln?"

The Rangers around him chuckled. Pecos leaned over to slap him. "The Tetley place is up ahead. From there we head on in to San Antonio. You're coming, aren't you?" His tone was anxious.

"Of course he's coming," Lincoln shouted. "We're gonna drink up a storm, then find us some hot women, right, Bragg?"

Bragg grinned. "Sorry to disappoint you, boys," he drawled, "but I think I'll just head straight west from the Tetleys'."

"Oh no! C'mon, Bragg, what's the rush?" exclaimed another Ranger, Anderson.

"Looks like we know who's wearin' the pants in that family," Pecos said loudly.

Bragg smiled, barely hearing the suggestive comments

that followed. "He'll probably never come into town with a gal like that warming his bed," someone said.

"If I had a little gal like that, I'd retire," someone else said. "Or take up a new occupation."

"Yeah! Making babies!"

Miranda. He breathed the name in his mind. God, but it had happened. He had fallen in love.

Maybe he had fallen in love the first time he saw her. She'd become a torment then, had been an obsession ever since the first moment he'd seen her. He smiled, remembering how she'd clung to him when he'd left, whispering that she was afraid—not for herself, but for him. And that kiss. He thought about the passion she'd shown, her desire, her caring . . . and his loins grew full, tight, aching. He needed her. He wanted her. Even if she still wanted him to hold to that promise, he would, but just to see her again . . .

He was glad they'd caught up with the small war party of Comanche in just a few days. He grew sober thinking about what had happened after they'd killed the Indians and freed the two girls and their mother. The older daughter, eighteen, had been such a beauty. She hadn't been much to look at when they'd found her. She'd been missing teeth, and her face was bruised and swollen. He knew she'd been raped repeatedly. She'd grabbed one of the Ranger's guns and killed herself before they had even left the battle site. He didn't want to think about it.

The Tetleys' small spread appeared around the bend, nestled in a long, open canyon shaded by oaks and birch, a lazy river meandering through the middle. Colonel Bent held up a hand. "Let's water the horses and give them a rest. I'll inquire after the Tetleys."

"Aw, Colonel, can I come?" someone joked. It was fairly standard practice for Rangers to stop in and check up on the settlers, but everyone knew that Tetley's fifteen-year-old daughter was blossoming into a very pretty woman.

"Everyone stay put, except for you, Anderson." The colonel and Anderson dismounted and strode up to the house. Mrs. Tetley appeared on the veranda.

Bragg dismounted and let the chestnut drink. They hadn't ridden hard coming back, so the horses were fairly fresh.

Rangers did not ride their mounts into the ground unless they had to. Horses were too important—to the ongoing war they waged and to survival.

"Still dreamin'." Pecos snorted.

Bragg smiled. He couldn't wait to pull Miranda into his arms and kiss those full, cherry-colored lips, run his hands through her hair—

"Captain Bragg!"

Bragg turned to see Anderson approaching swiftly. "Colonel wants to see you, Cap."

Bragg shrugged, handing Pecos his reins. "What's up?" he asked lightly, then grew dismayed. There had better not be another problem, because there was nothing that was going to keep him from seeing Miranda today. Nothing.

Anderson didn't respond, but his look was so dark that Bragg knew something was brewing. He cursed and hurried to the house. He knocked once, but Bent was there, looking very, very grim. "Come in, Bragg."

"What is it?"

Mrs. Tetley handed him a glass, and he saw that it was whiskey. His apprehension grew. "Colonel?"

"Derek, the JB's been burned to the ground."

Bragg stared, and slowly put the glass down. Shock numbed him only briefly. "Miranda?" It was a croak.

"Gone. They took her and that other woman. Killed the three hands and a fourth man. The old woman hid and survived."

Bragg was momentarily unable to breathe. *Not Miranda!* A red-hot rage flooded him. "How many men can you spare, sir?"

"I couldn't stop them from going with you if I wanted to," Bent said. "I just wish I could come with you. But I have to be in Galveston."

Bragg nodded. "How long ago?"

"Six days. And there were about twenty-five of them."

Two days after he'd ridden out, Bragg thought. He turned, striding out, his face a hard, tight mask. He reached the chestnut, swinging into the saddle. "We're riding out," he said clearly, but he knew that Anderson had already spilled the news, for everyone was wearing grim, deadly expressions.

They rode at a steady lope for the next two hours, and no one spoke. When they topped the final rise Bragg pulled up, to gaze down on nothing but stone hearths—all that was left of the ranch buildings. The twenty Rangers thundered down the slope, and it was only a moment before someone—Lincoln—called out. "Here! They've gone this way!"

As one, the prancing, stomping mass of horses and men wheeled and pounded after Lincoln, bits jangling, mounts snorting, saddles creaking.

Miranda had been captured by Comanche. The thought echoed again and again in his mind. Even now he couldn't think of it. He couldn't think of what was happening to her. Hang on, he pleaded silently. Just hang on. I'm coming.

Chapter 49

His touch on her shoulder awoke her.

Miranda started, instantly fully awake, aware that it was dark out, aware of drums and rattles and singing and laughter coming from outside the teepee. And aware of Chavez squatting beside her. She met his gaze.

He smiled, his teeth white against his coppery skin. The fire behind him illuminated him perfectly—and she gasped because he was naked. Naked and aroused. She quickly closed her eyes.

"Yes, *cara*," he murmured, slipping his hands over her shoulders, then up into her hair. His breath caught. Miranda lay very still, her heart pounding wildly. His hands moved down her back, then to her waist, and up to her breasts. He squeezed her gently, rubbing, lingering. His breathing was harsh.

He wrapped his arms around her and pulled her beneath him.

"No!" She began to twist, kicking, trying to buck him off. He laughed, shoving his knee between her thighs, forcing them open, her dress riding up. He kissed her savagely. She raked his back with her nails.

To her dismay, he groaned, trembling, shoving his hardness against her belly, excited by what she had done. Miranda didn't think. She clawed his face, breaking the skin by his jaw. Immediately, one of his hands captured

both her wrists and swung them over her head. She was
pinned helplessly beneath him.

He forced her mouth open and thrust in his tongue. She
bit down hard.

He cried out, jerking back, and struck her across the
face. The pain was brief; there was a faint explosion of
stars and then nothing.

The heaviness engulfing her was lightening, and she
was drifting up, out, but she didn't want to—she fought it.
Awareness with all its horror seized her. She opened her
eyes with a gasp.

He was kneeling between her thighs, breathing heavily,
staring at her. He lowered himself, shoving her dress up to
her waist.

"No, please." It was a pitiful whisper.

His arms went around her, pinning her own arms to her
sides, and he thrust in. She screamed—from pain as he
tore through her dry, tight flesh, and from humiliation. He
groaned. "Sorry, *cara,* so sorry . . ." and he cried out,
collapsing on top of her.

She began to cry, silently, tears streaming down her
face.

He moved away to sit beside her and stare down at her.
She averted her face. She could not stand to look at him.

"I'm sorry you are so determined to resist me," he
said. "I had no control then, for I have wanted you for too
long. Next time I will give you pleasure, I promise."

"Never," Miranda heard herself say. "I hate you, I
hate you . . ."

He was quiet for a while. She heard him moving about.
He returned to her side. "Here, drink this."

"No! Go away!"

"No, *cara,* the night is young, and it has just begun."

Miranda turned to face him. "You . . . you . . . dog!"

He smiled, held her head still, and forced some kind of
raw, burning liquor down her throat. She choked, swallowing most of it, although some dribbled down her face.
She slapped the jug away. He was amused and set it aside.
Then, before she could react, he pulled off her dress,
inhaling sharply. "So beautiful."

She tried to cover herself with her hands.

He chuckled. He reached for her, pried her hands off, and held her in an iron grip. "No," she moaned, but was helpless as he began to kiss her breast. She closed her eyes, a shudder of such revulsion shaking her that she felt like vomiting. The intensity of his mouth increased, and he released one of her arms and began to probe her womanhood.

She twisted, striking at him.

He caught her wrist, grinning, his eyes gleaming with lust. He shoved her down, pinning her, and began to tease her other nipple with his tongue. Miranda shrieked and kicked out. She knew it was hopeless, but it was all she could do—and she was so angry! She didn't realize, then, that her struggles excited him.

"*Cara*, God, I can't wait," he cried, his fingers probing into her, hurting her. "You're wet," he cried triumphantly, although Miranda had no idea what he meant. She was so sore, his touch burned. Then he thrust into her, and she screamed, this time in pure pain. Mercifully, she fainted.

When she came to, he was still there, but he was bathing her with a cloth. "Go away," she whispered, closing her eyes.

"You're bleeding," he said. "But I know you were no virgin. I hurt you. Dammit!" He threw the wet cloth down and got to his feet.

Miranda sat, feeling very, very dizzy, and reached for the cloth. It was bloody. She had bled with John. She wondered if something was wrong with her, if she was dying. She hoped so.

He came back to her. "Colchikehatta will bring you salve. I won't come to you for a few days, until you are healed. The next time, we will use grease to ease my way. I promise you, it won't hurt."

Miranda stared at her feet. Next time. God, please, help me. I do not deserve this.

He tilted her chin up. She was forced to look into his eyes. "Many women enjoy me. I do not understand why you fight me. Did you fight your husband too? Have you not learned passion?"

Miranda gritted her teeth and stared back defiantly. She refused to even talk to him. But when he left, she lay down, curled into a ball, and wept softly.

Chapter 50

Walking Tall Woman's attitude had changed after that first night in the village. She was no longer friendly; in fact, she was hostile. She brought some herbal ointment and indicated that Miranda was to apply it to her most intimate area. The next morning she half dragged her outside and set her to the task of grinding corn.

Miranda sat there outside the teepee, grinding the corn on the flat, oblong stone. It hurt her delicate hands. Walking Tall Woman was mending buckskin pants, not far from her. Other women sat in front of their teepees doing similar tasks. Children ran, playing. The few men who were about were taking care of their weapons—sharpening knives and spears, making arrows, and a few cleaning pistols. Miranda guessed most of the men were out hunting.

She paused to rest her hands. They were red and chapped, almost raw, and she had only been at it an hour or so. Before she even knew it, Walking Tall Woman was upon her, and she hit her so brutally across the face that Miranda fell onto her back.

"Lazy dog!" she shouted, and she kicked Miranda in the ribs.

Miranda cried out, gasping with pain.

Walking Tall Woman reached down and yanked her upright by the hair, hurting her again, and threw her toward her task. Miranda landed on all fours, gulping, her face

240

numb, her rib and hip throbbing. "Finish, dog!" Walking Tall Woman shouted. Miranda sat back and picked up the stone she was using to grind with, tears blinding her. What had she done to be treated like this?

She ground the corn methodically. She remembered that day at the pond, when Bragg had been so cruel, screaming at her for wandering alone. He had been afraid she would be captured by Comanche. ". . . wives are treated like dogs . . . and a second wife doesn't even have the status of first wife to protect her . . . the first wife beats her from jealousy . . ." Was Walking Tall Woman jealous? Because of last night? But she had been so kind yesterday afternoon. Miranda didn't understand.

Her hand started to bleed by the afternoon. Walking Tall Woman gave her the task of scraping hides. When she saw that Miranda was bleeding on the hides, she kicked her viciously, in the thigh. Miranda fell back, not able to move, not caring.

"Bitch!" Chavez roared.

Miranda struggled upright as Walking Tall Woman cried out in pain. She stared as Chavez struck her again and again, shouting in the Comanche language. He threw her to the ground. Then he left her and hurried to Miranda's side.

Miranda shrank away.

"God, what has she done?" he said, his face grim. "Your hands! Come, *cara,* stand. Here, let me help you. She will never touch you again. She has defied me, the jealous bitch."

Miranda let him help her to her feet, too battered and tired to care. He put an arm around her and led her into the teepee. He pushed her onto the hides, then cleaned her hands with a wet cloth. He let her apply the salve herself. He touched her hair.

She swallowed and looked at him, so afraid he was going to rape her again.

"I will not hurt you," he said seriously.

"You have already hurt me," Miranda said harshly, then was shocked at her bravery, her audacity.

"I did not mean to, *cara.* The second time, I did not

know you were bleeding. I thought you were ready for me.''

Miranda had no idea what he was talking about.

He suddenly smiled. ''You are still an innocent. That pleases me.''

She looked away. Please rescue me, Derek, she thought. Please come. Please.

He caught her face. She gasped, just as he lowered his mouth to hers, kissing her at first gently, then with growing insistence, until his mouth was savage and hard on hers. He released her, standing. ''You devastate me, *poquita.*'' Then he left.

I don't want to devastate you, I want to kill you, she thought, lying back on the hides. She touched her rib and found she was sore. She moaned. How long did she have until he came to her again?

Chapter 51

"Damn," Pecos said softly but succinctly.

Bragg didn't respond. As usual these past few days, his face was a hard, closed mask. Like Pecos, he was on foot, peering down into the valley and making a rough count of the teepees they saw. "Close to one-twenty, I'd say," Bragg muttered.

"More like one-forty," Pecos said. "How we gonna do this, Cap?"

"Miranda's down there," Bragg said, totally calm, almost detached.

Pecos nodded; he understood. A typical Ranger assault could endanger her—or kill her accidentally.

"You take the north end, I'll take the south. I want to know where she's being kept, how many other captives there are, and roughly where they are. Should be easy. Half the men look to be out hunting." Bragg turned and motioned. Anderson slipped off his horse, where he stood some twenty yards away with the rest of the Rangers. He came forward quickly. "Captain?"

"You're in charge. If we're not back in an hour and a half, we've run into problems. Launch an attack."

Anderson nodded.

Bragg nodded to Pecos, and the two men veered off in opposite directions into the heavily forested slopes. Bragg ran silently, easily, his knife in his hand. Not more than

five minutes later he had reached the bottom of the slope,
and keeping to the edge of the trees, he made a line for the
closest teepees.

He covered the perimeter of the camp easily enough,
merely by keeping out of sight. He didn't pray for luck,
but he suddenly had it. He saw Miranda instantly. She was
kneeling and sewing leggings, dressed like a squaw. His
heart went crazy.

She was all right!

It was his first coherent thought, and he reined in his
emotions, which threatened to explode or, worse, make
him do something foolish. He squatted behind chapparal
and studied her.

The teepee she obviously belonged to was two from the
outermost one—which was very lucky. He knew now
they'd attack Ranger-style, with an encircling but frontal
assault. He'd edge right up to her and abduct her before
the first shots were fired. There weren't very many men in
camp—maybe fifty warriors—when the village probably
boasted twice that number. He smiled grimly.

Miranda looked up directly at him.

Of course she couldn't see him, but his heart stopped,
and he wanted to cry out to her. Silently, in his mind, he
reassured her. She was so small, so fragile. Her arms and
face were no longer white, but a delicate peach hue. Thank
God she was alive! He got up and moved on, with determination, to complete the assignment he had given himself.

Forty minutes later he was back with the Rangers, who
all wanted to know what he had found out. They waited in
silence. "Is Pecos back?"

"No," Lincoln volunteered.

"As soon as he gets back we go in," Bragg said, the
Rangers crowding around. He gave his orders succinctly,
evenly. "There are fifty warriors to contend with. It's
possible, but not likely at this time of day, that the rest
may return in the midst of the battle."

"We can handle it." A wiry, lean Ranger grinned.
Luke Hollis was anticipating the fight with relish.

"I'm taking my wife out of the action." Bragg looked
up as Pecos materialized and repeated what he'd said.
Then, "How many?"

"Probably fifty warriors and about a dozen captives."

"I made four, including Miranda. The squaws who fight, kill. All other women and children are to remain untouched."

Bragg emphasized this last statement. It was not policy to kill squaws and their children, but sometimes it happened in self-defense. Then gender had nothing to do with it—an enraged Comanche squaw could be as deadly as a brave.

"Mount up," he said quietly.

Almost as one, the Rangers obeyed.

The villagers never knew what hit them. One minute it was peaceful, the morning silence broken only by the soft sound of chatter and the playful cries of children, and the next, Colts were blasting, men were falling, women were screaming, children were crying. The Rangers rode in like a hurricane, ignoring the squaws and the children, hunting down the braves like wild prey. Taken by surprise, few managed to do more than throw knives. In minutes it was over.

Bragg had ridden at a gallop for Miranda straight through the sea of teepees as soon as the assault was launched. Everywhere around him guns were blasting and smoking, and cries of terror and agony rose up. "Miranda!"

She was standing frozen next to the teepee.

"Miranda," he shouted, and she heard him.

Her face lit up. He reached her and swung her into the saddle at a dead run. Dragging his horse's head around, he turned to go back into the safety of the woods. His first concern was for Miranda's safety, he wanted her out of the danger, but with his practiced eye, he could see that the battle was almost over. The horse lunged back the way he had come, then screamed, the wild, eerie sound of a horse in pain.

Bragg knew his horse was hit even before the awesome shriek, and he was leaping from the saddle with Miranda in his arms as the great beast went down. They rolled into the dirt, unhurt. "Are you all right?" he said, looking into her eyes, his face inches from hers.

"Oh, Derek!" She clung to him.

Now was not the time, and he stood, pulling her up, as the melee around them quieted. He felt danger instantly, and shoved Miranda behind him. He saw Chavez and drew.

But Chavez's gun was already drawn. Bragg was fast enough that Chavez's shot only grazed his neck, although blood poured from the little wound. His own shot missed completely, and Chavez ran and dove behind a teepee. Bragg didn't hesitate. He tore after him.

He paused by the teepee, listening, but there were so many sounds around him—moans and sobs, horses stomping, jangling bits and creaking leather. He tried to block the noise out, straining to hear. He poked his head around the teepee, pulling back as Chavez fired.

Three shots left, Bragg was thinking. Chavez had a five-shooter, and he smiled with anticipation. Bragg darted forward, blasting with his Colt. Chavez was running for the trees. He hit him in the thigh, and Chavez went down.

Bragg ran hard across the open space. Chavez rolled, metal glinting. Bragg dove to the ground. The shot missed widely. Bragg rose, firing purposefully. He was close enough that he would never miss. He hit Chavez's gun, and it went spinning out of his hand. Bragg stood slowly, unbuckling his gunbelt and throwing it aside. "Get up, Chavez! Get up!"

Two Rangers came up, Colts in hand. "Cap?"

"No one interferes," Bragg said, never looking at them, his eyes only on Chavez, who was getting to his feet. He strode forward, only to stop some ten feet away. His smile was cold and ruthless. "If you can kill me, you might just live."

"You have the advantage, *amigo*," Chavez said easily. "I am hit, remember?"

Bragg smiled again, took out his knife, and before anyone could move, sliced into the back of his thigh—exactly where he had hit Chavez.

Miranda screamed.

Chavez smiled.

Bragg frowned. "Pecos," he said, not looking at anyone other than Chavez, "get her away from here."

He heard Pecos ride away, heard Miranda protesting, sobbing, screaming his name again and again.

Chavez moved, taking advantage of the distraction. His

knife appeared in his hand. Bragg leaped back, but not before a line of blood appeared on his chest through the buckskin shirt. They circled each other warily.

Bragg lunged. Chavez jumped back, but Bragg kept coming, and he slashed, opening a wide gash on the Comanchero's forearm.

The fight became a dance of movement, back and forth, blades flashing, just barely missing skin. Both men, although wounded, were agile, expert. Both men used their knives like the Indians whose blood they'd inherited. Soon both were drenched with sweat and breathing heavily, yet the intricate dance never stopped.

And then Chavez lunged. Bragg let him come, then blocked the knife-wielding arm with his own forearm, stepping around Chavez with one leg, locking him into place. He sank his blade into him. Chavez screamed and crumbled.

"He's a goner," Lincoln said conversationally. "It'll be hours before he dies, though."

"Give me your canteen," Bragg said, breathing heavily now, sweat pouring off his face. Lincoln complied. Bragg dumped the water on Chavez's face. The man came to, coughing.

"I want you conscious, *amigo,* while you die slowly." Bragg turned, then scowled. "What's she doing here?"

"She wouldn't leave," Pecos said.

Miranda was white and still, her eyes huge in her face, which was thinner—haggard. He strode to her with a definite limp and clasped her by her shoulders. "Did he rape you?"

She gasped.

"Did he, dammit?"

"Yes." It was a barely audible whisper.

He handed her to Pecos. "If you have to carry her, get her away. I don't want her to see this."

Pecos understood, and he lifted Miranda in his arms and strode toward the village. Bragg watched, waiting until they were too far away for her to be able to see. Limping heavily now, he made his way back to Chavez and stared down at him. The man stared back, refusing to beg.

Chavez's eyes widened with astonished fear as Bragg

slipped his knife out and held it, the sunlight dancing on the blade.

"I am dying," Chavez said.

"Yes, I realize that." Bragg bent casually and slit the man's trousers at the crotch.

"No!" Chavez cried.

Bragg grabbed him.

Chavez's scream was bloodcurdling.

Chapter 52

Pecos wouldn't let her turn around, and when Miranda heard the scream every hair on her body stiffened. What had Bragg done? She was still stunned by the rapidity of events, by how suddenly the village had been attacked, by Bragg's appearance and the fight with Chavez. Dear God, how she needed Derek now.

"Miranda?"

She whirled at the sound of his voice and ran blindly into his arms. "Derek!"

He held her tightly. His body was warm and hard. She felt so utterly safe. He smelled like sweat and horse and man, and she snuggled closer, his arms tightening around her, thinking she had never been more relieved in her life. She felt his hands in her hair, and then his lips pressing on the top of her head.

"Thank God," Bragg said heavily.

Miranda suddenly remembered his condition and pulled as far away as he would let her, which was only an inch or so. "Derek, you're hurt!"

"It's nothing," he said, gazing at her with sad, infinitely tender eyes.

But he was limping and bleeding, and it frightened her. "Let me care for you."

"We don't have time. Linc, fetch me a good horse, and my gear. How are we doing?"

"Just about ready to move out, Cap."

Bragg looked at Miranda. "You can bind up this wound on the back of my thigh, then we're riding out."

"There are more of them," she said anxiously.

"I know," he said.

"How could you, Derek?" she cried, examining the gash in the back of his leg.

He didn't answer.

She bound it quickly with buckskin. "This isn't good enough at all."

"My knife was clean. As soon as we stop, you can clean it and bind it properly." He smiled. "I know how much of a stickler you are for propriety," he said.

Miranda smiled, too. Her heart seemed to take on wings.

They rode all day until dusk. She sat on Bragg's new mount, a rangy bay. Two men scouted ahead, two rode behind. About eighteen women and children were with them, but Bragg didn't let that slow them down. Anyone who couldn't ride well enough to keep up rode double with a Ranger. Fortunately, only the elderly woman could not ride. They made a fireless camp as dark descended.

"I'm cleaning you up," Miranda said disapprovingly because Bragg had disappeared to give orders for four-man sentry shifts the minute they had stopped. "And let someone else unsaddle your horse."

"Yes, ma'am." He saluted, grinning, as if he were pleased to be ordered around.

"Follow me to the stream. Can you make it?"

"Certainly. You are a bossy wife, aren't you?"

For some reason, his tone of voice made her feel wonderful. She ordered him to sit and remove the blood-soaked bandage, then deftly sliced off the leg of his pants.

"Now why did you do that?" he complained.

"I'll repair it," she told him. "Turn over and lie still, Derek."

He obeyed.

The wound was quite clean and not deep. However it hadn't clotted yet, and she frowned, wishing he didn't have to be mobile and on horseback. She cleansed it with water, then whiskey, and Bragg didn't even flinch. She realized she was terribly proud of him. He was so brave, so utterly fearless, so strong. I'm going to try to learn from him, she thought as she bandaged the wound with linen strips taken from Lakely, who had handed her the material without a word.

"You'll be as good as new in no time," she said.

Derek gingerly turned over and sat up, keeping his bad leg bent at the knee and off the ground. He pulled off his shirt. "Aren't you going to clean up the rest of me?" he asked innocently.

His chest glistened, all hard, sinewy muscle. For a moment, Miranda couldn't respond, and then he chuckled. "Come here, I can't wait."

Before she even knew it, he had pulled her closer with one strong arm and was kissing her, tenderly but with rigid, restrained passion. She stiffened and closed her eyes, but didn't pull away. He wouldn't, she was thinking. He just wouldn't.

He released her and stared at her. He was no longer smiling. She was too familiar with that look of lust—she had learned what it meant from Chavez. Her mouth trembled. She didn't move. She felt concerned and trapped, afraid again.

His hand went to her hair, to tendrils that had escaped the one long braid she wore. "I want to make love to you," he said huskily. "I want to wipe out Chavez's print. I want to claim you for myself. I want you . . . so bad."

Miranda stood slowly. She tried to find the words she needed. All that came out was, "Please don't."

She saw the disappointment, and something like pain or grief, flood into his eyes. Then he lowered his gaze, a somewhat bitter smile crossing his features. "I can clean myself up now," he said evenly, and rose stiffly to his feet.

"Don't be silly," she said, breathless. "Please, let me take care of you." Her voice broke. She was suddenly shocked when tears started pouring from her eyes. She turned away.

"Hey," he said, startled, and wrapped his arms around her, pressing his chest against her back. "It's all right," he soothed.

She sobbed harder.

"Miranda, I'm sorry," he said, agonized. He kissed the top of her head, then tucked it under his chin. "Shhh, shhh, darling, don't cry."

"I'm sorry," she cried.

"I understand," he murmured. "I understand. I'll never hurt you, never." He rocked her from side to side in the cradle of his body.

Chapter 53

Bragg thought he did understand. She had been raped. Brutally, probably many times. He wanted to know all the details, for some damn reason. He wanted to share what had happened with her, but he refrained from asking. She was so gaunt and fatigued right now, and he wanted to protect and shelter her. He wanted to take away her grief and shame. The urge to make love to her was overwhelming. He felt that if he could take her in his arms, he could stroke and kiss away everything that had happened. He felt that once he buried himself deep inside her, he could remove Chavez's mark, his memory. He could claim her, truly, as his own.

But Miranda had always been afraid of sex, and now she was probably even more afraid. He loved her. He would never hurt her—he had meant that when he said it. He wouldn't ever force himself on her. He wanted her to want him, too. He would wait. He would comfort and care for her, cherish her, and they would start their lives anew, from this day forward. After all, making love was only one part of a relationship, and in this case it would be the bonus, he rationalized. Then he heard himself and laughed aloud. He sounded like some romantic fool. Certainly not like the crude rake, Derek Bragg, who had been taking women with the slightest provocation since he was sixteen.

The camp was quiet and everyone asleep, exhausted, especially the captives, who were a sorely abused, gaunt lot. Bragg approached his bedroll silently, and a soft smile crossed his features when he saw Miranda curled up there, on her side. He dropped down beside her.

She immediately turned over and sat up, facing him.

"Waiting for me?" he teased softly.

He wasn't sure, but he had the feeling she blushed. "Yes."

He raised a brow, absurdly pleased. "We both need to get a good night's sleep," he said, trying to be straight-faced. "But . . ."

"Oh, Derek, I meant . . . what I mean . . ."

He chuckled, sitting beside her. Putting his arm around her, he pulled her close. "I know what you meant, princess."

Miranda looked at him, her face inches from his. "Are you sleeping here, too?"

"Yes," he said. "Isn't this my bedroll?"

"But . . ." She swallowed nervously.

Bragg smiled and slid onto his side, pulling her down into the curve of his body. "Don't tell me you'd be more comfortable sleeping alone?" He hugged her gently.

She sighed. "No."

He pulled up the blanket and tried not to feel so much—so flooded with tenderness and caring that it made his eyes ridiculously moist. Worse, he tried not to feel the warm softness of her body, her little derriere firmly nestled against his belly, her silken hair teasing his chest and face.

"Derek?"

"Um?"

"What happens after San Antonio? After we drop off Bianca and the other captives?"

He hesitated. "How would it sound, Miranda, if it was just you and me? I want to take you up to the Pecos, into the country I was raised in. It's peaceful. You'll have time to . . . heal, and I'll never let you out of my sight." He kissed the back of her head.

"To your ranch?"

"There's nothing there, princess, just water and trees and meadows. But yes, I did mean that area."

"That sounds . . . fine."

"Do you mean it?" He felt tense asking the question. He wanted to take her there so badly, and his arms tightened a bit around her.

"Yes."

"I'm glad," he said quickly. "Now why don't we both get some sleep? I have last watch."

To his surprise, he fell asleep after only an hour or so, and his dreams were full of the woman he held in his arms.

Chapter 54

Miranda felt as if everyone was watching as they rode into San Antonio, and everyone was.

Of course, she realized it would be impossible for twenty Rangers and almost as many freed captives not to attract the notice of everyone on the streets and in the shops. People lined the boardwalks, and soon there was cheering and hollering. A man ran alongside them, asking for details, but the Rangers just grinned and answered cryptically. Bragg said nothing, but his hold on her was warm and reassuring.

He took a room at the hotel and went upstairs with her. "I have to make my report, princess, but on my way back I'll bring you some clothes. Tomorrow we'll go shopping together for everything we need." He flashed her a warm smile. His golden eyes were so tender these days. She knew he felt sorry for her, and it made her feel sorry for herself.

"Take your time," she said, and she looked longingly at the bed. Sweet Jesus! How long had it been? The endless riding, the week in captivity . . . no! She was not going to think about that.

"I'll have a bath sent up. I'll see if I can't talk one of the girls into lending you a wrapper."

Miranda smiled at him gratefully. When he left, she wondered what had happened to the gruff, crude, hard man she had met in Natchez. Then she knew she was fooling herself. She remembered how he had gone after Chavez. She still didn't know what he had done after Pecos had led her away, but she was sure it had been awful, and she didn't want to know. She climbed onto the bed and lay thinking about her husband.

She also marveled at herself. Who would have thought that the daughter of an earl would become what she was right now? Clad in buckskins, just freed from Indians, married to a half-breed Ranger—good God! And Bragg had told her the kind of life they were headed for. They would live in a wickiup, like his people, the Mescalero. They would hunt and harvest their own food, make their own clothes. It would be a very primitive existence. He didn't say it was forever. They didn't discuss the future.

For some reason, he wanted to take her up to his valley, as he called it, and live there for a while. She truly didn't mind. The JB was gutted. It was hers, and now Bragg's, because he was her husband, but she didn't want to go back there. Maybe later, in the future. She didn't want Bragg to leave her alone. He was resigning from the Rangers, and she was glad. She knew it was selfish, but she didn't care. She understood now how much a woman in this land needed a man to protect her. She never, ever, wanted to have to live again through a horror like that week as Chavez's prisoner.

Miranda had no tears left. She rolled onto her side and shut her eyes, but the memories were strong, vivid. They refused to leave. They haunted the back of her mind constantly and gave her nightmares. But there was always Bragg to turn to, to hold her, to say soft, sweet words and chase the awful dreams away. She had gotten used to sleeping with him, and she didn't think she'd ever want to sleep alone again.

Her bath came, and with it a servant bearing a flimsy wrapper of white wool trimmed with pink ribbons. She ordered a huge meal from the woman, thinking that if Derek came back he would be hungry. Then she soaked for a long time in the tub. After she had washed and dried off, she threw the robe over her bare skin. It wasn't sheer, but it seemed to mold itself to her lithe contours. Miranda didn't notice. It felt so good to be out of buckskins—at least out of those particular buckskins.

She was eating heartily when Bragg returned, tossing some packages onto the bed. "Eating without me?" he asked coming up to her and plopping a kiss on her mouth before she could blink. She was surprised—he hadn't kissed her since that time at the stream, days ago. And . . . she was pleased.

"There's enough for two," she managed, her body tingling deliciously for a moment.

"I can see that." He grinned, then sat down opposite her and stared.

"How did it go?" She began to serve him since he was just sitting there.

"Miranda," he began, then he looked uncertain.

She gazed at him calmly. "What's wrong? Oh! Another assignment?" She tried not to show her intense disappointment.

"No, nothing like that. Damn!" He dug into his pocket and produced a small padded box.

"What's that?" she asked, feeling foolish.

"It's not much," he said, grimacing. "I'm not a rich man, not like John. In fact, except for my land, I'm downright poor. But . . . here."

Miranda took the box and stared at him. "Derek, you are rich. You own all of John's properties now."

He waved at her. "They're yours. Are you going to open it?"

She suddenly smiled. They would discuss that issue later. She opened the box. Inside was an amethyst pendant shaped like a heart, hanging from a delicate gold chain. "It's beautiful!" she said, meaning it. She was truly touched.

"It's the exact color of your eyes," he said, watching her.

"Would you?" she asked, smiling, standing. She stepped over to him, lifting her hair and turning her back.

He sucked in his breath. He couldn't help it. He wanted her as he'd never wanted any other woman, and here she was, clad in such a lightweight, clinging robe, and it dawned on him that she had nothing on beneath it. Instead of looking at the nape of her neck, he found himself staring at her firm little behind, and his hands, of their own volition, settled on her hips. She gasped.

He hated the way she stiffened defensively. He quickly fastened the chain around her neck. He owed the jeweler just about every skin he could trap this winter, but he didn't care. He hated trapping, but he would do it. He wished he could have gotten her diamonds and rubies.

She turned to face him, smiling. "Thank you, again. I love it."

He wanted to tell her he loved her, but he had never said those words before, and he knew she didn't love him back. He just couldn't tell her, not yet. "Thank me with a kiss," he said instead.

She looked surprised.

"My kisses aren't so bad. In fact, I've never met a woman who didn't like them. Even you."

She colored faintly. "Derek, I . . ."

"I only want a kiss," he said gently, slipping his arms around her. "I know you need time, and I'm giving it to you. But kisses don't hurt. If you relax, I'll bet you like it."

Tears moistened her eyes. "You've been so kind."

"Not too bad for a savage barbarian, huh?" He smiled. The corners of his eyes crinkled.

She put her hands around his neck. "I take that back."

"You can't," he murmured, and lowered his face.

She met his lips lightly, their mouths just barely brushing. It was so hard not to tighten his hold, not to deepen the kiss, not to throw her onto the bed and take her. But he didn't. He hated her fear. He wanted her love. He flicked out his tongue to taste her lower lip, and she trembled. He hoped it was from pleasure. He was hard with agony. He pulled away with difficulty.

There was a knock on the door, and he was relieved or disappointed—he didn't know which. He admitted the boy who had brought fresh water. Miranda stepped modestly behind the table as the boy emptied the cold water, tossing it out the window, and refilled the tub. Bragg handed him a penny and began to strip. He reflected ruefully that hot water was not going to help his condition.

Realizing that she was watching him, he smiled. She

caught his eye and blushed, but stopped him. "What are you doing?"

He was amused. "What does it look like?"

"I don't want that wound wet."

"Oh ho. Back to being bossy, are we? I'm filthy. It's healed up enough."

"Derek, no." She put her hands on her hips and stared at him.

He laughed, delighted with her wifely demeanor. "Fine. Then you'll bathe me."

This time her color was really high. "You can bathe yourself," she said.

"Miranda, if I have to bathe myself, I'm climbing in that tub." He meant it. He had really wanted a bath, too, until this moment. He didn't care that a sponge bath from Miranda would be torture. He wanted to feel her hands all over his body.

"Let me see the wound," she said, a touch stiffly.

He began to pull his pants down. She inhaled sharply, but he didn't care. Women had always exclaimed and marveled over his physique and his manhood, which he knew was large. He wanted to impress her. He would certainly impress her now, when he was huge with need for her. He wondered if he would excite her. He stepped out of his pants and grinned.

She stared briefly before averting her gaze and pushing him around. He looked over his shoulder and saw that she was staring at his buttocks, not his thigh. He tried not to laugh. He was throbbing. "Well?"

"I just don't think you should take a bath," she said, flustered.

"Shall I sit or lie down?"

"Derek, I don't want to bathe you."

"Dammit," he burst out.

"All right," she said, glaring. "Fine. But wrap this around your waist, please."

He took the towel but turned to give her another view as he casually complied. Of course she had her back to him and was wetting the sponge. He sighed, straddled the chair, then closed his eyes as she washed his back.

Her touch was pure heaven, especially as he felt her

anger recede, replaced by a tense, trembling hand. Was it fear? Disgust? He didn't think so. He thought it was desire, even if she didn't know it.

"Turn around."

He obeyed. He watched her wash his arms, his shoulders, his chest. he was having trouble breathing evenly, and having even more trouble not grabbing and kissing her. "That's enough," he finally said gruffly.

She looked surprised. "What about your legs?"

He was afraid he'd embarrass both of them if she continued. "I'll do it myself." He took the sponge and turned away from her. He debated finding a whore for the night. It had been so long. Then he glanced at her, picking up a wet towel from the floor, and his heart twisted.

I will court her, he thought, and I will wait.

Chapter 55

"Why are you looking like that?" Bragg asked.

Miranda smiled, still studying the pyramid-shaped structure. "I just never imagined there would come a day when my husband would build us a wickiup to live in."

Bragg laughed. "To be honest, princess, I never thought I'd see the day when I'd build my wife one. You see, this is women's work."

"Impossible," she gasped. The wickiup was twelve feet high, and about eight feet in diameter. It consisted of eight very stout poles of juniper, stuck in holes in the ground and attached at the top. The sides were woven with brush. Miranda didn't see how any woman could possibly build such a structure.

Bragg grabbed her and planted a firm, quick kiss on her mouth, taking her by surprise. Just as quickly, he released her. "But no squaw is as small and thin as you." He grew serious. "I'll spend the afternoon hunting, and we'll have this covered with hides in no time."

Miranda looked at him. He seemed to be lost in thought now. His kisses took her by surprise. She had never even guessed that he was an affectionate man. Yet he seemed hard-pressed to go for long without touching her abstractedly, patting her shoulder, squeezing her hand, or fingering her hair. What a contradiction he was.

"Follow me," Bragg said.

They walked over to their packs and supplies, unloaded from their pack horse and covered by a tarp. Bragg rummaged through, found what he was looking for, and tossed Miranda a few leather pouches. "What's this?" she asked, curious.

"Look and see," he said, squatting by their supplies and grinning.

Miranda opened up one of the small pouches and gasped. It was full of seeds. "Derek—we'll have a garden."

"You bet," he said. "And we should get it planted as soon as we can."

Miranda looked around. The site Derek had chosen was a brief distance from a broad, sparkling creek. A small meadow filled with April's first blooms was bordered by forest. He had built the wickiup in a cluster of oak and juniper, where it blended naturally and unobtrusively into the landscape. "Over there," she said, pointing. "How will we clear it?"

"Easy. First thing tomorrow I'll burn a section, then plow it for you. We'll be planted by tomorrow night."

Miranda gave him a smile.

"Before I go hunting, princess, I want to give you a lesson in shooting." He beckoned. Miranda walked over, and he put a light hand on her shoulder and led her away from the wickiup. He left her to set up a target, a log standing upright on the ground. He paced back to her, took the Colt out of his holster, and emptied it of bullets. "Watch carefully."

He showed her how to load, then unloaded it again and had her do it. It was simple. "Good." He smiled. "Now, just stand nice and relaxed, sight the target, aim, and squeeze." He handed her the gun.

Miranda felt nervous. She had never held a gun before, much less fired one. She swallowed, pointed the gun at the target, sighted it, and fired. The recoil wasn't too bad. "How did I do?"

Derek looked at her. "Well, you only missed by a mile. Did you aim?"

"I most certainly did!"

He stood behind her, holding his hand on top of hers. "Aim carefully," he said, his voice in her ear.

His breath tickled her neck. His body was warm. Where his knees were bent, they touched the backs of her thighs. His chest was against her back. She was very aware of him, and it was distracting.

"Miranda?"

She sighted and fired. The slight kickback pushed her into his warm hardness. "Did I hit it?" she asked hopefully.

"Not quite," he drawled. "How's your eyesight, anyway?"

"That bad?"

"No, not too bad," he lied. "Again. Come on, we're wasting time."

Miranda tried to ignore the intimacy of how they were standing. This time, as she aimed, he put one hand around her waist, the other on her hand holding the Colt, and he told her to wait. He leaned into her, his face on a level with hers, trying to see how she was sighting the target.

"Jesus, Miranda! You're off by ten yards."

"To the right or left?"

"Left."

She adjusted her aim.

"Too much, sweetheart. Just a tiny fraction. There you go. Now, don't shake when you fire . . ."

She fired and missed. "I'm sorry," she cried.

"It's all right." he said, straightening behind her. But he didn't move away.

"I don't think I'm going to be much of a markswoman."

"Yes you are," he told her. "You're going to practice every afternoon for an hour. Try it again."

He stood there with her for what seemed hours, but she never once hit the target. Finally, he told her they'd done enough for the day. She stole a glance at him. He looked a bit displeased. He had been incredibly patient. And she wanted to please him. She felt miserable at being such a poor student. She was downcast.

"Don't worry," he told her as they strolled back to the wickiup. He put his arm around her shoulders, squeezing. "You'll be the best shot in west Texas by the time I get through with you."

"I doubt it."

He gave her a look. "Why don't you start up some bread?" He paused. "Do you know how to make bread?"

"Of course," she said indignantly. "I watched Elena."

Bragg smiled. This should be interesting. "What a tenderfoot I have for a wife!"

"How do we bake it?"

"Easy," he said cheerfully, picking up a rifle. "In the fire. You work on that dough. I'll be back in a bit."

Miranda watched him stride off into the woods, on foot, with a kind of animal grace. She smiled. They had spent so much time together in the last few days. She already missed him.

Chapter 56

Derek was gone, and she wondered where he was so early in the morning. She bathed in the creek, which was quite cold, then slipped on her plain cotton skirt and blouse. She made coffee and breakfast for him—she was never hungry in the morning. While she was making the batter for the pancakes, she began to hum. It was truly a glorious morning.

It was slightly cool, but that was because it was so early. The sky was almost a royal blue, without a single cloud. Birds chirped melodiously, sing-songing back and forth in the trees overhead. A wonderful aroma drifted around them, the scent of coffee, tanned hides, something sweet and floral—maybe all the columbine that had blossomed over the past week in the meadow, their riotous purple mingling with the yellow and blue of daisies. She was surprised to discover she was quite content.

Where had Derek gone so early in the morning?

Miranda was learning more every day. She had become a pioneer woman—or a squaw. Just the day before, Derek had spent the afternoon helping her make soap. They had brought soap with them, but their supply would run out eventually. The wickiup—which, Derek had told her, was called *gohwah* by the Apache—was completely covered with hides.

The door was made of a blanket swinging on a frame of

wood. It was really almost like a hut, she thought. She had even learned to make a decent loaf of bread. Her first effort had been a lumpy disaster. Of course, Derek had been kind and tactful, but she could see the laughter in his eyes.

Last night was the first night she had slept the night through without waking up from a nightmare about Chavez. Today was truly the first day she felt completely rested. She felt wonderful.

She couldn't help thinking about how it felt each night to have Derek crawl into their bed of blankets and hides with her. He would immediately pull her into the curve of his body, where his pulsing warmth distracted and confused her greatly. If it weren't for the fact that she was so utterly exhausted by evening after the day's travails and her nightmares, she was sure she would be up most of the night.

Derek didn't look like he was sleeping too well. Although his vigor seemed indefatigable, there were faint shadows beneath his eyes. She wondered what was keeping him up at night, and hoped it wasn't her and her awful dreams.

"Daydreaming so early?"

She leaped up, gasping.

He chuckled, his tone teasing, and squatted beside her, pulling her against him and kissing her full on the mouth. She leaned against him. He stiffened in surprise, then kissed her again, his mouth stroking hers with more intimacy this time, and she felt the tip of his tongue on her lower lip, circling it delicately, before slipping up to prod gently where her lips joined. A warm, liquid fire raced over her, completely pleasurable. She parted her mouth just a hair. His tongue probed the flat, porcelain surfaces of her teeth, and then he was gone. Disappointed, she opened her eyes.

Miranda gasped. He was standing staring down at her, and he was clad in his knee-high moccasins and a buckskin loincloth. It came almost to his knees, but it revealed the long, hard length of his legs on the outermost edges. His torso was bare. He wore only his knife, but he had been carrying the rifle. The sheer maleness of him mesmerized her. "What are you wearing?" she managed.

He looked away from her, but not before she saw the heat of his gaze, the unnatural brightness. Something plummeted fiercely deep inside her, achingly sweet. He stopped and poured himself coffee, sipping for a moment before he answered. "My clothes are dirty."

"Oh," she cried, flustered and ashamed. Color rose in her face. "Derek, I'm sorry."

"It's all right."

"No, I'll launder your clothes immediately."

"What's for breakfast?" he asked.

"Pancakes." She began methodically to make his breakfast. What was wrong with her? Had she expected a maid to materialize out of the sky to do their laundry? She stole another glance at him through her lashes. He was sitting on a boulder, graceful, so naked, so powerful. So male. He was staring at her.

"Make enough for two," he said.

"But I'm not hungry."

"You're wasting away, and I don't like it." His tone was sharp, the old Bragg, the one who gave orders and expected them to be obeyed. "I want you to put on some weight, Miranda." His tone softened. "I don't want you to get sick."

She thought about his wife, who had starved herself to death. "Yes, all right."

He smiled. "You slept well last night."

She handed him a tin plate and took one herself. "Yes."

He studied her with that penetrating gaze, one she was used to. Then he began to eat with relish, and she did, too, forcing herself to eat every bit. He wasn't asking much of her, truly. He was so kind, so patient. And it was true that she was thin. Her skirt was loose by an inch at the waist, and when she had bought it, it had fit perfectly. She wanted to please him. He had always thought her skinny. What would he think now?

She washed all their clothes that morning, including her buckskin dress. She mended his pants, the ones she had cut to tend his leg, and mended a few other holes she found. At least she could sew, and do it very well. It was something she could be proud of.

But he teased her. "Such fancy stitchwork." He laughed.

Miranda blushed. "It's the only way I know how to sew."

He was instantly contrite. "I'm sorry."

"I'm not a very good wife." She spoke aloud before she knew it.

He came over to her immediately, kneeling next to her, forcing her to look at him. "You're a wonderful wife."

"I'm an awful cook. I don't know how to do laundry. I can't clean game. My sewing is too fancy. I'm the worst shot, and I can't ride. Everything you need in a Texas wife, I'm not." She felt ridiculous tears welling up, and she tried to stifle them.

He cupped her face, his golden eyes tender and concerned. "Don't be silly. I wouldn't trade you in for anything. You're an English lady, and I've thrown you into a completely alien environment. You're doing wonderfully."

Miranda searched his face for the truth. "I just want to please you," she whispered. "I've been nothing but trouble . . ."

"No," he said firmly, adamantly. His mouth found hers. The kiss was soft but searing. She opened her mouth immediately, and he thrust his tongue within, exploring the inner recesses completely. Her heart began to thud, and his warmth assailed her. He still held her face. His tongue entwined with hers. She touched his tongue with hers, timidly. He shuddered.

"Miranda, please me," he said huskily, kissing the corner of her mouth.

She was floating. His mouth was becoming harder, more forceful. He pulled at her lower lip with his teeth, then instantly became tender, soft. He groaned against her lips. He pulled her against his body, knee to chest. "Let me love you," he rasped. "Miranda, please."

He cupped her buttocks and pulled her against his male hardness. The contact immediately ruined the euphoria of their heated embrace. She had a flash of Chavez hurting her as he raped her. She cried out in protest, pushing feebly against his chest. For a moment, a long moment, he held her hard against him, pulsating against her belly, his mouth taking hers with a savagery that was too heated, too brutal, too reminiscent. He released her suddenly and she scrambled to her feet.

He stood slowly, breathing deeply and unevenly. His eyes were burning embers. She felt so guilty, so afraid, and so needy all at once. Unable to sort through her jumbled emotions, she cried out inarticulately and fled into the wickiup. Her confusion turned into tears, and she wept silently, not just for herself but also for him.

Chapter 57

That night he slept under the stars.

He was at the limit of his self-control, and he knew it. The pleasure of lying with her, having her in his arms, so soft and fragrant, was outstripped by the agony. He hadn't made love to a woman since John's death, which had been more than six weeks ago. His physical discomfort was more than real. He was at the point where he feared waking up with a wet dream and embarrassing them both. And last night she had slept soundly for the first time since he had rescued her from the Comanche. He felt he could leave her to sleep alone.

He knew that if he could not forget Chavez, there was no way she could. The fact that she had those damn nightmares kept what had happened very alive for both of them. And it was the strongest reason for his self-control, which he had never even known he had. After all, he'd never gone celibate in his life until now. He'd never tested his capacity for self-denial. And, hopefully, he would never have to again.

The next morning, before she was up, he went hunting to test the bow he had made. He returned at midday with a wild turkey and two hares. He saw that Miranda was making him a pair of pants out of doeskin that he'd said she could have. He felt strangely warmed by the sight of her. She was wearing the buckskin dress and moccasins, her hair in two braids. Her skin was a pale peach now, but she was no less attractive. In fact, to him, every day she grew more beautiful. He worried about how thin she was, though. He knew she had lost weight since her capture by Chavez. If he had to, he would force-feed her, because she was not going to fall ill and waste away . . . not ever.

"Morning," he called out, depositing his game by the hides that were stretched and drying.

Miranda gave him a short glance, with no smile. He wondered what was wrong. He strolled over. "Good morning," he repeated.

She set aside the pieces of buckskin that she had cut and had just started sewing. She met his gaze. Her face was troubled and wan, and he hated seeing dark shadows beneath her eyes. "Are you sick?" He was immediately anxious.

"No."

He studied her, but she was toying with the leather, and he shrugged. Something was wrong, he knew it. Was she angry with him for making demands on her yesterday? Hell, it was his right. As far as he was concerned, he had gone beyond the bounds called for. No husband could possibly be more understanding or considerate than he was. He walked away and decided to clean the rabbits first, surprised when she followed him and knelt opposite him.

"What are you doing?"

"I want to learn," she said. "Cleaning game is women's work. Will you teach me?"

He suddenly smiled, wondering why she wanted to do it. "Miranda, it's okay. I'll do it."

"But wouldn't you rather I be able to do it?" Her violet gaze was direct.

He had never lied to her, and he certainly wouldn't start now. "Yes."

She smiled slightly. "Then show me."

Bragg studied her, shrugged, and decapitated the rabbit with one stroke of his blade. He didn't look at her, but he could feel her dismay. He quickly and efficiently sliced off the four paws. In another instant, he had slit the skin on the back of the four limbs and from the chest to the anus. In one more instant, he pulled the hide off completely.

Miranda cried out and turned away, stumbling and retching.

Bragg sat back on his heels. He had warned her. She was far too dainty for this. He reached into the belly cavity and pulled out the guts, tossing them in the pile of refuse, then set the hare aside.

"I'm sorry," Miranda said, turning back to face him. She looked truly miserable.

"Forget it," he said. "I told you, I don't mind cleaning the game." He picked up the other hare, setting it in front. He was about to decapitate it, then looked up when she was still standing there. "Why don't you go back to what you were doing?"

"No," she said, stepping closer. "I want to do it."

"Miranda."

She walked resolutely over to him, kneeling and taking the knife out of his hand. She was pale. She swallowed with obvious difficulty. He sat back on his heels, amused, and waited. A few moments passed. "Well?"

"It's still warm."

He took the knife out of her hand. "There's no reason for you to do this," he said. "Your sensibilities are too fine. I don't think I want you any other way."

She looked at him with tears in her eyes. "Give me the knife," she said.

He was amazed. "What the hell are you trying to prove?"

She took the knife. With clenched teeth, she made an incision along the neck.

"Lower," Bragg corrected. "In one slice."

She moved the blade lower on the animal's fur, hesitating. Blood appeared as she slowly, timidly pressed. Bragg glanced at her face and saw tears spilling out of her lashes. He angrily took the knife away and stood, pulling her up with him. "That's enough. This is ridiculous."

Miranda didn't look at him, but wiped her eyes with her bare forearm and pulled free of his hold. He watched her walk stiffly away to where she had been sewing, and sit, blindly picking up the doeskin. What was that all about?

Perturbed, he sat and cleaned the hare, then moved on to the turkey.

Bragg didn't understand her and began to feel guilty. He was making her into a squaw when she should be a fine lady. He paused as he pulled out feathers, thinking. He had wanted to bring her up here because it was beautiful, cleansing, healing. With just the two of them, they could start their marriage over. But had he made a mistake?

He imagined a beautiful home. It had always been on his mind, that if she became happy, he would take up ranching and build her a fine home to raise their children in. They would sell the JB easily, giving them some extra funds. Wild cattle were everywhere for the taking, so it would be easy to get started. He looked over at her.

Miranda was sewing determinedly, skillfully. Her beauty and vulnerability twisted at him. Yes, she deserved a ranch, and they would have children. . . .

Suddenly he stopped what he was doing, remembering how she had gotten sick, which made him think of pregnancy. What if she was already pregnant? He strode over to her, hard and tense.

"Miranda, when was your last monthly flow?" he demanded.

"What?" She dropped her sewing, startled. He repeated the question, his face dark.

"What . . . what is this about?"

"I'm your husband, and I have a right to know. When was it?" He watched her hesitate.

"Six weeks ago."

He felt as if he'd been shot. For a moment he couldn't speak. All he could think was, She's pregnant with Chavez's child.

Miranda got hastily to her feet, seeing his expression. "Derek, wait. I've always been a bit . . ." She blushed. "A bit irregular. Sometimes I've missed my month completely."

He stared, rigid. "You could be pregnant."

She paled. "I hadn't even thought about it," she whispered. "No, I'm not, I know I'm not."

He turned away. Then he looked back at her. "Maybe now is the time for you to say a prayer or two." He was angry, frustrated. What would he do if she had Chavez's child? How could he possibly be a father to a baby born of a man who had raped and hurt his wife? He strode away and finished plucking the turkey without thinking, in utter turmoil.

But he thought about her words. It was possible that she wasn't pregnant. It was ridiculous to get upset now, over something he couldn't control. But that was easier said than done. He looked over at her. She was bent over the doeskin, sewing fast and methodically. She had turned her back to him. He felt a pang of pity and an urge to protect her.

He couldn't see her face, which was just as well. Miranda was white and strained, managing not to cry, but her mouth trembled, giving away her distress.

Chapter 58

Her happiness had vanished. She was tense and afraid and realized now how content she had been for a while.

First Derek was angry with her for not letting him exercise his husbandly rights. Since that afternoon when he had begged her to let him make love to her, he had been sleeping outside, a silent message of anger. She had been so upset when he had chosen this means of communicating his disapproval that she hadn't been able to face him the next day.

Then she had failed again, and again. She so wanted to please him and be a good wife! She didn't know why, but it was the most important thing in her life. She desperately missed his comforting presence in their bed at night. She had wanted to clean the game to be a better wife, but he had laughed at her pitiful efforts, her weakness.

And he was raging over the possibility that she might be pregnant.

Miranda didn't want to sleep alone again. He had disappeared after cleaning the game. She stuffed the turkey with cornmeal and herbs, then baked it in the oven Derek had made from a pit, not far from the outdoor cooking fire. She made fresh bread and rice to go with the turkey, and roasted the hares for another day. When she had finished sewing the pants and bathed her face, he finally returned from wherever he had gone.

It was still light out, although the sun would be setting shortly. He was covered with sweat, as if he had been engaged in a great deal of physical activity. She watched him anxiously as he strode into their camp, and their eyes met. He gave her a smile.

"God, this place smells great," he said. "I could smell that turkey and stuffing two miles away. I'll bathe in a flash."

Miranda relaxed a little, absurdly pleased with the off-hand compliment, praying that she hadn't overcooked the turkey. She busied herself around the fire until he returned from the creek. She tried not to watch as he approached, naked. What a magnificent man he was. He took the clothes she had laundered, now dry and a bit stiff, and slipped on the pants. He shrugged on a shirt and came to the fire barefoot.

They ate in silence. Derek always had an appetite, and tonight was no exception. She could see that he was absorbed in his thoughts. Brooding, she thought. But he smiled at her and praised her cooking. She felt her heart flip at his words. The turkey was a bit overdone, she thought, but just barely. Her cooking was improving. She would be a good wife to him; she had made herself that promise. She knew she wasn't pregnant. She had prayed, as he had suggested. She also prayed he would come to her bed tonight.

Derek suddenly leaped to his feet.

"What is it?" she asked, turning to look in the direction he was staring. She saw a spiral of smoke some distance away. Her first feeling was terror. There were other humans, Indians, in the area!

Derek laughed. "Would you look at that!" he exclaimed.

"Derek, who do you think it is?" she asked anxiously.

"Apache," he said. "My people."

She gaped.

He made a very small fire and soon a thin trail of smoke was drifting up. He took a blanket and fanned the smoke into puffs, sending up smoke signals.

Miranda was stunned. "What are you saying?"

"I'm identifying myself. We don't want to be slaughtered while we sleep."

She stared. Then she looked at the puffs he was sending up, amazed that anyone could communicate by a code of smoke. She looked at the signals being sent from the Apache. "What do they say?"

Bragg didn't speak for many minutes. Then he laughed. "It's my brother's people, Miranda. It's Najilkhise's band."

"Your brother? Najilkhise?"

"I have a half brother," Derek explained, putting out the small smoke fire. "My mother was married to his father, then was widowed and married my father. His father was head man, as he is."

"I didn't know you had any family alive. So he's completely Indian."

"Yes. I'll go visit tomorrow or the next day." He smiled at her. "I would like to take you if you're up to it."

Miranda shivered, possibly from the breeze and coming darkness. She was thinking about the brutal Comanche. Derek seemed to read her thoughts.

"The Apache are not dogs like the Comanche. They do not torture women and children, nor do they rape. Ever. Women prisoners usually marry Apache men, and children are adopted, eventually marrying into the tribe. It's all quite civilized." He was watching her. He would understand if she refused to meet his people, but he wanted her to accept his invitation.

"Of course I'll go," she said softly, gazing at him levelly, with tenderness.

Her look made him tremble—a look of caring, concern.

Miranda's heart began to pound as she crawled into their bed in the wickiup. She strained her ears, listening to the night sounds—crickets and frogs. Bragg seemed to have recovered from the afternoon, and she wasn't sure if he was still angry or not. She waited anxiously for him to come to her, hoping he would. Tonight she would let him become a true husband to her—because she wanted to please him. But he did not come.

After an hour or so she got to her feet and wrapped a blanket around her shoulders, completely covering herself from head to ankle. If he would not come to her, she would go to him. She stepped outside.

She knew he slept just outside the door to the wickiup, a few yards away. She saw him there, on a blanket, lying on his back. Another blanket was pulled to his waist. His chest and shoulders and arms were bare; she knew he slept naked. She had never done so before, and had only disrobed in anticipation of letting him take her—as a husband takes his wife. She approached silently.

Miranda wondered if he could possibly be sleeping. The night was suddenly silent. The crickets and frogs seemed to have stopped their serenade. She could hear her own breathing. Could he really be asleep? It didn't seem possible. She knew he slept with one eye open and one ear attuned. She paused at his side, studying him.

His eyes were closed and his breathing was slow and even. He was incredibly handsome, his features almost finely chiseled, his ruggedness adding to his appeal. Even as he slept, she felt the power of his beauty. He was the first man she had ever felt attracted to. Her mouth was dry, and she was breathless.

How should she do this? Should she just climb beneath his blanket and lay beside him? She was flushed, apprehensive, excited by her daring, but afraid. She hated the thought of the pain, but she would bear it to please him. She got to her knees, then cautiously lifted one corner of the blanket. She let her own blanket fall, and holding her breath, slid in next to him. His skin was silk and sand and incredibly hot against hers.

Miranda had just stretched out beside him when he said conversationally, "What are you doing?"

She gasped. From the tone of his voice she didn't think he had been asleep at all. She couldn't find her voice. She lay on her side, her knees and lower thighs touching his hip, the tips of her breasts suddenly hard and touching his shoulder.

He moved like a snake. She was suddenly on her back, and he had his arms around her, his chest on top of her breasts, crushing them. His face was inches from hers, his breath hot. "What are you doing?"

"You're angry," she whispered, finally finding her voice.

"I'm not angry," he said huskily.

She became aware of his shaft, very hot and hard,

throbbing against the outside of her thigh. There was a constriction in her chest. "You're angry," she said. "Because I denied you yesterday. Please. Don't be angry with me, Derek."

"I'm not angry," he repeated, his mouth almost brushing hers. "And you still haven't answered my question."

"I want to please you," she said. "I want to be a good wife. You may . . . you may make love to me."

He stared. For a long moment he didn't move, didn't speak. She could see how brightly his eyes glittered, could see the tension on his face. And she could feel his heart against hers, the coarse hairs of his chest on her breasts, the throbbing tip of him against her leg. She couldn't breathe. She suddenly felt trapped. Images of Chavez fluttered through her mind, against her will. She tried to push them away. And at the same time the very core of her, her womanhood, was aching slightly, not unpleasantly. She closed her eyes.

"Do you want me?"

She opened her eyes in surprise.

"Do you want me, Miranda?" His voice was so hoarse. He threw his thigh over both of hers, and she felt his shaft between her tightly clenched legs.

"I don't want you to be angry," she whispered.

"I'm not angry," he groaned. "Frustrated, not angry."

"You slept outside last night."

"Because, Miranda, holding you is torture for my male body." He claimed her lips.

She didn't open them, her fright increasing. He moved insistently over them, shifting himself so that he was prodding between her legs. She clamped her thighs tighter together and lay stiff and unyielding in his arms. He stopped kissing her. She let out her breath, which she had been holding, in a sigh of relief.

He shuddered and rolled swiftly off her. "Dammit! Don't come to me like some kind of sacrifice!"

Miranda sat up. "No, Derek, please, now you're even angrier."

"I want you to want me," he said raggedly, staring at her with burning eyes. "And I chose to sleep out here because I haven't had a woman since that damn birthday barbecue. If you come to my bed, at least act like you're going to enjoy it! At least pretend!''

Tears trickled down her cheeks. ''I can't do anything right! Please, give me another chance.''

He stared, and then, before she could move, he grabbed her, pulling her against him and kissing her almost brutally. ''Damn! I'm only human!'' he cried, pushing her down, running his calloused hands over her breasts, kneeing her thighs apart before she could clamp them together. He kissed her so savagely she tasted blood.

All pleasant sensations were gone. She knew only fear, icy terror that he was going to hurt her terribly. His body shook on top of hers, his hands cupped and squeezed her breasts, and he groaned. He reached down and slipped his hand between her thighs, over her dry flesh.

''Damn,'' he said, ''damn!''

He couldn't take her like this, not when she was frightened and cold, but he had no control left. He was beyond almost all rational thought. He clamped his mouth on hers, grabbed her hand, and placed it against his shaft. ''Hold me,'' he ordered harshly. Her fingers closed around him. He moved her hand rapidly up and down his throbbing length, and then he was lost, exploding, releasing his seed onto her belly. He collapsed on top of her, slipping his arms around her and holding her tightly.

Miranda lay very still, not daring to move, shocked. She understood what had happened, but not why. But . . . she was grateful. He had saved her great pain. Still, why hadn't he taken her the way a man should?

''Are you all right?'' he asked softly.

''Yes.''

''I'm sorry. Miranda, it was too long, I lost control, I'm sorry.''

''Why did you do it that way?''

''I didn't want to rape you, and if I'd taken you so quickly, that's what it would have been.''

Miranda thought about what he'd said. ''But I don't think a husband can rape a wife.''

''You may have a point.'' He hesitated, then smoothed her hair and kissed her lightly. ''Did I . . . offend you?''

She paused. She was sure that what they had done was

wrong, sinful. But in a way, he had been protecting her. Had he offended her? She wasn't sure. She finally answered. "I don't think so."

He rolled onto his side, pulling her against him. He wanted to make love to his wife properly. He wanted to make her moan in ecstasy. But how was he going to do that when his passion frightened her? How could he breach her defenses, subtly, without her knowing? Hadn't he been trying to do that all along? He knew very well that she liked kissing, but he only kissed her in broad daylight, when they were dressed and doing their chores. A thought came to him, slowly forming in his mind. And he smiled.

Chapter 59

As usual, Miranda didn't hear him approach and didn't know he was there until he planted a kiss on her cheek. She leaped to her feet, startled only for a split second, while he laughed, turning her and holding her against him momentarily. "You need better ears, woman."

She smiled, suddenly shy. He had been gone all morning, gone before she had even awakened. She remembered the previous night with some embarrassment. "Where have you been?"

"Visiting," he said. "Can that stew hold till supper? I already ate, with my brother. But I want you to eat." He gave her a playfully stern look.

"You went to see . . . Naj . . ." Her voice trailed off.

"Najilkhise. Na-jil-ke-hi-say. Yep. I told him that tomorrow I'll bring my wife." He grinned.

Miranda felt relieved, but guiltily so. "You frighten me a bit, Derek, when you disappear for so long without a word." Her tone was reprimanding as she reached for the big iron kettle.

He intercepted her, taking the cloth holder out of her hand and moving the kettle off the fire. "Do I? Why is that?" He was teasing.

"What if you were hurt, or in an accident?" She was serious. As much as he liked to think he was invincible—as she sometimes did, too—he wasn't. He was only a man.

"Then I'd crawl back to my beautiful wife who would kiss me back to health."

"Be serious!"

"Eat up. We've got plans this afternoon." He ladled an overgenerous portion of the hare and root stew and handed her the tin plate.

"What plans?" she said, but sat on a chair of birch that Derek had made and obediently began to eat.

"A surprise," he said. He disappeared into the wickiup, then returned a moment later wearing his loin cloth and moccasins and carrying two of their smallest blankets. She finished eating half her meal, wondering suspiciously what he was up to now. She returned what she hadn't eaten to the kettle. She caught him scowling at her.

"I ate half," she said quickly, defensively.

"Let's go," Derek said, holding out his hand. Miranda took it, and he led her into the woods.

He slowed his pace to accommodate her. Spring was in its full glory. The sun was bright, the day perfectly warm. A faint, fresh breeze rustled newly green leaves. Chicks in nests overhead squeaked hungrily, and Derek paused once, putting a finger to his lips, pointing. Miranda searched the glade, and then saw a newborn fawn stumbling on long, stiltlike legs, the mother resting with heaving flanks in the tall grass.

"Is she all right?" Miranda whispered anxiously.

At that moment, the doe lunged to her feet and began licking her fawn, cleaning off the afterbirth. The fawn nuzzled its mother, searching, and began to suckle. Derek took her hand and they moved away.

He led her to a green, fragrant clearing where a sparkling pool graced a short waterfall, no higher than a tall man's height. "What a beautiful spot," Miranda exclaimed. "Is this our creek?"

"An arm of it," Derek said, smiling at her transparent delight. He bent and pulled off his moccasins.

She glanced at him. "What are . . .?" And she blushed as he dropped his loincloth, standing before her as if he didn't have a care in the world. She averted her face, but not before she caught a glimpse of that male part of him she had held last night. Only now it looked quite different.

"We're going swimming," he said easily, approaching her with a grin.

"Derek," she protested, and looked carefully at his face.

"Take off your clothes. The water's a bit cool at first, but you'll get used to it." He reached for her blouse.

"I can't swim," she said. She felt panic, and not entirely at the prospect of swimming. She backed away. She knew her face was red.

"Miranda, I'm your husband, so there's no need to be shy or modest. How I look is a natural thing, just like how you look."

"Modesty is godly," she said, grabbing his wrists as he began undoing the buttons of her blouse. "I don't want to go swimming."

"I'm going to teach you," he said firmly, pulling off her blouse as if she weren't trying to stop him. "And modesty does not please me."

She paused to think about that. In that instant, he had her skirt falling to her ankles. "Derek!"

"I refuse to have my wife drown on me someday," he said, reaching for the ribbon on her petticoat. He pulled it, and that item of clothing floated in a white cloud to the ground.

"All right," she said, becoming frightened of the actual prospect. "But if I drown now it will be your fault!"

He chuckled. "I have no intention of letting you drown, princess. Do you want to leave your chemise on?"

"Yes!"

He shook his head at the eagerness of her tone, but his mouth was twitching. "Take off those damn pantalets, though."

"Do I have to?"

"Do you want to drown?"

She pulled off her moccasins and pantalets, feeling naked. He looked at her. His face was expressionless, but she saw the hot vibrant light in his eyes. Her panic increased, and with it she felt a tumbling kind of quickening.

"C'mon," he said, stepping away from her.

She gasped as he put enough distance between them for her to see his aroused state, gasped and shut her eyes. But what she had seen remained a firm image in her mind. She was fascinated.

"I'm sorry," he said, "but you're too damn beautiful, and I can't help my reaction. Open your eyes!"

She did, but she looked at his face, then his shoulder. Her gaze started to drop—then she quickly met his golden glance again. He was laughing.

"You act like a virgin," he chuckled. "Do I . . . please you?"

She gasped, stunned at such a question.

His face fell. He frowned, then he took her hand and pulled her with him to the pool. As they got closer, she forgot about him and began to be afraid. "How deep is it?"

"Not deep," he lied.

"I don't want to swim," she said, digging in her heels.

"You'll love it," he told her, half dragging her.

"No, please," she said, pulling against him.

He stopped and looked at her. He didn't want to terrify her, just teach her a useful skill, one that could possibly save her life someday. That, and play around a bit. She was pale with fright. He'd forgotten that sometimes she had no backbone. He sighed and released her hand. Turning, he dove in. He swam across the width of the pond, which was about thirty strokes, pausing on the other side to see her standing still and watching. He swam back to her side until he was ten strokes from the edge, where he found sure footing. The water came up to his waist. "The water's great," he called. "And you can stand right up to here. I won't take you out past this point, I promise."

Miranda frowned. He could see her warring with herself, her natural timidity at odds with her desire to obey him, even please him. He dove under the water and swam back and forth hard a few times, until he strained his muscles, enjoying the tension. She had come to the edge and dipped her foot in. He dove under the water and swam to the edge. Reaching up, he grabbed her ankles.

She shrieked as she fell in.

He immediately put his arms around her.

"You bastard!" she cried, coughing and trembling and thrashing wildly.

Derek was shocked, but only for a moment. He had never heard her curse. He held her loosely, and his voice was soothing. "Miranda, you can stand."

She was clinging to him like a monkey.

"Miranda," he said in the same gentle voice, prying off her arms, "I'm standing, sweetheart."

Comprehension dawned, and she looked into his gaze with her wide, frightened violet eyes. He saw some of her panic recede. With her hands around his neck, she slid down his body, and he managed to bite off a groan at the feel of her thigh and hip rubbing his manhood. She was oblivious to his reaction—or too frightened to care. Her feet found the slippery rock beneath, her hold loosened, and she slipped, crying out.

Derek immediately grabbed her by the waist, but not before she got another mouthful of water. He pulled her up so that she was standing, sputtering and choking. Her hands were around his neck, digging in painfully, and she was practically crawling into his skin. He wished he wasn't so aroused. He wished she knew she was causing him agony by pressing her soft—if stiff—body against him. Maybe this hadn't been the best of ideas.

"Miranda, loosen your hands, you're hurting me," he said firmly. "You're standing. Look, the water only comes to your chest."

She began to relax. She loosened her hold fractionally, her breathing hard and rapid. Couldn't she feel the length of him against her belly? "Relax," he murmured, taking her wrists and prying them looser. The instant she gave him an inch, he moved his body back, away from hers. It was probably the hardest thing he'd ever done.

"Where are you going?" she cried.

"I'm not going anywhere. And I won't let you drown. You have my promise. Okay?"

She looked into his eyes and nodded.

"Are you ready to learn to swim?"

"No!"

He found himself staring at where the water lapped her erect nipples. She might as well have been naked for all the chemise hid. "I'm going to turn you onto your stomach," he began.

"No!"

"But I'm going to hold you, I will not let you go. Miranda, you'll float, I swear it." He reached for her.

She stepped back, toward the shore, and slipped. He caught her, and before she knew it, she was floating in his arms on her belly, her face turned aside so she could breathe.

"Relax. Is that so bad?"

"Don't you dare let go," she said.

Her hair was in one thick braid, drifting in the water. She was so small, he thought, resisting the urge to wrap her waist in his hands. He stared momentarily at the small, perfect derriere floating beneath his gaze. Without thinking, as she floated on one arm, he placed his hand on one of her buttocks, barely a touch, that became firmer, more tantalizing.

"Derek," she cried, "don't let go!"

He removed his hand. "Kick, Miranda," he told her. "And paddle with your arms."

"Do I have to?"

"If you don't, you'll sink when I let go."

She began to kick and paddle, her teeth chattering. "If you let go I'll kill you!"

Bragg smiled despite himself. "Good girl," he said a few minutes later. He wasn't even holding her, but she didn't seem to know it. His arm was beneath her, just a whisper touch. He removed it completely, taking her by her shoulders and turning her to face him.

"What are you doing!"

"Kick and paddle," he said soothingly.

"Don't let go," she pleaded.

He drifted back into the pond, pulling her with him while she thrashed fixedly. "Now I'm going to let go, but I'll only be a yard away."

"NO! You bastard!"

He let go and drifted back. She came at him like a locomotive. He tried not to laugh, drifted farther back, and she followed him with incredible determination.

"Derek!"

"You're doing great! A little farther!"

"I hate you!"

He stopped and she came to him, leaping into his arms with desperation, her arms going around his neck, her legs clamping around his waist, clinging like a vine. "You did great," he said, desire shooting through him. Her chemise had ridden up. He could feel the coarser hair of her womanhood pressed against his navel. God, it would be so easy . . . just slip her down a little, and he would be against her . . .

"You lied, you let go!"

"Miranda, you're going to learn to swim. Did I let you drown?"

She hesitated. "No." It was a reluctant admission.

He was having trouble thinking. He slid his hands down her back, to her bare flesh, capturing her buttocks, which he kneaded gently. She gasped, and he saw the dawning light in her eyes. Her skin was so smooth, so silken. He ran his hands down the backs of her thighs, to her knees, and then back up. He caught her buttocks and pressed her to him.

"Derek, please, not here," she said, and it was almost a sob.

He looked in her eyes and saw how afraid she was of being in the middle of the pool. There was no answering desire in her eyes. And maybe some of the fear was from him. He placed an arm around her waist, and as if she knew he was going to pry her loose, she clung harder. He decided she'd been through enough. "You did great," he told her again, his voice thick. He sidestroked to where he found footing, while she remained wrapped around him. The minute the water dropped to his waist she slid off, stumbling. She lunged for the edge of the pool, scrambling out, but not before giving him a wonderful, agonizing view of her perfect ivory behind. He sighed, turned, and proceeded to swim back and forth until his desire had ebbed. When he waded out, he saw she had gone.

Chapter 60

He returned to their camp a few minutes later, whistling. Miranda had pulled their bed of hides out of the wickiup and was airing the bedding. He saw her hard strokes as she swept dust from within and knew she was angry. She came out, set the broom aside, and marched to the creek with a pail, not looking at him. She *was* mad. He went after her.

She didn't acknowledge his presence as she filled the pail with water.

"What are you doing?" he asked casually.

She stood, ignoring him, and started marching back.

He took the pail from her hand and carried it. "Miranda?"

"Wetting down our floor," she said abruptly.

"I didn't notice it was getting too dusty," he said, regarding her set face.

She didn't answer, but took the pail from him at the entrance to the wickiup and disappeared inside. He followed and watched as she swept water across the floor. "I'm really proud of you," he said truthfully.

She swept the broom back and forth, back and forth.

"I've never seen anyone who's so afraid of water swim so well." It was the truth.

Her sweeping seemed to become a bit less determined.

"I'm sorry if you're angry," he tried, seeing her soften

and pressing home his advantage. "But one day you'll be a fine swimmer, just like one day you'll be a good shot."

She made a small noise, like a snort, her lashes lowered.

"If I were to die, I'd want you to be able to take care of yourself. When I met you, you were as helpless as a newborn babe. Everyday you're learning better how to fend for yourself."

She stopped sweeping and looked at him. He smiled. "Still mad?"

"Don't talk that way," she said, frowning. "You're young. Besides, you'll probably live to a hundred!"

He laughed. "I hope not, not unless you live to ninety."

She smiled slightly.

He grinned.

"Do you really think I did well?" Her gaze was bashful and hopeful.

"You did fantastic," he told her, exaggerating only a bit.

Miranda flushed under his praise. "If you really want me to swim, I'll learn," she said bravely and resignedly.

He beamed, coming toward her. "You know what would make me happy, too?"

She looked up at him innocently.

He took her face in his hands. "If you let me kiss you and touch you, just for a while?"

She started. "Derek . . ."

"All I want to do is kiss you," he lied, his mouth coming closer to hers.

"I already told you," she whispered, hesitant, "that you could . . . you know."

"I don't want to make love to you now, just to hold you," he said, a half lie. He slipped his arm around her waist and pulled her gently against him. His mouth found hers, caressing softly, again and again.

She was stiff, but she began to melt as his mouth moved gently and patiently, stroking her lips with a butterfly touch, his tongue flicking over their softness. Her lips parted, but he took his time, not invading, only kissing and tracing their outline, their parting. He moved his hands from her shoulders to her back. He felt her pliancy.

He didn't mind her passivity, as long as she wasn't stiff and afraid.

"What about chores?" she whispered some time later.

"Don't you like kissing?" His voice was husky. Her back was smooth, her lips incredibly sweet.

"Yes," she murmured, exciting him. "I like your kisses. I was surprised—"

He invaded her mouth with his tongue. She accepted him passively, and then, after a careful, leisurely exploration, her hands went around his neck, tightening. He increased the pressure, becoming bold, demanding. Her fingers wound in his hair.

He lifted her and placed her on the damp ground.

"Derek," she protested.

"All I ask is that you let me touch you," he said. "Is that too much for a husband to ask a wife?"

Her eyes were wide and questioning. "But—why?"

"It pleases me," he said, claiming her lips again, kneeling at her side.

She began to return his kisses, tentatively, timidly. He wanted to devour her, but refused to succumb to his lust. He was going to pleasure her. He was going to show her that she had nothing to fear. He was so glad he had found release last night, or he would have never been able to exercise the self-control he had now.

He heard her whimper deep in her throat, and fire flamed along his limbs. He kissed her throat, and she arched her head back to accommodate him. He could hear her soft, uneven breathing, and was triumphant. She's excited, he thought, elated. His hand stole from her shoulder to her chest, and he cupped one small, perfect breast. She gasped, stiffening.

"Let me touch you," he murmured against her soft throat. He captured her lips again, squeezing the soft globe in his hand, rubbing the nipple with his palm. She shuddered.

Deftly, he unbuttoned her shirt while he kissed her deeply. He claimed her breast again, fondling, massaging, relishing the soft swelling beneath his ministrations. She moaned, a barely audible sound. A roaring began in his head, and his loins were so full, so hot. He slipped his hand beneath the chemise, tempting and teasing the nipple. She writhed into his hand, wanting more.

He pulled her chemise down, baring both breasts, staring just for a moment. "You are so beautiful, Miranda," he told her huskily, and then he flicked his tongue over one hard nub.

She gasped. His kisses had heightened what had been a pleasant quickening of her body into a deep, throbbing ache. Because he only wanted to touch her and kiss her, what little fear had been in her mind had fled beneath his gentle mouth and hands. A moment ago she had wanted to protest, had tried to, at the shameful things he was doing, but now she couldn't think. He was suckling her like a babe. She was on fire, desperately yearning for something, for him, for exactly what, she didn't know, but the ache was so deep and unquenchable in her secret woman's place that she wondered if she was fevered and dying. She heard an animal moan. It was herself.

A part of her mind sought sanity when she felt his hand cupping her woman's mound through the folds of her dress. Not there! But the hot, myriad sensation washed away that thought, and she realized he was stroking that unmentionable place, stroking that was making her writhe uncontrollably, even through skirt, petticoat, and pantalets. She needed his hand. She arched against it.

She felt cool air on her bare hot flesh as he lifted her skirts and pulled down her pantalets. It happened so quickly she could only moan his name. She heard him say, "I love you, Miranda," his voice ragged and harsh. And then his hand was there again, slipping into the valley between her legs, which was wet and slick, causing a moment of coherent confusion.

"I love you Miranda," he said again thickly, his voice seeming very far away.

"Don't stop," she said, gasping, writhing, arching. Something incredible was happening to her; she felt as if every nerve of her body had taken wing. And then she cried out, again and again, a wailing keening, as her body soared, mindlessly, ecstatically, before bursting into a series of brilliant explosions.

"God," Derek said to himself, watching her passion-drained face. With trembling hands he pulled off her clothes, watching her flushed face, black lashes like a thick fan on each cheek, her breasts rising and falling unsteadily. Her eyes were still closed when she lay naked, and he knelt over her, slipping his arms around her. He kissed her lashes, her cheeks, her nose. He found her lips, shuddering with his own need. Her eyes flew open.

He smiled into her stunned gaze. "Miranda."

"I . . . what happened?"

He kissed her ear, her temple. "You just experienced a woman's pleasure, darling. It's what happens when two people make love. It's even better when I'm deep inside you." The thought and words made him want to die.

She stared, then blushed.

He cradled her face, kissing her slowly, holding himself on the very edge.

"Derek?" she said, and it could have been a plea or a protest, or a little bit of both.

He stroked her breasts, refusing to relinquish her mouth. She shuddered. He lowered his weight, still wearing the loincloth, not wanting to frighten her. "I won't hurt you," he said.

She stiffened.

He wanted to pleasure her again, he wanted that desperately, but he was so damn close himself. He slipped his hand between her legs, searching delicately, expertly.

"Derek?" she said, a half moan.

He groaned, slid down the length of her, cupped her buttocks in his hand and lifted her to him. He kissed the sweet, wet cleft, then began to search throught the pink folds with his tongue. She gasped, sitting upright and shoving at him. "No!"

"You taste so fine," he murmured, ignoring her feeble efforts to push him off as he tasted her essence, glorying in it.

She moaned and fell back in helpless defeat. He increased his efforts, and she began to shudder, arching herself at his seeking mouth. Her climax came so quickly it took him by surprise. She was there, open and wet, and then she was crying out, again and again, loudly, uncontrollably.

He lay very still, his cheek against her thigh, closing his eyes as she drifted in the aftermath. He had a few coherent thoughts. Soon he was going to take her there again, but this time while he was buried as deeply as he could be inside her. That thought made him touch her, and he slipped his forefinger into her, gasping at the small, tight size of her. Good God, he thought, probing gently, stretching her to accommodate him.

"Derek," she moaned.

With an age-old rhythm he thrust into her with two fingers. She shuddered, her hips rising. Excited beyond the point of any return, he rose, with one motion shedding his loincloth. He grasped her hips, gazed upon her flushed face, her closed eyes and plunged in.

He groaned at the sheer exquisite pleasure of it. Miranda, he thought, thrusting. Mine.

He moved slowly, trying to hold off, to prolong what was the most incredible, beautiful experience of his life, watching her perfectly featured face. He was in her, filling her up completely, she was his. Her eyes fluttered open, meeting his. He saw her expression of wonder.

"You're so small," he told her hoarsely. "How do I feel?"

Her lips were parted. Her eyes were smoky. She didn't answer, but closed her eyes and thrust her hips awkwardly at him. He went down on her, catching her hips, guiding her, thrusting faster and faster, lost in her, loving her, claiming her with every stroke. He cried out her name as he emptied himself into her, throbbing wildly.

And then he gasped when he felt her contractions and heard her cries, and he thrust again and again, reaching down to touch her and prolong her pleasure. Her cries trailed off and they both lay very still.

Chapter 61

Sleep left her in lazy, slow stages. She clung to it, so fatigued, not wanting to awaken, not wanting to leave the depth of her slumber. She dozed. Memories of Derek flooded her, waking her. A soaring joy swept over her. A hot flush brightened her cheeks. She opened her eyes and could see that it was late out, bright with midday light.

Derek wasn't in their bed. She flushed again, thinking. He had made love to her so many times that afternoon and evening, she couldn't count. She didn't think she had fallen asleep until midnight, maybe later. And then it had been in the warm, tender circle of his arms. Perhaps around dawn, when the sky outside was lightening to a rosy gray, she had awakened to find him kissing her, easing into her. She had welcomed him.

Something dark and hurtful pierced the warm, rosy haze of her thoughts. She shoved it away.

She stretched. She was stiff, but wonderfully so. And she was sore, she could feel it. She sighed, replete.

You are no lady.

She gasped, wanting to forget she had ever heard those hateful words. But he had said them and then his mouth had descended, and he had made love to her. The bliss that had followed had wiped out the content of what he had said. She tensed, searching her mind, trying to remember their exact conversation.

"I wanted you from the first moment I saw you," Derek had said, holding her, nuzzling her cheek.

"That's because you're a randy goat," Miranda retorted.

He chuckled. "You wanted me, too."

"I did not!"

"I remember how you kept staring at me, with that frightened fascination."

"That is not true." She was trying to recall if she had indeed looked at him that way.

He laughed, his hand sliding over her breast. "I'll never forget the day you almost fainted when I took off my shirt."

"You are no gentleman!"

"And you are no lady." His mouth had descended, cutting off all further conversation.

Miranda felt tears rising. Had he been teasing? Had his tone been playful? Did it matter? She *was* no lady! No lady accepted a man with such enthusiasm! And that was certainly understating her reaction to her husband. How could she have behaved like some cheap, ill-bred hussy? Like—a whore!

She pulled the covers up, turning onto her side, rolling into a ball, all the joy of discovering her husband gone. There was nothing left but shame and pain. Of course he had meant it. Because it was true. Not that he had meant to hurt her, but Derek wasn't a gentleman, so what did he care if she was a lady? But she cared! She cared tremendously.

Miranda tried not to think about her passionate response the previous night, her moans and cries. In a flash of insight she knew where that side of her came from. Her mother's father had been a notorious rake and rogue his entire life. He had had one mistress after another, despite his marriage. He had died in his mistress's apartments at the age of eighty-two, his last paramour a twenty-year-old actress. It was a well-known fact that traits skipped a generation. And now it made complete sense. She had inherited her grandfather's passionate nature.

She wanted to crawl into a hole and disappear.

Guilt vied with shame. She knew now how babies were conceived. When a man took his wife in the normal way, she supposed that was right, unavoidable. But Derek had trespassed far beyond those bounds with his hands and mouth. Dear God! What would Father Miguel say when she confessed? Could she even confess to such a sinful coupling? Would she get a chance to confess at all? She had to get to confession!

"Morning, sleepyhead." Derek smiled and reached her side, kneeling, pulling her into his arms. His gaze was warm and tender.

Miranda didn't look at him. No, she thought determinedly, not again!

"Miranda, how do you feel?" He tilted her chin up, forcing her to meet his gaze. His expression sobered when he saw her stern expression. "What's wrong?"

Tears welled in her eyes. She pulled away. "Go away." She pulled the covers up over her face, and moaned in anguish.

"Are you all right?" He grabbed the blanket, his concern razor-sharp. "Are you ill?" His hand was on her forehead.

She screwed her eyes tightly shut to prevent a full-fledged attack of weeping. She seized the excuse he offered. "No, I have a headache, and I feel awful."

He stared at her, afraid. He stroked her hair. "You don't have a fever," he said finally. "I'll bring you a cold compress for your head."

Miranda started to cry. She couldn't help it.

"Why are you crying?" he asked in an agonized voice.

She moaned, sobbing.

He turned her over gently, terribly afraid. "Are you in pain?"

She didn't answer.

"Miranda, where does it hurt!"

She heard the sharpness of his voice. "It's just a headache," she said, wishing he would take her in his arms and tell her he loved her. He had told her that last night, several times, but always in the thick of a torrid moment.

Bragg wondered if her illness was his fault. She was so delicate, so fragile. Was his lust responsible? A new thought occurred to him, one that he seized eagerly. "Miranda, could you be getting your monthly curse?"

"Yes, yes," she told him, anything to get him to leave her alone.

He sighed in relief and stood up. "I'll get you a compress. Are you hungry?"

"No."

He took one last look at her and left. The minute he was gone, her tears dried up, miraculously. She lay there depressed and ashamed.

Chapter 62

She could not spend the entire afternoon in bed. That was not going to change what had happened, or rectify anything. And it wasn't fair to her husband. Miranda got up, slipped on her clothes, and went outside to help with their household chores.

Derek was making some kind of stew. He brightened when he saw her. "You're feeling better?"

"Yes. I'm sorry for being such a child." She wanted to look away, but his gaze was so warm and caring that it held hers. A bittersweet stabbing went through her. "Here, I'll make supper."

"I want you to rest today," he said firmly. "How's your headache?"

"Better," she said. She actually did have a headache, a dull throbbing in her temples.

He dropped the knife he had been paring with and pulled her into his arms. "You scared me there for a minute," he said. His breath was warm on her face.

Miranda wanted to bury her face in his chest and forget her awful thoughts. As if sensing her desire, he pushed her head forward until her cheek rested there. He stroked her hair. She felt a tremendous surge of warmth and caring, maybe even love, for this man.

"Have you started bleeding?" he asked.

She held her breath. That hadn't been fair either, to let

him think she was about to start menstruating, not when he was so upset that she might be pregnant.

"Miranda?"

"Not yet," she said, wishing that she hadn't lied.

He tensed, and she wondered if he could sense her deceit. But he didn't bring it up again.

Derek wouldn't let her lift a finger the rest of the day, to her chagrin. He made their supper, did laundry, cleaned his weapons, and pulled down dried hides. He looked at her frequently. She wasn't sure what it meant. There was both concern and tenderness and a fixed brightness in his gaze.

Miranda was surprised that she was so tired, but she was eager to crawl into bed that evening—and worried. She didn't want tonight to be a repeat of last night, or at least her mind didn't. But she felt a tingling anticipation too, threads of desire that she knew he could spin into red-hot flames. She tried to quell that wicked side of her nature.

He came in after she was already under the covers, clad in her chemise. "What's this?" he asked in bemusement, fingering the ribboned edge.

"I'm tired," she said.

He sat there and gazed at her, looking very much like a disappointed little boy. "I know," he finally said. "Last night was my fault, I should have known better than to be so insatiable. It was just that . . . I'd waited for you so long, Miranda."

His words were thrilling. She didn't want to be thrilled or excited. Their gazes met. He bent and brushed his mouth over hers. Miranda fought the pulsing of desire. She raised her hands, pushed against his chest. "No," she said firmly. "I'm also sore." That was indeed the truth.

He clasped both her hands in his and sighed. "I'm a horny bastard, I guess. I figured you'd be sore, though, you being so damn small."

She flushed at his explicit reference.

He smiled, stroking her shoulder. "Still so modest. I'll go get some salve." He left.

Miranda lay there trying to deny that she wanted his loving. She wondered if her base appetite was some kind of punishment. How could that be? Since she had come to

Texas it had been one horrible thing after another. She
didn't deserve any more anguish, she was sure of it.

Derek returned with a small jar she recognized. Knowing what it was for, she flushed and reached out for it. He
didn't hand it to her. "I'll do it," he said.

She gasped and sat upright. "No you won't."

"Ssh." He eased her legs apart, and gently he spread
the salve inside her, soothing the raw tissues. "I didn't
mean to hurt you," he said hoarsely. His fingers stroked,
and when she began to arch he withdrew them, his hands
shaking.

"Damn," he said, dropping the jar on the floor and
crushing her to him.

He smothered what would have been a protest with a
very hot, hard kiss. Her body was like a finally tuned
instrument, responding instantly. She wanted him. Desperately. It was wrong—but she didn't care.

He rained kisses on her face and throat, stroking her
breast, then, irritated, ripping the chemise down the front.
She moaned as he captured both breasts with his hands,
kissing her deeply, passionately. Their teeth grated. She
returned his kiss, nipping at his mouth, holding his head,
then his face. She thrust her tongue in his mouth, touched
his.

"Miranda," he cried.

"Yes," she said.

His unspoken question was answered. He had already
shed his pants. "Let me know if I hurt you," he rasped,
stroking her moist, warm flesh with his fingers.

There was the slightest soreness as he eased in, controlling his urge to thrust hard and fast. She didn't care. She
wanted him, where he was, filling her up so completely,
becoming a part of her. He guided her legs upward, and
she clamped them around his waist. They moved together,
hard and fast, almost desperate, and reached a stunning
climax quickly, as one.

Miranda moaned when he left her, this time from real
pain. She was burning.

He held her close, tightly, kissing her temple. She
refused to think, tried desperately to block out ugly, guilty

thoughts, and buried her face in his neck. Wanton, she kept thinking, wanton. Soon he was fast asleep, still holding her in his arms.

But sleep eluded Miranda for a long time.

Chapter 63

It was a glorious morning, Derek thought exultantly as he lifted his wife astride her horse and handed her the reins. She gave him a small smile. To him, it was like a burst of sunshine. He was completely head over heels in love, he knew it, but it didn't matter. She was his wife—what he'd been waiting for his whole life.

They started out, Derek on foot beside the horse. It was about six miles to the Apache rancheria, and he enjoyed a brisk walk. He would have liked the short trip even better if he ran—endless energy coursed through his veins. But Miranda's seat wasn't very good yet, and he couldn't see her bouncing to a trot the whole way.

After a mile or so he noticed that she was very quiet. He had a stab of fear. ''Are you feeling okay today?''

''Oh yes,'' she said quickly.

He looked up at her and moved his hand to her knee. ''You're not frightened of my people, are you?'' His voice was quiet.

''Oh no,'' she protested sincerely.

''Miranda, I've been thinking.''

She looked at him curiously.

''How do you feel about this land out here?''

''What do you mean?''

''Well''—his heart began to pump harder—''the Texas frontier is always moving west and north. It won't be long now before there's a trading post closer than San Antonio. Damn! I'm beating around the bush." He flashed her a smile. "This is my land. I didn't think I'd ever be settling down again, but I want to."

"You want to settle down here?" she said helpfully.

"Yes." He plunged on enthusiastically. "I'd build us a fine cabin, one we could add on to when we need to. The cattle's for the taking, you know that. With two men I could round up a herd and start branding. Longhorns are real hardy, you know. Right now it's mostly a domestic market, but we could drive them to New Orleans, or even St. Louis. We'd live well," he added, and looked at her closely.

Miranda smiled. "Derek, you're my husband," she said softly. "And this land is beautiful. If that's what you want to do, then I say do it."

"Are you sure, Miranda? I know how citified you are. I could never live in the city. We'd starve and I'd go crazy."

She smiled at him, and the soft, tender emotion he saw in her eyes made him swallow, sending his pulse racing. "I think we should start on our ranch right away."

He laughed and stopped her horse, pulling her out of the saddle, making her cry out in surprise. He kissed her boisterously at first. Then, as his exultation faded, as she stood trembling in his arms, as love swept through him, he kissed her again, gently and tenderly, trying to show her with one kiss how much he felt. It was impossible.

"That is it," Derek said, almost an hour later.

Miranda stared curiously around her. There were about twenty wickiups just like theirs spread through the sparse glade. A few young children were running and playing together, both boys and girls. Squaws sat in groups, scraping hides, sewing buckskins, sorting gathered vegetables and berries—a scene very much like the one at the Comanche village, only smaller. An infant wailed.

"Are all the men out hunting?" she asked, surprised she felt no fear.

"Nope, they're over there. Looks like there's going to be a contest." Derek grinned, pulling her down. He took her hand.

Beyond the camp she saw a group of men, ranging in age from early twenties to middle-aged. Milling among them were six boys, in their early to mid-teens. Miranda was curious.

As they walked through the camp, a cry in Apache which she couldn't understand went up, and Miranda knew their presence was being noted. Derek paused and spoke to a heavily pregnant squaw, sitting with two others, all sewing.

"Miranda," he said, "this is Najilkhise's wife, Daglnike." Miranda smiled. "Hello."

The woman smiled back, then suddenly began speaking in Spanish, which Miranda understood. "Do you speak Spanish, señora? Welcome to our home. I am happy to share our fire with you."

"*Muchas gracias,*" she replied. "And yes, I speak the language, but not that well. Well enough to understand you."

"I didn't know you spoke Spanish," Derek said as they moved on.

"There's a lot about me you don't know," she said lightly.

He grinned. "And I'm looking forward to finding all that out."

"How does she speak Spanish?"

"Many Apache do speak some. In fact, many Apache have some Spanish blood, myself included."

"You do?" She was dubious, looking at his magnificent but unusual coloring.

He smiled. "My great grandfather married one of his captives, a beautiful Castilian girl."

"Really?"

"Really. Since the late sixteenth century the Apache had been warring with the Spaniards, and then the Mexicans when Mexico became independent in '21."

Miranda was silent. She knew nothing of this history of the new land except what little she had learned in a textbook.

"My brother," A lean, wiry man of medium height and piercing features stepped forth, speaking in English, and he and Derek embraced with real pleasure.

"This is my wife," Derek said proudly. "This is my brother."

Miranda searched the man's face for a resemblance to her husband, and found it only in the mouth—a sensual, firm curve of lips. Other than that, no two men looked more different. Even in build.

He smiled then, and Miranda saw the resemblance—it was Derek's smile, incredibly so. "Brother, she is more beautiful than the whole of this land."

"I think so." Derek grinned.

Miranda blushed. She was aware of his male interest, and was surprised that Derek was so unperturbed.

"You are just in time—the race is about to begin," Najilkhise said.

They moved forward to watch. Miranda saw six boys line up, all clad in loincloths and moccasins and headbands. Their red bodies were wiry and lean, their hair long and loose. A man went from one to the other with a bucket of water and a ladle, giving each boy a mouthful of water. Derek chuckled.

"Each boy is required to finish the race without drinking the water," he told her in a low voice.

"But that's impossible." Miranda gasped.

"Of course it's possible," he returned. "This is good training. Sometimes an Apache has to run for hours without water. This is probably a four-mile race."

The boys took off, running as lightly as deer. Soon they disappeared from view, down a slope. Miranda turned to her husband. "Derek, did you ever run like that?"

He chuckled again. "Of course. My father believed in Apache childrearing ways. And why not? Apache are tougher than any other breed on earth. We spent our summers with the tribe, and sometimes winters, too. I received the same training as any boy, maybe more."

Miranda was completely enthralled, so he continued. "Pa was an honorary member of the tribe. I'm considered a part of the clan because of my mother. My kin pushed me harder than the other boys to make up for the training I lacked, and, I guess, for my white blood. I'd wake up in the morning and my grandfather would make me run up a mountain and back down, before breakfast. If my performance was bad, he'd make me repeat it at dusk.''

"How cruel."

"No, it wasn't cruel, although maybe hard. It's made me the man I am today."

"They're coming back," Miranda said.

One boy was far in the lead, running furiously now. When he crossed the finish line, he opened his mouth for inspection, a cheer went up, and he spat the water out triumphantly. The rest of the boys finished, all closely behind, but one had swallowed his water. Miranda could see the misery on his face, and his father's tight-lipped anger as they spoke together. Derek told her in a soft voice that he had tripped and swallowed the water accidentally. "He has shamed not only himself but his father as well."

Miranda felt sorry for the boy, and he and his father walked away from the group, the youth hanging his head.

A wrestling match followed, between just two boys, the winner of the race and Derek's nephew, Najilkhise's son by his first marriage. Derek explained that there was heavy betting going on.

"What do they bet?" Miranda asked.

"Hides mostly, sometimes horses."

The two boys appeared evenly matched at first. Neither could get an unshakeable grip on the other. They battled silently for twenty minutes, first one on top, then the other, breaking apart simultaneously, to charge and wrestle again. Both boys were panting, their faces red. She was dismayed that no one called a draw.

Then Derek's nephew got his opponent in a headlock, one forearm across his neck, and he forced the boy onto his knees. Miranda realized that he was strangling him. "Derek! Somebody should stop them!"

He put his hand on her shoulder. "He can admit defeat, and it will be over. But he does not give up."

Miranda gasped as the boy's face turned first red then white, and then his eyes closed and he fainted. The winner released him and a cheer went up. Miranda was appalled.

Chapter 64

That night, back at their own wichiup, they sat outside in the moonlight and talked about the ranch, making plans. Derek had his back against a boulder, and he pulled Miranda into the crook of his arm. "To start with," he said, "I'll make it a two-room cabin, but we'll add on every year until it's a fine house."

"Two rooms is fine," Miranda said, surprised that she meant it. Life had changed so much for her.

"One room will be our bedroom, of course, the other for sitting and eating. We'll cook over a fireplace, but next year, if all goes well, I'll buy us a Dutch oven in San Antonio. And later, a stove." He reached for her hand.

She hesitated. "Derek, let's sell the JB. We can use the money from the sale for everything we need, even hiring help." She felt him tense.

"No, Miranda," he finally said.

"Why?"

He frowned. "I'm supposed to use another man's fortune to take care of my wife? I can't do it. And that's that."

She twisted to look at him. "It's yours, now, you know that! It's not mine, not even legally."

"It's yours in my mind," he said stubbornly.

"Then what do you want to do with the JB?"

309

"We can sell it and put the funds in trust for—" He stopped.

She gasped.

"You haven't bled. Don't deny it. It's two months almost, isn't it? You're with child." His voice was as bleak as his heart at the thought.

"Maybe not," she said. She felt cold fear. What if she was? What would happen to them? Would Derek turn away from her? She was so afraid that he would. She didn't even have to look at him to know how much he hated her having Chavez's child.

"Is there any way it could be John's?" he asked suddenly.

"No."

"But John died only two weeks before Chavez captured you."

Miranda didn't want to discuss Chavez. The nightmares had gone away, and she didn't want them coming back.

"It's not John's," she insisted, turning to look at him.

"How can you be sure?" he said grimly.

"John only made love to me three times," she blurted, then bit her lip.

Derek gaped.

She looked away.

"Why in hell was that?"

"I was reluctant, and he was kind," she said, her voice breaking. "I was an awful wife to him, Derek. He loved me so much, and I denied him."

Derek put his arms around her and pulled her onto his lap. "He loved you. You made him very happy, I know it for a fact. There's more to love than lovemaking, as we both well know. Don't torture yourself."

Miranda turned and slipped her arms around his neck and snuggled against him, closing her eyes. His scent was so intoxicating. She inhaled deeply. He stroked her hair.

"You are so giving," he suddenly said.

"What?"

"You never take, Miranda, and you're the only woman I know who's so giving."

"That's not true," she said, thinking he was crazy.

"You never ask for anything. Look at your life, what it's become. You came out here to marry a rich rancher, and now you've become something like a squaw. Our life is hard, at least for you." He tilted her chin up so their eyes met. "Do you want it differently? Do you . . . do you want to go back—to England?"

Miranda stared. "Are you giving me a choice?"

"I don't know," he said hoarsely. "I want you happy, but I don't think I can let you go."

"Then the question was moot."

"Please, answer it." He waited, breathless, his pulse pounding.

She seriously considered it. She knew she didn't want to go home to her father. But, if she went home married and separated, he wouldn't be able to marry her off again. Then what? Would it be possible he would let her return to the convent, maybe become a nun? Or go to live with her mother's kin in France? She tried to imagine what it would be like.

She would never seek Derek again.

Her heart leaped in protest at that single thought. She smiled, then, with the glad realization that she didn't want to be apart from her husband. What a wonderful thing that was! "No, Derek," she said, after a long moment. "I want to be with you."

He stared at her perfect face. It had taken her a long time to decide that, and he wished he knew how she had arrived at her decision. Was he the least of all possible evils? Something wrenched inside him. He loved her so much. He'd told her several times, but she'd never said those words back. He knew that she didn't love him, and it hurt, badly. He wanted to declare his love again, even without the protective cloak of passion, but he didn't have the courage. He couldn't face the silence such a declaration would surely bring, when what his soul and heart cried for was the same declaration in return.

"What are you thinking?" she said softly.

He held her tightly, and caught her mouth with his. He could tell her he loved her in this way. And maybe he could make her love him back, if he loved her enough, made her happy enough. His lips caressed hers, his thumb stroked her jaw. Her mouth opened beneath his, as she returned the innocent kiss. Instantly, his desire rose. She made him insatiable. When they were together, when he was inside her, she was his and his alone, a part of him. His need to claim her in that way was so fierce. His kiss deepened, with it his breathing. He began to tease one nipple with his thumb.

Miranda pushed against him. "No," she said, breaking free.

He smiled. "No?"

"No," she said, trying to get up, but his hold tightened, and she was a prisoner in his lap.

"I want you," he whispered, and holding her head still, he found her mouth again. He was shocked when she pressed against his chest, struggling against him. "Miranda?"

"Not tonight," she said, breathing unevenly, as much from trying to break free as from the pounding of her pulse that desire had caused. "I'm too sore," she lied, trying anything to save her the shame of her wanton ways.

He lifted her in his arms without a word and carried her into their wickiup, placing her on the bed of hides. She looked at his face and saw the hunger there. He knelt beside her, fumbling with her braid, and then her hair tumbled free. "Derek," she protested.

He was kissing her again, at the same time unbuttoning her blouse and slipping it off her shoulders. She was losing control, sinking beneath his onslaught, desire rising hard and fierce and almost frantic. How she wanted him!

"I can at least give you pleasure," he said huskily, and then he pulled off her chemise and nuzzled her breasts.

She stopped worrying as his tongue worked exquisite sensations across her body. She gripped his head as his mouth moved lower. She didn't protest when her skirts, petticoat, and pantalets were pulled off, and when he claimed the essence of her with his mouth and tongue she gasped and moaned and whimpered like an animal. She felt the magnificent flood tide rising, higher and higher, wanted it, craved it. The explosion was more scintillating and brilliant and lingering than ever before.

She lay limp and languid, becoming aware of Derek next to her, holding her loosely, watching her. She turned her head to see him gazing down at her intently, unappeased desire shining in his eyes. He bent, kissing her, and a tremor shook him. He raised his head and smiled tensely. He raised a shaking hand to brush the hair from her temple, then stood. "I'm going to go down to the creek," he said, and then he was gone.

Miranda couldn't believe it. She closed her eyes, her heart still pounding. She had said no, but he had taken her anyway, selflessly—but in the most sinful way he could. And she had loved every moment. He had denied himself to pleasure her, and what did that mean? He didn't care about sin, just the flesh. He probably didn't even realize how he was treating her, or that it was wrong. And she was shameless, too, there was no escaping that fact. Her mind was weak, her desires strong. She rolled onto her side and wondered how there could ever be a resolution to this issue. She wanted to be a good wife, but she wanted to be a Christian lady just as much.

Or did she?

Chapter 65

He took her by surprise the next day, in the afternoon. She was washing tubers she had resolutely gathered, trying to decide if two of them were the same edible species as the rest. She was on her knees, clad in her buckskin dress, when his arms came around her and he kissed her smartly on the neck. She almost jumped out of her skin.

His hands moved to her breasts, squeezing gently, while he nibbled her ear. She stiffened immediately, horrified that he would come upon her and grab her as if she was some trollop in a saloon. Even so, her body began to tingle and throb. "Derek!" Anger set in.

He rolled one nipple between his thumb and forefinger, and she felt his manhood swelling against her back, throbbing. She grabbed his wrists, anger outweighing the beginning of desire. He ignored her, his hand roving down her belly, still nuzzling her neck and ear. He cupped her womanhood and began to rub it through the soft buckskin.

With strength and fury she didn't know she had, she wrenched free and slapped him as hard as she could across his face. She rose to her feet, shaking. "How dare you!"

He was stunned.

"How dare you!" she screamed like a shrew, hysterical.

"Miranda," he gasped, his eyes wide, totally uncomprehending. He stepped forward, about to grab her by her shoulders.

"Don't touch me!" she yelled. "Don't you dare!"

He froze.

She whirled and raced away, running as hard as she could into the woods, tears streaming down her face. She sank to her knees when her lungs felt like bursting, and wept. What he had done was too much. To come up on her in the open, in the middle of the day, and paw her crudely, as if she was a whore. Is that what he thought? Why would he treat her like a whore if he didn't feel that she was one? She certainly acted like one—every time he touched her!

"Why are you crying?" he said stiffly behind her. He stood above her and stared, bewildered and helpless.

"Leave me alone," she ordered. "Go away!"

He hesitated and squatted by her side. "I know I haven't done anything wrong," he began, uncertain. "Or have I?"

Miranda raised herself into a sitting position, her face streaked with tears, her eyes huge and angry and incredulous. "Nothing wrong?! You treat me like a whore and you tell me you've done nothing wrong?" She clenched her fist because she wanted to hit him wildly.

Derek was shocked. "What are you talking about? What nonsense is this?"

Her face crumpled. Of course he didn't understand, didn't care.

But he did care. "Miranda, talk to me," he pleaded, touching her hand tentatively. "I can't believe you're reacting like this to my hugging you that way."

She stared and wiped her eyes with her fists. "Hugging me? You were pawing me!"

"I . . . I guess I was. But . . ." He stopped, not knowing what to say. She waited almost belligerently. "I love touching you," he managed, realizing as he said it that the statement was totally inadequate.

"I don't like the way you treat me."

"I don't treat you like a whore," he said with a flash of anger. "And I'm insulted that you think so."

"How can you deny it?" she cried. "If not just now, then what about last night? No lady is treated the way you treated me!"

Bragg stared, gaining an inkling of understanding. "I wanted to please you, make you happy."

Miranda knew he meant it. "I don't like doing those . . . things, Derek."

"You liked it," he said, trying and wanting to understand.

"My body is wanton, but not my mind," she replied.

He stared, comprehension dawning.

"I know you have every right to take me to your bed, but not that way. That is wrong! Your pawing me in the middle of the day, out in the open, is wrong! And sinful!"

"No," he said abruptly, grabbing her hand and pulling her toward him. "Nothing we do in love is wrong. How I touch you is good and right, Miranda."

"No, it's not!"

He frowned, but he didn't release her. "What are you trying to say? What do you want?"

"I want proper lovemaking." She saw a flash in his eyes and looked away. "It's God's will to make babies, Derek, but not for you to do the things you do to me."

"Crap," he said succinctly.

She stared, and their gazes met. She saw that his was hard and uncompromising.

"I love you," he said. "And you're the finest lady I know. And I don't want to make 'proper' love to you. I don't want a frigid lady in my bed. I want a lady of passion—the kind of lady you are. Your passion doesn't make you a whore, Miranda—how can you even think that? It just makes you incredibly beautiful."

"It makes me dirty," she said

"No!" He grabbed her, commanding her gaze. "Didn't you hear what I said? I love you—and that's why I want to touch you and give you pleasure. It's right—it's the way it should be."

Miranda felt herself weakening. He loved her. She could feel it, see it in his fierce eyes. She certainly felt it when he took her in his arms. Could anything so magnificent be so wrong? Maybe God intended two people who loved each other to find such pleasure in each other's arms. Would Father Miguel know?

"Miranda? I'm not much with words. But when I touch you it's my way of showing you how I feel." His gaze held hers. "And I know, sweetheart, how much you like my touch. That doesn't make you a loose woman. It makes you a real woman, not a hypocrite, that's all."

She thought about that, too. She wanted to believe him.

He wrapped his arms around her, holding her loosely. "What are you thinking?"

"I want to accept your ideas, Derek, but I was raised differently. Well-bred ladies don't act the way I have."

He smiled. "They say they don't. But, Miranda, have you ever thought that maybe you're expressing how much you care for me, too?"

She stared.

"If you were wanton, you would have liked Chavez's touch, and not been reluctant with John. Did you ever think of that?"

She hadn't. That thought relieved her immensely, and she felt guilt and shame flowing away from her like an ebbing tide.

Derek relaxed when he saw her features soften. "Also, you make me happy," he whispered. "Isn't that important, too?"

She smiled slightly. "You know I want to be a good wife."

"We're on our honeymoon, darling. And on honeymoons newlyweds are free with their love." He studied her. "Miranda, I won't change. I'm a virile man. Before you, there was never much time when I didn't take a woman to my bed. It's the way I am. I'm thrilled to death that you're so passionate because it fulfills my needs without going against yours. Don't you see? It's perfect."

Miranda sighed. He was so much stronger than she was, and she felt so good in his embrace, even now. It was like being home, safe and secure, but exciting and exhilarating, too. She leaned her cheek against his chest.

"We're perfect together," he whispered, stroking her back.

She raised her head to look at him. Tears of gladness came into her eyes. "I think I love you," she said, and then realized she did. If love wasn't this strange soaring of her heart, this need to be with him, the desire to please selflessly, the fear of being apart, the craving of union—then what was?

He trembled. He gently tipped her face up higher and then he kissed her with all the feeling in his heart and soul.

Her arms went around his neck, and their pulses quickened. Miranda returned his kiss, needing more, and tenderness vanished before the flood of hot need. "I'm going to show you how much I love you," Derek said, pushing her onto the soft earth of the forest floor.

She looked up at him, his long, hard body covering hers, his face inches from hers, his eyes golden, glowing. He didn't kiss her, but waited silently, his arms encircling her. She closed her eyes. The love was there, in his face, in his golden gaze. She wanted him, more than ever, wanted to love him in this way. In that moment, she decided that he was right. She opened her eyes to look into his. "Show me," she breathed.

He did.

Chapter 66

The next morning Miranda awoke with love in her heart, and she lay for a minute thinking about her husband and how much she loved him. He was already gone, to cut timber for their new home. She sighed. It was time for her to get up, too. She sat up, then stood, and a wave of nausea overwhelmed her.

She barely made it out of the wickiup before she began retching uncontrollably. After the spasms had passed, she lay still, curled on her side, naked, so sick that she was afraid to move. She knew she was deathly ill.

She lay there for hours, afraid to drag herself back inside, until she fell asleep. When she awoke she was startled to find herself outside, sleeping, with no clothes on, until she remembered what had happened. She sat, a touch groggy, but otherwise fine. What had been wrong with her?

She listened to the sound of a tree crashing not far away, then straightened and went inside to dress and begin her day's chores. She was immensely relieved that whatever had struck her was gone as soon as it had come.

The next morning she was ill again, but this time she had gotten dressed and made it to the creek before the dreadful sickness began. It was there that Derek found her. The day before he had felled enough lumber for the cabin frame, today he was hauling it into their camp. He saw her, dropped the horses' reins, and came running.

"Miranda, what's wrong?" he cried, panic-stricken, crouching beside her and about to take her into his arms.

"Don't touch me," she moaned, and then she moaned again.

But he did anyway. "You're sick. Let me get you inside," he said grimly, lifting her.

"No! Oh!" She began retching violently, and Derek promptly sank to the ground, waiting until it had passed.

"Is it just nausea?" he asked, his face tight, carrying her rapidly to the wickiup.

Miranda was afraid to talk. She was going to be violently sick again if he didn't stop. But then he gently laid her down on the bed. She curled up, moaning.

"Miranda, has this happened before?" Derek asked curtly, standing above her.

"Yes," she whispered, and closed her eyes tightly.

"I'll bring you some herb tea that will help," he said, wheeling and striding out. He felt incredibly angry as he yanked the herbs Apache used for morning sickness. He did not want to raise this child. He did not want to see Miranda grow big and swollen with this child; to go through the agony of childbirth for this bastard, the product of another man's violence and lust.

"Damn!" His fist hit the trunk of the tree he was kneeling before. The pain felt good. He wanted to break the damn tree, maybe even his hand.

Every time he looked at that child, he would remember how Chavez had raped his wife. Every time.

When he brought back a tea made with the leaves, Miranda was sleeping, so he let her be. He went to the horses, still standing with six huge pine logs attached to a makeshift harness, and led them down creek, to the site they had decided on for their house. Here the meadow spread out endlessly. It was actually part of a valley, and the vista was incredible, the sky etched by green-forested, white-tipped mountain peaks. The valley was lush and dense, too rocky for crops except on a small scale to meet their own needs, but perfect grazing for cattle. In fact, he mused, longhorn survived on much less than this. Maybe he would do some crossbreeding, something better for beef that would gain the longhorn's incredible durability.

But in the back of his mind he kept thinking about the child.

Miranda was preparing their noonday meal when he returned later, hot and sweaty and too angry to speak. He sat down wordlessly, saw her smile, but refused to acknowledge it. He felt like his whole perfect world had just crashed in.

"Derek? What's wrong?"

"Nothing."

She paused. "I don't understand what's wrong with me. I feel fine now." Her gaze searched his closed face innocently. Why was he so hard-looking?

"Haven't you ever heard of morning sickness, Miranda?" he snapped.

She flinched at his tone. "Are you mad at me?" Her voice trembled.

He stood, dropping his plate and kicking it aside. "No, Miranda, I'm thrilled to death to have you bear Chavez's bastard. Can't you tell?"

Her eyes grew wide, and there was no mistaking her shock. "Are you sure?"

"Dammit, yes! Women in the early stages of pregnancy have morning sickness, just what you have." He turned stiffly. "I'm not hungry. I'm going back to work."

She stared, watching him pace with tense, coiled strides, his body rigid with anger. He went over to the team, leading them into the woods for the felled lumber. Tears rose in her eyes. Dear God, she thought, why?

Why did You give me a child conceived out of violent, cruel rape? Why?

She held her belly self-consciously and tried to figure out how far along she was. Two tears trickled down her cheeks as she watched her husband disappear into the woods. We've only just discovered each other, and now this, she thought. I don't want a child conceived out of violence and brutality. I want my husband's child. She started to cry.

The tears were soft, helpless, self-pitying. When she had gotten them all out, she felt better, stronger. She gathered their laundry and took it down to the creek, all the while thinking about God's will, and how no man could possibly understand it. This child was His will, and He worked in mysterious ways. There was a reason. She didn't know what that reason was, but she did know that this babe was completely innocent of any wrongs his father had done. She felt a surge of protective maternal warmth, and realized that she wanted this child.

As she pounded the clothes with a large paddle, she thought of Derek's son, and was struck by instant understanding. His son was half Apache, raised by Comanche. This boy was partly Comanche, and would be raised by a man with Apache blood. She almost threw the paddle aside. It was as if God was giving Derek back his son.

He returned later than he ever had before, almost at dusk, and she'd begun to worry he had had an accident. He had not come back with any lumber, so she didn't know what he had been doing. But when he sat down, she saw instantly that he had been drinking. She could smell an alelike odor, although he was not staggering. She had waited to eat with him, but he didn't speak. Barely glancing at her, he ate ravenously. She felt incredibly hurt, and wanted to cry.

This isn't my fault, she wanted to say. Why are you being so cold and mean?

After their meal, he put out the fire, leaving her with all the cleanup, and stalked into the wickiup. He always helped her at night, and if he was trying to get his point across, he was doing very well. When she crawled into bed with him she knew he was awake. He was lying on his back, staring into space. She wanted to crawl close and seek the warmth of his body, wanted to be reassured that he still loved her. She was afraid, because since their marriage he had been nothing but kind and gentle. Still, she slid toward him, placing one hand on his chest, her head on his shoulder.

He rolled over onto his side, his back to her. "Not tonight, Miranda," he said.

She rolled over too, facing away, and silent tears welled up in her eyes and fell.

Chapter 67

"Would you consider giving the child to some childless family?"

Miranda stared, horrified. "No!"

His jaw clenched. "Just thought I'd ask." He turned away.

She grabbed his sleeve, not about to let him go. She had been too ill to discuss this with him earlier, but she was fine now. "I want to talk."

He glanced at her, his face expressionless. "There's not much to talk about."

"Yes, there is! Derek, I'm going to have another man's child, and you're treating me as if it's my fault."

He softened slightly. "I know it's not your fault."

"Then stop being so cold and cruel! I can't take it!"

He stared. "I'm only a man, Miranda, not a saint. What do you want, for me to be thrilled to raise some bastard as my own?"

Miranda slapped him across the face. "Don't you ever refer to my child that way again!"

He stood a moment, shocked, and then he said, "I apologize." He turned on his heel. "I've got work to do." He strode away.

She was angry—angry and upset. How long was he going to be like this? For the rest of his life? Was he going to take out his anger and hatred on the child when it was born? She ran after him.

"Not now, Miranda," he said, not looking at her.

She was out of breath, and she clung to him with both hands until he stopped. "Yes, now!" she exclaimed, panting.

"All right." He wouldn't give an inch.

"The baby is innocent, Derek, innocent, and it's God's will."

He grimaced. "I don't believe in God's will."

"But surely you agree the babe is innocent."

He nodded. "What's the point?"

"Will you be a father to this child? Will you give him your name, protection, and caring? Will you?" Her voice rose. She had to know.

"I told you, dammit, I am no saint. Every time I look at this child I'm going to remember what Chavez did to you, and I'll be filled with anger and hate. Yes, I'll give the child my name. But don't ask me to give him love, because it's not in me to give!"

Miranda stood trembling, feeling sick deep within her heart. He was cool. "Anything else?"

She shook her head, watching him leave. She walked back to their camp, everything a blur. I never knew this man, she thought. He is not who I thought he was. He is a selfish beast, like any other man. He is kind only when it suits him. What am I going to do?

It was all she could think about all day. How could she raise this child with a father who would hate him, or at the very least be coldly indifferent? She knew she couldn't, and her heart ached unbearably with that knowledge. There was only one solution, one that broke her heart. She brought it up after supper.

"Derek?"

He was sitting in the growing twilight, his profile to her, looking amazingly handsome, his bronzed face still. He glanced at her.

She was afraid. Her heart was pounding wildly. But she had to do this for the baby. She wet her lips. "Derek? I would like to return to England."

He stared, completely attentive. "What?"

"I would like to return to England . . . please. It would be for the best." She looked into his stunned eyes and wanted to cry. She didn't, with great effort.

He regained instant control, looking away out over the mountains. "I see."

Did he? She should speak, explain, but no words came.

"You choose the child over me." The words were final. He looked at her. His gaze was so cold, so remote.

Miranda took a deep breath. "The child is innocent and defenseless. You can survive without me—easily."

He laughed, shortly, with bitterness. He looked away. "And if I refuse? We were married in the church—your church, more than mine. There are no divorces."

"Why would you refuse?"

He stood. "The answer is no." His gaze was hard, steady, a look she knew well. There was no compromise in it.

"You're not being fair," she cried, standing.

"No one said life was fair." He walked away.

Miranda felt defeated. A part of her felt relieved—and she knew she still loved him. But she had the child to think of. How could she get to San Antonio without him to begin her journey back to England? It was impossible, and she knew it.

She had just fallen asleep when she felt him slide into bed next to her, and she was instantly awake, frozen, pretending sleep. She felt him looking at her. Then she felt his hands, stroking down her arm, her hip. She was shocked. It wasn't possible, with all the anger between them, that he should want to exercise his rights tonight.

His lips brushed her temple, her ear. She twisted to face him. "No," she said firmly.

He took advantage, catching her face with both hands and kissing her. She tried to turn her head; it was impossible. The kiss deepened, and she tried to push him away. He grabbed her hair with one hand, coiling it around his wrist, the other holding her tightly around her waist. He threw one thigh over hers, pinning her. What was he trying to prove?

Miranda stopped caring. Her body began to respond eagerly, as if it had been years since they had been with each other, not a day or two. She pressed against him, accepted his tongue, probed his mouth with her own. She was desperate, starved, frantic. His passion matched hers. They kissed wildly, savagely, and she moaned. His breathing was ragged and harsh. He pulled up her skirt and thrust into her. She cried out with the sheer splendor of union. He plunged almost viciously, and she wanted it faster, harder. He sensed it, and drove himself like a rutting bull. She climaxed first, crying out wildly, and then he joined her, groaning, shuddering, collapsing.

She listened to their heartbeats, holding him lightly, and found her fingers stroking his hair. She wanted to weep with sadness. She wanted to break down the wall the child had created, but she didn't know how. She wanted to love him.

He rolled off her, and she waited anxiously for some tender sign, some words of love. He lay still on his back, eyes closed, breathing even. She moved to him. His arm curled around her. She lay her head on his chest, glad at least that he hadn't turned away, and sad that there was no tender, loving aftermath. She listened to his breathing, and realized he had fallen asleep.

Chapter 68

He was bitter, still, that she was choosing the baby over him. It proved to him that she didn't love him, and that was a stabbing truth. He felt less angry today. It was as if her asking him if she could return to England had jolted him back to his senses. But the bitterness was there, hurting.

He couldn't let her leave, because that would be giving up something more precious than his own life. He couldn't imagine living without her, not after he'd had her and her love, even if for a short time. Last night he had wanted to show her how much she needed him, but he knew he wasn't approaching her in the right way. If anyone knew the difference between lust and love, it was he. It was so ironic. He had lusted after women his whole life, then fallen in love with a complete innocent, who in return only lusted after him! If it wasn't so heartbreaking, it would be funny.

He wanted things to be right between them. If it meant his accepting the baby, he would try like hell. He had seven months, maybe a bit less, to come to grips with raising Chavez's son. He would turn to her. She could help him. But it was unfair of her to expect him to love the child as his own. That he couldn't do. What he could do, what he could try to do, was care.

That afternoon, after she had recovered from her morning sickness, he found her plucking the quail he had brought in that morning. He took her hand, stilling it. When she looked up at him, he saw the hope flaring in her eyes, and the anguish. He hated himself for being so selfish, for making her so unhappy. If he was unhappy, he resolved, he would keep it from her from now on.

"Miranda, I've been thinking."

She looked deeply into his gaze, waiting. She was so vulnerable, he thought.

He exhaled. "I want things to be right between us. I'll try to be a good father. I . . . I would never let harm come to any human being, not an innocent one, you know that, and that includes this baby. I can't pretend I can love it, but I . . . I will be a good father. You can help me, show me how. Please."

Miranda looked at him, and he saw sadness filter into her eyes.

"What is it? Haven't I told you what you want to hear?" He heard the desperation in his tone.

"I never assumed you wouldn't give my child protection and creature comforts, Derek. But you offer yourself because of me, not because of the child. What you want to do is right, but for the wrong reasons, selfish reasons."

He heard her and knew she was right. "Miranda, how do I get your love back?"

"You don't trade on love," she said softly.

He felt miserable.

She saw his unhappiness. Her hand came out to touch his cheek, and he caught it, holding it there. "Derek, we'll do the best we can."

"I'm a selfish bastard," he said. "I've always known it, but it never bothered me before. But when I met you, you became more important than my own needs. Or so I thought. Maybe I was wrong."

"I don't doubt your love," she said. She sighed. "Maybe when the baby is born you will find it in your heart to love an innocent child."

"Maybe you can help me." But even as he said the words he felt torn—he didn't want to love Chavez's son, he just wanted to love his wife. But another side, a deeper side, told him to let go of his anger.

Suddenly he lifted his head, every nerve ending in his body alert.

"Derek, what is it?"

He grabbed her arm and began propelling her toward the pile of logs and the framed cabin. They had taken three strides when an Indian war cry split the air, and the ground thundered with pounding hoofbeats.

"Miranda, behind the logs!" Derek yelled, propelling her, dragging her, shoving her forward. There was no time to think of what Comanche were doing this far west. He saw Miranda dive behind the logs, then fired just as the Comanche released his spear, riding down on him. The spear took him high in the chest, then the Comanche fell, dead. Miranda screamed.

Derek turned, firing at another attacker. He hit him and the pony raced off, riderless.

Miranda screamed in warning. "Derek!"

Too late, he felt the knife in his back, driving him to his knees. He raised his gun and fired. The attacking brave slumped over his galloping pony's side. Bragg hadn't had a chance to see how many there were, and now he was too weak, too hurt, losing blood. He was starting to have difficulty focusing. Then he heard Miranda scream again.

He was on his side, half sitting, when he saw that he was being rushed by three Comanche on ponies, all with raised spears. With great effort he focused and fired once. One warrior fell, his aim deflected, and the other two missed, galloping past. He had only two shots left. He waited. The Comanche rushed, then raised his bow. Derek fired, hitting his target. He knew it was a lucky shot because his world was a blur.

He heard her scream again. He couldn't lift his head, couldn't see, heard thundering hoofbeats, close, retreating. Everything was gray and growing black.

"Derek!" It was a shriek.

"Derek!" Fainter.

"Derek!"

Chapter 69

Miranda sobbed helplessly. She had no strength left to fight. She had seen everything, had watched her husband slaughtered before her eyes, had seen him fall as she was thrown up on a pony in front of an Indian who smelled like rancid grease. To leave him lying there destroyed her. What if he was still alive, but bleeding to death?

How could a man live after being lanced and stabbed that way?

There were only six of them, she realized dimly, and they rode through the day and into the night. She stopped thinking. Her heart was broken. She couldn't think because then she would die from the pain. Derek. Derek. She wanted to die.

They stopped the next day. Miranda wasn't sure if it was the next day or a week later. She felt utterly exhausted. She was confused, dazed. Derek was dead. Derek! Pain throbbed steadily within her. Someone pulled her off the pony, and she crumpled to the ground.

A hand coiled in her hair. She whimpered from the physical pain as she was dragged by the hair, then released, falling on her face. She heard male voices, excited voices. They were arguing. She opened her eyes, raising her head. A big man in buckskins, a white man, was talking to the Indians, gesturing with his hands. What was happening? Where was she? Where was Derek?

This wasn't happening. She was with Derek in their beautiful meadow, safe, secure. No . . . Derek was dead! No . . . soon he would come, rescue her . . . Derek, I love you. . . .

The floating, drifting sensation deepened. A fog curled around her. A misty fog . . . England. Her mother, a park, beautiful, manicured lawns. Her mother loved her. She was young, so young, a little girl. The fog was cool and soft, like a fluffy cloud. She didn't want to leave it, but someone was shaking her. Miranda forced her eyes open, and her heart leaped at the sight of a buckskin-clad chest. "Derek."

The man smiled. "This is your lucky day, l'il gal. Come on. We got some traveling to do."

Miranda blinked and stared at the big, dirty stranger. Derek was dead. Nothing mattered. The Comanche had already ridden off. When the man pulled her to her feet, she moved as if she were drugged.

Chapter 70

He didn't know how long he'd been unconscious. That was his first coherent thought—that he was conscious. His next was of Miranda.

He focused. He was hurt—dying, if he didn't do something about it. His back was in agony. His chest burned, but that pain was insignificant to the rest. He was weak, and when he opened his eyes, it was dawn, red, rosy, and very blurry. He closed his eyes and fainted again.

The next time he came to, the sun was high and very, very hot. He managed to pull his knife from his sheath. He had to rest after that effort. He made an incision in his shirt. He was panting, and desperately thirsty. He was going to faint. No! He had to live . . . to find Miranda.

He fought the encircling blackness. He cut through his shirt, slicing it into awkward rags. Then he fainted again.

But only for a few hours, he saw, when he came to again. He still had the knife in his hand, and he released it, with great difficulty placing both his hands on the spear protruding from his chest. It was in a good spot, he noted, below the collarbone, above his lungs. He was lucky. In his mind he smiled at the complete irony of the thought. He needed strength. He yanked, moaning in pain, fighting wave after wave of dizziness.

It took him half a dozen tries to finally pull the spear out, and then the blood gushed anew. By sheer willpower he managed to place a wad of his shirt on the wound and rolled onto his stomach, still clutching the material to his chest. He refused to pass out.

He knew the knife was still in his back, because he had fallen against it before twisting half consciously to his side. The pain was unbelievable, high in his back, in his shoulder, in bone and muscle. He was so weak. He had to get it out, but he knew he didn't have the strength, not yet.

He crawled to the creek. He passed out twice, and it took him hours to go thirty yards. His body was burning, and he knew fever was setting in. But he wasn't going to die. He slithered into the water.

He drank deeply.

With his knife he cut off the rest of his shirt in strips. The process took him a long time. All the while he sat in the creek, letting the water bathe his wounds. He bound the wad to his chest with a strip of his shirt, still bleeding. He was weaker than ever, but his determination outweighed everything. He ignored the knife in his back; he knew without trying that there was nothing he could do to get it out, not now.

He could not think about Miranda, either. But he did wonder, briefly, if his people had been attacked, too. He fell asleep.

He awoke burning up with fever, but he had expected it. Desperately he hung on to sanity. His chest wound had stopped bleeding and was clotting. He knew he shouldn't get it wet, but he also knew he could die from the fever. He had already determined that the chest wound was the more serious injury. He crawled fully into the water until it coverd him, clear and cool, and he slept again.

He awoke as cold as he had been before, but he didn't move, he wasn't able to. The chills alternated with burning heat. At some point he began to thrash and murmur and dream, mostly of Miranda. He relived their time together. He could actually feel her touch on his forehead, so cool and soft.

He saw his son as a newborn infant, and he felt thrilled with pride. The boy howled with lusty vigor from his first moments in the world. Derek held him. His wife smiled tiredly. She was Apache. Then, before his eyes she turned into Miranda. The boy in his arms became Chavez's bastard. He stared, holding the infant, unable to put it down, but not wanting to touch it. The infant changed, became his own flesh and blood, then turned back again into the unwanted bastard. Finally he saw his son, tall, a teenager, a Comanche. Derek was protecting Miranda from his son who was charging, wanting to kill her. Bragg prepared to defend Miranda from his own flesh and blood.

He awoke to a sparkling day, the pleasant, tepid warmth of a late setting sun. He focused, remembering. He was in the creek, covered up to his neck, but he was no longer feverish. He was very, very weak. He didn't have the strength to move, but he tried to take a mental inventory of his wounds. The bandage on his chest was as clean as if he had never bled. He became aware that there was no knife in his back. Had he pulled it out? Or had the water loosened it? He didn't remember pulling it out. How long had he fought the fever?

And, God, was Miranda okay?

He knew he needed strength. He dug with his fingers in the mud to find worms and bugs, which he ate. He was too weak to spear a fish with his knife, which was tucked in his belt. But if he built up his strength he would be able to catch a fish and eat it raw. Until then he would live on worms and bugs. He sank into sleep.

Part Four

The Beloved

Chapter 71

"What's wrong with her?" the woman asked suspiciously, her hands on her ample hips.

"You can see she's a beauty," the big, buckskin-clad man said, scratching his lice-ridden beard.

The woman was short and plump, clearly a prostitute, clad in a scandalously low-cut black satin gown. She was not young and not old. Her hair was red and natural, her face heavily painted. Her eyes were hard and old. "Chester, what did you do to this girl?"

They both looked at Miranda. Her hair was nothing but snarls, her dress filthy tatters. Chester had washed her face, the better for Mollie to see what a beauty she was, but nothing could change the vacant look in her eyes. If she saw them looking at her, or heard them, she didn't give a sign. In fact, she never looked at them, but through them, as if they didn't exist.

"I didn't do nuthin'. She's an idiot, I guess. She don't talk, don't smile, nuthin'. But she's a beauty. Hell, she don't need to talk, Moll, you know that. Men don't pay a whore to talk."

Mollie frowned and walked up to the girl, then around her, inspecting her. "She's thin." She wanted to ask how Chester had come by this girl, but she wouldn't—she never asked. Never before had she even wanted to know. "Girl, you got a name?"

Miranda looked at her blankly. She was in such pain. Why couldn't they leave her alone with her grief?

"I told you, she don't talk. But me an' Will named her Belle, 'cause she's such a looker. Listen, you don't want her, I can unload her in Chihuahua, I know that."

Mollie frowned. "I'm short two girls, Chester. Damn bitches run off and got married, can you believe it? The way this town is growing, damn, I need all the girls I can get."

"You sure do," Chester encouraged her. He wouldn't tell her that he privately thought the wench was insane. Crazy like a loon. At night she'd moan and whimper, saying the name *Derek* over and over. Her man—the one killed by the Comanche. He'd always been afraid of crazy folks, and it was too bad, because if she weren't crazed from her grief he'd have bedded her. What a waste. "Galveston's three times the size it was five years ago," he said.

"There was nothing here five years ago, practically." Mollie snorted. "All right. I'll take her. Maybe with some food and sleep she'll snap out of it. Let me ask you, though, how long she been like this?"

Chester hesitated. He didn't want to tell her she'd been like this from the first day he'd seen her and bought her from the Comanche.

"I see," Mollie said astutely. "Well, I ain't giving you the standard price, not for this one. Seventy-five, and that's it."

"Damn! That's robbery! You know I don't sell a girl for less than a hundred fifty. You make that much in six months."

They bickered back and forth and agreed on a hundred, as they had both known they would. Chester left. "Well, girl," Mollie said, taking her hand. "I'm going to have one of the girls bathe you and bring you up a fine meal." She led her out of the office behind her saloon, which served also as her sleeping quarters. There was a back stairs up to the rooms where her girls lived and work. There were eight girls—now this one made nine. Better than nothing, she thought.

"Lil, follow me," Mollie said to a tall, willowy brunette. Lil had been standing in a doorway clad in a sheer wrapper, talking to a plump Mexican and a thin redhead. She obediently followed Mollie and Miranda into a small room containing a bed, a washstand, a chair, and wardrobe.

"Who's this?" Lil asked curiously, her blue eyes friendly.

"Belle. She needs some care. I want you to fix her up, see if you can't get her to talk. Maybe she's deaf and dumb, I don't know. I don't think she's a dimwit, myself. Something so damn empty about those eyes." Mollie stared at Miranda, scowling. Then, "See she eats, too. I want her fattened up good." Mollie left. She was disturbed about the girl, and she didn't like it. She was a businesswoman, and a cold one. If she hadn't been, she'd still be on her back every night like her girls, instead of just when she felt like it.

"Hello, Belle," Lil tried. "Gee, you are dirty, but truly beautiful. Let's get you out of these clothes." She wondered if the girl even heard her. She didn't seem to, just standing there in the middle of the small room where Mollie had left her.

Lil undressed her after sending for hot water and a tub. The girl was thin and bruised. She felt sorry for her. She knew the girl had been brought here by Chester. She herself had chosen her life, which was different. She sighed and helped Miranda into the tub, talking all the time.

"Things really aren't so bad here. Mollie pretends to be mean, but she's not. We have plenty of food and we get one day off a week. Mollie says its important for us to get a day of rest. It's better for business, she says. She wants us fresh. You're so pretty you'll be real popular—well, maybe not. Don't you ever talk?"

Miranda looked at the woman bathing her, seeing her as if through a haze. The woman was speaking to her, and the words came from a great distance away. She wondered where she was. Oh yes. Galveston. Chester had bought her from the Comanche. Sold her into a brothel—just like Derek had said. Derek. She had never told him how much she loved him—and now he would never know.

"You have such pain in your eyes," Lil said compassionately. "Did he hurt you?"

It would take too much effort to answer, so she didn't
respond.

Lil washed her with soft caresses, as if she were a frail
child. Even her compassionate touch couldn't stir Miranda
from her grief. Lil helped her out of the tub, chattering
now about the latest gossip in Galveston, gently toweling
her dry. When Lil wrapped her in the thick towel,
pushing her onto the bed, Miranda was pliant. Lil began to
comb through the tangles of her hair.

"Good Lord! I never seen so much hair on a head!
You're lucky, Belle, do you know that?"

Lil finished and spread Miranda's hair out along her
shoulders to let it dry. She removed the towel, handing
her a wrapper, much like the one she was wearing, from
the wardrobe. Miranda looked at it without curiosity. It
was sheer and hid nothing. It brought home the fact that
she was indeed in a brothel. But she slipped it on. She
didn't care—she couldn't care. Nothing mattered anymore.

Chapter 72

Miranda looked up as Lil returned to the room with a tray of food. Lil smiled brightly. "Hello again, Belle. I've brought you some food."

Food. She wasn't sure when she had last eaten, but the aroma of chili and beans was pungent, and even though she didn't care whether she ate or not, her stomach growled. Despite herself, she looked at the tray. She sighed and said to Lil, "My name is Miranda, not Belle."

Lil's eyes widened with surprise. "You *can* talk! Oh, dear, I was so worried about you! Are you all right?"

In answer, Miranda felt tears coming again. From deep inside, deep in her soul. Oh Derek.

"What's wrong, dear?" Lil's tone was compassionate.

"My husband."

Lil sat down on the bed next to her. "Do you want to talk about it? Maybe it would help."

"It won't bring him back," Miranda said softly.

"I'm sorry."

Miranda shook her head. "I don't think I can go on without him." Her voice broke.

Lil put an arm around her. "You've got to, honey. If he loved you as much as you loved him, he'd want you to."

Those words rang true. And there was something else, something she'd avoided thinking about all the time, and

341

her hand went unconsciously to her belly in an age-old protective gesture.

Lil gasped. "Honey—you're with child?"

Miranda nodded.

"Then you just have to eat and get on with living," Lil said firmly.

Miranda knew she was right—but didn't know if she could. "It's so hard."

"No, it's not." She set the tray on her lap, and handed Miranda a spoon. "One bite at a time."

Miranda ate.

"Honey, I'll see if I can't get you a few more days to grieve, to pull yourself together, before you have to start working."

Miranda stopped eating. Fear pierced her numbness. "Lil—I can't."

Lil grimaced. "Honey, you're going to have to earn your keep."

Miranda shook her head and gulped back a sob, seeing Derek's golden image. Did it matter? Did anything matter now?

Lil watched her, frowning. She coaxed her through most of the meal, told her to get a good night's rest, and said she would be in to see her in the morning. She left, and Miranda fell into another light, dozing sleep, broken by nightmares about Derek's murder. Once she woke up screaming, and Lil rushed in half clad to comfort her.

The next few days passed in a kind of haze. Lil came to visit often, and introduced her to other girls—prostitutes— who seemed kind and cheerful, if curious and sympathetic. Miranda's grief and lack of animation tugged at everyone's compassion. She rarely smiled, and when she did, it was soft and slight, barely there, a sad, pain-filled smile. Lil wasn't the only one to pity her and want to protect her. Most of the other girls did, too.

The day came when Mollie decided that Miranda was ready to work. Lil brought the news that afternoon, and Miranda stared at her with a twinge of fear. "What am I to do?"

"I'll help you dress," Lil told her. "You'll serve drinks downstairs, and when a man wants to take you up to your room, you get the money first, and give it to Cleeve. Never spend more than a half an hour with any man; twenty minutes is better. Soon as he's done, give him the boot.''

Miranda's heart started to pound.

Lil hugged her. "You'll do just fine."

The dress was a rose satin, faded and worn. It was cut very low, exposing almost all of Miranda's small bosom. Lil brushed out her hair into a shining, waist-length mass. Because Miranda was so pale, Lil added rouge to her lips and cheeks. Lil regarded her handiwork and thought Miranda looked like a painted porcelain doll. She felt a pang of pity and regret. They went downstairs, Miranda looking more and more frightened every moment.

The saloon was loud with raucous laughter, rank with male body odor and cheap whiskey. Lil felt Miranda stiffen, saw her face pale, and took her hand. "It's all right."

Men stopped talking and they all looked at Miranda. She was new, and thus an object of considerable interest. Miranda's fear increased as the reality of what was happening registered. "Miranda, this is Cleeve," Lil said. "You bring Cleeve the money, three bits, before you go upstairs," she repeated.

Cleeve was tall and stocky, balding and mustached. He looked at Miranda. "Hey, she all right, Lil?"

Lil bristled. "She's fine. Ain't you, honey?"

Miranda looked at Cleeve, then Lil, scared to death.

A big man in stained buckskins, bearded and with broken teeth, sauntered forward. "Hey, little lady, I'll be your first."

Miranda looked at Lil. "Lil—I can't."

He reached in his pocket and tossed some coins on the bar, toward Cleeve. "What's your name?" He grabbed her hand.

Miranda felt his touch and was terrified. She paled and tried to pull away.

"Her name is Miranda," Lil said, worried. "It's all right, honey, you take Moss up to your room. He'll know what to do."

Moss laughed, revealing yellow teeth, several missing. He grabbed Miranda by the waist.

Miranda's heart began to race. She looked at Lil pleadingly, and began to struggle. "No!"

"A fighter!" Moss was delighted. He laughed again and picked her up as if her weight was meaningless to him, carrying her up the stairs. She hadn't stopped struggling, in fact, she was fighting with hysterical strength. Lil couldn't stand it.

She raced up the stairs, knowing that she had to stop Moss. She reached them as they went inside Miranda's bedroom, and followed them. Moss threw Miranda on the bed, reaching for his belt buckle.

"No, Moss," Lil said. "You don't want her, you want me."

"Hell no, Lil. I want the new one. She's prettier."

Miranda huddled on the bed, panting and tensed, her painted cheeks stained with rouge and tears.

"She's been ill," Lil snapped, and placed herself between Moss and the bed. "We thought she was well enough to work, but she ain't."

"Get out of my way," Moss growled.

Lil struck a provocative pose.

Moss snorted.

Lil gave him a surly look, and began to unhook her gown in the back.

"It won't work, Lil," Moss said, but he was hard and grinning.

Lil slid the gown down to her waist, revealing a partial corset that thrust her breasts up, the nipples just visible. "You know how good I am," she said huskily.

"Damn," Moss said. His eyes were hot.

Lil slid the gown the rest of the way down. She wore no petticoats—nothing, in fact, but stockings and garters. Moss stared at the hair curling between her thighs, then inhaled sharply as Lil touched herself intimately. "Tell me who you want now, Moss," she whispered.

He grabbed her. Lil darted free, out the door, and into her room next door. Moss followed.

Lil returned sometime later, and found Miranda still on

the bed, her eyes closed. "You all right, honey?" she asked, picking up her dress and slipping it on.

Miranda looked at her with gratitude. "Thank you."

"I've got an idea, Miranda, one to keep you off your back. I'm going to go back downstairs, but I guess you'd better stay here until I talk to the other girls and then to Mollie."

"You can talk to me now," Mollie said grimly from the doorway, clad in her usual black satin. Her gown, unlike her girls', was new. "Why is she cowering up here alone?"

"Mollie, Miranda just lost her man. She's only a child, look at her! She needs time—"

"She'll get over it," Mollie said.

"Yes, she will—with time." Lil stared, hands on hips.

"Lil, you have gotten too bold," Mollie said, frowning. "I paid money for her, and I expect her to earn her way."

"I'll take up her slack," Lil said. "If me and the other girls all do one extra trick each night, it'll be the same as if she was working."

"The rest of the girls would never agree."

"I think they would. They all feel for her."

Mollie hated to admit it, but ever since she had first seen the girl, she had had doubts about buying her, because of her strange mental state. It had made her wonder just what had happened to the girl, that she was so vacant and detached. Now, of course, she knew, for Lil had told everyone. The girl disturbed her and made her feel sympathy—something totally out of character. "If you can talk the other girls into it, we'll try it for a while. But she still has to serve drinks."

"We can say she's your niece," Lil said eagerly. "And that's why she's off limits."

Mollie just walked away.

Chapter 73

Derek was too weak to search for Miranda, but he set out anyway, while the trail was still fresh. A week had passed since the fever had abated, and he could only guess how many days had gone by before that, since the attack. A week at most, he thought, but with luck only three or four days. Miranda was a week and half or two ahead of him. His wounds were bound tightly, healing, but he was weak and his movements stiff and sore. He was half a man right now, and he knew it. But he had his guns. He could shoot as straight as ever, and he had his eyes—he could track.

Their trail was old, and he lost it time and time again. Because he was weak, he had to travel slowly, stopping often to rest in exhaustion. But he pushed on. There had been six Comanche carcasses around the camp, and he soon saw that he was following six other braves, one riding with extra weight—his wife. He was terribly afraid.

He knew this time was worse than Chavez. Chavez had been obsessed, and had wanted her for himself. He knew it was the Comanche way to rape every female captive, each brave taking a turn if he so desired. What if they killed her from repeated rape? He felt sick inside.

If he ever found her, he would send her back to England. That was where she belonged. She didn't deserve the punishment this savage land inflicted on its frontiersmen. It was a promise he made to himself, one he would keep.

He also prayed to God, once, before he set out. It was the only time in his life he had ever prayed. He got down on his knees, his hands clasped as he'd seen her do, and closed his eyes. He begged God for her life, for she was pure and good and faithful. He didn't try to make a bargain, didn't offer anything in return, he just begged. He had never been so humble.

Five days out of camp he found signs of a Comanche campsite. He saw where the extra-weighted horse had stopped, its rider dismounting, and then the scuffed area where Miranda had obviously been dropped, or had fallen. From there he saw she had been dragged a short distance away, on her back. He could see heel marks and claw marks—her fingers. The spot she had been dragged to was surrounded by footprints, moving back and forth in a circle around her. He was sick, because these signs unfurled the story as if he were seeing it, and he did, with his Apache eye. They had all raped her, there, where he was standing.

There were also signs that two riders had approached, big men on loaded-down horses, at least one of whom was white. One man had worn boots, a man lean and light. A big, heavy man had worn moccasins. There were empty jugs of whiskey scattered around, chewed tobacco, the remains of a fire, and a deer carcass. He understood. Miranda had left with these men, had been sold to them. And these men had walked over to her too, inspecting— and perhaps even raping her.

His resolve outweighed his physical fatigue, and he pushed on, following the two men who had headed south and east. These tracks were easier to follow, for the horses were so heavily burdened. He rode until it was too dark to see, and then he fell from his horse, forcing himself to eat the smoked venison he had brought with him. At dawn he rode again.

Chapter 74

He rode into Galveston with grim determination.

He had lost their trail a day ago, but by that time, there was no doubt in his mind that they were heading for Galveston. They had avoided all other towns, settlements and even farms and ranches. Derek knew why. It was because Miranda was their prisoner.

He was afraid. There was a strong possibility that Miranda wasn't even there, but had been sold again and shipped south, to a Mexican brothel. He quelled the rising sickness and dread such thinking brought. He knew he must be about a month behind her. He had been making bad time, especially at first, and he had also lost the trail time and time again, having to double back to find it.

He intended to comb every saloon and brothel in Galveston before heading to the waterfront. He had prayed to God before that she was all right. Now he just prayed—to anyone who would listen—that he would find her here.

A few hours later he was at the end of his rope, feeling despair, losing hope, having covered every saloon and brothel except for the two closest to the waterfront. He rode up to the Red Garter as dusk was settling in. The streets were quieting down, but the din from within the saloon was increasing. He slipped off his chestnut gracefully, his stiffness and soreness having gone away. Sometimes at night the stab wound in his back ached when it was damp.

He brushed through the wide swinging doors, scanning the room. Already the saloon was full of rugged, dirty men—sailors and travelers and men in buckskin, shouting and laughing, slamming empty glasses down and demanding more. Three girls floated among the men, serving drinks, all in garish satin dresses revealing almost complete expanses of bosom. He had a sinking feeling, then walked to the bar and found a spot between a sailor who didn't speak English and a huge man who smelled like bear and grease. The bartender saw him, and came over some moments later.

"A whiskey," Derek said.

The man poured.

"I'm looking for a woman," he said as the man pushed the glass at him.

"You're in the right place." Cleeve grinned.

"This woman is young, seventeen, with violet eyes and black hair. She's beautiful, but thin. Her name is Miranda."

Cleeve squinted, taking the money Derek had flipped onto the bar. "No gal like that here."

His heart sank.

"Why you looking for this particular one?"

"She's my wife," Derek said. "And she was abducted by Comanche, then sold to white slavers."

Cleeve made a noise of sympathy and walked away to serve another customer.

Bragg gulped the whiskey down in one shot. He had one last place to try. He wouldn't hang out here, he was impatient. He pressed away from the bar.

And then he saw her coming down the stairs. *Miranda.*

He froze, taking her in, unable to believe his eyes. She was pale and thin, but breathtakingly lovely in a fragile, delicate way. She was wearing a whore's red satin dress, and he became angry—angry at what she was showing, angry that she was coming from upstairs; he knew damn well what went on up those stairs. He reached her in four strides, just as she hit the bottom step, and grabbed her, crying, "Miranda!"

She saw him, and rushed into his arms, clinging, trembling, crying his name.

"You're alive," Derek groaned. "Oh God . . ."

"Derek, Derek, I thought they killed you," she wept.

"I'll never let you out of my sight again," he said harshly. And a second later, he felt a steel barrel in his back.

"Let her go," Cleve said.

Derek froze, releasing Miranda.

"Cleeve, he's my husband, don't!" Miranda cried.

"You gonna leave by yourself?" Cleeve drawled. "Or do I escort you outside?"

Derek stared at him.

Cleeve smiled slightly, waving the gun barrel. "Get lost, mister."

Derek saw her moving before he could stop her. With a look of rage, she leaped for Cleeve, her nails going for his face. As Cleeve tried to defend himself, Derek knocked the gun away. He grabbed his wife like a striking snake, one arm clamping around her waist, pulling her off Cleeve, holding her against his body, his other hand drawing his Colt. Miranda relaxed against him. The men at the table nearest them leaped up and away from their chairs. Cleeve stared, and everyone in the saloon turned their attention to him.

"My name is Derek Bragg," Derek said to Cleeve. "And in case my reputation hasn't preceded me, I'm a Ranger." He paused to let the implication sink in. "This is my wife. Anyone who tries to stop me will precipitate mass slaughter, because nothing would give me greater pleasure than to shoot up this saloon and everyone in it."

There was absolute silence. No one moved. Derek smiled grimly. Then a woman in black satin stepped into the space where the bar ended.

"What's going on?" Mollie demanded, stepping forward into the middle of the saloon. "Release my niece at once!"

"This is not your niece, ma'am," Derek said, "but my wife. And right now I'm not taking too kindly to finding her here, whoring for you."

Mollie was quick. "Miranda only serves drinks, ask

anyone. She needed a job. I gave her one, out of the kindness of my heart.''

Derek didn't take his eyes off the men in front of him. "Miranda?"

"I never . . . never, Derek."

He smiled grimly. "It's your lucky day. You have earned the right to live by not allowing her to whore for you, but don't press your luck. My trigger finger is itching.''

"Humph," Mollie said.

Derek backed out of the saloon with Miranda pressed tightly against him, daring anyone to even think of trying to stop him. No one did.

He set her up on his horse, then leaped behind her, clutching her firmly again. He wheeled the horse, and they rode off.

Chapter 75

Derek looked at Miranda, choking up from deep inside. They were in a hotel room in Galveston. She was weeping. "I thought you were dead. They took me away, and I thought you were dying." She rushed to him. "Oh, Derek, thank God you're alive!"

"I'm alive," he said huskily. "Very much so. I couldn't possibly die without rescuing you first." He felt something wet on his face and was shocked when he realized it was his own tears.

"I wanted to die," she moaned into his chest. "I didn't care anymore, not without you. We rode for a day, days, I have no idea how long."

He held her tighter. "Miranda, are you all right?" He had to know.

"Oh God, yes!"

He caught her face before she could press her mouth to his. "The Comanche—did they hurt you? And the child?"

Her eyes met his. "I wasn't raped. They sold me right away, and the man who bought me was afraid of me—he thought I was crazy."

His breath expelled. "And the baby?"

Miranda searched his gaze. "He's fine."

For a moment he just closed his eyes. "I have you back," Derek said, the relief in his voice immense. He cupped her face.

"No," she cried. "I have *you* back." She slipped her hands up into his hair, clutching it. Pulling his head down, she kissed him frantically.

He was surprised, even more so when she forced his mouth open and began a fierce assault with her tongue.

"Miranda . . ."

"Love me," she gasped, pulling him down onto the bed. "Love me!"

She still held his head, and she was partly on his chest, seeking his mouth again, desperately. She kissed his face all over, his eyes and his nose, his cheeks and then his mouth, and he exploded in response to her passion, needing her as much as she needed him. Desperate, mindless, except for the soaring, overwhelming sensation of loving each other so completely, they shed their clothes, stroking each other frantically, reeling, gasping, their tongues entwined.

"I love you," Derek cried, shuddering, holding her face still in both his hands so he could imprision her mouth with his.

"I love you, too," Miranda breathed, and he caught her hips, pulling her down to where he wanted her, kneeling between her thighs, poising his thick, straining shaft against her wet pink flesh. He looked into her eyes and she gazed back breathlessly. "I love you," he said again, and then he glided into her.

As his length and width slowly filled her, he saw tears start, and she began to cry, harder and harder. "Miranda," he gasped, not understanding, about to spiral out of control.

"I love you so much," she sobbed, holding his head tightly, kissing him. He could taste her tears. "Never, Derek," she said, her face still wet. "Never leave me—I never want us to be apart."

"I'll never leave you," he said huskily, meaning it. He wrapped her in his arms, closing his eyes, thinking, feeling, knowing how much he loved her. And then his life seed burst from him in an explosion, draining, emptying. He shuddered into her, giving her everything he had, everything he could, and they were truly one.

Chapter 76

He leaned on one elbow and smiled down at her. She met his gaze and smiled back; they held hands. "I love you," he said huskily.

"I love you," she said.

He reached out to touch her cheek. He let his hand drift down to cup her breasts, feeling hunger rising in him again. He stroked the smooth, swollen flesh, marveling at her beauty. He ran his hand down her torso, to the slight swell of her abdomen. He rested it there, then slowly began to rub the faint mound.

"I was afraid you had died before I could ever tell you how much I love you," she said.

"Tell me now."

"I could never live without you," she said. Their eyes met, held.

"Your skin is so smooth," he whispered, exploring her belly, fascinated with its shape, its firmness, its silkiness. He bent over to flick a nipple into hardness with his tongue. She took it into his mouth, sucking gently. His encircling caresses expanded, dropping lower. He slid a finger into the wet, moist valley below. She trembled.

He stroked her gently, his mouth playing with her nipple. She clutched his head and spread her thighs, arching for him. Gently, he rolled her onto her side, her back to his chest. She was confused.

"Raise your leg," he murmured, lifting her upper leg so it was bent at the knee. And then he eased into her wet, throbbing passage from behind, cupping her hips, pausing, full and heavy and straining inside her.

"Oh, Derek," Miranda breathed.

He chuckled, a laugh of sexual power and desire. He moved slowly, languidly. "How does it feel?"

"So full. Derek . . ."

He reached up to fondle her breast as he stroked her slowly. He kissed the nape of her neck, her shoulder, the side of her throat. She gasped, unable to move because of their position, but wanting to, wanting more. She whimpered.

He understood, moved harder, with more determination. His hand stroked downward from her breast, over her belly, to the swollen pearl. He began moving faster and faster. When she cried out, he wrapped his arms around her, thrusting once, twice, shuddering, emptying all of himself into her, as much as he had to give. They lay damp and still except for their heavy breathing and their pounding hearts.

She turned onto her back. "And to think I once thought our lovemaking wrong."

"You don't anymore?"

Her eyes were older, wiser, hinting of sadness, tragedy. "Am I a fool?"

He wished he had been able to spare her the trials she had suffered. He put his arm around her, kissed her lightly.

"Derek?"

"Yes?"

"You don't seem distressed anymore about my child."

He took her hands. "I won't lie to you. It's hard. But I think I've conquered my anger, mostly." He gazed at her seriously. "I'll do my best, Miranda. I swear."

"I know you will," she said, smiling, faith glowing in her eyes, faith and love. "I think of your son sometimes," she added.

He suddenly remembered a dream in which his newborn

son had changed into Chavez's son. He frowned. "What do you mean?"

"It occurred to me a long time ago that some Comanche family is raising your boy, and you're going to raise a child with Comanche blood. Maybe this child is a gift from God."

He stared at her. He didn't believe this baby was a gift from God to replace his own child, but it struck him how the situations were exactly reversed—almost too much so to be coincidence. He was part Apache, Chavez part Comanche. . . .

"God does work in mysterious ways."

"You know," he said thoughtfully, "forget about God for a minute. Someone took in my boy and raised him as their own, undoubtedly needing him for lack of sons. Someone gave him care, and hopefully love." He stared out the window.

"Just like you're going to raise our child and care for him," Miranda said. She knew he was struck by the coincidence of the parallel situations. She knew it was meant to be, and one day he would realize it, too.

He pulled her closer. "I can't wait to take you home."

She raised herself up. "Home?"

He looked into her eyes and saw her distress. "We'll rebuild the JB," he said. "It will be much safer than my own land, being close to San Antonio. That other time was a fluke, Mir— "

"No!"

They stared at each other, his heart sinking, her face fearful and set. When he spoke again, his voice was very calm. "Miranda, the JB was attacked because of Chavez—"

"No!" She was sitting, pulling the covers up. "I can't. Derek, I love you. But I hate this land."

He was afraid. "What would you like to do?"

"Let's live in the city—any city. Even San Antonio. But I won't, Derek, I won't go live in that godforsaken wilderness, not now, not after I've found you again, not with the baby— Derek, you were almost killed!"

"I see," he said.

Miranda reached for him. "Please. For me. Please."

He tried to smile and failed. "All right, princess. You

know I would never force you to do something against your will.''

With a sob of relief, she catapulted into his arms.

He held her, wondering how they were going to make their marriage work. He then vowed that he would, no matter what.

Chapter 77

Derek took her back to San Antonio, then proceeded to rebuild the JB.

Miranda's protests were at first vocal, then silent. He left her in the care of an elderly seamstress, a widow, who lived in town. On the journey back he had realized he'd never be happy living in the city—nor could he let her go back to England. Not ever. He would rebuild the JB, which was close to San Antonio and had never—until Chavez—had a problem with the Comanche, because of its size and location. And somehow he would get her to change her mind, no matter how long it took.

He rode into town once a week to see her. Because he had no cash—indeed, few Texans did—he had to rebuild alone, from scratch, and he started with the house. Because he was the legal owner of the JB, his credit was good for the supplies he needed. By early August the ranch house had been rebuilt, on a smaller scale—one story, three rooms, a kitchen and dining room, a parlor/study, and their bedroom. It helped that all the hearths were still standing. The house could be added on to later. His neighbors had come for a barn raising, and the smokehouse had been finished as well. He had framed the bunkhouse, but decided he would finish it at his leisure. He did need to hire hands to round up the JB cattle, but he had no money for wages, so until he could sell some beef, he would have to wait and do it himself. He sold his own land on the Pecos. After everything that had happened, he knew that he could never live there again—much less with Miranda.

She was now obviously pregnant—five months, or more. It was so hard living apart from her, and his weekly visits were just not enough. He knew she felt the same way. He loved the way her eyes lit up when he appeared Sunday mornings to call on her. Sometimes, even though he was exhausted after a full day's work, he would ride into town to see her on a Saturday night—take her to dinner and for a stroll in the moonlight. They would find a secluded spot down by the river and make love as if it were the first time. It was only when they were together that he felt complete, and even though she listened with polite interest to his report of how the rebuilding was going, he knew she was still upset by what he was doing. He didn't know how he was going to get her to come around. He was rapidly reaching the point where he was losing his patience.

Miranda had been spending part of her time helping Mrs. Leander, the seamstress, in exchange for her keep. She had offered to do so after the first two weeks, when she realized that Derek had no cash. She knew she was imposing on the woman—who was not immune to Derek's charm—and she was excellent with needle and thread. Mrs. Leander was thrilled to have an assistant for the price of room and board.

Miranda spent her spare time making maternity clothes for herself and clothes for the baby. Sometimes she and Derek would sit together in an easy silence and he would watch her knitting a pair of booties, her face glowing with an expectant mother's joy. He had reached the point where he didn't think he cared that the child wasn't his, or at least not much. He was so glad to see her happy at times like these. If only she could be happy at his side, instead of living apart.

The time came when he felt he had to put his foot down.

The JB was ready. It was a warm summer morning, and Miranda flew into his arms when she saw him, surprised, for it was the middle of the week. "Derek—what are you doing here?"

He held her firmly by the shoulders. "It's time to pack your things, princess."

She stared.

"I'm taking you home with me."

She backed away. "I told you—"

"No, Miranda. You're my wife and you belong at my side. You're miserable without me, and I'm miserable without you. We can't go on like this. I'm taking you back with me. I'd rather you have an open mind. I'd rather you want to please me, to make me happy the way I've bent over backwards to make you happy. But failing that, I'm taking you back anyway."

Their gazes locked. She flushed.

He kept on, ruthlessly. "I've never asked much of you. I've treated you like the princess I think you are. When John died I gave you time, when I was so in love with you I couldn't stand it. Even up on the Pecos, I didn't push you—not when it would have been my right. I've accepted this child. Tried my damndest to feel like a father. I know I let you down a few times and damn, I'm sorry, I wish I could do it over. But now I'm asking something of you. I've never asked you for anything before. As your husband I'm not even required to ask you for anything, but I am. Please come home with me—please try to make a life with me, at my side."

Her beautiful violet eyes were wet, and two pink stains crept along her cheeks. "I'll try, Derek," she said softly.

Chapter 78

"Derek, it's beautiful!"

He smiled, ridiculously pleased, and swung down from the wagon. "I've still got a lot of work to do," he said modestly, looking at her to see if she meant it. "Here."

Miranda slid over to him, and he carefully helped her down.

"Are you sure you're okay?" He was worried. They had traveled at a snail's pace, even though he had been assured by two doctors that a wagon ride would not hurt Miranda in her condition. Every rut had made him wince.

"Fine," she assured him, smiling and looking around. When she had said she'd try to make a life with him out here in the wilderness, by his side, she had meant it—thoroughly ashamed of herself when she realized that everything he had said was true. She loved Derek, and in the course of their relationship he had done nothing but give—while all she had done was take. Now she was going to give everything she had because she loved him so dearly.

"Let me show you inside," he said, taking her elbow.

He showed her the kitchen. The hearth was as before, a great iron kettle hanging inside it. He had made a round table big enough for eight, and eight chairs, all of oak. The floors were oak planking. There was a large work space, and Derek had installed an indoor pump.

"An indoor pump," Miranda breathed, going over to it and trying it. She smiled when water dripped out into the tin basin on legs.

"I don't want you having to run back and forth to the well," he said. He turned as Elena burst into the kitchen with a cry.

"Soon a *niño*," she cried, overjoyed. Like everyone else, she thought the child was Derek's. "A big, brave boy, to grow to a big, brave man, like his father."

Miranda smiled, hugging her. "It's so good to see you," she cried. Derek had told her how Elena had hidden and survived Chavez's raid. She had been living these past months in town, and had been eager to return to Miranda and the JB.

Derek took her arm and led Miranda into the parlor, which boasted a couch in front of the hearth and two chairs, all purchased on credit. "We'll just keep adding until the place is exactly the way you want it."

Miranda smiled. "I love it," she told him, meaning it, surprised that she did. "I love it because you did all this by yourself, for us." She rubbed her belly.

Sometimes, every now and then, her maternal and expectant pride would cause a rising feeling of anguish, bitterness, and dismay in Derek. Like now. He quickly quelled it. He was going to be a good father. He was going to make Miranda happy.

"I think you should lie down and rest," he said, taking her hand and leading her into the bedroom. "Elena can bring you in some lunch."

Miranda stared at the bedroom, the coziest room in the house. The bed was a four-poster of oak, and she knew it had been made to order in San Antonio from the Swedish cabinetmaker. There was a plush chair and footstool in front of the fireplace, and a fur rug both there and on one side of the bed—her side, Derek told her, so her feet wouldn't get cold when she got up in the morning. A beautiful quilt coverd the bed, handmade, many different pieces sewn together. There were two windows on either side, both with cheerful curtains, tiny pink roses with green stems on a cream background. There was a small table on her side of the bed, too, with a candle and a book.

In a far corner of the room, past a pine wardrobe, was a lacquered screen. Behind that was a washstand and chamber pot and a copper tub. The bedroom was by far the largest room in the house.

She walked around the bed and picked up the book on the nightstand. It was a Bible. She felt tears rise, and she opened it and saw the inscription. "From your loving husband, always, Derek."

She turned to him. He was waiting, his eyes so intense, so warm and loving. "Thank you," she whispered. "This is—so beautiful, Derek." She clutched the Bible to her breast.

He smiled. "I want to give you more, Miranda, and I will, one day. Jewels and silks and—"

She reached him in time to cut him off, placing one finger on his lip. "This is enough."

He hesitated, then lowered his face, touching her mouth very softly with his. Their love enveloped them, soaring.

Chapter 79

A few days after he had brought her back to the JB, Derek was out riding to take a count of his stock to see what was left on his land, and where. He was about ten miles from the house, high on a ridge overlooking his valley. He turned his gaze to the northwest, disturbed, and instantly saw why. Some ten miles away, there was a great group of riders coming at an easy pace, probably a trot, indistinct except for the cloud of dust. An awful feeling seared him.

His eye was trained. Even at such a distance, he could tell there must be two hundred riders. So many riders had to mean trouble. Miranda was back at the house—alone except for Elena and one teenage boy he had hired on for room and board and the promise of wages. He spurred the chestnut into a gallop and raced back to the ranch at breakneck speed.

He couldn't help but think: *Comanche.*

They had been too quiet for the past few months. The twelve renegades who had attacked their camp on the Pecos didn't count—that kind of raid was a part of Comanche life, the way they lived. There could be no other explanation for several hundred riders than a Comanche war party heading toward San Antonio. And the JB was almost in their path.

He galloped into the yard, yelling for the boy, Jake, and

immediately gave instructions. He shouted for Miranda, who had already come running when she heard him arrive. "Derek, what is it?" she cried.

"Start pumping water," he said, "and douse the house down."

"What's happening?" She became frightened.

"Now," he roared. "Have Elena help you."

They closed the shutters on all the windows of the house, bolting them. The shutters were made of six-inch-thick oak, with just such an emergency in mind. The original house had been built to withstand a siege if something so unthinkable should ever occur, and Derek had rebuilt it the same way. All smoked meats were brought in from the smokehouse. The four horses were brought into the parlor and hobbled. Ammunition and guns were laid out. Then Derek and Jake helped the women throw pail after pail of water over the house. He was glad it wasn't larger, and thanked God that it had rained the past two nights in a row.

"It's Comanche, isn't it?" Miranda cried, leaning against a pillar and rubbing her back.

"You've done enough," he said sharply. "Go inside, stand by the hearth in the parlor. Do you remember how to load rifles, Miranda?"

"I don't know," she said tightly, her face white.

"Just go inside," he said.

"Jesus!" Jake yelled. "I can hear them!"

So could Derek. The thundering was like an earthquake underfoot. He saw the mass of riders, and his heart leaped to his throat. He had been wrong. There weren't two hundred, but twice that number. "Everyone inside," he said, his voice even and cool now. He slammed the thick oak door behind him, bolting it, and he and Jake pulled all the furniture in front of it. "Jake, you take the bedroom," he said.

He went to stand by the one window in the parlor, now shuttered. Each shutter had a small window to fire from, something quite common in Texas. "Elena, you show Miranda how to load, in case she's forgotten. I want both of you to keep a steady supply of loaded weapons for me and Jake."

"It's done," Elena said.

Miranda couldn't move. She was frozen with fear. She realized that Elena was talking to her, and she looked at her, staring without seeing. Then she heard the war cries, and Derek and Jake both firing.

Something snapped inside her. Her husband, whom she loved, was standing there defending her, their baby, and their home from these savages. Anger rose in her, furious and boiling over. She reached down, picked up a rifle, and ran to the window to stand by Derek's side.

"What are you doing?" he said, glancing briefly at her.

She gritted her teeth and poked the rifle through the square opening in the shutter, peering through. She gasped, fear filling her up again. Never had she seen so many Indians at once, all painted and screaming. They were shooting arrows at the house. A few had muskets, and a very few had modern rifles. They had torched the outbuildings, and were torching their home. Anger welled anew in Miranda's heart. She aimed and fired, crying out when her target fell from his pony.

"Great shot!" Derek exclaimed, tossing his Colt to Elena, picking up a rifle. He handed Miranda his other Colt. "Use this. You were always better with the six-shooter than the rifle."

They stood side by side for what seemed like hours to Miranda, but in truth was less than thirty minutes. Over half the Comanche had not even stopped when they rode up to the house, had kept on going toward San Antonio. The house did not catch fire. Miranda didn't know how many Comanche Jake and Derek had shot, but she herself had hit at least six. Then as suddenly as they attacked, they wheeled and rode away, south.

The yard was littered with wounded and dead Indians, two dozen or more.

Miranda placed her Colt on the windowsill and brushed the sweat out of her eyes. She realized that Derek was staring at her, and she managed a wan smile. "My back is killing me," she said.

"Miranda," Derek breathed. "Miranda, look what you did."

She looked at him and suddenly smiled, a smile so

triumphant that his heart leaped wildly. "We showed them," she said fiercely. "Those bastards will think twice about ever coming here again!"

Derek threw back his head and roared with laughter, then swept her into his arms. "God, you're magnificent," he said.

Chapter 80

The war party of Comanche, numbering five hundred, swept past San Antonio to obliterate Victorio, then proceeded to destroy the coastal town of Linnville. The Comanche then headed back to their plains with two thousand stolen horses, leaving twenty-four Texans dead.

Every able-bodied male Texan rallied, including Derek. At Plum Creek the Texans avenged their dead, killing fifty Comanche, not losing a single man. Derek returned home to the JB, but some ninety Texans pressed their advantage, riding deep into Comanche territory. In October they launched a surprise attack, killing some one hundred and thirty Comanche, including women and children. The policy for dealing with the Comanche became settled, one of aggressive obliteration. It was the end of the Comanche heyday.

On New Year's Eve, Miranda went into labor. It was a long and difficult labor, twenty-two hours, but she delivered a squalling boy into Elena's waiting hands, with Derek white-faced at her side, encouraging her. The baby instantly howled his protest at entering the world. Miranda collapsed on the bed, exhausted. Derek closed his eyes, just as fatigued. Elena began speaking excitedly in Spanish as she washed off the child's afterbirth, praising all his attributes.

"Derek?"

"I'm here," he said hoarsely. Never, ever did he want to go through this again. Never. He held her hand. Never in his life had he been so helpless, able to do nothing but encourage his wife while she suffered in agony. He was thoroughly shaken.

"A boy?"

"Yes, princess, a boy." He bent and brushed his mouth across her wet temple. He was ready to collapse. Watching his wife give birth had been worse than running seventy miles a day for days on end!

"Señor," Elena cried, and before Derek knew it, she had handed him the squalling red-faced infant, swathed in a thick white towel.

He stared, stunned, at the baby in his arms. Just what in hell was he supposed to do? "Elena, I can't . . . let me do that," he said. Elena was cleaning up Miranda, but he wasn't watching. Instead, he found himself staring at the tiny baby, who was still howling. Tiny fingers moved on tiny hands. Incredible. Had his own son been this small when he was born? He couldn't remember. He found himself rocking the child—he couldn't let it cry. But the baby still howled. "I think he's hungry," he said in a soft voice. At the sound of his voice, the baby stopped crying, looking at him out of blue eyes. Derek smiled.

"Derek," Miranda whispered, too exhausted to speak any louder.

He responded, moving quickly to her side, carefully handing her the infant, afraid that he might drop him, afraid the child would break by mere transferral. He watched Miranda take him into her arms, her eyes shining.

"He's beautiful," she whispered.

Personally, Derek thought he was rather unattractive, but he kept his opinion to himself. He looked at his wife's face, then stared at her son, fascinated. The infant was making sucking motions with his mouth. "He's hungry," Derek said, somewhat awed.

Miranda shifted her baby, and he found her breast and began to suck greedily.

Derek watched and thought about his son, wondered where he was, if he was all right. He felt grief trying to raise itself from deep inside, and he was surprised. He thought he had conquered his loss a long time ago. Suddenly he felt a surge of protective warmth for this tiny, vulnerable baby.

Miranda cooed to him, making motherly noises. The baby finished nursing, but he didn't sleep. His little fists flayed against his mother's breasts.

"What does he want now?" Derek asked, sitting by her side, unable to stop staring at the child.

"I don't know," Miranda said, looking at her husband and seeing both the pain and the warmth there. Her heart turned over. She had known Derek would love little Nicholas.

"Nick," Derek said, and he took his finger and touched the boy's hand. Nick immediately grabbed the proffered finger, his tiny hand wrapping around it. Derek laughed, trying to move his hand away, but the baby wouldn't let go. "Look at that! He's a strong little fella."

Miranda smiled.

"I think he likes me," Derek said, his pleasure showing on his face as Nick still clutched his finger.

Miranda had no intention of informing Derek that she'd been told that all infants seemed to have this grasping instinct. She just smiled, never having felt more serene in her life.

"How are you feeling?" Derek asked, transferring his attention to his wife. He saw that her eyes were closed, and she had already fallen asleep. He leaned forward and kissed her tenderly, then paused to study the baby. He, too, had fallen asleep. He smiled, glanced at the door to make sure that Elena wasn't about to burst in, and kissed Nick's forehead. Then he crawled into bed on the other side of his wife and collapsed into a deep sleep.

Epilogue

"Pa, she's following us!"

Derek smiled. "And making enough noise to stampede a herd of buffalo," he said softly. But he was exaggerating, and he was very proud of his daughter. Storm was barely making a sound as she followed Derek and Nick through the woods. Not only was she as silent as a deer, she was also as fast as one. Why, she was almost as capable as her brother. Even little Rathe moved like an Apache. Derek was filled with pride.

"Pa," Nick whispered tersely, his brown, gold-flecked eyes flashing. They both stood motionless, peering through the forest at the grizzly, which was standing very still—squatting, actually, and sniffing. He had sensed them.

Derek touched Nick's shoulder in unspoken communication, well aware of Storm's precise location. He should punish her for disobeying his orders and following them while they hunted the killer bear, but he didn't have it in his heart. At least Rathe was too young to be up to such mischief—but the instant he thought that, he knew it wasn't true. That boy was always in trouble.

Nick and Derek crept forward for a clear shot, both holding their rifles ready. The bear stood, growling, and saw them. Nick stood side by side with Derek, both raising and cocking their rifles automatically. The bear gave a vicious cry of attack and lumbered toward them.

Neither the man nor his son moved, or even flinched. The bear came into range. Nick's bronzed face was sculpted with grim concentration. He sighted between the beast's eyes. He fired.

The beast gave a death roar and took two more steps before falling.

"Great shot!" Derek cried, clapping Nick on his back. "Right between the eyes. Nick, I'm proud of you!"

Nick grinned, flushed with his father's praise, tossing a wave of black hair out of his eyes.

"I could have done better," Storm announced, coming out of the woods behind them.

Nick snorted.

"I'm just as good a shot as he is," she cried. "Isn't that so, Pa?"

"You wish," Nick said, but he was smiling in amusement, and so was Derek. They both exchanged glances, then simultaneously broke into laughter.

"I've never met another girl with more braggadocio than five men put together," Derek told his daughter, trying to look stern.

"But I'm as good a shot, and as good a tracker, and a better rider!" Storm placed her hands on her buckskin-clad hips, blue eyes flashing. Except for her eyes, she had Derek's incredible golden coloring.

Nick smiled. "You're in trouble, Storm," he told her. "Pa, are you going to let her get away with this?"

"Nope," Derek said. "As long as you're here, you can help Nick skin and butcher the bear."

Storm made a face. Nick grinned, and Derek supervised both children while they proceeded to obey him.

Sometime later, the three of them rode across the valley and up to the sprawling, two-story ranch house, surrounded by barns, corrals, two bunkhouses, and a smokehouse. The land was green, spotted with oak, fir, and wildflowers. Five years ago they had sold the JB and built this ranch—their ranch.

They dismounted, and Derek restrained Nick as Storm raced up the steps and across the veranda. Nick looked at his father questioningly. "You outdid yourself today,"

Derek told him, slipping his arm around the boy's shoulders. Nick grinned, and they walked in together.

"Pa," Storm shrieked, racing across the foyer to greet them at the front door. "We have guests! Grandfather—and a cousin of Mother's!"

"Slow down," Derek said, and followed his two excited children into the drawing room.

Miranda rose immediately to her feet, and as always, he felt a flush of warmth at the sight of her. At twenty-seven she was rounder, shaplier than she had been, an incredibly breathtaking woman. He smiled, instantly feeling her distress, and understanding it. A long time ago Miranda had told him everything about her there was to know.

"Derek, this is my father, Lord Shelton. And my cousin, Paul Langdon."

The two men stood. Shelton stepped forward, a tall, handsome man with silvery gray hair and sad eyes. "Bragg, this is a pleasure."

They shook hands. "My pleasure," Derek said. "I'm so glad to finally meet you after all these years."

Shelton smiled. Derek meant it. Now that he was a father, he wanted to see Miranda reconciled with hers.

Nick stepped forward, extending his hand. "I'm glad to meet you, sir," he said with characteristic intensity.

"And I am thrilled to meet you," Shelton said softly, staring. He glanced at Derek.

Derek felt anger rising up in him, defensive anger. Anytime someone compared him and his son, he knew they were wondering about Nick's parentage, and he didn't like it, not one bit. Nick's hair was blue black, darker than Miranda's, his skin showing both Mexican and Indian blood. As Nick stepped back, Derek instinctively touched the boy's shoulder, resting his hand there.

"And you must be Angeline," Shelton said, smiling.

"Storm," Storm said, grinning. "No one ever calls me Angeline. Except Ma, when she's really mad."

Shelton laughed. "You have your father's coloring but your mother's eyes. Dark blue—almost purple. Your grandmother had those same eyes." His voice was sad.

Miranda saw and heard the sadness as he discussed her mother, and felt surprise. There was no mistaking the

depth of his grief, even now, after so many years. In that
instant, she felt she had been wrong about her father.

"Where's Rathe?" Derek was asking, after shaking
hands with Langdon—a tall, dark man in his late thirties.

There was a crash from upstairs and the sound of pounding footsteps. Miranda and Derek looked toward the ceil-
ing at the same time, both frowning. "I think your question
has been answered," Miranda said.

Derek walked to the open doors and called, "Rathe,
Rathe, come down here this instant." His voice was loud
and stern.

"My youngest has a penchant for mischief," Miranda
told her father, smiling ruefully. "I thought Nick was bad
when he was younger, then I thought Storm was bad, but
Rathe makes them seem like angels."

"Your children are beautiful, dear," Shelton said, looking proud. "I wish Angeline were here to share your
family with me."

Miranda had a tremendous urge to cry and to hug her
father. She remembered as if it were yesterday her father
slapping her mother and calling her a slut, then hitting her.
But here he was filled with a grief that wouldn't die. She
was confused.

"Here's the scamp," Derek said, propelling forward a
boy of about five who was the golden image of his father,
except for his sapphire blue eyes.

"It was an accident!" Rathe yelled. "I swear!"

"Don't lie and swear in the same breath," Derek said.
"And we'll discuss your mother's broken vase later."

"Oh, Rathe!" Miranda cried, frowning.

"Rathe's in trouble now." Storm grinned.

Rathe tossed a defiant look at her. "It was an accident! I
swear!"

"Rathe, this is your grandfather," Miranda said, taking
him firmly by the hand. The boy seemed to be bursting
with energy, barely able to stay in one place.

"Hello there, Rathe."

"So you're my grandpa. Do you really live in England?
Are you really an earl? How come Nick gets to be an earl,
and I don't? Can I come visit? Do you have horses?"

"Yes, Rathe, I do live in England, and yes, I am an

earl.'' Shelton smiled at him warmly. ''I'm afraid only the oldest son can take the family title, but you are most certainly welcome to visit. Perhaps you'll come visit your brother when he is earl of Dragmore.'' Shelton winked at Nick.

Rathe whooped, jumping up and down.

''I hope you'll be staying for a while,'' Derek said. ''I would love my kids to have a chance to get to know their grandfather.''

Shelton looked at Miranda. ''It's possible, although Paul will be leaving from Galveston in a few days.''

''Gold fever.'' Langdon smiled.

''Going to make your fortune?'' said Derek.

''Don't see why not,'' Langdon said easily.

''C'mon, Langdon,'' Derek said. ''Me and the kids are going to give you a tour of the ranch.'' He looked at Miranda and Shelton. ''I think these two have some catching up to do.'' He took Rathe's hand firmly, and Langdon followed the troop of Braggs. At the door, Rathe broke free of his father's hold, shrieking, running into the hall. Derek grinned back at Miranda with a little shrug before closing the door behind their guest.

Father and daughter looked at each other.

''You have a beautiful family, Miranda,'' Shelton said softly. He gazed fixedly at his daughter.

''Thank you, Father. How about something to drink?''

''Yes, please.''

Miranda poured them both a brandy and sat on a divan that was covered with floral chintz. Her father sat on a sofa upholstered in striped silk.

''I'm so glad you're happy,'' Shelton said. ''Even though your letters were few, your love came through in every sentence.''

''I am happy,'' Miranda said. ''Completely. ''I'm in love with my husband, and I adore my children. We have a wonderful home.'' She gestured. ''It hasn't been easy.''

''You look exactly like Angeline,'' Shelton said, shakily. ''It's like gazing upon a ghost.''

Miranda saw the pain in his eyes and her heart went out to him. ''You loved her.''

''Very much.''

She thought about that and realized that what a little girl had seen might have been an isolated incident. As if reading her mind, Shelton spoke. "I would like to share the past with you, Miranda."

She looked at him. "I would like that too," she said, tears coming to her eyes. "But you don't have to, not if you don't want to. I can see how much you loved her. I realize that I was wrong, Father."

He gave her an understanding smile.

"Are you going to California?"

"No. I had considered it, though, I must admit. The past ten years have been painful for me. But I can't neglect my estate, my duties." He smiled. "Paul's decision to go to California gave me an opportunity to come here that I couldn't resist."

"I'm glad you've come."

A silence descended, sad yet warm. Miranda wondered how she had ever been afraid of her father. He was no beast, no terrible monster, just a man.

From outside, there was an explosion of noise. Nick shouted, Storm shrieked, and Rathe gave a perfect imitation of an Apache war cry. Through it all could be heard the sound of Derek's rich laughter. Then the three children started yelling at once, vying for their father's attention, and Derek's laughter could still be heard. Miranda smiled.

"What's going on?" Shelton asked, startled.

Miranda shrugged. "Who knows? Sometimes I think Derek believes the children are here to amuse him, his personal circus troop." She was smiling tenderly.

Still, she couldn't resist. With her father at her side, they went to the window and peered out the long velvet drapes. Derek had Rathe perched on his shoulders, laughing helplessly. Langdon was at his side, and they were watching Storm and Nick, both astride the same horse. Storm was in front, standing, slipping, the horse snorting in protest. Nick moved the horse into a trot. Storm yelped. The mare broke into a canter, and Nick stood gracefully. It looked extremely precarious.

"Bravo!" Derek shouted.

With laughter, Storm slipped, taking Nick with her, and they went tumbling to the ground. Derek was still laughing, and Miranda tried not to smile.